YA Kramer
Kramer, Stacy
From what I remember--

WITHDRAWN

$16.99
ocn757483220
1st ed.   06/06/2012

FROM WHAT I REMEMBER....

FROM WHAT I REMEMBER...

STACY KRAMER & VALERIE THOMAS

HYPERION
NEW YORK

First Edition
1 3 5 7 9 10 8 6 4 2
G475-5664-5-12060
Printed in the United States of America

This book is set in Adobe Garamond Pro
Designed by Marci Senders

Library of Congress Cataloging-in-Publication Data
Kramer, Stacy.
    From what I remember— / Stacy Kramer and Valerie Thomas.—1st ed.
    p. cm.
    Summary: Just before her graduation from La Jolla's exclusive Freiburg Academy, valedictorian and scholarship student Kylie Flores inadvertently ends up in Ensenada, Mexico, with Max, one of the most popular boys in school, where, in twenty-four jam-packed hours, their lives dramatically change.
    ISBN 978-1-4231-5508-9
    [1. Self-realization—Fiction. 2. Self-perception—Fiction. 3. Family problems—Fiction. 4. Love—Fiction. 5. High schools—Fiction. 6. Schools—Fiction. 7. Ensenada (Baja California, Mexico)—Fiction. 8. Mexico—Fiction.]
I. Thomas, Valerie. II. Title.
    PZ7.K85892Fr 2012
    [Fic]—dc23   2011032892

Reinforced binding
Visit www.un-requiredreading.com

To David and Henry . . . for everything

GRADUATION DAY: FRIDAY, JUNE 25

PROLOGUE

"Happy endings are just stories that haven't finished yet."

—MR. & MRS. SMITH

kylie:

I am jolted awake by sunlight flooding the room.

What time is it? Where am I?

Disoriented, I attempt to open my eyes. The light is stabbing. My head is throbbing, my throat is raw, and my stomach is roiling. Is this what a hangover feels like?

I wouldn't know. I've never had one. Until now.

I close my eyes, take a few deep breaths, and lie still, trying to get my bearings. Last night was one of the greatest nights of my life. I think. But then again, it could have turned into one of the worst. I don't remember much past a certain point.

I can hear kids' voices a few rooms away. The smell of

bacon wafts into the room, a distinct reminder that I'm not home, in my bed, where I should be. My mother grew up in a kosher, Jewish home. Even though she's more agnostic than Jewish these days, old habits die hard; she'd never cook bacon.

I give it another go, allowing my eyes another peek at the world. Slowly, gradually, without making any sudden moves, I glance around, taking in my surroundings. A partial view of an unfamiliar bedroom comes into focus. There's a dresser in the corner, where a mess of snow globes, stuffed animals, and Barbie dolls fight for space. A poster of a fuzzy white kitten with a huge purple bow around its neck is taped to the wall, between two windows. One window has a shade pulled halfway down, the other has no shade at all. Light pours in mercilessly. Is it always this sunny in the morning?

I turn my head to avert my eyes, and that's when I see him. The gorgeous, half-naked boy lying next to me. Asleep.

Oh. My. God. Max.

I am now wide awake, and it's all rushing back at me.

I'm in Ensenada. Mexico. With Max Langston. At Manuel's house.

I'm not at all sure how I got here last night. And I'm not at all where I should be, at home, in my bed, preparing for my valedictorian speech, this afternoon. This is so not the ideal scenario for the morning of graduation.

The final throes of last night appear in spiky flashes. Glimpses of scenes flicker in and out, staccato and in no particular order. It's like watching a movie trailer, except, instead of Kate Hudson or Kristen Stewart, I'm the star. Swimming in the ocean with Max. Drinking (*lots* of drinking) on the dock.

And kissing (*lots* of kissing). Then . . . the screen goes black.

I try to sit up, but the effort makes me woozy, and I lie back down. Why on earth would anyone drink if this is what it feels like the morning after? Maybe because the night before felt pretty damn great. That much I remember.

To say I'm not the kind of girl who normally finds herself in a situation like this is an enormous understatement. I play by the rules even when there aren't any. I listen. I do as I'm told. In four years of high school, I haven't dated, drank, or partied—though I seem to have done all three with wild abandon last night. To prove the point, I'm lying here, next to a boy I barely know, in a strange house, in a foreign city. I'm pretty sure this kind of thing doesn't end well. At least not for girls like me.

Oh God, what was I thinking? I suppose I wasn't. For the first time in my life, I allowed myself to unplug. Utterly and totally. I went way off the rails. It was exhilarating. Addictive. But not the best idea on the day before graduation.

I look at my watch. It's nearly seven o'clock. Graduation is in five hours, in La Jolla, California, which is a good two hours away. And that's without border traffic. *Think*, I tell myself. But my brain isn't cooperating. I'm getting very little except the low, dull sounds of static. Much of the blame for this mess falls squarely on my shoulders. If only I hadn't chased after the guy on the bike, or climbed into that truck, or lost Will, or drank so damn much tequila . . .

I am interrupted from my free fall by Max's firm, bronzed arm reaching across my waist. My breath catches in my throat. Beautiful, sexy Max Langston—whose green eyes are lethal weapons, whose lopsided smile is impossible to resist, whose charm is legendary, and whom I've barely spoken to in six years of school until three days ago—is lying next to me. If I knew anything about statistics, I'd say the chances of this actually happening are improbably low, and yet here we are, against all odds, our bodies grazing each other, my face flushing with heat.

Max is wearing only boxers, sliding down so low on his hips I can see his V-line. He moves closer. All my senses are on high alert as our limbs intertwine, finding their comfort zone. His body fits perfectly into mine. His fingers inch their way under my T-shirt and gently stroke my stomach. He makes circles around my belly button. His touch is tender and yet totally electrifying. It's almost too much to bear. His soft, full lips brush my neck. He doesn't even have morning breath, as I'm sure I do.

"Hey, you," Max says, smiling lazily. "We got pretty messed up last night."

"Yeah," I say, hoping he'll offer more, giving me a better picture of what exactly happened toward the end of the evening, when my disk got erased.

"I hope we didn't do anything stupid," I say, fishing for information.

"Yeah, pretty sure we did." Max laughs softly, and then his eyes close again.

That's all I get?

It's hard to know if he remembers much. Although I can't help taking pleasure in the fact that he doesn't seem at all upset to be waking up next to me. I gaze at him, wondering how someone can look that good first thing in the morning. I am in way over my head. I haven't a clue what happens next.

Max takes my hand in his, which is when I see them—two

identical gold bands. One on his hand. One on mine. The rings catch the sun; light shoots off the gold and bounces around the room.

What exactly happened last night? I am ablaze with an unsettling mix of passion and panic. I'm sweating now, which can't possibly be appealing. What have I done? I've got high school graduation, a summer internship at the San Diego Arts Council, New York University in the fall, and parents who are going to freak. I've been MIA for the past twenty-four hours. I'm in Mexico with Max. And we're wearing rings that look suspiciously like wedding bands. This is bad. Very, very bad.

I've never even been on a date.

Or had sex.

Or have I?

I rack my brain, but the things I can't remember skirt the dark edges like storm clouds. I turn back toward Max, and for a fleeting second the dread dissipates. He looks so lovely and content as he drifts back to sleep, his chest rising and falling with each breath. It's heart-stopping.

I turn away, and the panic sets back in, full-throttle.

I sit up, intent on hatching a plan, and that's when I see Lily Wentworth standing in the doorway, staring at me.

TWO DAYS EARLIER:
WEDNESDAY, JUNE 23

CHAPTER ONE

"Today's forecast?
Dark and cloudy, and
chance of drive-by."
—THE 40-YEAR-OLD VIRGIN

kylie:

Ms. Murphy drones on, partnering up our English class: "Brendon and Julie, Nadia and Sam, Kylie and Max . . ."

Wait, what? Kylie and Max? Terrible idea. I've managed to escape all interaction with Max Langston in six years at Freiburg, since I got here in seventh grade. We're at opposite ends of the social spectrum, which is probably why Ms. Murphy put us together. She's spiteful like that.

"An assignment? No way," Lily Wentworth blurts out. Lily has her head buried in a huge leather bag that probably cost hundreds of dollars. She never looks directly at anyone. She always looks past people, her eyes flitting around, searching for something or someone better.

"But tomorrow's the last day of school. . . ." Lily whines. While I hate Lily, bitch extraordinaire, she makes an excellent point. Right now, in classrooms all over the country, teachers are handing out candy and patting self-important seniors on the back for a job well done. Not Mistress Murphy, as Will and I call her. (We're pretty sure she works nights as a dominatrix.) She has found new and inventive ways to torture her students year after year.

"We're not supposed to get any more homework," Charlie Peters adds.

All bets are off. No one seems to care that they're talking back to Mistress Murphy. Something no one would have dared last semester, when grades mattered a whole lot more.

"And that is precisely why I am giving you this assignment, Mr. Peters. I'm tired of seniors riding out spring semester like school is over. If you stop exercising your mind, it atrophies. And next thing you know, you'll be on the street begging people like me for spare change. And I won't give you any," Murphy says.

Harsh.

A flicker of a smile crosses Murphy's face, which is all sharp angles and pinched features. She's enjoying this. She *definitely* dabbles in S&M. I can see her now, clad in leather, holding a studded riding crop as some poor guy pleads for mercy. There are sighs all around. But unlike everyone else in class, I don't mind one last writing assignment. If I'm going to be an Oscar-winning screenwriter, I might as well hone my craft. What I do

12

mind is working with Max. It's clear he's not into it.

"Crap, not Kylie Flores. She'll actually want to do it," Max says, loud enough for everyone around him to hear, including me. What an asshole.

A bunch of people laugh. Ha-ha. So witty. He may be perfect on the outside, but inside it's a different story. If he had a thought in his head, it would perish from loneliness. Max, as always, basks in the attention. He tips back in his chair and tosses his shaggy, sandy locks, like a preening bird.

Like everyone at Freiburg, Max is a spoiled rich kid, floating in a vapid sea of privilege, completely and blissfully ignorant of how the rest of the world lives. Everyone, that is, except for Will. Thank God for Will. God knows, I wouldn't have survived without him.

Luckily, two more days and Freiburg Academy is in my rearview mirror. I will fly off to New York University knowing the worst is behind me and the best is yet to come. The world will embrace what Freiburg didn't, couldn't, wouldn't— my biting sarcasm (which, unfortunately, is often on the fritz at Freiburg), my fiery temper (which I consider a sign of a passionate soul rather than a lack of self-control), and my offbeat looks (I'm half Mexican, half Jewish, which looks great on paper, less so in the harsh white light of La Jolla). I will shed this coat I've been forced to wear that reads Token Scholarship Student. I will reinvent myself and become someone fabulous, fascinating, and ecstatically happy. I will be unrecognizable to all who knew me, including myself. The Freiburg class of 2012 can kiss my ass. I will finally be free of the social chains that bind me.

Okay, that's a little over the top. Not my best prose. It sounds more like a bumper sticker or a fortune cookie than actual insight. But it's all I've got right now, and it paints the picture. Life at Freiburg sucks. Plain and simple.

"You will interview your partner and write a thousand-word essay about the two books that made the biggest impression on them during their years at Freiburg. The paper is due tomorrow, the last day of school. If you choose to abstain, I will fail you on the paper, which will count toward your final grade in English this semester and could impact your total GPA. Let's see how your college of choice feels about that," Mistress Murphy announces.

Surely the administration wouldn't condone this move, but Murphy is a renegade. She's been teaching in these hallowed halls for so long, her outrageous behavior goes unchecked at this point. While everyone else can slack off, Murphy's threats tap right into my own particular brand of crazy. I will have to do this paper. I'm currently number one in my class with my GPA, a long-held goal of mine, but an F could throw things wildly out of whack, dropping me to number two. The top is a precarious place at a competitive private school like Freiburg, and it requires constant vigilance.

"Does *Playboy* count?" Luca Sonneban shouts out. Jesus, he's dim. How did he get into Freiburg, anyway? Aren't there some basic requirements for one of "the nation's premier learning institutions," which is what is etched into the massive granite arch at the entrance of the school? I guess when your dad owns the country's largest chain of grocery stores, admission standards tend to be waived. A bunch of guys high-five

14

Luca, like he's just said the most scintillating thing ever.

Mistress Murphy sucks in her breath and glares at Luca. "Go directly to the headmaster's office, Mr. Sonneban, and do not bother to return to class. Ever. You will receive an F on the paper."

Luca saunters out of class, all confidence and swagger. He couldn't care less about the F. The rest of his life is taken care of, and he knows it. I wonder if I would be cavalier and cocky like that if my parents had more money than God? I hope not. But who knows? If I didn't have to prove myself every damn minute, maybe I'd be dancing on a desk with a lampshade on my head. Students cheer Luca on as he exits. He lifts his fist in the air in salute. Really, people? Do we want to encourage this guy?

I'm sure Max's favorite book is something so glaringly obvious it'll feel like a blunt object to the back of my head. *The Catcher in the Rye* or, worse, *The Guinness Book of World Records*.

After class, I walk straight to Max's locker, where he's standing with Lily (über-girlfriend) and Charlie Peters (sidekick). Max and Lily have been dating since the beginning of senior year. It was only a matter of time before the most beautiful boy and the most beautiful girl coupled up. If they hadn't gotten together, the world would have spun off its axis or something. Everyone treats them like royalty. It's so predictable and irritating, it makes me want to scratch out my eyes. As I approach, I can hear them discussing this weekend's postgraduation party at Charlie's house, to which I am not invited. The DJ, the songs, the food. You'd think they were planning a moon landing, they're so intense about it.

Of course I'm invited to the official Freiburg Graduation

Fiesta, as are all graduating seniors, but in keeping with the fascistic social code that is life at Freiburg, you only go to the Graduation Fiesta if you're not invited to the nonofficial, thereby cool, graduation party, which is being hosted by Charlie. Hence, losers only at the Fiesta. No, thank you very much.

Will and I have decided to make our own party. A John Woo movie marathon preceded by an In-N-Out Burger run. It's an end-of-the-year tradition for us. I get teary at the thought of it. The end of an era. I am so going to miss Will next year. Could there be another Will for me at NYU? Probably not. I don't make friends that easily.

"Seriously, no Lady Gaga. I'm so over her. I'm all about the Gorillaz and the Dirty Projectors," Lily insists, fiddling with her gold door-knocker earring that has no business on her moneyed, white ear. The fact that these rich kids like to slum it by dressing faux ghetto bruises me to the core. The ghetto is not particularly cool. I know. I've been there most of my life.

"You are just so ahead of the curve, Lil. No one can keep up," Charlie jokes.

"I know. It's sick. I'm, like, setting trends all over the place," Lily says.

I'm standing right next to them, but they've yet to acknowledge me. So typical. I don't want to deal with them as much as they don't want to deal with me, but what choice do I have?

"Just make sure you get some old-school mash-up in there. Like Prince and Parliament," Max adds.

"Prince? Seriously?" Lily whines. "Maxie, c'mon, your music taste reminds me of my dad."

16

"We can't all be as hip as you," Max says with a smile, though I think I sense a hint of annoyance in his voice, which surprises me. Max and Lily are so sickeningly enamored with each other all the time. I'm probably just projecting.

"No, baby, we can't," Lily snaps back, with bite. And then she takes Max's face in her hands and kisses him, long and hard. Charlie just stands by, the lonely job of the loyal third wheel. I guess this is part of Max and Lily's very public game of romance. I have to look away. I'm afraid I might gag.

I clear my throat. I need to say my piece and get the hell out of here.

Max, Charlie, and Lily turn to me, bemused.

"Let me guess: you want to talk about Murphy's assignment," Max says, laughing in my face.

"Uh, yeah. I do," I say, holding my ground.

"Dude, you called it," Max tells Charlie.

"Give it up, Kylie. Grades don't matter anymore," Charlie tells me.

"They do to me. I don't want an F in English. I'm doing the assignment, and since it requires a partner," I say, turning to Max, "you're going to have to do it with me."

What I don't say is that because I'm not sporty or arty or a theater geek, the one thing that distinguishes me at Freiburg is my valedictorian position, and I'm not about to lose it. I happen to know that Sheldon Roth is a mere .02 points behind me, nipping at my heels, and Patrick Bains is on Sheldon, and Lily is right behind Patrick. (As much as I'd like to write her off as an idiot, I can't. She hit the jackpot: rich, beautiful, and smart.) My name may be printed on the graduation ceremony program as valedictorian speaker, but the numbers can change at any time. With one bad paper in English, Sheldon could pull ahead. This is a war and I intend to win it.

"You're kidding, right?" Max says. "Murphy can go to hell."

"I'm sorry. It's just, I've got an academic scholarship to NYU and I really need to keep my grades up. . . ." I wish I didn't feel the need to apologize. I wish I could drum up a genius comeback that would shut them up. Tragically, I've got nothing. My wit goes into hiding with these people. It's not like I care about their approval; it's more like we're different species and I'm not sure how to communicate with them. Popular people are from Mars. The rest of us are from a distant galaxy that no one has ever heard of.

The great irony here is that I can *write* a brilliant character. I just can't play one in real life. In the world of my screenplay, the one that earned me a full scholarship to NYU's Tisch School of the Arts, I created the most kick-ass female protagonist ever, one who nails the perfect line every time. One who never finds herself in situations like this, flush with humiliation, begging Max Langston to find a shred of decency somewhere inside the cavernous, empty space that is his soul. You'd think I would have picked up a few tips from her. Sadly, that's not the case.

Lily rolls her eyes. "Oh my God. You are such a geek, Kylie. Just blow it off. One stupid paper from Murphy doesn't matter in the scheme of things. She's just trying to freak us out because she knows it's her last chance to mess with us."

Lily's right. Mistress Murphy's threat is empty and baseless. My scholarship won't be affected; I'll still be valedictorian. But I can't ignore an assignment. I didn't achieve an Ivy trifecta

18

(Brown, U Penn, and Princeton, all of which I rejected for NYU and their star-making film department, much to my parents' chagrin) by blowing anything off. Ever. I'm not going to start now.

"Seriously, Kylie. No one's doing it," Max adds, flashing his pearly whites. I stare at the floor, afraid I'll lose my courage if I have to look at him for a second longer. He's too hot. It hurts the eyes.

"I have time after sixth period. We can meet then. It shouldn't take long. I, uh . . . can write yours, if you want." I am getting this done. No matter how low I have to go. And frankly, with the offer to do Max's assignment, I've hit the floor. Hopefully, NYU will be more of a meritocracy. "Ten minutes. That's all I need and I can write both papers at home tonight," I say.

"Okay. Cool. Write my paper," Max says.

Whatever. I'm never going to be friends with these people. I'm here to graduate first in my class and get the hell out of Dodge.

"Later," Max says. And then he throws his arm around Lily, pulls her close, and they kiss again. This time with tongue. Thanks so much. Once just wasn't enough.

Forty-eight hours and counting . . .

CHAPTER TWO

"Do you prefer 'fashion victim' or 'ensemblely challenged'?"
—CLUELESS

will:

Kylie doesn't even see me as she rushes down the hall, staring at the ground. She's wearing her daily uniform of gray jeans, white T-shirt, and that lame-ass ratty knit scarf her grandmother made her, like, a million years ago. Girlfriend needs a makeover. I'm so the guy for the job, if Kylie would just give fashion a chance. But all the beautiful clothes I've given her over the years are marooned in her closet, tags on, waiting to get off the island and back into civilization.

At least she's not wearing those Uggs anymore, which look like huge suede foot tumors, as far as I'm concerned. I tossed them in the garbage last time I was at her house. Saving Kylie from herself is a full-time occupation, let me tell you. I was born for the job. Too bad I can't do it professionally.

"'Hey, girl,'" I call out. "'If you're from Africa, why are you white?'"

Kylie looks up at me. "'Oh my God, Karen, you can't just ask people why they're white,'" she says.

Mean Girls. We know the script by heart. That movie and about a million others. The number of hours we've logged together watching films is appalling. There have been times when we've watched the same film four times in a row. There have been lost weekends when we've barely come up for air. I would say this is because we are ardent film lovers, but I know it's more than that. Both of us, for our own reasons, would prefer to live embedded in the silver screen than in the real world of high school. At least, that's what my therapist says. Kylie is going to be a screenwriter and I'm going to be a . . . who knows? I've got time and money, so I'm not particularly concerned, unlike Kylie.

Kylie keeps walking. I rush to catch up with her. A few stray curls poke out from her signature ponytail. Girlfriend wears her gorgeous fro so tightly slicked back it looks like a helmet. She needs to embrace those kinky Latina curls. With her bronze skin, her golden eyes, and those massively long black lashes, she could look like a movie star. Sister is hot even in an outfit that could make Marilyn Monroe look neutered. Sadly, she doesn't have a clue. She thinks she's ugly. It kills me.

"You've totally outdone yourself today," Kylie tells me, giving my ensemble the once-over. "Are you trying to push Alvarez over the edge?"

"You know he secretly lives for it."

I'm driving the headmaster crazy. Freiburg is a straight-ass school in a straight-ass town, and my dresses and skirts do not please Headmaster Alvarez. He talked to my parents last year, but he's kind of given up at this point. Just like my parents.

"Hot or not?" I ask Kylie as I spin around in my vintage platform black patent heels (purchased on eBay). I am wearing lime-green skinny jeans with a gorgeously tailored Marc Jacobs black dress, borrowed, without permission, from my sister. I know. It's so out there. I was kind of born out of the closet. Way out. Every year I've taken things a little further in my insatiable need to push this conservative crowd to their limit. And this year I went all out. Full-frontal fashion. I'm about to blow out of town; might as well do it in style.

I'm not an idiot; I'm aware of what people say about me. I know they think I'm a screaming queen, which, oddly enough, I'm not. I'm just a regular gay boy. I'm not insatiably drawn to women's clothes or anything, but this is one way to distinguish myself at Freiburg. I don't have many other marketable skills. I mean, I tried the volleyball team, at my dad's insistence, and it was . . . a freaking nightmare. Large, hard balls coming at me from every direction at high velocity.

But this cross-dressing thing has been kind of a boon for me, a solid extracurricular, with all the Internet shopping, studying of fashion blogs, and even learning to sew. It's been a good distraction and a résumé builder. People still tease me about my voice and my boy crushes, but it's died down as I've amped up the fabulosity quotient. My outrageous outfits allow me to take center stage in character, which is far better than being the lone gay guy in the corner.

"Yeah. You're rocking it. Even in this hideous fluorescent light," Kylie says. Kylie is the one person who has always accepted me just as I am.

"I have a gift. Speaking of which, I've got a little something for Charlie Peters. A graduation present. I just need you to help me get him into the boys' room."

Kylie and I always call Charlie Peters, Charlie Peters. We could just call him Charlie, but it's another one of those things that stitches our friendship together.

"Shut up. You are all talk. Besides, Charlie Peters is so not gay," Kylie says. "You think everyone's gay."

"Most people are. They just don't know it yet."

"Okay. Whatever. Listen, Will, I'm kinda in a hurry. I've got to get to the library."

She's not in the mood to play.

"The library? We're done, baby. Stick a fork in us."

Kylie is such a grind, it worries me. Who's going to make her kick back and watch *Modern Family* and *Fringe* at NYU? I may have to fly in from Berkeley and physically force her to chillax.

"Mistress Murphy gave us one last assignment."

"Please tell me you're not going to do it. It will build character *not* to do it. I promise."

"I am going to do it. And I'm doing Max Langston's as well. We're partners."

"Kylie, Kylie, Kylie."

"He won't do it if I don't do it for him. I can't not do it. I can't. I'll be better at NYU. I promise," Kylie offers.

"Doubt it." Maybe New York City has the answers for her. God knows San Diego only had questions.

"Yeah. You're probably right. I need to get to the library. I'm meeting Max there."

"Oh, we get to meet Max Langston at the library?" Mortals like us don't normally interact with the Max Langstons of the world.

"We?" Kylie says, shooting me a warning glance.

"I'm coming with." No better view than staring at Max from a neighboring carrel.

"Will, don't you have anything better to do?"

"Sadly, no."

"C'mon, this is only going to make things more difficult."

"You'll barely notice me."

"Impossible." Kylie sticks her tongue out at me.

I stick my tongue out at her. It's an interchange we have about seven hundred times a day. I love her. I would give her a lung and a leg if I had to. Hopefully, I won't have to.

"Okay. Here's the plan. You have sex with Max over in biographies, and then I can go down on him by the microfiche," I suggest.

"Gross. I wouldn't touch Max with a ten-foot pole. I have no interest in sex with Max, at all."

"Um, hello . . . you have no interest in sex whatsoever. It's a problem."

"Not everyone thinks about sex twenty-four seven," Kylie says.

"I beg to differ, darling. Most seventeen-year-olds are not only thinking about sex, they're actually having it, unlike us."

24

I think about sex every single minute of every day. Not that it's getting me anywhere. Kylie and I are both virgins, but for very different reasons. It's not normal for a seventeen-year-old girl to turn that whole part of herself off. She's going to explode one day. I just hope I'm there to pick up the pieces.

We take a seat at a table in the library to wait for Max. I reach into my pocket, pull out a fabulous pair of long, gold chandelier earrings, and offer them up to Kylie.

"You *have* to wear these for graduation. You need something that's going to stand out on the podium. These will look major with your hair all wild, and—"

"Will, you promised me you wouldn't steal any more of your sisters' stuff."

"You're the valedictorian, darling. You need some kind of something. Annie will never know they're gone. She has gobs of them."

"The thought is sweet, and I love you for it, but I won't take your stolen goods. I'm sorry."

Damn Kylie and that moral compass she wears around her neck. My sisters have so much stuff, it's embarrassing. I'm just trying to share the wealth.

"At least let me buy you a dress for graduation."

"Will, seriously, drop it."

I do drop it. But I vow to pick it up again before Friday. Kylie deserves a slamming dress when she stands up there at the podium and blows us all away with her speech. Of course, no one will see it under her gown, but it's the principle of the thing that counts.

Kylie and I are an unlikely pair. I'm one of the richest kids in a school filled with La Jolla's most moneyed families, while Kylie is one of five scholarship students. We met on the first day of seventh grade, in the far north corner of the cafeteria, having both been pushed out of all the prime real estate. Kylie was new and I was, well, me. We ended up at the same empty table, along with Justin Wang, who just sat there, in a trance, communing with his Nintendo.

Neither of us spoke for about ten minutes. When I couldn't take it any longer, I turned to Kylie and said, "'Did you know without trigonometry there'd be no engineering?'"

Without missing a beat or even glancing up from her pizza bagel, Kylie said, "'Without lamps, there'd be no light.'"

"No way," I said. What were the chances the new girl could quote *The Breakfast Club*?

"Way," Kylie said. And then she looked up and smiled at me. Girlfriend has an amazing smile. Her whole face lights up. "*Breakfast Club* is one of my favorite movies of all time."

"It's a masterpiece," I concurred. And we've been best friends ever since.

Our family's relationship, unfortunately, is a whole different story. Our parents have only spent one miserable evening together in the past six years, and it will never happen again. Kylie's mother insisted on having us over. She made spaghetti with meatballs. It was, how do you say *en anglais*? An unmitigated disaster.

My sisters and my mother are all vegans, so they just nibbled on salad. (You'd think with all our money they'd fill up on lobster, caviar, and filet mignon, just because they can; but no, they spend their money on dried lentils and tempeh.)

Since only beer was on offer (which is to say, there was no wine served, a crime worse than murder in my parents' opinion), only a handful of words were exchanged all evening, unless you count my incessant blathering, which filled the silence but annoyed everyone to no end, including me.

At some point, toward the end of the long day's journey into night, Jake, Kylie's little brother (who I love more than my own siblings, and who is challenged in his own special ways), launched into a thirty-minute exposition on the San Diego bus schedules. I think it was right after that that my parents made some pathetic excuse about a previous engagement they'd forgotten. They were out of there so fast the wind shook the shelves. I stayed and played Yahtzee with Jake and Kylie, rather than head back to Cloudbank (that's right, our house has a name).

Kylie is staring at the clock in the library, twirling her hair. She's pissed. We've been waiting here for thirty minutes, and still no Max. I'm so not surprised. Kylie springs up from her seat and bolts for the door. And she's off. Uh-oh.

Kylie's temper is not something to mess with. She looks like she's going to blow, in a big, operatic way. I live for these scenes. As we're getting precariously close to graduation, this could be Kylie's final performance. I race to catch up with her, no small task in these crazy platform shoes. I seriously need to get some sneakers.

CHAPTER THREE

"I'ma get medieval on your ass."
—PULP FICTION

kylie:

I hate when people are late. It's at the top of the list among my many pet peeves. I am also infuriated by selfishness, narcissism, and stupidity. Hard as it is to believe, Max appears to have all of these traits in spades.

He cannot get away with this. I don't care how hot or popular he is. A force beyond my control seizes me, and before I know it, I'm running toward the sports center. For anyone else it would be social suicide, but I was dead on arrival years ago.

I'm working hard at controlling my anger, but it has been sorely tested at Freiburg. Just this year, I've had minor eruptions at least three times: when Isabel Tornet cheated off of me in AP Calculus and then tried to pin it on me when she got caught;

when Oscar Mezlow taunted Will for being gay; and when I saw Jemma Pembolt teasing Anna Salington about being overweight.

I rush across the quad, pretty sure I'll find Max on the squash court. Will weaves and bobs behind me in his ridiculous shoes. I hope at Berkeley he will feel less of a need to display his sexuality like a merit badge. I know for a fact Will loves tailored suits and his old worn-in Levi's. Maybe someday he'll feel comfortable enough in his skin to wear them. Or, at the very least, choose more sensible shoes.

A Frisbee slams into my head. A bunch of kids stare at me, pissed. I realize I've just crashed the Ultimate Frisbee championships. I apologize and veer off, out of the line of fire. I know I should appreciate the beauty all around me, but something about the blazing green lawn and the stately brick buildings, surrounded by towering palm trees, makes me want to hurl. I watch for a beat as Lauren Jacobs leaps into the air to snatch the Frisbee. She's wearing such short shorts I can see her butt cheeks, and a pink T-shirt so tight her nipples are practically visible. Why must Lauren constantly dress like a stripper? She's hot. I get it.

Lauren tosses the Frisbee back to Chase Palmer, whose white-blond hair glistens in the sun and whose perfect teeth sparkle like diamonds. All these happy, shiny people. I will never adjust to this world, ever.

"Hey, Kylie, wait up," Harriet Zoles yells to me. I pretend not to hear her and pick up the pace. Harriet Zoles is one of the precious few people at Freiburg who relentlessly seek out my company. Her and a few other Crofties. Crofties are so named because they spend their time in the undercroft, an inside archway beneath the main building. Will and I tried to hang with them for a while. As it turned out, aside from being unpopular, we had very little in common with them. They're kind of extreme geeks. I'm sure they'll go on to create the next Facebook or Google, and I'll be kicking myself that I didn't cozy up to them more when I had the chance. But as much as Will and I tried, we just couldn't make the connection happen. Talking to Harriet Zoles is like torture, or "water-boring," as Will would say. And, unlike Franklin Peterson, I don't build elaborate, historically accurate structures out of Legos competitively. Nor do I think Mandarin is the *only* way to get ahead in this "global rat race" we now live in, as Sheila Nollins insists, every chance she gets.

No woman is an island, but together, Will and I are a very tiny atoll, floating peacefully off the Southern California coast. Sure, it can get lonely. And maybe in a different place, at a different time, we'll visit the mainland. But for now, island living suits us just fine, thank you very much.

I yank open the door to the sports center and march down the stairs, toward the squash courts. Will takes a step, his heel gives, and he tumbles down the stairs, landing in a heap outside the court.

Lily looks down at Will and snickers. "Maybe that's why men don't wear heels, William." Lily's two BFFs, Stokely Eagleton and Jemma Pembolt, sitting at her side, giggle on cue.

If this were some kick-ass action movie, the main character—that being me—would yank up her pencil skirt and, with one long sweep of her leg, incapacitate all three of these girls with a swift kick to their heads. Then she'd straighten her skirt, freshen her lipstick, brush a little lint off her sleeve, and saunter off with a wink and a smile. But this is not a movie. This is my dismal life. And I'm no hero.

So I glare at Lily and company, and then look down at Will and ask, "You okay?" Hardly Oscar-worthy.

"Never better."

I help Will up and onto the bench. He bites his lower lip and rubs his leg.

"You sure?" I ask again.

"I'll be fine. Don't stop the show on my account. You know how I live for the climactic second act break," Will says to me.

I leave Will and march onto the squash court, where Max is in the middle of a heated match with Charlie. I know this is such a bad idea, but I'm so over it. Max Langston and his crew do whatever they want, whenever they please, to whomever they choose. Enough already.

I'm so caught up in my fight for justice, I am completely oblivious to the squash ball flying around the court until it smacks me in the butt.

I hear Lily and her harpies laugh hysterically.

"Kylie, what the hell are you doing?" Charlie asks. He and Max continue to whack at the ball as if I'm not there.

For the second time today, Max looks at me and rolls his eyes.

I feel naked and ridiculous standing in the middle of the court, the ball whizzing around me.

"Max and I were supposed to meet forty minutes ago," I say, holding my ground in what is increasingly becoming one of my worst ideas ever.

"Oops, my bad. The game went long. Obviously we're not

going to do it now. So can you get off the court?" Max asks.

"No. I cannot get off the court. You are so unbelievably rude it's mind-blowing. I mean, were you raised in a barn?" I know this is an odd comment, but, as usual, I'm not on my game with these people.

"No, Max wasn't, but a barn is better than a trailer. Or do you people call them double-wides these days?" Charlie says.

Charlie is referring to the fact that I live in Logan Heights, not exactly the posh part of town. It's twenty miles outside of La Jolla, but more like worlds away. My family's shabby little rental house could be shoehorned into Charlie's guest bathroom. I'm guessing, of course, since I've never seen any part of his house and never will.

Charlie's comment sends me into the stratosphere. I go from angry to apoplectic in a split second, losing my pride, my dignity, and all sense of decorum in the process. Sure, I've got a temper and it flares up at inopportune times, resulting in verbal fireworks, but I've never gone completely postal. Until now. Maybe it's graduation jitters or anxiety about my speech. Whatever it is, my fury has come to a rolling boil and just bubbled over onto the court. I can't control my urge to pummel Charlie. I haul off and kick him in the shin. I swear I can hear Will gasp from outside the court. Charlie grabs his leg and yelps in pain. What a drama queen. It wasn't that hard, was it? I am embarrassed by my slide into violence, but at least I've got their attention.

"What the hell?" Charlie says.

"What is your problem, Kylie?" Max adds.

"You are my problem, Max."

A few other students have wandered over and are watching

the show. I'm turning bright red. But I'm not putting my tail between my legs and backing away now. I've already gone too far; might as well go all the way. *Right is might.* I think. I hope.

"Actually, now is a perfect time for us to talk," I say, whipping out my notebook. I poise my pen above the page. "You're here. I'm here. What could be better?"

Max and Will gape at me like I'm some kind of creature from a horror movie.

"So, what's your favorite book?" I ask Max.

"Kylie, let's do this later. I'll be done in half an hour." He sounds almost conciliatory.

"Screw you, Max. You're such an asshole. You've wasted enough of my time today. We're doing it now."

Jesus. Who says this kind of stuff in real life? Me, apparently. I'm not filtering. I've gone completely off the edge. I just wish I could have waited until after I delivered my valedictorian speech. I'm going to be standing at the podium, the laughing-stock of Freiburg. Will anyone even want to listen to a speech I've labored over for months? Too late to worry about that now.

Max's expression switches from placating to pissed. "You know what, Kylie, *screw you.* The deal is off. You're on your own because you're the only idiot who cares about doing the assignment. I was trying to be nice, but fuck it. And I'm in the middle of a game. So get the hell off the court."

At this point, Max whips the ball at the wall, missing my head by only a few inches. He's a very good player, so I have to assume that was on purpose. I've lost the battle *and* the war. I skulk off the court. I'm still livid, but my anger is now mixed with the sour taste of humiliation. I keep my head down and hurry toward the exit, ignoring the peanut gallery.

Will catches up with me outside. He loops his arm through mine. "You had me at 'Screw you, Max.' You were brilliant!"

I don't say anything. I'm too busy beating myself up. Why can't I just let go for once and kick Murphy's stupid assignment to the curb? Will can tell I'm in the middle of round five of one of my self-boxing matches. He's been ringside many times before.

"His ass isn't what it used to be. Freshman year, it was tight and sweet. He's getting soft. Doesn't bode well for middle age," Will says, trying to cheer me up.

"You know that's not true."

"I know. He's got an amazing ass, not to mention his six-pack abs and those guns—"

"Is this supposed to help?"

"Sorry. Sorry."

"I'm getting worse. That was ridiculous."

"They deserved it. No one else stands up to them."

"I hate this place."

"Me too. But you're gonna kill at NYU."

I love Will for trying to prop me up. But I worry I'll be just the same at NYU, or anywhere else I go, for that matter. What if it's not Freiburg? What if it's me? What if I just don't fit in anywhere, like my brother, Jake? Don't get me wrong: Freiburg sucks and has, rightly, been an endless source of blame for most of my social shortcomings. There's very little here for me besides Will. But I can't help wondering if, at a certain point, it's partly my fault.

34

"Yeah. Whatever . . ." I say to Will, my insecurity creeping across my skin like a bad rash.

"Stop it. Do not let these people make you feel less than extraordinary. You are one amazing human. Don't forget it," Will insists.

"I don't know. It's just, I can't believe I lost it like that. It was totally mortifying."

"It was inspiring. You're my hero." Will pulls me into a hug. "Wanna go to Pinkberry? My treat."

"Can't. Gotta watch Jake," I say, unhitching myself from Will and heading toward the street.

"'Loser,'" Will calls to me.

"'Blow me.'"

"'Call me later?'" Will finishes the line from *Cruel Intentions*. He waves and disappears into the quad.

I need to get home. I'm already running late. But before I get on the bus, I've got to pee. So I hustle my way to the arts center. Everybody has their favorite bathroom at school, and this one is mine. It hasn't been modernized like the rest of Freiburg. It's shabby and creaky, with deep sinks and rusty metal doors on the stalls. And no one's ever there. It's a great place to hide away from the world, unlike Freiburg's other bathrooms, most of which have been commandeered by various social groups. The bathroom in the basement, beneath the cafeteria, is where all the smokers go because, not surprisingly, the smell of institutional food overwhelms the smell of smoke, and no one ever gets caught. The bathroom in the main hall, near the lockers, is controlled by Lily and company. They freeze people out with old-school mean-girl tactics—staring, giggling, and whispering—which are somehow always in vogue and ever effective. I avoid that bathroom like the plague.

I am sitting on the toilet, peeing, when I hear someone enter.

"What, Mom? This is, like, the tenth time you've called in the past hour."

It's Lily. I'm surprised to find her here.

"No. I can't come home right now. We're all going to Stokes's and then out for dinner. We can talk later. Or tomorrow."

I don't know what to do. Lily clearly doesn't know I'm here. But the longer I stay, the more awkward it gets. I don't want to appear like I'm eavesdropping, but any way you slice it, it's not going to be good when I suddenly appear. The sooner I can get out of here, the better. I have no interest in Wentworth family drama.

"What's the big secret? Why can't you just tell me now?" Lily barks into the phone.

I flush and exit the stall. Lily glares at me. I keep my head down and pretend I haven't heard a thing.

"I've gotta go. I'll call you back," Lily says, hangs up, and turns her high beams on me. Ugh. I'm not in the mood. I'm worn out from my earlier outburst.

We stare at each other for a beat, neither of us pleased to see each other, both for different reasons. Underneath Lily's fierce bluster, I sense fear and embarrassment. It's weird. So not Lily.

"What the fuck, Kylie?" she says, as if she owns the whole damn place.

"Sorry, I . . ." And my voice trails off. I'm thrown by the whole strange scenario. What I should say is, "What the fuck, Lily?" I mean, she's the one yelling at her mother in the bathroom. Not me. But as usual, I'm on the defensive.

"Were you spying on me?" Lily demands.

"Of course not. I was going to the bathroom. I was here first. You walked in on me," I remind her.

"Why don't you get a life instead of listening in on other people's?" And with that, Lily turns and marches out before I can come up with a witty rejoinder.

Bitch.

Hopefully, this will be our very last exchange for the rest of our lives.

CHAPTER FOUR

"You shouldn't
take life so seriously.
You'll never get out alive."
—VAN WILDER

max:

"That was wack, bro," Charlie says.

"Girl's a freak!" I say to Charlie. But what I don't tell Charlie is that Kylie is right. I *can* be an asshole. It's a role I'm pretty comfortable with. Bottom line, I get away with a lot of shit around here 'cause people let me.

The thing is, everyone's always wanting something from me. If I worried about everyone's feelings, I'd never get anything done. I've got to take care of myself. I can't be dealing with everybody's junk all day long. And Murphy's assignment is definitely Kylie's junk.

I should put it out of my head. Normally I would. But I

made a promise to myself when my dad went into the hospital for the second time, that I would stop being such a selfish prick, because maybe that isn't the way to go through life. It didn't work out so well for my dad.

"She kicked me. Hard. Chick has issues," Charlie insists.

"Totally," I say. But I can't help feeling sorry for Kylie. She takes everything so goddamned seriously. No one wants to hang with her, except for weird Will Bixby. I mean, who gets that worked up over an assignment? I can't remember ever giving that much of a crap about any homework. Ever.

Charlie gets another point off of me. He's in the lead. It's eight to seven. Kylie totally messed with my head. I don't need that kind of distraction, with tryouts for UCLA coming up next week. That's a whole lot more important than some stupid paper for Murphy.

"Get your head in the game," Charlie says.

"I'm trying," I say. But it's easier said than done. Charlie serves and I miss. Twice. It's not even a good serve. It bounces off the back wall and stays high. I could have easily scooped in and slammed it. Instead, I'm wasting brain space on Kylie.

I jump up and down a few times. Shake my head. Okay. Moving on.

Charlie serves. I rush in, power driving the ball down the line. Charlie dives for it. Misses. My serve. I slam the ball. It hits the back, then the side wall, and dies on the floor. Ace. An impossible return. There's nothing Charlie can do but appreciate my mad skills. I'm back. Kylie Flores is gone.

CHAPTER FIVE

"Honey, just 'cause
I talk slow doesn't
mean I'm stupid."
—SWEET HOME ALABAMA

jake:

Hopefully, Kylie is getting on the 3:13 right now at the corner of Buchwald and Center. Otherwise, she's going to be late, and Mom will be mad. The bus will stop fourteen times before she gets off. The ride is fifty-two minutes long. Unless the bus hits all the green lights; then the ride is forty-one minutes. But this only happens five times a year.

Just like me, Kylie likes to sit by the window and look out as the bus cruises toward Logan Heights. There are 186 buildings downtown. More than twenty-nine of them stand taller than three hundred feet. The tallest building in the city is thirty-four stories. One America Plaza. It may not sound very tall if you've been to Chicago or New York. I haven't. So One America Plaza seems really tall to me.

Kylie puts in her earbuds and listens to music so she doesn't have to talk to anyone. I like to talk to people when I'm on the bus. Sometimes they get up and change seats. Mom says not to be upset, people just don't like to talk to strangers. Lately, I've tried not to talk as much. But when Mom or Kylie aren't in the mood to talk, it's hard to know what to do with all the words. There's always something interesting to talk about, like why certain cacti lean way over but don't fall to the ground (I suspect this has to do with the moisture content in the cactus fiber), or how the labels on most soda bottles are exactly the same size as the labels on ketchup bottles, almost all of which are manufactured in Malaysia.

I wish I were on the bus right now with Kylie. She always likes listening to me. We could talk about the Great Pacific Garbage Patch that I read about in school today.

I hear a key in the lock. Kylie's home.

CHAPTER SIX

> "Traveling through
> hyperspace ain't like
> dusting crops, boy."
> —STAR WARS

kylie:

"October 1972," I say to Jake as I enter the house and see him waiting for me on the maroon chair next to the couch, a bowl of carrots on his lap. I hang up my backpack and step over the enormous pile of laundry deposited at the bottom of the stairs, wondering if it's clean or dirty.

Jake smiles at me like it's been ten years since we've seen each other. Still, it's nice to be greeted every single day with such enthusiasm. Even if Jake's brain is a little scrambled from Asperger's, it feels good to be loved this much. There aren't a lot of people who feel so positively inclined toward me.

"Hurricane Dimitri," he yells out triumphantly. "Seven

"Me too." Jake smiles, genuinely pleased. "I like when we both have good days."

I point to the carrots on the floor. "How about those carrots?"

Jake reluctantly gets down on all fours and gathers up a few carrots. He flicks one under the couch, for fun. He watches to see what I'll do. I pretend not to see. I'm too wiped to care.

Jake stands up and looks at me expectantly.

"Okay. November 1932," I say.

"There was no hurricane that month. Just a tropical storm. That's boring." Jake peers at me, eager. Too eager. "Give me another one."

Just once, I'd love to come home, disappear into my room, listen to some Arcade Fire, and spend some quality time writing.

"Okay, here's a reverse one. Hurricane Dana," I say.

"Oooh. I know that one." Jake is so excited, he starts to vibrate.

Jake is smart. Scary smart. People assume he's stupid because he's got a disability, but they're dead wrong. If anything, he's disabled by his superbrain. The carrots are back on the floor.

Mom rushes down the stairs, her uniform hanging open, her overstuffed purse dangling from her arm. "Can you make dinner, Kyles?"

She kneels down and picks up the carrots.

"Mom, please don't do that. Jake can pick them up. Right, Jake?"

Jake says nothing.

Mom continues to gather the carrots into the bowl with one hand as she buttons her uniform with the other. "Oh, people died in Galveston, Texas, and there was twelve inches of precipitation over two days." Jake eyes shine with excitement.

"Okay . . . December 1956."

"Hurricane Meredith. Jamaica lost power for six days. Winds up to 146 miles an hour." Jake jumps up. His carrots spill across the floor. At thirteen, he's my height, his jagged energy bouncing off him like electric currents. On the heels of my enormously bad day, I am feeling irritated by Jake, which I try to hide.

"Pick up the carrots, Jakie," I say.

Jake scowls at me. "No. I won't."

I soften my tone. "Please pick up the carrots. And then we'll keep playing." I wrap my arms around his hulking frame and pull him close. "Did you have a good day?"

"Yeah. We learned about the Great Pacific Garbage Patch," Jake responds, eager to tell me more.

I smile. No matter how bad my day is, Jake can always make me smile. His passion for minutiae is infectious. Until it gets annoying.

"Did you have a good day, Kylie?" Jake asks. He's been learning about manners and empathy at school, things that don't come naturally to him. It seems like it's finally sinking in. Jake is usually so immersed in his own world, he forgets t ask me about mine. Not that I mind. It's a relief to spend son time in someone else's reality.

"My day was great," I lie. I know the truth will only conf and depress him, just as it does me. He has a limited capa to understand complicated social interactions, and my l chock-full of them.

Kylie, it's just carrots. Don't be so hard on him."

Jake looks at me, and we have a moment of understanding. He's gotten away with it, as usual.

"Here, honey." Mom hands me a piece of paper with an elaborate chart sketched on it. "He's got to do three sets of fifteen each, okay, and that includes the arm stretches and the hopping thing the doctor showed us the other day. He needs it to improve his balance. And don't forget the pills." If Mom paid one tenth this much attention to me, maybe I wouldn't have lost my mind on a squash court this afternoon.

"Okay," I say.

"I want to play guitar tonight. I don't want to do the stupid exercises." Jake's mood is shifting.

"You can play guitar, honey, after you and Kylie do the exercises, and after you eat dinner. Kylie, I left some salad in the fridge, but you can make some pasta or something. And Dad should be home in a half hour. He came back a day early."

Mom works as a nurse at Piedmont Retirement Village four nights a week. I'm in charge of myself and Jake those nights. And Dad, whenever he's around. God knows what will happen once I leave. Dad doesn't spend a whole lot of time taking care of anyone but himself. He mows the lawn and takes out the garbage, such classic dad duties it would be funny if it weren't slightly tragic.

"And can you do the laundry, Kyles?"

"Is that clean or dirty?" I ask, pointing to the mound of clothes on the floor.

Mom stares at the pile, confused. "Can't remember. Can you poke around and figure it out?"

"Sure," I respond. What else can I say?

Mom pecks Jake on the cheek and then rushes out the door with a wave. "Bye, guys. Love you."

I look at my watch. Mom's going to be twenty minutes late to work. Typical.

This has been my life for as long as I can remember. Mom is so distracted by Jake, everything else is an afterthought and I'm forced to pick up the slack. Normally, I don't complain. It's pointless. It's just, today I'm so not into sifting through a heap of potentially smelly clothes and then whipping up dinner for three. I comfort myself with the thought that I'll be gone soon.

But that comfort is fleeting. As much as I want to escape, I worry about how Mom will handle things on her own. On the one hand, it makes me want to enroll at UCSD and just live at home. On the other, New York City doesn't seem far enough away. The moon doesn't seem far enough away.

I'm interrupted from my roundelay of anxieties by Jake tugging at my sleeve.

"Can I tell you the answer? Can I tell you? Can I tell you?" Jake has been waiting patiently, and now he's bursting to answer the question I've long forgotten. Still, he's made impressive progress at his new school. I am reminded what Jake is capable of when he sets his mind to it. A year ago, he never would have had the self-control to wait. "September 1987. Grenada had bad flooding. Grenada had bad flooding!!"

"You're amazing, Jake," I say. And I mean it.

Jake could do this for the next ten hours. He will do this for the rest of his life, actually. This, and recite every iteration of the dozens of bus schedules that service the greater San Diego area.

I wade through the laundry and realize, to my relief, that it's clean. One less thing to do. I grab the clothes and start to head up to my room. "Jake, I'm going upstairs for a little bit. You want to watch TV? Or read your book?"

"I want to tell you about the Garbage Patch," Jake whines. "You have to hear about the Garbage Patch. You just have to. . . ."

I can feel myself shutting down. I just want to proof my valedictorian speech one last time, and get back to my screenplay. But then I see Jake's hands trembling. He's verging on a tantrum. I look at his sweet, open face, pleading with me for more time. I plop onto the couch with the laundry.

"Tell me, Jakie," I say.

I fold the laundry as Jake settles onto the floor.

"Well, it's twice the size of Texas and located in the middle of the Pacific Ocean. It's made up of plastic and other forms of debris, like fishing nets. Garbage from all over the world gets sucked in by an oceanic gyre, which is a huge system of rotating currents." He speaks with the zeal of a true believer. It's not so much the words I'm hearing, it's more the cadence.

"It takes about five years for a piece of garbage from the west coast of North America to be carried into the gyre. So if I lie down on a raft tomorrow, I could get to the gyre by 2017. Nobody knows how long it's been there, but it's growing larger every day. At some point it might just fill up the ocean so that *we* are the island and *it* is the land. I don't understand why someone doesn't just clean it up."

He makes a good point.

Two of Jake's friends who also have Asperger's, have the same lilting quality to their speech. When all three of them are together, it can sound like a spoken symphony. They say people with Asperger's can't understand basic human signals, the little things we all do that mean "I don't understand" or "You are standing too close." They are always bumping up against a world that confuses and thwarts them, and occasionally, this foreign planet and its people can be too much for them, and they can rage, as Jake does sometimes, when his brain erupts into flames. Pure pain and anguish shoot out of him in the form of a tantrum. Despite the fact that I'm the "normal" kid in the family, I understand Jake's behavior only too well. I experience it myself, albeit in a muted form. Sometimes I wonder who the normal sibling is. I'm rarely ever as happy or comfortable with myself as Jake can be. I wish life were easier for both of us. It would be nice to slip through the world, smooth and slick as arrows whizzing through air, instead of always crashing into things.

As Jake buzzes on, my mind drifts back to the worry stream, and I find myself lost in the current again. How will Jake deal without me? What if he can't find his blue sweatshirt, which happens at least twice a week? What if Jake spits on his teacher again, Mom can't leave her shift, and Dad is traveling? That happened last year, and I skipped my math test to pick him up.

And, on the B side, what about me? Wouldn't it be ironic if Jake was just fine when I left, and I turned out to be the basket case, all alone in New York City? Who will be excited to see me when I return to my dorm after a long day of clawing my way through the city? Who will comfort me? Who will I confide in, without Will and Jake around?

But if I stay, I'll never leave. And then what?

This is the drain of being me. I can't seem to find the joy, just the dilemmas. A Möbius strip of crazed thoughts loops through my brain on constant rotation. I've wanted to go to NYU forever. When I got in—with a full ride, no less—my parents weren't the least bit pleased to hear the news. Especially in light of the fact that I'd gotten into Brown, Princeton, and the University of Pennsylvania the same week. Mom and Dad were dead set against NYU, which is pretty funny since they know nothing about it. Unlike all the other Freiburg parents, they weren't really involved in my college applications. Still, they knew enough to be alarmed that I was turning down a scholarship to an Ivy League school. They begged me to go to Brown, where I got a substantial amount of money. They didn't fight for Princeton or UPenn, because, frankly, we couldn't have afforded it. New York City scares the shit out of them, despite the fact that neither has ever been there.

"Be premed. Or prelaw. Do something practical," Mom pleaded.

She can't understand why I want to write movies. Though she hasn't come right out and said it, she doesn't think I have a chance in hell of actually succeeding at it. As far as Mom and Dad are concerned, I might as well sell cotton candy at the circus. But I am like a dog with a bone. Sheer tenacity won out over their eventual fatigue.

The front door opens and Dad walks in. He's carrying a huge box of medical supplies.

"Hey," I say.

"Hey, guys. Kylie, want to help with this?"

I get up and help him with the box. Dad's been trying to

49

sell medical equipment lately. I say *trying*, because it's not going very well. Even though people still get sick, nobody wants what he's selling, which is some new sonogram machine that's twice the price but ten times more exact.

"So, how'd it go?" I say.

"Not great. Better luck next week, hopefully." Dad gives me a weak smile.

Dad used to sell electronics at Circuit City, until they went out of business. (Which is kind of weird, considering everyone at Freiburg seems to have a house full of the latest, greatest, shiniest electronics. Rumor has it Deborah Sneeden has a retractable flat screen television in every room in her house. I guess the Sneedens didn't buy their electronics at Circuit City.)

"Dad, Dad, I learned to play 'Sergeant Pepper' on the guitar, wanna hear?" Jake has grabbed his guitar and is swinging it around manically.

"Whoa there, buddy, let's put that down. Don't want to break it."

Jake ignores Dad and starts strumming the guitar. It's not exactly music, but it's something. I'm proud of the fact that Jake is trying hard. Who cares if he can hit the right chords?

"I'll tell you what," Dad says, preparing for his exit. "Let me relax for a bit, and then maybe we can have a concert. Okay?"

Jake keeps playing, but Dad is already en route to the garage to fiddle with one of his beloved motorcycles, none of which he even rides. He's much more interested in his old bikes than his kids. He'll come back into the house for an awkward dinner—made, served, and cleaned up by yours truly—and then settle onto the couch with a six-pack, and be lulled to sleep by the dull sounds of episodic television.

I get that his life sucks (having doors slammed in your face every day must be soul-crushing). I get that selling medical equipment may not have been his lifelong dream (not that I have a clue what he'd rather be doing, since he never talks about his past). But I'd be a lot more sympathetic if he were more pleasant on the rare occasions when he was home. And if he took the time to talk to me or Jake about . . . anything. Maybe it's a chemical thing and he just needs some pharmaceuticals (not likely that will ever happen). Or maybe this is just the way Dad is drawn. Anyway, I've kind of given up trying to get to know him. I'm outta here. But Jake's not. So as long as I'm in this house, I'll fight the good fight for Jakie; not that I actually expect it to yield results.

I follow Dad out the back door.

"You know, Jake notices that you're always disappearing into the garage. You could spend a little time with him every now and then."

"Kylie, I do not want to have this conversation. I've had a long day."

"It's like you avoid him. How do you think that makes him feel?"

Dad turns around and looks at me.

"I don't ignore him. I'm just tired. Working on the bikes helps me relax. I'll come back in soon."

Same old story. I've been hearing it for years.

I think Dad blames Jake for his unhappiness. Maybe if he

had the perfect son, with whom he could play football or ride bikes, he wouldn't be hiding away in the garage. Or maybe that's not it at all. Maybe Dad's just a complete jerk. I'm not sure. Neither option is particularly appealing. I'm holding out hope for the former, but as the years march on, I have to say, the latter is gaining ground.

"Whatever," I say, turning and making my way back into the house.

"Kylie . . ." Dad calls out, feeling a tinge of remorse, I'm guessing. Maybe he is human.

I turn around. "Yeah?"

"I'll come in in a half hour. And I'll listen to Jake play. Tell him that, would you?" Dad looks sincere, like he wants to be a better man. I think it's just an attempt to assuage his guilt.

"'Kay. Sure," I say. What I don't say is, *I'll believe it when I see it*. Which is never.

Dad has cut himself off from the world. It occurs to me that I cut myself off from the world, too. I may have an inherited tendency, but I'm hoping I'll outgrow it. Or I'll learn to fight against it. The one time I saw a different side to my Dad was when my grandmother, my Dad's mother, was alive. She would come over every Sunday for dinner and Dad would dote on her. He was warm and sweet with Nana in a way he seems incapable of with me or Jake.

I return to the living room, where Jake is now watching TV. I sit back down on the couch to fold the rest of the laundry. My cell begins buzzing like a cicada.

"Hello?"

"Kylie?"

52

"Yeah."

"Hey, it's Max."

Max? Seriously? How bizarre. I say nothing, though I'm rolling my eyes.

"Kylie?"

"What?"

"Listen, about today. You were right. I, uh, shouldn't have blown you off."

I'm a cynical, cold little bitch a lot of the time, but as soon as it's clear Max is apologizing, I feel a swift rush of warmth spread through my body, and my initial temptation is to forgive him immediately. What a wimp.

"Kylie? Did you hear me?"

"Uh, yeah. And, uh, I'm sorry about walking into your squash game and kicking Charlie. I got a little carried away." Breaking no records here for verbal dexterity and imaginative retorts, I'm folding like a house of cards.

"Yeah." Max laughs. "You were pretty worked up. Anyway, if the paper means that much to you, I'll do it. Or, at least I'll give you what you need so you can do it for me."

Max is sorry, but not enough to refuse my idiotic offer to write both papers. It's my own fault. Several moments of awkward silence go by.

Finally, I manage a weak, "Okay. Whatever." Jesus, that was lamer than lame.

"How about we meet at Roland's Coffee Shop down by the pier tomorrow morning?"

"Um, I don't really know where that is. Can't we just meet at Starbucks on Randle, at seven thirty?"

"Sure, my treat."

"I can pay for my own coffee," I shoot back. I'm so sick of everyone reminding me that I'm the scholarship student. "I already agreed to meet you once, and you didn't show up. How do I know it won't happen again?"

"I'll be there. If I'm not, you can come find me in Shuman's Calculus and beat the shit out of me."

"Okay. Whatever." I've got to stop saying that stupid word.

"See you there," Max says, and then he's gone.

THE NEXT DAY:
THURSDAY, JUNE 24

CHAPTER SEVEN

"I'm kind of a big deal."
—ANCHORMAN

max:

It's 7:55 and she's not here yet. I've downed two espressos and now I've got a caffeine buzz that's making me tweaky. Her payback for yesterday, I guess.

I look around the Starbucks and can't help but feel annoyed. I wish we could have met at Roland's. I should have just given her directions. Starbucks just pisses me off. I know it's a cliché to hate Starbucks, and while I try not to be a cliché, I can't help it. Starbucks is ruining what used to be great about the city. They're taking the cool old buildings down and replacing them with big brown boxes.

This one used to be a run-down little doughnut shop with the best coffee ever. It was a stumpy, two-story, red brick building. I used to come in once a week to check out the crowd and take some pictures. All kinds of people came in for coffee, from cops to football players, from Westview High to homeless people. The old guy who owned it weighed, like, three hundred pounds. He had long dreads and a goatee. I took some pretty awesome photos. But then Starbucks swooped in, offered him cash, and leveled the place to make room for the caffeine heads. Like they didn't already have enough places to go.

Charlie's dad said there are Starbucks in China now. All those old Chinese ladies who used to squat outside their homes, sipping tea, are now going to Starbucks and ordering up Mistos. Depressing. The whole world is one big strip mall, separated by large bodies of water. What is there to see if everything looks the same? Gaps, Starbucks, Panera. At the very least, it makes me feel better that I never seem to get out of La Jolla. But does that make me a part of the problem?

I'll give Kylie two more minutes and then I'm out of here. It's the last day of high school and I'm stuck at Starbucks waiting for Kylie Flores. I should be in the quad right now, hanging with Charlie and Lily. I should be carving my name into the palm tree on the Great Lawn, which is one of those stupid Freiburg rituals that has gone on for, like, eighty years. I swore I wouldn't participate, because it's kind of pathetic, but now I'm feeling kind of sentimental about the whole thing. I want to leave my mark just like all the other seniors.

Okay, where the hell is she? I've lost all interest in being a good guy. I don't know what I was thinking. I should have blown the whole thing off. I'm supposed to be kicking back. I'll have enough to do next year at UCLA, between Lily, squash, and classes. It's my fault for taking pity on her. Nice guys totally finish last.

I get up and head for the door, which is when Kylie literally walks into me. Her backpack falls to the ground, smashing my foot.

"Shit. What do you have in there?"

"Just . . . stuff. Sorry. You okay?" Kylie asks me.

I don't say anything. I mean, it hurt, so, no, not really.

"Anyway, sorry I'm late. I had to get my brother to school, and it, uh . . . just took longer than usual today."

"It's cool," I say. But I don't mean it. I'm over it. She's late. She hurt my foot. It's easier to be an asshole. "You wanna get some coffee or something?" I ask, hoping she'll say no and we can get on with it.

"Yeah, okay. I'll be right back," Kylie says.

As Kylie gets into the line, I take a seat at a table and see Lacey Garson and Sonia Smithson walking over. They're both wearing green and blue, Freiburg's colors, which is another last-day tradition. Unlike carving my name on the tree, I'm not warming to this one.

"Hey, Max. Can we join you?" Lacey asks.

"I'm kinda here with someone," I say, feeling weird because it's Kylie.

"Oh, right, Lily . . ." Sonia smiles at me. "We'll give you your privacy."

"Actually, I'm here with Kylie Flores. We're doing Murphy's assignment," I add quickly.

"Seriously?" Lacey says. She and Sonia laugh.

"I know. Kylie wouldn't stop hassling me until I agreed. She's doing both papers."

"I'm sure she just wanted to hang with you," Lacey says, winking at me. Lacey is always winking at me. It's kinda freaky. It looks more like an eye tic than anything sexy. Lacey has had a crush on me since seventh grade. I considered making out with her once, in ninth grade. I was pretty buzzed, but still couldn't pull the trigger. There's just too much going on with all that dyed blond hair, makeup, and jewelry. And all she ever talks about is clothes.

Kylie returns with coffee. Lacey and Sonia walk off, ignoring Kylie completely. They whisper to each other and giggle as they stand in line, glancing over at us. It's obvious they're talking about Kylie. Man, girls can be brutal.

Kylie looks uncomfortable. She lives somewhere around the seventh layer of social hell. It's got to be a drag.

"You know what I don't get about Lacey and Sonia?" Kylie asks me.

"What?"

"Lacey must spend more time with personal grooming than any other girl at Freiburg. Her hair is bleached to within an inch of its life. Her makeup is caked on so thick she probably has to remove it with an ice pick. So you'd think she would have turned her attention to Sonia and plucked that animal tail between her eyes."

I bust out laughing. Kylie nailed it. Sonia does have a freaky unibrow.

"Okay. Let's get started," Kylie says, suddenly all business.

She pulls out a notebook and pen. I don't take out anything. This is her show.

"So, uh, the book that most impacted you?" Kylie says. I can tell by the look on her face that she's not expecting much from me.

"I guess, maybe *Catcher in the Rye*," I say, though I don't mean it. It's just an easy answer.

Kylie smiles, biting her lower lip, like she's holding back laughter.

"What?" I say.

"I just figured you'd say something like that."

I'm not loving the smirk on her face or the condescension in her voice. She thinks she knows me. She doesn't have a clue.

"And I figured you'd say something like that," I respond, looking her in the eye. "Actually, it's not really true. I just said it so we could be done. That was the first thing that came to mind."

"If we're going to do this, let's do it right. I mean, we're here."

She's right. Why am I hedging? Because I don't do books with people. It's not my thing. I talk sports and shit. It's who I am. It's what people expect from me. No one cares what I think of T. S. Eliot. Even though the truth is, I like him. I just don't really want to talk about it.

"Pick something else. Impress me," Kylie adds.

Yeah. Right. She should try impressing me. Like I need to prove something to her. And yet, here I am, thinking about what I'm going to say. Fine. Let's play.

"'Death is always the same, but each man dies in his own

way.' You guess the book," I say. "C'mon, impress me."

Kylie doesn't say anything for a minute. I've totally stumped her. She looks so shocked, I have to laugh.

"What?" She says.

"You don't have a clue and that's kinda funny."

"Why's that so funny?"

"I don't know. It's just, you usually have all the answers in English, so I would have figured you'd know this."

"Yeah, well, I don't."

Kylie's not used to being caught off guard like this. She's used to being the smartest person in the room. She's not amused.

"Maybe I'm not as predictable as you thought," I say.

"Okay. What I said before was bitchy," Kylie admits.

"Yeah, a little."

"So, what's the book?"

"*Clock Without Hands* by Carson McCullers."

"Wow, I could barely make it through that book. I thought it was really depressing."

"I liked it. I thought it was . . . hopeful. In a weird way."

"Really? Why?"

"I don't know. . . . I guess because it's about coping with, you know, dark shit, stuff no one wants to talk about. The lies we tell ourselves to get by." It's stuff I can relate to. But I'm not going to admit that to Kylie. She doesn't need to know my business. Instead, I just say, "Yeah. I guess it's depressing. But, you know, we gotta deal with it. None of us are getting out alive."

"That's deep. Did you steal that line from Taylor Lautner?"

"Actually, Clint Eastwood. Give me a little credit. Taylor Lautner?"

Kylie laughs. "Good point. Too deep for Taylor. But I still don't get it. What's the hopeful part?"

"I guess just that there's dignity in death. That if you live your life right, maybe it makes the dying part not so bad. It's comforting, somehow. It made me less afraid of death."

"Intense. I never figured you for a Carson McCullers fan," Kylie says.

"Why? Because I'm a dumb jock?"

"I'm not saying you're a dumb jock. I don't even really know you. It's just, you don't say much in English. I assumed you weren't into reading. But you obviously got more out of the book than I did. I mean, I didn't get any of that." Kylie grins. She's got a sexy smile with her big, full lips. I don't think I've ever seen her smile in school. "It's just . . . not what I expected you to say. At all."

People are rarely what they seem, babe.

"This is great. I figured I was going to have to do all the heavy lifting, but you gave me some stuff to work with. The only thing I remember about Carson McCullers is that her best friend was Truman Capote, which is the coolest thing ever. That guy had more style and wit than anyone, ever," Kylie says.

I've actually read Truman Capote. I loved *In Cold Blood*. But I'm not going to mention it. That could take up a whole lot of time. Kylie seems a little too eager to talk about books. We don't need to start bonding all over the place. I'm just here to get the job done.

"So, one more book," Kylie says. "And then you never have to talk to me again."

"Promise?" I'm just messing with her.

"Trust me, I'm as psyched about it as you."

"*Infinite Jest*," I say, without pausing to think.

"Okay. Why? I haven't read it."

"It's about addiction, tennis, escaping life. I don't know. I can relate."

"Why would *you* want to escape life?" Kylie asks.

"No one's life is perfect," I say. I want to leave it at that, but Kylie looks like she's dying to ask me more questions. "I have my stuff, like everyone else. Anyway, those are my books. That's my deal. Are you still cool with writing both papers?"

"Uh, yeah. Sure . . . I'll just do it during study. I should be able to get them both done by class today. I guess . . ." Kylie doesn't seem super into it anymore, but it was her idea. I'm sure not writing the paper. I'm already in deeper than I need to be. It's time to get back to the last day of school.

I stand up, ready to blow out of here, when I see Kylie looking up at me, all puppy dog eyes.

"Don't you want to know what book had the biggest impact on me?" she asks.

Not really. I thought we were done. I was walking out the door, in my mind. "Uh, sure." I sit back down, not wanting to be a total dick.

"Well, if I had to choose . . ." Kylie looks like she's about to give some kind of major speech. I'm wondering what Charlie and Lily are up to. Doughnuts and coffee on the front steps? Frisbee on the lawn? "It's a hard choice, but I guess I'd say *The Stranger* by Camus, because it felt so true to me. It's about understanding that no one cares, but once you accept that, you can actually move on and be happy."

66

"That's depressing."

"Right back at you."

Girl's got a point. We both like bleak shit. Who'd have thought I'd have anything in common with Kylie Flores?

"And then I loved this book *Disgrace*, by a South African author named Coetzee. I read it last year. I think it's the most perfect book ever written. Every single word in that book should be there. It's so honest. And real. It's about racial oppression, which I don't think we ever escape."

I can't believe we're still talking about books. I've never talked about books with anyone outside of class. It's weird. I'm not sure what I'm supposed to say next. I don't really have the time or the interest to get into a whole long thing about literature. I've got places to go. People to see.

"Anything else you need from me?" I ask. I'm feeling kind of bad, but what am I going to do, offer to write it myself? Miss out on the last day of school? No thanks.

"I think I have enough," Kylie says.

I stand up again. "Okay, then, I guess we're good to go." I'm about to head out when I realize that Kylie is looking around in a panic. Oh no. Now what?

"What's up?" I ask her.

"My backpack's gone. . . ." Kylie jumps out of her seat and races toward the exit, nearly knocking down two old women in the process.

I rush after her because . . . well, I'm not really sure why. I feel like I should, somehow.

Kylie bolts out the door and runs down the street. I'm right behind her.

"Where are you going?"

"That guy stole my backpack." Kylie points to a small fig-ure in a black leather jacket racing down the sidewalk a few feet in front of us.

"Don't follow him," I pant as I try to keep pace with Kylie. "He's a criminal. Why don't we call the cops?"

"No time. I need my computer. . . . It has my life in it." And with that, Kylie sprints around the corner, chasing some thug who most likely has a gun. I stop and watch her go. While death may be part of life, it has no part in mine at the moment.

CHAPTER EIGHT

"I don't know. I'm making this up as I go."
—RAIDERS OF THE LOST ARK

kylie:

'm running for my life. Because that's what's in the computer. My screenplay, my valedictorian speech, my journal—my life. And nothing's backed up. What can I say? I know there's no excuse, and yet . . . I didn't do it. This would be funny if it weren't so tragic, which is kind of the story of my life. I look back and realize Max must have given up. Not like I expected his help or anything.

The thief is wiry and fast. He looks younger than me. What is he doing stealing backpacks from Starbucks? He should be in school.

I push with everything I've got. I'm gaining on him. Just a few more feet and I'll be able to grab it. I'm closing in. I reach out for my backpack, which swings around on his arm like a monkey. I miss. I try again. This time, my hand latches on to the strap. But he tugs and the backpack slips from my grip. I stretch forward as far as I can, trying to catch the strap in my fingers, but I lose my balance and crash to the sidewalk. I'm going at such a fast clip, I roll over a few times before coming to a stop on the pavement, my jeans, wrist, and elbow etched with cuts and scrapes.

I watch helplessly as he jumps onto a dirt bike parked at the curb, and peels out. He must be one of those street kids who hangs around the beach and spins on his bike all day long. San Diego is crawling with them. I've never given them much thought. Now I understand how they afford their designer sweatshirts and tricked-out bikes. I fall back onto the sidewalk, defeated. I am so royally screwed.

"Hey, get in," a voice calls out.

I lift my head to see a car pulling up to the curb. Max stares at me from inside a sparkling new Beemer.

I don't respond at first. I'm too stunned that Max is actually here.

"C'mon, Kylie. I'll take you to school."

"I'm not going to school. I've got to get my computer back. There's no point to anything without it."

"Don't you think you're being a little melodramatic?"

"No! I need my computer. . . ." And then I burst into tears. So humiliating.

"Okay. Fine."

"Fine what?"

Max gets out of the car and helps me up.

"Shit, you're bleeding."

"It's just a scrape." I take a few deep breaths and try to pull it together.

Max puts his arm around my waist and helps me into the car. I hurt all over from the fall. I'm completely embarrassed from my emotional outburst, and yet the only thing occupying my mind is Max's proximity. He's really close. Close enough to make me flush. His touch is soothing—warm and firm. He smells like coconut shampoo and coffee. I can feel the blood rushing up my spine. This is too strange. Max Langston has his arm around me. Even stranger, Max Langston is going to help me.

"For the record, I think this is a terrible idea," Max says as he gets into the car.

I don't say anything, because Max is right. Still, the fact remains that I've got to get my computer back. There really is no alternative. Max guns the engine and the car shoots forward. I guess it's a good thing he's got a Beemer, because my Mom's old Honda takes about an hour to gather speed.

"Thanks. I really appreciate this," I say.

"Yeah, well, if we make it out alive, you can buy me a drink or something."

We power down the street, hugging the road. Before long, we catch sight of the guy on his bike, expertly weaving in and out of traffic. Max is on him in minutes, but he's elusive. First we see him, then we don't, as he darts around cars and through lights. He's obviously done this before. Max is switching lanes like crazy, trying to keep pace.

"So what's on the computer that's so important?"

"For one, my valedictorian speech for Saturday . . ."

"But you backed it up, didn't you?"

"No. I didn't back it up. I have a ton of stuff on my plate. So, no. I messed up. Okay?" Max is helping me out and I'm yelling at him. What is wrong with me? This is so not the way normal people behave. Then again, I'm a little stressed at the moment. Hopefully, I can chalk it up to that. Though I doubt it. More likely, I can blame it on my extreme lack of social skills.

Max doesn't say anything. There's an awkward silence as we trail the bike for a few blocks. I've got to learn to edit myself. If I get my computer back, I vow to try.

"Sorry, I didn't mean to bite your head off," I say. It's the second time I've apologized for being a bitch. At a certain point, if it walks like a bitch and talks like a bitch . . . "It's just, I spent five months writing my speech, and then I've got a screenplay I've been working on for two years, and it's . . . it's kind of a big deal—"

"Also not backed up, I'm guessing." Max smiles. He's got a really beautiful smile. Perfect white teeth, dimples. No wonder every girl at Freiburg has a crush on him.

The bike makes a sudden turn off on Kearney Villa Road, maneuvering through three lanes of cars.

"Quick, he's turning," I cry out.

"Yeah, I see. It's gonna be kinda hard to get out of here. There are cars everywhere."

There's a lot of honking as Max snakes his way through five lanes of traffic, nearly colliding with several cars. At one point, I shut my eyes, not wanting to see what I've wrought.

But then, miraculously, we're on the exit ramp, unscathed.

"Impressive," I say.

"Yeah, I've got mad driving skills. Don't know shit about American history though."

Unfortunately, we're about thirty seconds too late.

As we turn onto Kearney Villa Road, the bike pulls up to the side of an orange-and-white U-Haul truck. Two guys climb out of the truck and approach the biker. They look exactly like the kind of guys you don't want to mess with. Muscled up, bald, badass. They almost look like twins except that one is crazy tall, maybe over six-three, and the other one is at least a head shorter. Kind of a Mini-Me. If they weren't so scary looking, it would actually be kind of a funny sight gag.

The biker pulls stuff, and more stuff, from his seemingly bottomless backpack and hands it off to the men. iPods, small electronics, and my backpack are among the stash. One of the men presses a wad of cash into the biker's hand. And then, as fast as it all began, it ends, and the biker disappears down the deserted street.

All we can do is pull over and watch.

"That is some serious shit going down," Max says.

"It feels like we're in a Michael Mann movie or something. I didn't think this kind of thing happened in real life."

"Welcome to the other side of the tracks."

"Ah, news flash, I live on the other side of the tracks and I've never seen anything like this."

We watch as the two men load their newly acquired goods into the back of their truck, jump into the front, and drive off. Forget the Michael Mann movie. That's too good for these guys. It's more like some cheesy action movie on TNT. Except it's real. It's happening to me. And it sucks.

Max starts up the car and makes a left turn. "What are you doing? Where are we going?" I demand.

"Back to Freiburg. This thing has just blown up. This is not some kid on a bike anymore. He's working with other people. Probably very bad people. We don't want to get involved. And we're missing the last day of school. This is actually the one day this year I didn't want to miss."

"Stop the car. I want to get out."

"No way. Are you kidding me?"

"Maybe you didn't hear me, but my valedictorian speech is on that computer."

"So, write a new one."

"Oh, okay, I'll toss off another one this afternoon."

"Just say whatever comes to mind. I'm sure it'll be fine."

"Yeah, well, thanks for that brilliant advice, but that's not how it works. If you knew anything about writing, you'd know it takes weeks, months, to get something right."

"If you say so," Max says, clearly not really listening, not really caring. Screw him.

Max is about to head back onto the freeway, which is when I jump out of the moving car. Not smart. Especially since I'm already banged up from my fall.

Max pulls over and rolls down his window. "I will buy you a new computer and a backup drive, okay? Just get in the car."

I don't respond. I turn and walk down the street. I can see the U-Haul stopped at a light, heading the other way. Max jumps out, rushes up to me, and gets right in my face.

"Seriously, Kylie, what are you doing? You're going to run after the truck? Like some kind of superhero? Why don't you quit while you're still alive?"

"I can't." I wish I could. But it's true. I can't. Max obviously doesn't understand.

"I know it's a huge drag, but there's nothing you can do."

I know he's trying to be nice when what he'd really like to do is dump me right here on the side of the road. I'm sure he'd rather be anywhere but here. And frankly, so would I.

I keep walking. Max follows me.

"Let's call the police," he says.

"We don't have time. We'll lose them."

It's at this point that I glance over at the Beemer. The driver's side door is wide open. I can see that Max has left the keys in the car. I make a snap decision to do something I know I will regret later. But I just can't help myself.

I turn, race back to the car, and jump into the driver's seat. Max figures out what I'm doing a split second too late. I'm already gunning the engine.

"You coming?" I ask.

"Kylie, you are totally extreme," Max says. Strangely, he doesn't seem as annoyed as I thought he'd be. More surprised. He doesn't protest as he slides in shotgun and looks over at me. "So, what're you gonna do, Scooby-Doo?"

I laugh, despite my desperation. "Follow them at a distance. See where they're going. If it seems dangerous, I'll bail. Promise."

Max looks at his watch. "I'll give you a half hour."

CHAPTER NINE

"If I'm not back in five minutes, just wait longer."
—ACE VENTURA, PET DETECTIVE

max:

Time's up.

Nothing much has happened. We've been following the truck for a half hour as it heads south. The U-Haul isn't in any hurry, just cruising. We're keeping a safe distance.

"Do you, uh, wanna turn around?" Kylie asks as she glances at the clock.

"Not yet."

Kylie looks relieved. I'm giving her a little more time. I'm not sure why, exactly. I guess I'm kinda digging the adventure. I don't usually do crazy shit like this, but once Kylie jumped into the driver's seat, I was kind of into it.

I always thought she was such a weirdo. She's barely spoken to anyone but Will in six years, but suddenly she's all crazy tough. It was hot, the way she took control. Lily would never do that. I know I should make Kylie turn the car around, that this can't lead anywhere good, but I'm not ready. Things have been so stressed lately, with Dad, college, squash, and graduation. I'm happy to skip out on real life for a while, follow a U-Haul, and play action hero. It feels good to get out. So what if it's the last day of school? It's not like anything that great happens. It's all about the parties after school, and I'll definitely be back for that.

We're cruising through parts of the city I never see: National, Chula Vista. Taking back roads south, toward the border. Maybe that's where these guys are headed. Over the border to Mexico. A good place to sell stolen stuff. Nowhere I want to go.

"Do you wanna drive?" Kylie asks.

"It's cool. You can drive."

"Okay. Thanks."

She's on best behavior. She knows I could shut this thing down anytime. I don't know why, but I don't want to let Kylie down. At least not yet. She's thinking she's somehow going to win this thing. I'm sure she's going to lose. Still, I'm willing to wait it out a little longer, on the off chance Kylie knows something I don't.

"This is an amazing car. Our car is, like, a hundred years old. We've still got a cassette player in the stereo."

"What's that?"

Kylie laughs.

"So how come you don't act like this in school?" I ask her.

"You mean, like, carjacking and playing cops and robbers?"

"No, just . . . I don't know, cooler, less uptight. You're always looking at the floor, avoiding everyone. Unless, of course, you're going insane on someone in a squash court."

Kylie smiles at this. Maybe she doesn't take herself as seriously as I thought.

"I mean, I've never even seen you at a party."

"No one's ever invited me. And I hate parties."

Kylie looks over at me, and I can see her big golden eyes poking out through a mess of curls. Her usually tight, prissy ponytail is all messed up. She looks good. Not so geeky.

"They're pretty casual. Everyone just kinda shows up," I say.

"Yeah, it would be weird if Will and I just showed up."

"Maybe." She's right. It might be weird. "Why do you spend all your time with Will?"

"Because there's no one else worth my time."

"So we're not good enough for you?" I can't believe I'm even asking her this question. Like we care what Kylie Flores thinks of us.

"Let's just say you're not right for me, and leave it at that."

I can't tell if she's bluffing. Does she actually think she's too good for us? It's pretty hilarious when you think about it.

"So what's the plan? Do you really think you're going to get your computer back? Those dudes looked pretty serious. We don't have guns or knives. I may have a Frisbee in the trunk, but that's it."

"Decapitation by Frisbee. I like it."

I laugh. She's funnier than I would have thought.

"I don't know. I'm hoping I'll come up with a brilliant idea any second now."

"Good. 'Cause I've got nothing. Maybe you can talk the guys into giving you back your computer. Like you talked me into doing Murphy's paper."

"And look where that got us," she says, pushing a few stray curls off her face.

She's got a birthmark above her lip, and the longest eyelashes I've ever seen. She's kinda hot. Not Lily hot. Hot in a different way. I never noticed it before.

The truck slows down and pulls into a 7-Eleven. Kylie parks a few cars away.

"What are you thinking? 'Cause I'm thinking we're at the end of the road here. It's been fun. But now we're done. I mean, seriously, what are we going to do? Jump the bad guys?"

"Probably not the best idea," Kylie admits.

The two dudes exit the U-Haul. From the back, they look like father and son. One of them towers over the other. They're seriously inked; even their bald heads sport tattoos. I so don't want to have anything to do with these guys. I watch as they head into the 7-Eleven, thinking to myself, I am out of here.

Before I have a chance to say anything, Kylie's out of the car and heading toward the truck. I follow her because I'm wondering what the hell she's thinking.

"What are you doing?" I ask.

"You wanted a plan, here's my plan. I'm going to get into that truck and get my computer back."

"That's a bad plan, Kylie. These are bad guys. We are way out of our element. We need to get out of here. Like now."

Kylie isn't listening to me. She runs around to the back doors of the truck. Shakes them. Locked. She moves to the driver's side door. Locked. Yeah, people with stolen electronics tend to lock their doors. But then, Kylie manages to open the passenger door.

"Kylie, get back here. Seriously. We gotta get out of here. . . ."

I'm talking to myself. Kylie ignores me and disappears into the truck.

This is no longer fun. Or cool. I'm not into it at all. It's freaking me out. Kylie is even crazier than I thought. She's going to get herself killed. And me along with her.

A couple of minutes go by and she's not out of the truck. I can't decide if I should just drive away and never look back, or go in after her. Stupidity wins out over common sense, and I climb into the passenger side. I can't see much. A partition separates the back of the truck from the front. There's a small window between the cab and the back. Kylie must have crawled through it, because she's nowhere in sight.

"Kylie, what is your problem? You are going to get us killed."

"I found it. I've just gotta dig it out. But I need help," Kylie calls out.

I peer through the window, but can't see her because she's hidden behind about a million dollars' worth of stolen electronics. There are wide-screen TVs, DVD players, cameras, iPads, speakers, desktops, laptops, printers. It looks like an electronics store warehouse. I want to run away as fast as I can. This is messed up.

"Please, Max!" Kylie begs, because I haven't moved.

The desperation in her voice draws me in. Knowing full well this could be the biggest mistake of my life, I crawl through the opening and land on the face of an enormous flat-screen television. I make my way over the equipment, toward Kylie, where she's attempting to pull her backpack out from under an iMac. We can't have much more time. Those dudes have got to be on their way back to the truck. I mean, how long can it take to pee and buy a Coke? I push the iMac to the side, freeing Kylie's backpack, and that's when the front doors to the truck open.

The two dudes climb in, slam the doors, and rev the engine.

FUCK!

The truck slowly pulls out. With us inside.

We're hidden from view by all the equipment, at least for now. What happens next is anyone's guess.

Kylie and I stare at each other. She looks like I feel—freaked and terrified. I'm sure I must look like that as well. I've never been this scared in my life. Frantic, I quietly crawl my way to the back door, but it's locked from the outside. We're totally trapped. I take Kylie by the arm and maneuver us into the corner. She doesn't seem so tough anymore as she peers up at me. We crouch behind a huge pile of speakers as the truck picks up speed.

CHAPTER TEN

"Oh, we're so dead."
—TRANSFORMERS

kylie:

think I might throw up. I've been through some pretty bad stuff: Jake's seizures, getting mugged at knifepoint on Crosby Street, and Nana's heart attack. But now that all seems minor league in comparison. I'm pretty sure we're both going to die.

It's weird what comes to mind when you think your life is about to end. I'm wondering who will be at the memorial. Definitely Will. But anyone else from school? I kind of doubt it. Will would call it an "intimate" affair. The perils of dying young when you're not super popular. I'm sure Max's funeral will be standing room only.

I force myself to try to think positive. I am not going to die.

Everything will be all right despite the absurdly ridiculous odds against that possibility. People say positive thinking can save your life. I doubt it will help, but I might as well give it a try. I attempt to focus on the fact that, best-case scenario, I'll have some good material for my next screenplay. Unfortunately, it doesn't take hold. And I'm back to freaking out.

It's dark in the truck, with only a few slashes of light piercing through the seams of the back doors. A huge television looms over us, dangerously close. If the truck swerves or stops suddenly, we could be crushed to death, which might be preferable to being beaten to a pulp.

I am so stupid. And reckless. And selfish. What about graduation? NYU? Jake? Mom? My life is just beginning. It's not supposed to be ending. How could I have just climbed into this truck? Max was right. It was a bad plan. A terrible, awful, horrible, idiotic plan that I didn't think through. As usual. I have my computer, but I'm about to lose my life. What on earth is wrong with me?

Max is sitting next to me, his arms wrapped around his knees. As I look at him not looking at me, I feel even worse. Nausea and tears well up inside me. I feel like I might burst open—raw, ugly emotion splattering all over the truck. We are so screwed, and it's all my fault.

I'd never write a lame scene like the one I've managed to find myself in. I sure as hell wouldn't have let my protagonist jump into the bad guys' truck without a plan. At the very least, I would have made sure my hero had a gun or a knife hidden in her boot. The only thing I've got is my computer. And it isn't even turned on. I suck as a real-life action hero.

I'm feeling more and more despondent. I try to play things out in my head, to ferret out a good ending, but it's just not happening. Even if we can somehow escape, that would probably involve jumping out of a moving truck onto a road with high-speed traffic bearing down on us. If we survive that—and that's a big if—we'd most likely be in San Ysidro, a border town filled with drug runners, where massacres are a daily occurrence. And that's the happy ending.

As for the bad scenarios, take your pick. We're discovered by the bad guys, dragged to a deserted location, shot, knifed, or strangled, and then left for dead. I'm overcome with images of Max and me riddled with bullets, lying in a ditch. I'm trembling. I can't get the gruesome picture out of my mind. I shake my head to stop myself from spiraling into the abyss. So much for the power of positive thinking.

I glance over at Max, looking for some kind of solace. But he seems even more terrified than me. It's disconcerting. Panic doesn't suit him.

"What are we going to do?" I whisper.

Max doesn't respond. He continues staring straight ahead. It's wigging me out. I wish he would just scream at me. Or punch me. Something. Anything. I need him to be present. He's all I've got. I am about to say something else to Max when he shoves his hand over my mouth. His palm is sweaty from nerves.

He holds up his iPhone and taps into it. My phone vibrates. I pull it out. He's texting me.

84

MAX: WTF WER U THINKING?

KYLIE: IDK. GUESS I WASNT.

MAX: YEA.

KYLIE: IM REALLY SORRY. REALLY. REALLY.

MAX: SAVE IT. NOT GOOD ENUF WEN IM DED.

KYLIE: I KNOW. I MESSED UP.

MAX: BIG TIME.

KYLIE: I GET IT. YOU HATE ME. IM AN IDIOT.

MAX: OK.

KYLIE: U DONT HAVE TO B SUCH A DICK.

MAX: IM GONNA DIE CUZ OF U. HOW SHD I B?

KYLIE: NICER?

MAX: R U SUICIDAL??

KYLIE: NO!! JUST WANTED MY COMPUTER. IT WAS STUPID.

MAX: WHTEVR.

KYLIE: U CLIMBD IN BEHIND ME.

MAX: N BY THAT U MEAN THANX?

KYLIE: IT WAS UR CHOICE.

MAX: I WAS TRYING TO HELP. WONT DO THAT AGAN.

KYLIE: SORRY. REALLY, REALLY SORRY. I AM.

MAX: WATS UR PLAN NOW?

KYLIE: DUNNO. U HAVE ANY IDEAS?

MAX: THIS IS UR PLAN, UR FAULT. U COM UP W SUMTHING.

KYLIE: WISH I CD. BUT HOW? WHAT?

MAX: GUESS U SHD HAV THOT OF THAT B4.

I shoot Max an exasperated look. How is that helpful? He's acting like a petulant child, and refusing to be part of the solution. Max won't meet my gaze. He's too angry at me. I can't blame him. I deserve it. He'd be at school, basking in the limelight, celebrating the last day of classes, comfortably inter-twined with Lily in an ostentatious show of public affection, if it wasn't for me. Still, if we're going to spend our final hours on earth together, it might be helpful if we could get along. Or at the very least, work together.

KYLIE: I GET THAT I MESSED UP BUT UR GONNA HAV TO HELP ME OUT HERE.
MAX: HOW???? ID B OUT OF HERE IF I CD. DOORS R LOCKD. NO WAY OUT. WERE SCREWD.
KYLIE: SHD WE CALL 911?
MAX: NO! 2 RISKY. IF THEY C COPS, THELL FREAK. MAYB SHOOT US.
KYLIE: THEN WHAT?
MAX: WE WAIT. MAYB THELL STOP AGEN. N WE RUN.

The truck makes a sharp left turn. I fall on top of Max as both of us are thrown against the wall by the centrifugal force. The television falls to the ground. The edge of it nails my knee, which throbs in pain.

Something seems to shift in Max, and his anxiety shoots through the roof. He is gulping air like he's struggling for breath. His eyes are glassy. His jaw is tensed. I look down to see his hand gripping his pant leg. He reminds me of Jake when he's seen a snake. Too frightened to move or speak. I text him.

MAX R U OK?

Max doesn't text back.

"Max? What's wrong?" I whisper in his ear.

86

He doesn't respond. He turns away from me and stares at the floor. I don't know what to do. I want to reach out to him. I'm just not sure how. I barely know the guy. Amid this nightmare, and despite all my better instincts, my heart swells a little for him. I can't help it. He looks so vulnerable. It's a whole different side to a guy who I thought was made of stone.

CHAPTER ELEVEN

"If somebody told you I was just your average ordinary guy, not a care in the world, somebody lied."
—SPIDER-MAN

max:

For the past ten minutes we've been moving at a pretty fast clip. I'm deep breathing to keep the anxiety at bay. Kylie keeps looking at me, but I want nothing to do with her. Seriously, what do we have to say to each other at this point? I'm having a hard time just maintaining.

I hear one of the guys in front yelling into his cell in Spanish. I don't understand anything except the word "Tijuana."

Tijuana? Jesus. I know Kylie understands Spanish. I text into my cell.

MAX: R THEY GOIN TO TIJUANA?

KYLIE: YES

MAX: WHAT ELS DID THEY SAY?

KYLIE: JUST SOME ADDRESS. I THINK THEY'RE DROPPING STUFF THERE. NOT SUR.

Mexico?!

I read the papers. I know what's going on in those bor-der towns. People are being slaughtered, entire police forces are quitting, journalists are murdered just for showing up to work.

I feel dizzy. My vision starts to pulse in and out. There's no more keeping anything at bay. The dam breaks and an enor-mous wave of fear spreads through my body. I sit on my hands to stop them from shaking. I'm having a panic attack. It's not the first time. I've been here before. My chest cramps up. My heart whirs out of control. Red-hot anxiety courses through my veins. I just need to breathe. Count to ten. Slowly. Focus on something. I can will myself off the ledge. I've done it before.

I wish Kylie would stop staring at me. It's making things worse.

For the most part, I'm pretty chill. I can get intense during squash, but that's different. Nothing like this had ever hap-pened, until last year. I didn't have a clue what was going on. I thought I was having a heart attack. Luckily, I was in the hospital at the time. My mom and I had been sitting in the waiting room for hours. She was zoned out on some kind of meds, and powering through a stack of gossip magazines. I was reading On the Road. We were mostly ignoring each other. To fill the dead air, Mom would occasionally ask me about school or squash. Not about Dad. Stupid stuff. We were pretending that everything was okay. That's what my family does. We put all our shit away into some dark place where we never go, and plaster on our game faces.

Dr. Stein was still wearing his scrubs when he came out and headed toward us. I could tell it wasn't good news. I wanted to get the hell out of that hospital. Just jump in the elevator, slip outside, into the sunshine, and go for the longest run of my life. But I stayed there next to Mom as Dr. Stein told us more than I wanted to hear about Dad's condition.

That was when my body first seized up. It felt like I was suffocating. Like my organs were shutting down. I thought I was just sitting there suffering in silence, but it must have been pretty obvious, because all of a sudden, Dr. Stein grabbed me by the shoulders and pulled me to my feet.

"Breathe, Max," he said. "Slowly. Blow the air out through your mouth. In through your nose. Stare at the nurse's station. Put everything else out of your mind. You're having an anxiety attack. It'll subside in a few minutes. Keep breathing with me."

Dr. Stein was right. After about ten minutes, I came out of it. It didn't feel like the world was pressing down on me. I could move and breathe normally again. For the next few hours I was still a little shaky. The whole thing really messed with my head. Once something like that happens to you, you start to wonder if you'll ever feel normal again. You wonder if you even *are* normal. Or if something is seriously wrong.

Dr. Stein had me talk to some woman psychiatrist for a few weeks. She was pretty useless. She asked me a million questions. Mostly I lied to her, told her everything was cool so we could end the sessions. She prescribed Xanax for me, but I threw them down the toilet. Mom was already taking way too much of that shit. We didn't need two robots in the house.

For weeks afterward, I felt like I was always waiting for it to happen again. Where would I be? Somewhere embarrassing, like school? Or squash? Or wherever. Worrying about it drove me crazy. But then it didn't happen. I forgot about it. Until six months ago, out of the blue. Lily and I were at the movies, some horror film. All of a sudden it felt like the walls were closing in on me. I got this weird sensation of being outside my body. The blood, the gore, the violence started getting to me. Which is weird because I usually love that stuff. I had to get up and leave the theater. I told Lily I'd be right back.

I went to the bathroom, sat on the toilet, put my head between my knees, and stayed there for about fifteen minutes, until it all blew over. When I went back in, the credits were rolling. Lily was all worried. I lied and said something about food poisoning. I couldn't bring myself to tell Lily the truth. I'm sure she would have been sympathetic and everything. It's just, I wasn't ready to tell her. I was kind of hoping I'd never have to tell her. Who wants a boyfriend who can't keep his shit together? Besides, Lily can be such a drama queen. I didn't need her freaking out about my freaking out. I figured I'd let it ride. Hopefully, it wouldn't happen again. And if it did, I'd deal with it then.

It's all been good. Until now. I'm wishing I had some of that Xanax on me.

I suddenly realize Kylie's been rubbing my back. How long

has she been doing that? I was so in my head I didn't notice at first. Her touch feels nice, soothing. It's bringing me down off the ledge. It's weird. I barely know her, but somehow she's able to calm me. My breathing slows down. My heart stops fluttering. I feel better.

And then the truck stops. I hear voices. The driver is having a conversation with someone outside, in English. We must be at the border, probably customs. We need to act fast. We could escape or be rescued. But I feel completely paralyzed. What do we do? I mean, it's not like I've been in this kind of situation before.

"We're at the border," Kylie whispers.

"What should we do?"

"I don't know."

"Should we say something?" I'm speaking incredibly fast now. The panic presses to get back in; I can feel it start to flood my brain again.

"Maybe we should scream or start pounding on the door," Kylie suggests.

I'm not sure that's such a good idea. Fear is flaming through my system. I'm not in any condition to make rapid-fire decisions. I know this is our chance. Maybe our last chance. What do we do? What do we do?

Okay. I'm going to do this. I'm about to yell at the top of my lungs. The truck begins to move again. Fast. *Are you kidding me?*

We're picking up speed. Moving away from customs. From the people who could have saved us! Shit. Shit. Shit. We've missed the moment. We're as screwed as two people can be.

Kylie picks up her phone and punches into it.

KYLIE: NOT GOOD.
MAX: YA THINK? CANT IMAGIN HOW IT CD GET WORSE.
KYLIE: THEY CD KILL US.
MAX: YEA. THAT WD B WORSE. THNX 4 THAT.

At this point, things are so bad, I have to smile. Kylie smiles as well. Gallows humor, as they say. We're out of options, for the time being.

KYLIE: THEY'LL STOP AGAIN SOON. WE'LL JUMP OUT THEN.
MAX: IN TIJUANA? PERFECT. BEEN DYING TO GO THERE.
KYLIE: I HEAR IT'S NICE THIS TIME OF YEAR.

I don't know how we got into this head space, but I guess it's better than the place I was a little while ago. Might as well suck the last bits of humor out of our lives.

Kylie texts me again, punching away at her phone. I look down at mine and realize I'm getting nothing. I look at her. She looks at me, confused, and tries again. Still nothing.

She leans in to me and whispers, "I think we lost service."

I don't respond. I mean, what can I say?

"You have to let your service provider know when you're going to another country," Kylie whispers, like she's some kind of official Verizon rep or something. Is this somehow supposed to be helpful information? She looks at me expectantly like one of us might want to get in touch with our "service provider" right about now, request international service. Genius plan, babe.

We sit in silence. I'm no longer feeling the humor.

Soon we'll be buried among the cacti, our bodies laying waste in the desert, dinner for coyotes. Fear gives way to anger. I am suddenly aware of how pissed I am at Kylie. Man, I cannot believe she got us into this. I'm dying to lose my mind on her. Tell her what I really think of her for making me do Murphy's assignment, meeting her at Starbucks, following the biker, and then climbing into this stupid truck. For a smart chick, SHE IS A TOTAL IDIOT. But then again, I followed her into the truck, so, really, what is my problem? I do a silent scream in my head. It doesn't help.

Kylie tugs at my sleeve. I shake her off. Let her sit in her own shit. I'm sitting in mine. Even if she's the last person I get to see before I die, I'm not really interested in conversation.

"I heard them say they're pulling over soon," Kylie whispers.

I don't feel the need to answer. There's nothing I can possibly say that will be at all helpful. Besides, we shouldn't be talking. If we're quiet and they don't notice us, maybe somehow, miraculously, we'll make it out of here alive.

"We could make a run for it," Kylie suggests, as though she's had some kind of inspired breakthrough.

"Whatever," I say, rolling my eyes. Shit. That's the best she's got? Obviously, if there's any opportunity, we're going to make a run for it. I'm going to run like hell. I just don't think it's very likely that we'll be able to run without the two dudes noticing us.

"What is that supposed to mean?" Kylie asks. Her eyes bore

into me, big and sad, like some kind of wounded animal. She thinks we're a team and I've just let her down.

"Nothing," I say. I'm not going to make this any easier for her by pretending we're in this together. If we're going down, it's each man for himself. I'm not interested in making her feel better. Or being a hero. What Kylie does is up to her. I'm taking care of number one.

"I know this is my fault," Kylie whispers, "but we have to work together if we're going to survive. I can't die. I can't. If I die, my entire family falls to pieces."

Yeah, tell me about it. "It's not like my family will be thrilled," I shoot back.

And then she starts crying quietly, her shoulders shaking.

Oh, man. What am I supposed to do now? I feel bad. Immediately, I backpedal.

"We're gonna figure this out," I say. I'm not sure why, but I reach out and take her hand. I guess because, if this is the last thing I do on earth, I don't want to be a complete asshole about it. "We'll get out of here alive. I promise."

I'm trying my best to believe what I'm saying, but it's a pretty empty statement. I'm really not feeling it, though it seems to help Kylie. She stops crying, wipes away the tears.

The truck stops. The front doors pop open and then quickly close. The two dudes have left, for the moment. We hear them talking as they walk away.

Kylie shoots up, pulling herself together. It's as if the crying somehow bolstered her. She's definitely rising to the occasion. I am not. I'm feeling defeated before I've even begun to fight, which is totally lame of me.

"This is it. It may be our only chance," Kylie tells me. Shit. What's she doing this time?

Kylie straps on her backpack and crawls to the window that divides the front from the back of the truck. She peers out and, without warning, shimmies her way through the window, landing in the front seat. I'm not sure whether to follow or stay put. I mean, the guys could be right outside. With guns.

"What are you doing, Max? C'mon," Kylie insists.

I'm terrified. I don't move at first. I can't believe Kylie's got more balls than me.

"I don't see them. We need to go. Now," Kylie commands.

There's something firm and reassuring in her voice. It urges me on. She's all badass again. The way she was earlier. The girl is totally bipolar, but she does manage to get me going. I push myself up and over the pile of electronics I've been sitting on for the past hour and pull myself through the window.

Kylie and I are crouched down in the front seat. We peek out through the windshield and can see that we're parked on a small side street, somewhere in Tijuana, presumably. All the signs are in Spanish. Across the street is a store that sells phone cards; I can make out the words *Lagos, Nigeria* and *Sin limite*. I look up and see blue sky above.

I realize we've been in the dark for a long time. Something about the purity of the light and the brash blue reminds me of Sunday mornings on the beach with my Dad. He used to take me and my brother to explore the tide pools, in the days before he got too busy to hang out on weekends. I would stick my finger into the middle of the rubbery sea anemones until they snapped shut. I thought it was the sickest thing ever. Those mornings, the sky looked like this.

I am jolted back to the present by the sight of a kid running down the sidewalk, followed by two scraggly dogs. The street is deserted except for the kid. The dudes are nowhere in sight. Maybe we can catch a break here.

"We're going to make a run for it. Into that store," Kylie says, as though she's had the whole thing planned out all along. She's confident and determined.

Kylie opens the front door of the truck and jumps out. I'm on her heels. We sprint toward the store. We're nearly there. Almost in the clear. Home safe. And then I see them. They're hard to miss, with their shiny heads and multiple tattoos. They're standing in a doorway, talking to a skinny guy with a full beard and a baseball cap.

There's one of those interminable pauses where time slows way down as they turn and stare straight at us.

CHAPTER TWELVE

"I know it may look like I had become a bitch, but that's only because I was acting like a bitch."
—MEAN GIRLS

lily:

What part of "meet me on the front lawn at noon" didn't Max understand? We had a date. We decided to blow off third period so that we could carve our initials on the palm tree, go to the mall for lunch and a quick shop, and then make it back for senior assembly. Somehow, I'm the only one who remembered. Alone on the front lawn. This is so not where I live.

I really need Max now. This is not the time for one of his disappearing acts. Last night was possibly the worst night of my life, and I haven't even told Max about it yet.

I've already given up on lunch, but I need to hit the mall.

I've got nothing to wear tomorrow. Mom's been so completely wrapped up in her own stuff, she didn't get me a dress for graduation. I get it under the circumstances. But still . . .

This is not even close to the fabulous last day of school I had in mind. I call Max for the fifth time in the past two minutes, but it goes straight to voice mail. I'm sure he's playing squash with Charlie and completely spaced on our date, which has happened too many times to count.

Max and I have been together for almost a year now. People we don't even know in La Jolla are always telling Mom and Dad how amazing we are together. It's weird to find your soul mate in high school. But it happened. It's done. And I'm not letting go. Especially not now, with things so seriously wrecked on the home front. I don't even know the full extent of it.

When I walked in the door last night at midnight, Mom's eyes were red and puffy. I thought she was going to tell me she and Dad were getting a divorce. I wish she had. That, at least, I could deal with, get over eventually. This is worse. Way worse. I'm not sure how I even hurdle this one. Ever.

Mom kept talking and talking. There was too much information to take in. After a while, I couldn't listen anymore. How could I go from having everything one day to nothing the next?

"Your father is being investigated by the federal government. There's going to be a trial."

Those were Mom's exact words. I'm still not entirely sure what it even means. But I know we're in trouble. Big trouble.

"Dad is declaring bankruptcy. We're going to put the houses on the market. We're looking for a temporary place to live, maybe a condo somewhere downtown. We're going to be okay. I promise. But we'll have to rethink things. Pull back . . ." It was all coming at me fast and furious, like a tornado.

In a heartbeat, my life had gone from awesome to awful. We were broke. Dad was potentially a criminal, and how in the hell were we going to afford Stanford? I know I should have been more concerned about Dad, but honestly, Stanford was the first thing that came to mind. It so isn't fair. I worked my ass off to get in, and now it seemed like it was being snatched right out from under me.

I got nearly perfect scores on my SATs. I got into Stanford, Swarthmore, Pomona, Michigan, and Williams. I took more AP classes than anyone in the history of Freiburg. I was captain of varsity tennis, I tutored inner city kids for two summers straight, and for what? So I could attend the local community college in preparation for a manager's position at Burger King?

How could Dad do this to me? To us?

I should have seen the early warning signs. But the truth is, I wasn't interested.

About three months ago, Dad came home from work in the early afternoon and said he was done working for people. Done with the bank. He was going to start his own business. He set up shop downstairs, in the media room. I'm not sure, but I think he may have been fired. He didn't want to talk about it, and I certainly didn't want to talk about it. With him. Or anyone else, for that matter. The less said the better. I just assumed he would figure it out.

He was trading stocks, I think. Sometimes he was down there all day and all night. For a while, nothing seemed to change. Mom and I still went shopping, Janice cleaned and cooked for us, we went to Cabo for spring break. And then, about a week ago, Dad got all psychotic. He took away my credit cards, stopped delivery of all the flowers, fired the house-keeper, traded in his Porsche convertible for a Ford Focus (a Ford Focus?!), and sold the yacht.

In retrospect, Mom's news shouldn't have come as a surprise. But it's hard to grasp the worst-case scenario until it smacks the shit out of you. At the very, very, very least, thank God the world came crashing down on the last day of school and not any earlier, because as soon as word gets out, the vultures will be circling. Schadenfreude. Deriving pleasure from other's pain. It's horrible, but it's sport at Freiburg. And I'm about to be the ball. They're all going to take a whack at me, and there's precious little I can do about it.

I'm not sure how Max is going to react. I'd like to believe that he loves me unconditionally, but I'm no fool. I know the bells and whistles help. He likes the yacht, my Audi convert-ible, the house in Aspen. What am I going to tell him? Or anyone, for that matter. Maybe I'll just keep it a secret until it absolutely, positively can't be kept quiet anymore. And just maybe, some kind of miracle will happen and everything will turn out okay. Like it always has for me.

Jesus. Dad isn't actually going to go to jail, is he?

When I asked Mom what Dad did wrong, she said, "He didn't do anything everyone else wasn't doing. He just got caught."

That didn't clarify things at all. And the morality of that statement was questionable at best. But I didn't even go there with Mom.

"Don't worry. We'll fight this, and we'll win," Mom insisted in that Pollyanna way of hers. But her unflagging enthusiasm was flagging, for the first time ever. She knew things weren't going to be okay and she didn't have a clue how to deal. Her thinly veiled horror was written all over her face.

"People are just jealous of me, pumpkin. They want what we have. We're going to come out on top, though. Don't worry," my dad told me a little while later when he came up to my room. It was probably one in the morning by then. It all sounded suspiciously like the words of a guilty person. When I asked him about Stanford he said we'd "figure something out." I'm pretty sure it was his way of just pushing off the inevitable difficult conversation.

I want to believe he's innocent. I mean, he's my dad. But it wouldn't surprise me if he did something wrong. He's never played by the rules, even with us. When my brother was spending too much time on the bench in basketball, Dad took his coach out for dinner, and after that, Jordan never warmed the bench again. He once paid three times the fee for some stupid horse camp that was full so I could get in. Another girl was probably yanked out to make room for me, and I don't even like horses. Dad always gets what he wants, one way or another. And Jordan and I have learned to do the same.

I curse Max again for making me wait. I don't want time alone today. I don't want to have to be thinking, ruminating, worrying. I want to keep moving. I call Max again. Surprise, surprise. Voice mail. Screw it. I'm going to the mall with Stokely. She won't blow me off.

CHAPTER THIRTEEN

"I feel just like
Julia Roberts in Pretty
Woman. You know, except
for the whole hooker thing."
—SHE'S ALL THAT

will:

It's fourth period and I am standing in the dressing room of Forever 21, surrounded by piles of discarded clothes. I had to flee the festivities at Freiburg. It's insufferable enough on a normal day, but the last day of school is truly beyond. Seniors were marching around singing the Freiburg anthem, like brainwashed North Korean soldiers. The library had been strafed with toilet paper, and everyone was wearing green and blue. Gag me.

Maybe if Kylie had shown up for school today I could have handled it with aplomb and a dollop of snark, but on my own, it was just too much. Which brings me to the burning question: where the hell is Kylie on the last day of school?

I hold a formfitting, black spandex mini-thing up to my body, the sixth outfit I've considered. I can't help but wonder if I'm making any progress. The question is, would Kylie rock this outfit the way I could? It would have been enormously helpful to have her here with me as I try to find her the perfect graduation dress. But we can't always get what we want. How well I know that old adage. It should be my theme song.

I'm on a mission, with or without Kylie's blessing.

I'm surprised Kylie didn't show up for first period, or second or third, for that matter. I can't remember the last time my little chica missed school. She's really anal about attendance. Hopefully, she's not sequestered in her bedroom, rewriting her speech for the thirtieth time. She's been working that thing like it's the inaugural address. I keep telling her that it wouldn't be so bad if she riffed a little bit at graduation. Maybe everyone else would realize what I already know: girlfriend rocks the house with her brains and beauty. She could talk her ass off without ever preparing a thing, if she'd only trust her instincts. But Kylie's not into doing anything on the fly. Her life is all about planning and über preparation. I'm just worried that if she reads the speech straight off the page, it's going to be missing soul. Kylie is full of soul and I want everyone to know it.

Predictably, she hasn't responded to any of my fifty texts to meet at Forever 21. She is relentless in her quest to look sexless. But I am going to pack her smoking-hot bod into a fabulously sexy frock for the ceremony, or die trying. I like playing Kylie's own personal stylist. It gives my life purpose and shape—at least for the next hour—something that is sorely lacking from most of my day. The ennui and the existential angst will set in again when I leave the mall. But for now, I'm dancing to the party in my mind and having a swell time.

I stare at myself in the mirror and realize that Kylie will never go for this black number. It's too tight, too sexy, too too. Maybe I should buy it for myself. It would definitely be a game changer. This look is even more outré than usual. As a rule, I don't do dresses alone. We all have our limits. I usually try to tone things down with jeans, combat boots, a blazer, or a necktie. Something masculine. Something feminine. Something borrowed (from my sisters). Something blue (usually my mood). It's my own secret homosexual recipe.

I'd love to wear this dress simply for the sheer impact of the visual at graduation. It's not that I like women's clothes so much—it's more that I like shaking up the status quo in our traditional little town. But I'm not sure I can do it to Mom and Dad. They've finally stopped badgering me about my clothes, but do they really need their son wearing a black spandex mini to his high school graduation? Seems like cruel and unusual punishment.

Mom and Dad have come a long way since they sent me to Dr. Chan in ninth grade, after I renounced my heterosexuality and officially proclaimed myself as gay as the Roaring Twenties. I've known forever. I kind of figured they must have figured it out somewhere along the way. I just thought it was high time to get it all out in the open.

While they weren't particularly surprised, they were both disappointed to have it articulated so clearly. They were hoping I'd have a change of heart.

Enter Dr. Chan. Handsome in a professorial way. He was my first real crush. Dad insisted I could talk through "my issues" with him. I insisted I didn't have "issues," just "preferences."

"Same thing. It's all semantics," Mom said.

Hmmm. Methinks, not so much. Dad thought I was "confused." Mom called it "conflicted." They both chalked it up to adolescence, not nature. It was kind of soul crushing to realize my parents couldn't accept me for who I was. I mean, I was fine with it, why couldn't they be? So, like it or not, off I went to yak it up with Chan, who was, fortunately, easy on the eyes, thus making the hour a lot less painful than it otherwise would have been. The good doctor and I spent weeks trying to work out why I "thought" I was gay. He urged me to try and date women before coming to any rash conclusions. He talked in this very slow, calm way that often lulled me to sleep during the session. He'd wake me by nudging me with his foot.

It soon became clear to both of us that I yam what I yam: a devout and dedicated homosexual. Chan threw in the towel and we quickly changed course. We spent our time discussing the best online shopping (Chan was a bit of a metrosexual), new music, and my rage and resentment at my parents.

I've never been so mad at them. They didn't like who I was. It was insulting, offensive, hurtful. I expected more from them (or at least from my mother). At one point, I stopped speaking to both of them for sixty-two days, which for me was quite the feat. I'm a champion chatterer. I literally had to bite my tongue at times to stop myself from talking to Mom.

Before Chan, Mom and I were the best of girlfriends. We could hang together without getting all shrill on each other, like she does with my sisters. I listened endlessly to her litany of complaints, unlike either of my sisters, both of whom are way too self-consumed to ever bother with someone else's issues.

During the "Silent Talks," as I fondly refer to those sixty-two days, I would e-mail or text in emergencies. Otherwise, my lips were sealed. It broke my mother's heart. She went into therapy herself. Eventually, Chan told my parents that I was fine. Not the least bit "confused or conflicted." And the sessions ended. I'm here, I'm queer, get used to it. And they have, mostly.

I knew Mom would come around, but Dad surprised me. He's a little bit to the right of Attila the Hun. It's a minor miracle how well we're getting on these days, considering who and what he is—a Republican to the core. I think he came out of the womb in khakis and a blue blazer. His great-great-great-great-grandparents came over on the *Mayflower*. He was in an eating club at Princeton. He is so white, they've named a shade of Benjamin Moore paint after him (Bright, Uptight White #7). He runs a private equity firm that specializes in crushing the spirit of middle management. He buys companies, strips them of all their employees, and then sells off their assets, leaving people unemployed, hapless, and helpless, all in the name of making money. Lots of it. It's kind of unconscionable. And yet, I blithely live off the proceeds, which kind of makes me hate myself at times. But the alternative, not living off it, is a nonstarter.

Despite it all, Dad and I have come to terms with the fact

that we are inextricably father and son. We're loving each other the best we can. It's not always a perfect scenario, but what is?

I'm coming up empty-handed on the Kylie front, and starting to feel frustrated, when a red dress calls to me from the hanger. I hold it up to my body and immediately feel I've found a friend. It's a T-shirt style and surprisingly demure, despite the fact that it's screaming red sequins. It's not too plunging, not too short. It would show off Kylie's curves without strangling them. I love it immediately. It's the perfect podium look. It says, "I'm smart, chic, and sassy. Call me."

The problem is, Kylie's not really a red sequins kind of girl. Or a dress girl. Kylie's not really an anything kind of girl. She is an extremely fluid concept. For once, I'm happy she's not here, negative nabobing in my ear. I'm inclined to buy one for her and one for me. We should show up to graduation in matching red sequins. It would sure give Freiburg something to remember.

I throw on a black chain necklace, very eighties. And spiky black patent heels.

Ding ding ding. We. Have. Got. A. Winner. People.

I exit the dressing room to admire the look I've just curated, ignoring the tweaky stares I'm getting from tweens and their moms. I stand in front of the three-way, staring at myself from every angle, which is when it hits me. I'm actually kind of over the whole cross-dressing thing. At first it was fun—lots of shock and awe, which was a kick. But lately it's been less satisfying as people have become slowly inured to my look.

Girls' clothes feel different on the body. They cling, they hug, and they drape. It's sexy and pleasurable to have a different relationship to fabric, but I'm kind of starting to miss the fit and feel of a finely tailored men's suit. Nothing like a European-cut Tom Ford to make you feel dapper. The honest truth is, I like stylish men's clothes as much as the next guy. Maybe even more than I like women's clothes. Maybe it's time for a change. Maybe I don't have to shove my gayness down everyone's throat. Maybe I should consider the possibility of a suit at graduation. Maybe. Maybe. Maybe. The kid needs to give this one a good think.

The one thing I do know is that Kylie absolutely must wear this dress. It rocks.

"Will Bixby, what the hell are you doing?"

I turn around to see Lily Wentworth staring at me. She is wearing the exact same dress. Stokely Eagleton hovers behind her like some kind of military helicopter, ready to whisk her away in case of emergency.

Lily Wentworth? What is she doing slumming at Forever 21? She's such a label whore.

"What's wrong with you? You look totally gay," Lily says.

"I am totally gay, Lily," I remind her. "I'm buying it for Kylie."

"I don't think so. I'm buying this for graduation, so you might as well just put yours back," Lily insists, like she's the boss of me or something.

Stokely nods in solemn affirmation, as though the word of God has just been handed down.

I am suddenly back to wanting to shove my gayness right up Lily's ass, along with the stick that's been in there for a while now. So much for the suit.

"Kylie will be wearing it to graduation. Deal with it." I flash Lily a toothy grin just because I know it will drive the knife even deeper. "If I were you, I'd find something a little more . . . forgiving. Maybe try the plus sizes or something."

Lily doesn't say anything. She just glares at me. I turn and sashay back into the dressing room like I'm working the runway.

"Does this make me look fat, Stokes?" I can hear Lily asking. Mess with me, beyatch, and I will mess you up.

"Not at all. You're a size two. It looks great on you. He's just jealous. He knows you'll totally show up Kylie if you wear the same dress. I mean, Kylie Flores? Please," Stokely says.

"You're right. Besides, who cares what weird Will Bixby thinks, anyway?"

"Totally," Stokely echoes.

Man, I hate Lily Wentworth. I can't believe we were best friends in kindergarten. What was I thinking? I walk out of the dressing room, firmly clutching my red dress, and march over to Lily, getting all up in her grille. I am so over being called a loser.

"Hey, Lily, shouldn't you be at Dolce or Prada?" Lily noticeably flinches. I've hit a nerve. "I mean, wearing a dress from Forever 21? Everything all right at home?"

Mom and Ms. Wentworth are friends from The Casino, a hideous tennis, golf, and swim club that I haven't dared to set foot in since sixth grade. They play doubles together every week. There was a juicy tidbit of gossip that Mom let slip to Dad over dinner last week. It seems the Wentworths haven't paid their club bill in months. Looks like someone's family is having financial troubles. Oh, the horror.

"Go to hell, Will," Lily says. And it's bingo, baby. Something is definitely up over at the Wentworths'. Has Daddy gone bust?

I wave and smile as I strut off.

Mission accomplished.

CHAPTER FOURTEEN

"Movies don't create psychos. Movies make psychos more creative."
—SCREAM

kylie:

We are going to die.

For a fraction of a second, the four of us stare at each other. I'm sure the two guys are trying to figure out what the hell we were doing in the truck. Max and I share a quick look, both scrambling for a Plan B. We have no idea where we are or what we're doing. There's no one around. And we have absolutely no time to think, so it's not much of a plan—more of an instinctive desire not to die—when we simultaneously turn and dart back up the street, running for our lives. The two guys take off after us. We don't stand much of a chance.

Max catches my eye, and for the briefest instant we are

connected. I know it's utterly inappropriate and odd, and yet I can't help but think that it's the first time I've connected to someone from Freiburg other than Will. My mind is a strange place. Even stranger when faced with imminent death.

When my computer was snatched, I had a moment to consider whether going after it was a good idea. The same could be said when I crawled into the back of the truck; I could have walked away. That's not the case now. This is it. The end. I look back at the men—they're closing in on us. And then I remember something. The keys are still in the truck. The keys are still in the truck. Oh my God. No way! A minor miracle. I don't usually have the best luck, nor do I believe in fate or God watching over me. But I may have to rethink my position on all that, because there, on the dash, is a gift from . . . someone. I sprint toward the truck.

For the second time today someone has left keys in their vehicle and I am carjacking. I don't have time to figure out the larger implication of this. Maybe it just means people are idiots. Or I have a bright future in car theft.

Max isn't reacting. It's like someone turned off his radar and he's not picking up signals. I grab his arm and pull him toward the truck. He's moving as if by rote, following me as a last resort. My being in charge must be pretty cold comfort to him.

I'm terrified. Nonetheless, my synapses are firing on all cylinders. I know exactly what to do. Even though I've never been in this situation, something about it feels familiar. I've been training for this moment most of my life. Obsessively watching and writing action movies just might save my life today. And Max's.

I jump into the truck and start it up. Max hops in shotgun. As soon as I turn on the engine, the guys charge us like a hurricane. We slam the doors shut. I jerk the gearshift into reverse. We buck backward. Shit! How do you drive this thing? My budding confidence starts to ebb.

The short guy grabs on to Max's door and tries to pry it open. He's screaming in Spanish. Max presses down the lock and pulls the door toward him for good measure.

"Forward. Go forward," Max yells, as if I don't know that.

"I'm trying!" I scream.

Shit! The gear is stuck. As I wrestle with the gearshift, the tall guy reaches through the open window and tries to pull my hand off the wheel. I let out a kind of animalistic, guttural screech. It doesn't even sound like it's coming from my mouth. And then, without thinking, I smash my fist into the guy's face. It's right out of a Jet Li movie. It's like I've been body-snatched. The guy falls back, grabbing his face. His nose is bleeding. I've just bought us a few crucial seconds.

Max thrusts his hand on top of mine and throws the gear into drive. I hit the gas. We plow forward, crunching the bumper off the car in front of us and nearly swiping several parked cars. I have never, in my life, punched someone. Sure, I've screamed at people during one of my angry spells. But nothing like this. I slammed this guy with a fury and force I had no idea I possessed. I'm equal parts scared and excited by my newfound powers. I'd almost believe I'm part superhero if my hand weren't pulsing with pain.

Out of my peripheral vision I see Max gaping at me, as stunned as I am. We are both silent. This is no time to talk.

I keep the pedal to the metal as we career down the street. In the rearview mirror I see the two guys chasing after us. They're receding into the distance. They'll never make it on foot. Miraculously, we have survived. Against absolutely the worst odds imaginable.

We are moving at a pretty fast clip when I suddenly realize that the street is about to end. I nearly crash into an old man selling food from a metal cart. I jerk the wheel hard to the right. We hug the corner. The truck lurches dangerously to the left, threatening to overturn. Max slides into me. I slow down a little and the truck rights itself.

"Just keep driving," Max tells me.

"What did you think I was going to do? Stop for an enchilada?"

"Who knows? You're pretty unpredictable." A smile creeps up the side of Max's face.

Max isn't so bad. As it turns out, neither am I. I just saved our lives, by the way.

The situation, however, is a whole 'nother thing.

We speed down a street, somewhere in Tijuana, no idea where it will lead. It doesn't matter. We are alive. We are not going to die. Maybe in five minutes, an hour, but not right now.

"That was pretty awesome! I cannot believe I hit that guy. And hard!!" I blurt out. And then, because I can't hold back, I let out a quick little holler and slam my hand down on the steering wheel. "I'm like La Femme Nikita. Jason Bourne—"

"Uh, let's not get carried away."

"Angelina Jolie in *Salt*?"

"Tina Fey in *Date Night*?"

115

"Shut up. I saved your ass, white boy."

Max bursts out laughing. I laugh along with him. The tension ebbs.

"You definitely did. It was like that chase scene in *The French Connection*."

"I've never seen *The French Connection*," I say.

"Wait. You've never seen it? You're the film snob, not me."

"Yeah, well, we all have gaps in our education. I can't believe you've seen it."

"Guess I'm not the cultural retard I appear to be."

"Guess not. And I'm not the social retard I appear to be."

Max and I share a quick smile, followed by silence as we absorb what just happened. We may be safe, for now, and my performance was outstanding, if I do say so myself, but the whole thing was so stressful and scary, I think we're both still reeling.

As we take in the streets of Tijuana, heaving with people, merchandise, and smog, I'm feeling pretty stoked even though my hand is throbbing. Kind of like I saved the world. I've never felt particularly cool, but I'm feeling it now. For once in my life, my academic career is the last thing on my mind.

"So, now what?" Max asks.

"Dunno. We try to figure out a way out of here, I guess."

"This is way messed up. The last day of our senior year and we're in Tijuana!" Max's mood suddenly shifts.

I couldn't care less about the last day of school. I mean, I want to get back, but I'm hardly broken up about it, like Max. It's just another day in the salt mines for the socially obscure,

116

like me and Will. But it's a momentous occasion for a high school celebrity like Max.

"We've got no GPS, no cell service, no passports, and no plan, a truck filled with stolen electronics and two dudes who are extremely pissed at us," Max reminds me. As if I need to be reminded.

"Yeah, it's probably not the best way to see Mexico."

I can now recall the only other time I've been here. When I was four or five, my Dad and I took a bus from San Diego into Tijuana. We met my grandmother and went shopping. We made our way through the colorful, winding alleys, and my dad bought me a tiny clay donkey painted white, some castanets, and a beautiful wooden doll. It was one of the nicest days I can remember having with my father. He seemed comfortable and relaxed, in a way he doesn't in San Diego. I remember wondering why we didn't come here more often. My grandmother moved to San Diego soon after that, and we never came again. In my mind, Tijuana was a magical place. Beautiful, dynamic, spirited. It wasn't the crowded, dirty, chaotic noisy place I am encountering now.

Okay. I'm starting to get frustrated. I'm turning left and right, no clue where the streets will lead, seemingly going in circles. So much for handling the situation. My brief moment of control has been snatched from my clutches all too quickly. There seems to be no way out of this labyrinth.

"Where are you going?" Max asks, in an accusatory tone. Like I know. Like there's something I'm not telling him. And just like that, the mood sours again.

"I'm trying to find a road or a sign or something that will tell us which way to go. Feel free to contribute any ideas you have."

"I don't have any. I didn't get us into this in the first place," Max says.

Oh no, here we go. Back to the blame game. We'd taken a brief respite, but Max is eager to play again.

"I don't remember you thanking me for saving our lives. I didn't see you punching anyone in the face, or getting behind the wheel." I turn away, annoyed. I mean, really. We'd be lying in a ditch right now, our bodies riddled with bullets or knife wounds, if it were up to Max.

"Thanking you? For nearly getting me killed in Mexico? For bringing me along on your psychotic road trip?" Max stares at me, incredulous.

Connection officially severed.

"No. Thanking me for the fact that you're alive," I spew.

"You are unbelievable, Kylie. I wouldn't be in this huge freaking mess if it weren't for you. I'm pissed. I'm supposed to be with Lily at the mall."

"Oh my God. The horror. I had no idea I screwed up your big plans to go to the mall. Can you ever forgive me?"

"Maybe if you ever had any plans, you'd understand."

"Screw you, Max," I say, for the second time in two days.

"Screw you, Kylie."

I don't bother to tell him that's not the most original comeback. I let him have the last word. I'm too exhausted, mentally and physically, to keep going at it. Max could probably go another few rounds, but I'm no one's punching bag. I know it's my fault, but, really, what's the point of going over the same

118

particulars? Been there. Done that. We need to move on and focus on getting out of here.

There are no lanes. No signs. No one follows any rules, as far as I can tell. People bolt across the street whether there's a car coming or not. A minivan is actually parked in the middle of the street, with no one in it. It takes all my concentration not to collide with the various elements coming at me—bicycles, clumps of schoolkids in blue uniforms with little backpacks, old ladies carrying armloads of plastic bags full of stuff. I watch as a guy in a window a few stories up dumps a bucket of dirty water onto the sidewalk below, disregarding the fact that he's dousing a crowd of people. Toto, we're definitely not in Kansas anymore.

And then, as if by some weird intuition, I take a left down a wide, tree-lined boulevard, at the end of which the tangle of downtown Tijuana clears and we find ourselves on a highway. Before we can do anything about it, we are motoring down what appears to be a major interstate that rings the city, heading God knows where.

"Why are we taking this road?" Max wants to know.

"Doesn't look like we have a choice."

Max seems to think I've got this whole plan to go on some crazy Mexican road trip, with him as my hostage. Uh, news flash, dude, I'm so done with this country. And you. I'm like a charred steak at this point, just get me off the grill. I want to go back to never speaking again. At Freiburg.

"We're heading away from the border," Max says, agitated.

He's right. I look to my left and realize we are going in the wrong direction, heading farther into Mexico, away from the

States. But there's no off-ramp. This road seems to only go in one direction.

"Yeah, well, this is our only option at the moment." I take a deep breath and stop myself from saying anything snarky, which is so my inclination. It's not going to do us any good. Our annoyance with one another hangs in the air like humidity, thick and sticky.

"I have no idea where we're going, but at least we're getting away from those guys. Besides, I can't imagine it's a good idea to try to cross the border in a truck that we stole, filled with stolen electronics that we didn't steal. We'd have a hard time explaining that one to the border police. We need to find a bus or something back. I'm sure there'll be some kind of sign soon. And we'll figure it out from there. Right now, we just need to stay on the move." I'm proud of myself for my composure and restraint. I'm thinking so clearly under pressure, it's kind of trippy.

"You're right," Max concedes. "It's just . . . all so epically insane."

"I know."

He's right. It is. There's no denying it.

"Maybe we'll find it funny in a few days," Max says. "If we're still alive, we can have a drink in San Diego and laugh hysterically about how we thought we were going to die in Mexico."

Max is offering up an olive branch, I think.

"If we're dead, I'll take a pass on the drinks."

Max smiles. The clouds part again, letting in a little bit of sun.

120

After a few silent minutes, we pass a sign that reads ENSENADA . . . 83 KILOMETERS.

The sign whizzes by, but I'm sure I saw it correctly.

"We should head to Ensenada," I say, gesturing back at the sign.

"Ensenada? Why should we go there?"

"My father grew up there. My grandmother used to live there. According to the sign, we'll be there in less than an hour. I know there's a bus we can catch back to San Diego. My grandmother took it all the time. We'll leave the truck and get on the next bus."

I've just come up with an actual plan, and I, for one, am psyched. Max just stares at me blankly.

CHAPTER FIFTEEN

"Well, we're not in the middle of nowhere, but we can see it from here."
—THELMA AND LOUISE

max:

wake up. I must have fallen asleep, as Kylie's been driving. I look at my watch. It's only been about twenty minutes. Cool of her to let me sleep. For the first time in two hours my body is relaxing. My shoulders are so sore. They've been scrunched up around my neck for, like, an hour. Man, I could totally use a beer right now. Maybe this nightmare has a happy ending. Maybe Kylie's latest plan is better than some of her earlier ones.

I look over at her. She's staring at the road. I feel bad. I should cut her some slack. She did save our asses. If it had been up to me, we'd be in a Dumpster somewhere in Tijuana. Instead, I don't say anything. I'm too proud to beg. It's one of

122

my less attractive qualities. Besides, I wouldn't be here at all if it weren't for her. Then again, nobody held a gun to my head. I was right there with her all the way over the border. So, really, I've got no one to blame but myself. I'd just prefer to blame Kylie. It's a shitload easier.

It's embarrassing that in the moment of truth, I caved and she rallied. It's my dirty little secret—cool on the outside; soft, wimpy center. It's the reason I never leave La Jolla. I like things to be predictable. It's a lot easier to be a player when you know the game.

I look out the window, taking in the scenery. I'm not sure I'll be passing this way again, might as well try and enjoy the ride. The highway stretches out like a lazy black river. The tar ripples in the distance as the heat bears down on it. It's pretty much a desert landscape, spotted with the occasional beaten-up roadside attraction—a taco stand, a souvenir shop, a run-down motel. I see a roadrunner clipping along, his legs pumping so fast they blur. A hand-painted sign reads GASOLINA.

I crane my neck to check the gauge. It would really suck if we ran out of gas. The last thing we need is to end up by the side of the road, crouching under the truck, bait for bandits. Half a tank. Should be enough to get us to Ensenada, and then we're on a bus back to San Diego. I have never been so excited to get to school.

Okay. I'm being a prick. It's been, like, five minutes and I haven't said jack to her. I should say something. This sucks as much for her as it does for me. I turn to Kylie and am just about to get it together for an official apology when she flips on the radio. Mexican music blares, fast, syncopated, and hyper.

She punches another button—a sad ballad in Spanish. Weird place to land, but she seems to like it. Kylie starts to sing along.

"You know this song?" I ask.

"It was one of my grandmother's favorites. It's about a guy whose best friend stole his wife. He can't seem to get over her."

"That's pretty dismal."

"Yeah. We Latinas love us our melodrama. You ever seen a *telenovela*?"

"Heard of them. Never watched one."

"They're these serial television shows, kinda like soap operas. My grandmother watched them constantly. You can figure out the entire plot in the first three minutes. There's always the cheating wife, the jilted lover, the bereaved widow, usually with heaving breasts. They're awesome. They make *Desperate Housewives* look like *Dora the Explorer*."

"I wouldn't think that would be your thing. Cheesy romance."

"I like all kinds of stuff," Kylie says, a little defensively. "I'm full of surprises."

"Yeah, you are."

I mean it in a good way, but I'm not sure Kylie's picking up on that.

"So who's this guy singing?" I ask her.

"Luis Miguel." Kylie looks at me expectantly, as if I know who that is.

I stare back at her. *"No comprendo, chica."*

"Ahh, ¿habla usted español, amigo?"

"Not at all. I'm taking Chinese with Bernstein. So that's pretty much the extent of my Spanish."

"Chinese? Really? You and Sheila Nollins."

"They're taking over the world. Or so my dad tells me." What I don't say is that it was his idea. And in our house, Dad's ideas rule.

"'Kay. Whatever. I still can't believe you don't know Luis Miguel," Kylie insists.

"I'm a serious gringo. In case you haven't figured that out."

"Actually, I have." Kylie smiles. She's not being bitchy. I'm pretty sure of it.

"He's not bad," I concede.

"He's, like, one of the most famous Latin singers ever. He's won about a million Latin Grammies."

"Yeah, I've missed the Latin Grammy Awards these last few years," I say, wondering why I would ever watch them.

"You'd be surprised how good the music is. Luis Miguel is amazing. I mean, it's not like I go running to him or anything, but I really like his storytelling and the passion. At least it's about something real. I mean, Lady Gaga could learn a thing or two from this guy."

"Lady Gaga wouldn't know a genuine emotion if it hit her in the face," I say, which seems to surprise Kylie. She grins.

"So, who do you listen to?"

"I don't know. I am into lots of different stuff. I'm kind of all over the map. I like Johnny Cash, Jack's Mannequin, Vampire Weekend, Thirty Seconds to Mars, Radiohead, PiL, Fleet Foxes, Led Zeppelin. . . ."

Kylie looks like she's trying to make sense of it. My music taste isn't as one-dimensional as she assumed. I'm totally into music. Latin music as well. Award ceremonies just aren't my thing. Music and old movies help me escape my shit, even if it's fleeting. Nothing else takes me out of my head in the same way.

"What are you into?" I ask. Not because I'm trying to be polite, like in Starbucks, but because I actually want to know. The girl is a total mystery to me.

"I like almost everyone you just mentioned, with the exception of Radiohead, who I just don't get. I'm a little annoyed by how precious those boys of Vampire Weekend are, but I can't help liking their music."

"Totally agree."

"And . . . it's majorly queer, but I secretly love Shakira and Enrico Iglesias. And . . . Gloria Estefan. It's a Latino thing."

"Yeah, must be."

I laugh, because it is queer. And no one I know would ever admit anything like that without a gun to their head.

"'You know my hips don't lie. And I'm starting to feel you boy . . .'" I sing, shimmying my hips as best I can in a car seat. Okay, so I know the song.

"The boy knows his Shakira." Kylie smiles, really smiles, with her whole face.

"Shakira is seriously hot. I mean, I wouldn't turn down a private concert."

"Get your mind out of the gutter, Langston. I'm talking about her music. I have a total soft spot for Latino pop. I'm genetically inclined toward it. That and Israeli folk songs."

"Seriously?"

"I'm kidding. Though my mom is Jewish and made me listen to them when I was little. But they're awful."

Thwack. A seagull hits the windshield, recovers, and then

zooms away. It's so surreal and surprising that Kylie and I start to laugh. And soon, neither of us can stop, we're releasing the stress. It feels good. Scratch that. It feels great.

Eventually, we both catch our breath and chill.

"Wow. Kind of beautiful," Kylie says, pointing outside the window.

We've been talking so much I haven't even noticed the awesome coastline that stretches on, endlessly.

"Some nice swells out there," I say.

I can spot surfers in the distance waiting on the waves. It would be nice to come back and shred. Like maybe when I can come by choice, on a vacation or something, instead of having been abducted.

"So what's in this amazing speech we almost got ourselves killed for?" I ask Kylie.

"You know, just lots of brilliant insights and sage advice that will change your life."

"That really paints a picture for me."

"I can't give it all away now. You have to be surprised tomorrow."

"Just tell me one thing you've got."

"Okay, well, I quote a lot of people. You know, like Winston Churchill, Bill Clinton, Desmond Tutu. And one of my favorite quotes is from Golda Meir. 'Create the kind of self that you will be happy to live with all your life. Make the most of yourself by fanning the tiny, inner sparks of possibility into flames of achievement.' I kind of use that as a jumping-off point."

"Sounds interesting." And that's all I say, which is probably not what Kylie wants to hear. But the truth is, I'm thinking she's not blowing me away. I mean, do we really care what Golda Meir has to say? Who even knows who she is? And the quote sounds pretty standard-issue graduation speech.

"What? You don't like it?"

"No. It's good. It's just . . . I'm sure it'll be great. Really." I so don't want to get into it. I know less than nothing about graduation speeches, except the shorter the better. "Seriously, it's a good quote. I know you'll do an amazing job tomorrow," I say, eager to put this conversation to bed.

"You bet I will," Kylie says. She looks out at the road. I can tell she's annoyed.

I never should have brought it up. Jesus, she's sensitive. Conversationally, we've hit a standstill. Luckily, we don't have much farther to go. I see a sign for Ensenada on the left. Kylie pulls off the highway. End of the road.

Kylie flags down a guy crossing the street, and in impressively fluent Spanish asks for directions to the bus station. He's wearing a T-shirt that says "Jessica Bernstein's Sweet Sixteen—June 16, 2007." It's pretty hilarious. I mean, I probably went to that stupid party, and somehow the T-shirt ended up on this guy's back. Most likely some cleaning lady who takes the hand-me-downs from rich people gave it to her brother's family back in Ensenada. What a long, strange trip that T-shirt has been on. I pull out my iPhone and snap a quick picture of him.

We drive about a mile down the road, turn in to the center of town, and park on a street that runs along the side of a big plaza. Kylie throws the keys onto the front seat.

"I am so done with this truck."

"Tell me."

"Now we just have to find the bus station and we're good to go."

"If you say so." It's all too easy to be believed, after the day we've had.

"We just have to hope the bus won't be hijacked."

"Shouldn't be a problem for you. You'll just do a Keanu and take it over."

"So, what? You're like a connoisseur of action movies? *Speed, The French Connection?*"

"Not really. But I know stuff. Yeah."

We leave it at that.

As we walk toward the bus station, I keep looking over my shoulder, thinking the dudes are going to pop up at any moment and shoot us dead. But it doesn't happen, and we make it to the station in one piece.

I feel a huge sense of relief as I watch the woman slide two tickets for the three o'clock bus to San Diego under the glass divider. It's all good. Everything is going to be okay. An hour ago, I was shaken to the core, shivering in my own sweat, convinced I was about to die. And now, all I have to do is kill a few hours in Ensenada.

Sweet.

The ticket seller leans forward and says something to Kylie in Spanish. I watch as a look of concern sweeps across her face, wiping away her smile. It's like a shade being drawn. Kylie slides the tickets back under the divider and then looks at me. Jesus. I don't know if I can take another hitch in the plan. I'm already running on fumes.

"What?" I ask. I hate not being able to understand. I should have studied Spanish and just ignored Dad. I live on the border of Mexico. I can say maybe ten words in Spanish, and one of them happens to be the word for hand-job. Pathetic.

"She asked me if we have our passports or birth certificates," Kylie says.

"Jesus, I didn't even think of that. We can't get over the border without them?"

"No." Kylie takes in a sharp breath and doesn't seem to exhale.

I feel dizzy, like the floor is spinning. This day is really beating the shit out of me.

Kylie thanks the ticket seller and walks away. What is she thanking her for? Reminding us that we are once again totally screwed?

Kylie heads over to a wooden bench in the corner and collapses onto it. I sit down next to her. I can feel myself slipping into the panic and fear. The sitting is only making it worse. I get up and walk out of the station, leaving Kylie behind. I don't want to look at her. I don't want to talk to her. I'm back to being pissed at her for getting us into this. I can't help myself. I don't want to be here. And it's starting to look like there's no way out.

I wander out to the street. My mood has dipped dangerously low. I look around the town. It's not a bad place. There are bars and restaurants everywhere, and little pastel houses. It's the kind of place I expect to end up in on some crazy spring break during college, slamming back shots of tequila and cruising the streets all night. But not today. Not now.

"I know this sucks. I'm really, really sorry. I should have never gotten you into this," Kylie says, appearing at my side. She seems eerily calm. And genuinely sorry.

"It's not all your fault. I mean, I'm a big boy. I could have bailed," I say.

I both do and do not mean this. She didn't want any of this to happen any more than I did. At least she's not whining about it like me.

"What are we going to do?" I ask. Because hell if I know.

"I have a passport at home. But I can't call my parents and tell them what's going on. I just can't. They'll freak."

"Yeah. Me too."

"Couldn't you tell them you came to Mexico on, I don't know, some kind of senior prank or something, and they could come down with our passports, or meet us at the border?"

"Not gonna happen. Listen, I can't let them know any of this. It's just . . . it's a long story. Trust me. It would be a very, very bad idea."

My eyes meet hers. I want to make sure I'm getting my point across.

"Shit." That's all Kylie says. And then she walks across the road to a little park. There are about a million pigeons and a few old guys playing dominos. Kylie sits down on a mound of grass and stares out at the harbor. I lie down on the grass next to her, staring up at the sky. It's a cloud-free day, perfect for surfing, biking, running. Instead, I'm stuck at a dirty bus station waiting on a miracle.

"Things are, like, hanging by a thread at my house. I seriously think this would push my mother over the edge." Kylie

131

lies down, rolls onto her side, and stares at me. "Just when we thought everything was going to be okay, it all goes to hell again."

"What do you mean, hanging by a thread?"

Kylie heaves a sigh. "My brother Jake is special needs. He has Asperger's syndrome. He requires a lot of attention. I mean, he goes to school and stuff, but everything is really hard with him. It's practically my mother's full-time job to worry about him, except for the fact that she actually has a full-time job as a nurse. And my Dad is always away, working out of town."

Kylie pauses to make sure I'm still with her. I am.

"I'm kind of the glue that holds things together. Between taking care of Jake and working as a nurse, Mom doesn't get around to doing things like making dinner or laundry. Anything, really. So that's all me. I don't know what they're going to do tonight if I don't get home."

"That's a lot of shit to deal with." No wonder Kylie never smiles.

"Usually it's okay. I've got systems for getting things done quickly. And I really like spending time with Jake. The worst part is the mental stuff. I feel like they've got all their hopes pinned on me, since Jake will never become the doctor they wanted him to be. I've already kind of disappointed them by choosing film school over premed at Brown. So I try not to stress my mom. If I call and say I've been smuggled into Mexico illegally in the back of a U-Haul, I might as well be hurling my entire family in front of a moving train."

Heavy.

"I'm sorry. That sounds shitty. I'll give you an eighty-nine on the life-sucks scale," I say.

"I didn't even crack ninety? Are you grading on a curve?"

"Totally. You get an A minus in overall suckage."

"Cool. I feel so much better. Okay, your turn."

"My Dad is sick, with cancer."

I blurt it out, just like that. I'm not sure why. Maybe because we barely know each other. And, most likely, we'll never see each other again after today. It's easier to be honest.

Kylie looks startled. Cancer has a way of doing that to people.

"My Mom, who kind of has a compulsive need for everything to be perfect, is in denial. So she never talks about it. My older brother is an outcast because he refused to go to law school and join my dad's firm. Instead, he plays guitar in a crappy band in dive bars around Seattle. I am the last remaining beacon of hope, kind of like you, I guess. I'm expected to go prelaw at UCLA and join the firm. If I do what I want to do, like my brother did, it would be the ultimate blow to my dad."

"Wow. That sucks."

Kylie looks at me with such sad eyes that I actually feel bad. So I lie to her.

"You know, they cure cancer all the time these days, so, hopefully, he'll be okay."

"Yeah, hopefully."

Neither of us says anything for a minute.

"So, what *do* you want to do?" Kylie asks.

"I don't know. Lots of stuff. I'd like to try a few different things. Just not law." I hedge. I don't want to go there.

"Congrats. You're the big winner, Max Langston. Cancer trumps disabled sibling. Cancer trumps everything. I'd say that's a ninety-seven on the suckage scale." And just like that, Kylie changes the mood. I'm grateful, because I'm not sure I could have done it.

"Excellent. I love winning."

I don't mind talking to Kylie. In fact, I'm digging it. If this were any other day, I'd say we should kick it and grab lunch. But it's not any other day. It's the last day of high school, the day before graduation, and we're stuck in Ensenada, Mexico.

CHAPTER SIXTEEN

"Life moves pretty fast. If you don't stop and look around once in a while, you could miss it."
—FERRIS BUELLER'S DAY OFF

kylie:

"**W**hat if I ask Will to drive down?" I say. "He'll be totally into it. He can go to my house, get the key from under the mat, and then grab my passport. Can he get into your house?"

"Definitely. Our housekeeper's always there."

"He can probably cruise down here in a few hours," Kylie says.

"That's very cool that he would do that." Max sounds surprised.

"Whose best friend wouldn't do that? Charlie would do it, no?"

"He would. He totally would. Should I call him?"

"No, Will would be mad if I *didn't* call him. I don't know why I didn't think of it before. You might call him Weird Will—"

"He knows about that?"

"He's not an idiot. Anyway, he's an amazing guy. And an amazing friend. He'd do anything for me. Besides, he lives for a good story. He'll dine out on this one for years."

"Okay, I'll call the housekeeper and tell her a buddy of mine is coming by to pick up something. She's gonna be a little weirded out about the girl's clothes. Any chance Will will wear jeans and T-shirt?"

"Not a prayer," Kylie says.

"Man, I do not get that. What is up with the cross-dressing? It feels like he's just making things more difficult for himself, you know?"

"He likes to make a scene." That's all I say because explaining Will Bixby to Max Langston is like explaining quantum theory to Jessica Simpson.

I rush back into the bus station and buy a phone card. Max is right behind me. I slip into a tiny booth with an old-fashioned phone. It's caked with years of dirt and grime, a leftover from 1985.

Max stands outside, leaning on the glass. Damn, he's sexy.

I'm pretty sure he doesn't see me the same way. Guys find me neutered, detached, invisible. I'm Switzerland. The girls Max dates are Brazil. Still, it's hard to ignore the facts that 1) I'm stranded in Ensenada with him, 2) he's not the total asshole I assumed he was, and 3) he's undeniably hot. I push out this train of thought. I can't let myself go there. What's the point? He's got a girlfriend. We're worlds apart. And, technically, I don't even like him.

I call Will on his cell. He picks up immediately. Just as I predicted, he's thrilled with his task, positively giddy that I seem to have found myself marooned in Mexico with Max. He acts like I've just won the Nobel Peace Prize. He can't stop telling me how proud he is of me. It's so Will, I have to laugh. I tell him where to find the extra key and the passport at Max's house, and before I can say good-bye he's out the door and on his way. He sounded a little too excited at the chance to paw his way through Max's bedroom. I just hope he's discreet. I look at my watch; it's a little past one. He should be here by six, at the latest.

I exit the phone booth and Max squeezes inside. His large frame looks pretty funny squished into the diminutive booth. He calls his housekeeper, and we are good to go.

"I cannot believe my new hero is a dude who wears dresses and combat boots," Max says.

"It's true. Will is a superhero."

I slip back into the phone booth.

"Who are you calling now?"

"My mom. I've gotta come up with a reason I can't watch Jake after school today."

I'm dreading this call. Dad will have to pitch in. At the very least, he's a warm body in the house. I shut the door to the booth for a little privacy, and dial Mom's cell.

"I'm gonna be a little late," I say.

"How late?" Mom sounds irritated, frustrated.

Wasn't she ever in high school? I mean, really, it's the last day of school. I shouldn't have to get home right away. If I were even the least bit normal I'd be going to one of a million parties. Of course I don't say any of this. I never do.

The conversation is blessedly short. When I tell her I have to attend a "valedictorian meeting," there's not really much she can say. We hang up and I exit the booth.

"How did it go?" Max asks me as we leave the bus station and walk toward town.

"My dad is going to have to watch him."

I can't help but wonder if Mom would be concerned for my welfare if she knew the truth, or just worried about what time I'd be punching in tonight. Sometimes I feel more like her star employee than her daughter. She has complete faith in my competence, and since I never complain, she assumes it's all going well. Well, it's not. And I'd really like to talk to her about it, but I know it would just stress her out. She needs to see me as independent and strong and happy. The complaint department is closed, and I just have to deal.

"Excellent. Problem solved," Max says.

"Jake is probably going to freak out. He likes things to be predictable. If his schedule changes at all, he usually throws a tantrum."

Nothing I can do now. Got to put it out of my head before my brain travels to the worst-case scenario: Jake lying dead somewhere in the house. Dad completely oblivious.

I shake my head to clear out the bad juju. That's just absurd. Dad may be out of it, but he's not going to let anything bad happen. Is he?

"Your dad will deal with it."

"Maybe. But not particularly well. My dad doesn't really deal with much. Especially not Jake. I think Jake scares him. My dad just wants a kid he can toss a ball around with in the backyard. Jake is not that kid."

I stop myself because I feel like I'm about to vomit out all my family drama, and that could get messy. I've already said way too much. There's no need for Max to know any of this. Why am I even telling him? No one knows anything about me, except for Will. It's better that way. Max and I may be sharing stuff for the moment, but I remind myself that it's just an illusion. We're not friends.

"Aren't you going to call your mom?" I ask, changing the subject. "You should let her know you're not coming home."

"Nah, she won't notice."

He obviously doesn't feel the same need to over-share.

CHAPTER SEVENTEEN

"I am not under
any orders to make the
world a better place."
—REALITY BITES

will:

know Kylie would not want me snooping around in Max's
bedroom, but what she doesn't know, she doesn't know. And
this is too juicy an opportunity to pass up. The housekeeper
was much more of a problem than Kylie indicated. It was like
getting past the Gestapo. Clearly, the old Mexican woman does
not like boys in kilts. I've now been through Max's closets, his
drawers, his bathroom, and I'm not really coming up with
anything that floats my boat. Lots of squash shit, random tech-
nology (like old iPods and PSPs), trophies up the wazoo. But
nothing scandalous, salacious, or even mildly interesting. No
porn, no sex toys, no drugs, nothing I could use to start nasty

rumors on the Internet. Damn. Max Langston is as clean as a whistle. A closed book.

Time to rock and roll. Just need the passport and then, *vamos a México*.

I open Max's desk drawer and easily find his passport. I'm about to close the drawer and be on my way when I catch sight of a stack of photographs. Really cool photographs. Funky landscapes. Strange portraits with only one eye visible or half a face or just a mouth. I open the other desk drawers and discover a treasure trove of pictures, hundreds of them. There's a whole series of feet. Another of what looks like garbage on a beach, some dogs. And they're all really freaking awesome. I feel kind of depressed. Max Langston isn't only gorgeous, he's talented. The guy has an eye, and possibly even some depth. I came here hoping to be able to ridicule him and his stupid possessions. As it turns out, Max has a more impressive interior life than I do. I have no intention of telling anyone about this. Max doesn't need any more positive reinforcement.

My work here is done. Well, almost. Just one more itsy bitsy teeny weeny thing to do . . .

"You finish in there? Is taking a long time," Hitler's little helper calls out to me from the hallway.

"Just grabbing the passport and then I'll be out of here," I say. Seriously, bitch, chill. I'm not a terrorist.

I pull out a tube of lipstick, purloined from my sister's overstuffed cosmetic bag (she's only thirteen, but the girl can paint her face like a pro). I go into Max's bathroom and write on the mirror. After all, what's the point of a visit to the great Max Langston's bedroom if I can't leave my mark? I may not

141

have found anything spicy, but the least I can do is leave a little drama in my wake. I cover his mirror with red lipstick scribblings.

"Thanx for the blow job, dude. You're the best. I owe you one. XXOO Charlie."

Maybe the housekeeper will stumble upon my little gem. Maybe his mom or dad. I'm sure it will find an appreciative audience.

CHAPTER EIGHTEEN

"I've got moves you've never seen."
—MY BEST FRIEND'S WEDDING

kylie:

People wander in and out of stores and sit on benches eating. It's a lively scene. Not a bad place to get stranded. Too bad Dad never brought us to Ensenada when Nana was living here. I'd actually know where to go now and what to do. Not to mention the fact that it might have been nice to get to know my father's hometown. But just like everything else with Dad, it's a blank page, and I'm just a tourist with a few hours to kill in a foreign city.

"So what are you in the mood for? Mexican, Mexican or . . . Mexican?" Max asks.

"Mexican sounds good."

"Excellent. Me too. Let's head down that way. Looks cool."

Max places his hand on the small of my back, guiding me down a narrow alley.

I like the feel of his hand on me, guiding me, taking control, even though it's bound to be fleeting. Max seems comfortable with the role of alpha male. I guess this is what it must be like to be Lily Wentworth, famous other half. Max takes my arm and steers me around a huge mound of garbage that I was seconds from plunging into. Not only is he not an asshole, he may actually be nice. Or nice-ish. Or maybe he just plays a nice guy in Mexico. For years, I was so sure he was a complete jerk. Maybe my snap judgments of people aren't always so accurate. Is it possible they have more to do with me than with them?

Max points to an old-fashioned *taquería*. It's less of a restaurant, more of a cross between a street vendor and a storefront. It's probably a good choice. I remember my grandmother telling me that the best tacos are made right on the street.

Thoughts of Jake and Dad surface again. I push them down and away, but it's not so easy. It's like tying a brick to a body and forcing it to sink. I've got to do it or I'll never get through the day.

We walk inside to find two tables, an overhead fan, and a poster of a motorcycle race on the wall. Not the most inviting atmosphere. The counter girl looks over at us, annoyed we've stumbled into her lair.

"*¿Qué quieren?*" she asks, like she'd prefer not to know.

Max looks at me.

"She wants to know what we want," I tell him.

"What is there?" Max asks.

"*¿Un menú, por favor?*" I ask.

"*No menú. Tacos.*"

The girl stares stonily back at us. I gather she's not going to be much help. I'm guessing this is the kind of place that serves about three or four dishes to their regular customers. Cheesecake Factory it is not. They've got tacos and more tacos. Luckily, I've got an advanced degree in tacos.

I decide to mess with Max a little. I'm not sure why; it just feels right. I sense he'll appreciate a little game playing. Maybe this is what normal people do? Or maybe not. It's all so strange, having lunch in Mexico with Max Langston. I'm orbiting a whole new universe, just feeling my way in the galaxy, hoping I don't crash the ship.

I order two tacos. The girl disappears into the kitchen.

"Did you just order for me?" Max asks.

"Yep."

"Cool. I like it when a girl takes charge."

"Does that happen to you a lot?"

"Not usually, but today it keeps happening."

"Well, I'm not into being submissive. I like to call the shots. So get used to it."

"Noted. Flores calls the shots. I'll try to fall in line."

"Yeah. You do that, Langston. 'Cause I don't want to have to mess with you."

What am I saying? Who am I? It's my voice coming out of my mouth, but it doesn't sound like me. It sounds distinctly like I'm flirting. I'm not really sure why I'm doing this, or even *if* I'm doing it. I'm new at it. I could just be embarrassing myself. I should shut up now.

"So what are we having?"

"It's a surprise."

We take a seat at one of the rickety tables. There's a plastic red-and-white-checked tablecloth covered with cigarette holes. This place has seen better days.

"Love it. It's all very *when in Rome*," Max says.

"Yeah, too bad we're not in Rome."

"Ensenada isn't so terrible. Now that we've got a ride home, I'm into it."

Max is into it? Suddenly I'm nervous. That feels like pressure. Can I keep up my end of things? My confidence of only five minutes ago starts to drain away. The worries are back. Does Max think I'm a weirdo who's trying too hard? Why do I care what he thinks? I shouldn't. I'm sure he's not neurotically worrying about what I think.

The girl returns with two heaping plates of food. Soft tacos with meat, cabbage, and a little sauce. It looks innocuous enough. But that's kind of where my surprise comes in. Was this a bad idea? I should have just ordered him something normal. Too late now.

"So what is it?"

"Eat it first. Tell me what you think."

I know if I tell him, he won't eat it. I also know if he eats it, he'll like it. That's how my grandmother got me to eat it. Hopefully, he won't think I'm a freakazoid for making him eat it.

"Wait," I say, and squeeze a little lime onto the tacos. "Okay."

Max takes a bite. I wait a beat as he considers it.

"Whoa. Amazing. You can order for me anytime."

Max devours the entire thing in a matter of seconds.

"Okay. Hit me. What did I just eat? Cockroach? Poodle?"

"Nope."

"Just tell me."

"It's tripe." I pause for effect. Max looks at me, confused. "Cow stomach lining."

Max takes out his napkin and wipes his mouth. "You're shitting me?"

Oh, no. Is he going to throw up into the napkin? Is he pissed?

And then Max bursts out laughing. "Cool. I like cow stomach lining. Who knew?"

"You never would have eaten it if I had told you what it was."

"Never." Max signals to the girl. *"Por favor, uno más."*

"Nicely played. I thought you couldn't speak Spanish."

"Learned that at a bar in San Diego. Otherwise I never would have gotten another beer. *Una más Tecate.* So, tell me more about your food fetishes."

"I wouldn't call them fetishes. Let's just say I have an open mind."

I'm enjoying myself, which is so not me. I rarely enjoy being in the moment. I'm usually ten to fifteen moments ahead of myself, worrying how things will turn out.

"Tell me about your open mind," Max prods me.

"Well, I have a thing for goat. It kinda tastes like—"

"Wait, don't tell me . . . chicken? Everything weird always tastes like chicken."

"No, more like lamb. And I've been known to eat fish eyeballs on occasion."

"Okay. That's freaky. Seriously?"

"Too much information?"

"I love it. Did you ever watch that show with that crazy chef, Anthony Bourdain? Where he travels around the world eating lungs and ants and shit?"

"*No Reservations*. Love that show."

"He is the coolest dude ever. I totally want to travel to wack places like that and eat funky fish-tail stew with the locals. My family basically eats roast chicken and vegetables every night. And, you know, everyone at Freiburg just wants to go out for pizza. So it's not going to happen anytime soon."

"Except for today."

"Yeah. Except today. Thanks."

Max smiles at me. Our eyes meet. An electrical current shoots up my spine as we take each other in for a moment. I have to look away, afraid I'm blushing. It feels too intense, staring at him that way. I'm pretty sure any intensity is one-sided. Goose bumps form on my arm. I pray Max doesn't notice—it's all so teenybopper.

"Okay, tell me about the fish eyes," Max says.

"They're really good with sprinkles and a little whipped cream." I stare at the table, willing myself out of this adolescent schoolgirl behavior. Max and I are just friends. New friends hanging out.

"You're kidding."

"Yes. I've only eaten them a few times. You know, when there's a whole fish on a plate, I'll dig out the eyeballs and take little slices out of them. They don't really taste like much of anything. Kind of salty. It's a parlor trick, to freak people like you out."

"You're going to have to try harder next time. Because fish eyes don't even faze me."

The girl hands us two more tacos. Max takes out his iPhone and snaps a picture. I lean over to see it. Then he takes a picture of me as I'm staring at my taco.

"Oh my God. Delete that. I must look terrible."

I hate getting my picture taken.

Max looks at his iPhone. "No way. It's a keeper. You look adorable."

Adorable? I don't think anyone has ever called me that. I've gotten *interesting*, *appealing*, and a few times, *beautiful*, but it doesn't really count because it was from construction workers or the *cholos* down the block. They call any girl with a pulse and boobs beautiful. Most people think I'm too prickly to be adorable. Maybe adorable like a porcupine.

"Let me see that."

I hold out my hand. Max gives me the iPhone. He's right. It's not a bad picture. I look good. Pretty. Happy.

Max is on his feet. He leaves a twenty-dollar bill on the table, way too much for a couple of tacos, but that's life on the other side of the world. I wouldn't know about that. I'm always counting out change, hoping to find an extra dollar in my backpack.

"We should head out. We don't have a lot of time and we've got shit to do."

"Like what?"

"It's a surprise. Payback for the tripe."

I stand and follow him out the door, eager to go where he leads, which is just too bizarre. Before today I hated Max Langston. I'm still not exactly sure how I feel about him, but I definitely don't hate him. Though it was a lot more convenient when I thought he was a stupid asshole. It made it easier to write him off. My general policy is that I don't need many people in my life, besides Will and Jake. There's too much that can go wrong when you start depending on people. But really, what's the worst that could happen? We've only got a few more hours together, and then we say good-bye forever.

Outside the *taquería*, back on one of the main streets, I get my first real look around the town. Driving in, I was still so nervous, I didn't take much in. The town bends around the harbor, where huge cruise ships vie for space with sailboats and rickety fishing crafts. Craggy cliffs jut out above the water, which is dark green and shimmering in the afternoon sun.

"We're going to just jump in the water. Right off the dock. 'Kay?" Max asks me, like it's practically perfunctory.

"I don't think so," I say. I'm so not jumping off the dock right now.

"Give me one reason."

"I don't have a bathing suit. That's just off the top of my head. But give me a minute and I'll come up with several more."

"We can buy bathing suits."

"Uh, yeah. I'm not a big ocean swimmer. I'm afraid of eels."

"Eels? I surf all the time; I've never seen an eel."

"I was swimming at Ocean Beach once and an eel wrapped around my leg."

150

"It was seaweed."

"It was an eel. I swear to God."

"So, you'll eat a fish eyeball, but you won't get in the ocean. Have you ever heard of managing risk?"

I laugh. In the space of ten minutes Max has gotten me to laugh three times. It's wild how people can surprise you. But I'm still not going in the water. The truth is, I'd rather throw myself under a bus than have Max see my big Latina butt in a bathing suit. Putting on a bathing suit and jumping off a dock is not the kind of thing I just do spontaneously. It's the kind of thing I plan for months.

"Okay. I've got another idea. A lot safer. No eels, no fish eyeballs. I think you'll like this."

Max turns and heads down another street. I follow. People are in the process of decorating their storefronts with streamers and balloons, like they're preparing for some kind of party. Max walks with purpose. He seems to know where he's going. Must be nice to go through life always feeling like you're in charge. After a minute or two, he stops in front of a bar. He turns to me and smiles.

"I've got excellent news. I'm finally legal. The drinking age in Mexico is eighteen, and so am I. We're gonna celebrate with a drink."

Max ushers me into the bar. It's housed in an old warehouse with huge wooden beams across the ceiling. I've never been in a bar. I'm not much of a drinker. Sure, I've had a glass of wine or a beer at Will's house, but it wasn't particularly pleasant. The whole thing always seemed like a big waste of time.

"I don't really drink," I say, fully aware of how lame it makes me sound, but what am I going to do, lie? Tell him I'll have a martini, neat? It's so not me, it's laughable.

The bar is dark and cavernous. A few weathered drunks nurse drinks. Otherwise, the place is empty. Funky wooden stools line the black stone counter. Photographs of crazier times are tacked up on the walls, pictures of people drinking and dancing at the bar. Serious partying has happened here. We're probably a few hours away from a wild night.

"Kylie, you don't have to drink. Whatever. Get a Coke. I don't even drink that much. But I really want a margarita in Mexico. You know, when in Rome . . ."

Max plops down on a stool. I take a seat next to him. It's not going to kill me to hang out in a bar for an afternoon.

No one seems to work here.

"Hello?" Max yells out.

From the back we hear, "*Hola.* Be right there."

A few seconds later a barrel-chested man appears. He looks about fifty, ruddy cheeked, with a full bushy beard and a little black hat, kind of like a Mexican Santa Claus crossed with an aging hipster.

"Sorry about that. My dog ran away, slipped out of the kitchen. *Bastardo.* He'll come back when he's hungry. I just hope he doesn't eat a kid or something in the meantime." At this, the huge man chuckles. "I'm Manuel," he says, shooting a beefy hand at Max and then at me. "You two from the States?"

Max and I nod.

"Welcome. Welcome. Great day to be in Ensenada. Hope you're enjoying yourselves in our humble little town."

152

"We are," Max says.

Manuel grins. I can tell he's the kind of guy who smiles easily.

"Ensenada is an easy place to have fun."

I like this man immediately. Good vibes circle around him.

"I'm Kylie," I say in English, since Manuel is speaking English.

"I'm Max."

"What are you guys doing here? School's not out in the States for a couple of days. I wasn't expecting anyone here until next week."

"We dropped out. And eloped," Max says.

I stare at Max with a look of disbelief. Max peers back, a look of mischief dancing across his face.

"The thing is," Max continues, "we were going to have a big wedding, you know, white dress, tux, cake, and all, but then we thought it would be more romantic to come to Mexico and get married on the beach."

Okay. Now I want to play. Is this more flirting? Or something else entirely? Whatever it is, I could get used to it. It's challenging and fun, forcing me to think on my toes. I would have thought Max Langston was too cool for games like this. I'm certainly not.

I interrupt Max. "And with the baby coming and all, I just wasn't up for a big wedding anymore." I have no idea who this person is talking. But I want to be just like her someday.

Manuel's eyes crinkle into a smile. "You had me until the baby."

Max and I crack up.

"Tell you what. I'm going to make you guys the best margaritas you've ever had. And you celebrate whatever it is you want. Wedding. No wedding. Baby. No baby."

"Thanks, man. That sounds great. But she doesn't drink," Max says, pointing to me.

"So there really is a baby?" Manuel asks.

"No. She just doesn't—"

"Actually, I'd love a margarita. Salt. No ice," I tell Manuel. It's high time I tried one.

CHAPTER NINETEEN

"When life gives you lemons, just say fuck the lemons, and bail."
—FORGETTING SARAH MARSHALL

lily:

"Oh. My. God. Check it out!" Stokely screams as we approach school.

I turn to see Jason Simon and Billy Stafford streaking through the quad. Completely freaking naked. They must be totally high. Last day of school, indeed. Everyone is standing on the lawn watching.

Ms. Glades, head of the upper school, appears out of nowhere.

"Okay, show's over, people. Back to class. Let's try and get through the last day with a minimum of wreckage. We've already had a lunchroom table and two chairs destroyed.

Let's see if we can't keep our bodies calm for the last hour," Ms. Glades tells us, like we're five.

Our bodies calm? Lady, our bodies haven't been calm in years.

Mr. Cane and Mr. Yarrow, the Rec Arts teachers (otherwise known as "gym" in public school) flank Ms. Glades like bodyguards. She signals to both of them and they break into a run, easily overtaking Jason and Billy. They throw towels around the boys and haul them off to God knows where. Detention? A dungeon? Seriously, what can they do? It's the last day of school. We're seniors. No one cares.

Stokely and I file into the building with the rest of the sheep.

I head up to my locker to finish cleaning it out. I get to the sixth floor and find people partying like it's the end of the world. Justin Brandt and Lola Kellogg are making out in the stairway. Shirah Lang, Ella Bing, and Nicole Collins are singing along to Eminem, which they've got blasting from mini speakers hooked up to an iPod, and Charlie and his crew are tossing around a football. The inmates are running the asylum. I gather Ms. Glades has yet to visit the sixth floor.

"Wanna scratch our names on the bathroom wall?" Celia Higgins asks me as I'm throwing crap from my locker into a garbage bag. I don't really care what it is. It's all got to go. I'm not in the mood for memories.

"Already did it last week," I say. That is so Celia—a day late and a dollar short with every idea. She's got middle management written all over her. But then again, so do I now. Maybe we can job share at McDonald's. God, how depressing. Dad has seriously got to figure something out.

156

"Wanna, maybe, go grab a smoothie at Jamba Juice?" Celia's desperation drips from her like a leaky faucet.

"I'm actually going to class," I say, throwing the stuffed garbage bag into a corner already loaded with garbage bags, and head toward math, pointless as it is.

Celia trails me. *Please, Celia. It's over. We're not friends. Never will be. It's just not going to happen for us.*

"Why? You totally don't have to."

"I know. But I'm going anyway."

The thing is, I'd rather sit in Calculus than talk to people right now.

I slip into AP Calculus without saying anything more to Celia. Mr. Daimler is standing at the chalkboard writing up some formula.

"I was thinking as a graduation present I'd show you all a little trick that helped me with college calculus."

There's an audible groan. I mean, seriously? Give it a rest. Everyone's texting on their phones. Mr. Daimler looks out at us for a minute, throws up his hands, and takes a seat. He opens a drawer, pulls out a bag of chips, and sets them on his desk.

"Fine. Do what you want. Just don't let it get too loud."

Everyone gets up and starts to mingle, like we're at some fabulous cocktail party. I sit at my desk and stare out the window, ignoring Charlie and Shirah, who wave at me from across the room. Isn't the last day of school supposed to be the best day ever? I want a do-over.

I'm going to try my damnedest to wring some kind of small joy out of graduation, but I'd be shocked if it happens. My life is in shambles. My future is completely uncertain.

And Kylie Flores and I will be wearing the exact same cheapo dress when it becomes official that she's done better than me in school. Sure, I'm one of the valedictorians, one of nine, but Kylie's at the top of the heap, giving the speech. No medals for trying. Yeah, tomorrow is pretty much a wash. Soon, all of Dad's dirty laundry will be public information. I might as well write off the rest of the year, the rest of my life. Jesus, it's been a day, and it's not even two o'clock yet. And where is Max? I mean, what is up with the disappearing act? I haven't heard from him since last night.

"You okay, Lil?" Charlie asks, taking a seat next to me.

"Yeah, just . . . tired."

"I hear you. Last night at Joe's was pretty crazy."

"I'm not sure I can keep this up every night."

"It's good college prep. It'll build up your tolerance. Make you the best drinker at Stanford."

"That'll make my parents proud." If only Charlie knew the half of it. But I've got to love Charlie for trying. He's a glass-half-full kind of guy, which can be nice to have around at moments like this.

"Have you seen Max?" I ask Charlie.

"Got a text from him this morning. He was at Starbucks. But haven't seen him yet."

"I haven't heard from him. And he's not in school."

"You know how Max can go off the radar sometimes. Maybe he needs a breather."

I'd be worried, except I know Charlie is right. Max is most likely lying low, not wanting to deal—with me, with the last day of school. He's not into all the rituals. He'll appear at the

158

party when he's good and ready. It's so Max. I'm pissed just thinking about it. The last we spoke, at Joe's party, I wanted to talk about next year—how things were going to work when I was at Stanford and he was at UCLA. We need to figure these things out, but Max never wants to talk about it. He said it would all work out, which is just so Max. In March, the night after a big fight (where I told him he needed to spend Friday nights with me, not playing squash with Charlie), he went surfing with Charlie instead of meeting me at Stokely's birthday party. He said he forgot. But the truth is, he just didn't want to deal.

Emotions freak him out. I wish it weren't the case, because I really need to unload on him about . . . absolutely everything. I have no idea how he'll take it. I'm going to have to go slowly. Really slowly. Because he cannot break up with me now. I need a boyfriend, a rich boyfriend. I know how awful that sounds, but I'm fighting for my life and I've got to play hard.

"Luca Sonneban's having a pre-party at the new house. After school. Full liquor cab. No one home. His house is sweet, right on the beach. I'm sure Max will show up."

"Sounds good. I'm there."

Maybe getting drunk is the answer. Might be helpful if I knew the question.

CHAPTER TWENTY

"It's beer o'clock, and I'm buying."
—MEMENTO

kylie:

'm sucking down the last of my margarita and laughing so hard at something Max said I almost pee in my pants. When I realize that I can't even remember what it was he actually said, I laugh even harder. Max looks at me and then bursts out laughing.

"Settle down, Flores," he says.

I kick Max in the leg to show him I'm feeling a little feisty. Ready to tussle. Max kicks me back, gently.

"Don't make me get off this stool."

"Ooooh, tough guy."

I have to assume I'm flirting again. I may be new at it, but I know it when I see it. I'm also not stopping to consider why I'm doing it. Whatever. It's fun, that's why, nothing more.

The truth is, I'm feeling pretty good. Great, even. Warm and relaxed. I totally get this drinking thing now, why everyone wants to spend all weekend doing it. I could hang here, at this dive bar, forever. It's the most beautiful place I've ever been.

"Whatever. We're in Mexico. Go crazy," Max says, a grin slipping across his face. "So what do you think?"

"What do I think about what?" I bite my lip so that I won't laugh. I'm finding everything funny.

"Did you hear what I said?"

"Not really. I couldn't stop thinking about your addiction to blue Play-Doh in kindergarten and how your mother freaked out when she looked in the toilet."

"Funny stuff. Hard to top that."

"I don't think I want to."

"I asked if you're going to miss Freiburg."

"God no. I hate the place."

Max looks surprised by my answer. "Really? That sucks."

"It's no biggie. I learned to deal."

"But you'll miss Will, right?"

"I'll talk to Will all the time, so there's nothing to miss."

"Yeah, but it's different after high school. You can't hang with people like you used to. I mean, for the first time in fifteen years, Charlie and I will be in different schools. It's weird. I'm gonna miss him. He's, like, my better half."

"Better half? I don't think so."

"Trust me, he's a much nicer guy. What do you have against Charlie?"

"Nothing, really."

"You think he's a dumb rich jock, like me, right?"

I don't reply. What can I say?

"That's a cheap shot. You may be right about me, but there's a lot more to Charlie than that. He's always been there for me. And I'm not sure I can say the same thing."

"For the record, I don't think you're a dumb jock. And I'm sure Charlie's a great guy once you get to know him." Ugh. Whatever. How did we get to the place where we're talking about Charlie Peters? It was much more fun when we were discussing blue Play-Doh. "You know what? I think we need another margarita," I say, pointing to our empty glasses. I want to get this party back on track. We seem to have veered off course.

"I thought you didn't drink."

"Yeah, well, I'm a bundle of contradictions."

"You sure are."

I'm not sure what he means. Is that a good thing?

"What do you say? Another margarita? Or should we try a shot? I'm buying," I say. I'm out of my comfort zone and drop-kicking the rulebook.

"You don't want to pound tequila first time out of the box. I've been there. It's not pretty."

"I'm fine. Don't worry about me."

I'm liking the buzz and I want it to keep on keeping on. The circuit of worries looping through my brain has stopped for the moment. I'm not thinking about Jake or Mom or Dad or school or . . . anything, really. I'm just hanging, without a care. Is this what everyone else feels like all the time?

"We should pace ourselves. Tequila can give you a crazy headache."

162

Max puts his hand on my arm as if that will slow me down. It doesn't. Instead it speeds everything up. My whole body is spinning from his touch. I don't want him to ever move his hand.

"I'd like one more, please," I say to Manuel, ignoring Max.

Max interrupts. "Could we get some water first? And maybe some chips?"

"Water and chips coming right up," Manuel promises.

"And then another margarita," I remind Manuel.

Manuel looks at me askance. "Only got two hands, darling. All in good time."

Manuel's been watching us, since there's no one else here. He's probably nervous I'm going to puke all over his bar.

He sets two glasses of water in front of us and then pulls out an iPod and puts on some music. He's obviously delaying the margarita. Whatever. I can wait. I'm having the second margarita, and possibly a third, if Will doesn't get here and spoil the fun.

Hard-core Mexican rap blasts from the speakers. It's kind of brain numbing, or maybe that's the alcohol.

"What do you guys think of this?" Manuel says. "It's my nephew's band. I told him I'd play it. But I think it's going to drive customers away."

"I like it," Max says.

"I don't," I say. "Can you put on something else?"

"Don't hold back, tell him what you really think, Kylie," Max says.

Manuel laughs. "It's fine by me. I'd rather hear the truth than some bull."

"Sorry," I say.

"Even without alcohol, she can be kinda harsh," Max tells Manuel.

Max squeezes my shoulder playfully. I guess he's kidding. I can't help but notice it's the second time he's touched me in the past five minutes. But who's counting?

Manuel fiddles with the iPod, and soon we're listening to this incredible guitar music, sort of classical meets gypsy meets Jimi Hendrix. I like it. It's a lot better than the nephew's band.

"This is Rodrigo y Gabriela, right?" Max says. "I love them."

"They're fantastic, no?" Manuel asks Max.

"Totally. My brother used to play them all the time. He took me to see them in San Diego. They killed it," Max says.

"They used to be in a Mexican thrash band, like heavy metal. But now they're totally acoustic."

"They live in Ireland, right?"

"Yep. Dublin. They're huge over there."

"My brother says they're about to blow up in the States."

"I knew them when they were nobody. They played right here in the bar a bunch of times."

"No way," Max says, impressed.

They are still nobody to me, but their music is freaking awesome. It's sexy, fast, and rhythmic. It's a good soundtrack for hanging out in a bar in Ensenada with a boy I barely know. It's the kind of music, in a movie, that underscores scenes where people go off the rails and do the unexpected, like skydive, bungee jump, or fall in love. The kind of movie I'd love to watch. The kind of life I don't lead.

And yet, here I am. In the bar. With the boy. Listening to the music. What exactly it means, I have no idea.

164

CHAPTER TWENTY-ONE

"It's really human of you to listen to all my bullshit."
—SIXTEEN CANDLES

max:

I'm not sure what to make of Kylie. She's not at all what I thought she'd be like. She's not at all what she was like an hour ago. She's not at all like anyone I know. She's totally unexpected, wicked smart, funny, off-the-wall, way more fun than she is in school. Different, in a good way. And kinda awesome.

"Where you guys from?" Manuel asks us.

"La Jolla," I say.

"Actually, I'm from San Diego," Kylie corrects me.

"What about you?" Max asks Manuel.

"Born and raised in Ensenada. I moved to New York for a year, but I hated it. Missed Mexico too much. Came right back to Ensenada and opened this bar. Been here ever since."

Manuel still hasn't served us the second margarita. He's waiting for the water to soak up Kylie's first. She was laughing her ass off, but she seems mellower now.

"First time in Ensenada?" Manuel asks us.

"First for me. But Kylie's grandmother used to live here. And her dad grew up here. You've been here before, right?" I say, turning to Kylie.

"Uh, no. I haven't." Kylie looks like she doesn't want to talk about it.

"What's your dad's name?" Manuel asks Kylie.

"Javier. Javier Flores," Kylie says, softly.

Manuel's face lights up like a Christmas tree. "Il Maestro?"

Kylie stares at him blankly. "Il Maestro? I don't know what you mean. I think you've got the wrong guy."

"Is your grandmother Lola?" Manuel asks.

"Yes," Kylie says.

"Then it's the same Javier Flores. Your father is Il Maestro. I knew him really well. He was one of my best friends. You must be Kylie."

Manuel rushes around the bar and pulls Kylie into a hug. Kylie lets herself be hugged, but she looks completely weirded out. I'm kind of stunned too—Kylie's dad and Manuel know each other? I mean, what are the chances?

"Your father and I grew up together. You're like family. I can't believe I've never met you!"

"Yeah, my dad doesn't talk about Ensenada much," Kylie says.

166

I have a feeling this is a loaded subject. Kylie's body language has changed. She's stiff, awkward, much more like the Kylie from school.

"That's too bad," Manuel says.

"Yeah, well, that's my dad."

"Your dad is a complicated man."

Like father, like daughter, I'm thinking. Damn, I never should have said anything. I was just trying to be friendly. Now I've messed with the vibe. Wish we could roll back fifteen minutes, before I brought up Kylie's dad.

"I haven't seen your father in years. He's only been back a few times since he moved to the States. How is he?"

"Um, he's good, I guess. Why did you call him Il Maestro?"

"That was his soccer nickname."

"Soccer?"

"You know, because he was such a virtuoso," Manuel tells Kylie, as if this will suddenly jolt her memory.

"My dad doesn't play soccer."

"Are you messing with me? Your dad was one of the greatest soccer players to ever come out of Ensenada." Manuel doesn't seem to believe Kylie. He thinks she's bullshitting him. I'm pretty sure she's not. "You really don't know about your dad?" Manuel asks, the disbelief hanging awkwardly in the air.

"No. He's never said anything, nor has my mother." Kylie looks kind of stricken.

"Wow. Okay. . . ." Manuel looks thrown. I am too. "When he was younger, he was a soccer hero. He played in the World Cup in 1982. Kicked a few winning goals. Mexico didn't

167

win, but he came out of it an MVP."

The World Cup? An MVP? That's some big stuff to keep hidden. We did not need another curveball. This day seems to have a mind of its own.

"Maybe we could get those chips?" I say to Manuel.

"Sure thing."

As Manuel grabs some chips, none of us say anything for a minute or two. Manuel watches Kylie out of the corner of his eye. I'm keeping an eye on her as well. I can't figure out what she's thinking. I want to find a way in, but I'm not sure how. It feels like she's shutting down.

Manuel places the chips and salsa in front of us.

"I'm sorry if I've said too much. I was so excited to meet Javier's daughter, and I figured you would have known about his past. I'm surprised your dad never talks about soccer."

"My dad doesn't talk about much. Period."

Manuel looks like he's about to say something else, when his cell rings. He picks it up and goes in the back to talk.

I turn to Kylie. "You okay?"

"I can't believe I didn't know any of this."

"It blows."

I instantly regret my clumsy reply. I want to say more to make her feel better. But this isn't really my thing, propping people up. That's Charlie's job. It's why I like him by my side. I could use him here right about now.

Kylie looks like she's about to cry. She deserves better than me, sitting silently next to her, racking my brain for some words of comfort.

"It's embarrassing," Kylie says.

"I'm sure some stranger in a bar could tell me a lot of crap about my dad that would surprise the hell out of me."

Kylie smiles, which makes me feel a little less lame.

"Before he got sick," I say, "he was never really around, and I was so caught up in my own stupid stuff, I never asked him questions about himself."

Kylie's listening, taking it in. Maybe I can help in my own feeble way.

"This is kind of huge," she says. "It's freaky. I mean, a soccer hero? I've never even seen him hold a ball. What else isn't he telling me?"

"I'm sure he's got his reasons. You can ask him about it when you get back."

"He probably won't answer. He's like that."

Manuel is back. "Look, I'm sorry if I upset you. I just assumed you knew all of this."

"Yeah, that would make sense. That I would know that about my dad."

"Tell you what: why don't you guys come to my house. We're having a late afternoon barbecue, in celebration of St. John the Baptist. It's probably getting started about now. I'll take you over there and we'll show you how we party, Ensenada style. Maybe I can dig up some old pictures from your father's glory days."

"We're getting a ride back to the States in a little while. So we'll be gone by dinner," I say, jumping in to save Kylie. I'm thinking there's no way she wants to go.

And then Kylie looks at Manuel and says, "Thanks. We'd love to come."

She turns to me. "We can go for a little bit, right? Will won't be here for at least two or three hours."

"Yeah, sure."

This girl is a total mystery.

CHAPTER TWENTY-TWO

"I think it's safe to say you know the least about anything of anyone in this room."
—HOODWINKED

jake:

Dad is staring at me as he drinks his second beer. He's not saying anything and neither am I. I don't know what to say. I'm not happy. I wish I were. I like being happy. People can get frustrated with me. I don't do what they expect, and that can make people like Dad mad. I'm not trying to be difficult, it's just that everything's wrong and that makes it impossible for me to eat my dinner.

"Hey, Jake, eat up, it's your favorite," Dad says, pointing to my bowl.

"I can't. It's not right."

171

I haven't touched the pasta. Dad put my glass of milk on the left side of the place mat, not the right side, where it belongs. He put my fork in the bowl, not next to it, which is where it goes. And he gave me an apple. I don't eat apples. They aren't on the list.

"I did everything your mother told me."

Dad is using that voice, the one he uses before he gets angry and leaves the room. I wonder if he's going to leave the table and go to the garage, like he usually does.

"I'm trying here, Jake. Are you listening to me?"

Of course I'm listening to him. No one else is talking.

I wish Kylie were here. She would have done it right. She knows what I like. She doesn't get mad at me.

Kylie hasn't come home yet. She's late. Really late. That makes it even harder to be happy. I like seeing Kylie and talking to her about my day. We learned about the Trojan horse in school today. I wanted to tell Kylie about it. It was a big wooden horse that the Greeks built. They hid inside it and entered the city of Troy and won the war. I don't think Dad would be interested, so I'm not going to say anything to him. I'll just wait to tell Kylie later. I hope she comes home soon.

When Kylie didn't come home after school, I told Mom to go to work and leave me alone until Dad got here. It was only ten minutes. At first she didn't want to do it. She never leaves me alone. I knew I would be okay all by myself for ten minutes. And I was. I took off all my clothes and ran around the house. I went from room to room. It was so quiet, like being underwater. I like the feel of the smooth carpet under my feet and the cool air on my body. It was the first time I've ever been alone in the house. It wasn't scary, it was fun. I think Mom is afraid I'll do something stupid. I'm not stupid. Kylie knows that.

Mom told me Kylie was still at school. She had to stay late for something. It's Thursday. She's usually done with Advanced Chemistry by two forty and then home by four. When Dad came home he didn't seem very happy to see me. He was angry that I was naked and he made me put my clothes on. I think I make Dad feel sad.

"Why don't you eat the apple, buddy?" Dad says.

"No, thank you," I say, remembering how they told me to try to be more polite in school.

I won't eat the apple. Fear of fruit is called carpophobia. I don't have that. They don't scare me, I just don't eat apples. I don't like their shape. I will eat watermelon, though, and cherries. Fear of vegetables is lachanophobia. I don't have that either. Fear of the number 666 is hexakosioihexekontahexaphobia, and I definitely don't have that. I think I have neophobia, the fear of anything new.

"Okay, so what are we going to do about dinner?" Dad asks.

"I'm not hungry. Can I just watch *Star Wars*?"

"You always watch that. Why don't you do something else tonight?"

"I don't want to do anything else."

I'm starting to get mad. I wish Kylie were here.

Dad finishes off the rest of his beer, gets up, tosses the can in the garbage, and grabs another one. He takes a long swallow and looks at me for exactly eleven seconds. Dad doesn't understand that I watch *Star Wars* at least eight times a week, sometimes twice in a row. He doesn't understand that I don't want the apple, and that I want my milk on the other side of the place mat. He doesn't understand anything. I don't want to look at Dad anymore. I just want to watch *Star Wars* and wait for Kylie to come home.

"You know what? Watch *Star Wars*. Don't eat your dinner. I don't care. I'm going out to the garage." Dad walks out the back door and he's gone.

Fine.

CHAPTER TWENTY-THREE

"It's weird that chairs even exist when you're not sitting on them."
—KNOCKED UP

kylie:

"Y our dad and I had some crazy times when we were your age. They called us *Los Buscarruidos*."

"Troublemakers?" I ask.

"Yeah, basically." Manuel laughs.

We're walking away from the harbor and the main part of town. The crowds are thinning, the streets are narrower, quieter. The air feels lighter, fresher. Somehow, it all seems more authentically Mexican. No more tacky souvenir shops, no more bars. Kids are playing soccer in the street, people sit outside on lawn chairs, talking to their neighbors. The houses are pressed close together, with only a sliver of grass between them. They look like little Lego homes that Jake would build, with their bright colors and blocky construction.

"We used to climb out of our windows at night and go to clubs in Tijuana, stay up all night, and sneak back in before our parents got up. We surfed The Killers during a hurricane. We even jumped out of a plane on our last night of high school. Crazy times. We were bad. Don't try that at home, kids. I probably shouldn't even be telling you all this. But it's so long ago, I figure you'll get a kick out of it."

I'm getting a lot more than a kick out of it. More like a sucker punch. I'm listening to Manuel and wondering who this guy is that he's talking about, because it doesn't sound like my dad. At all.

"We know about getting into trouble on the last day of high school, right, Kylie?" Max asks me, pointedly.

"Yeah . . ."

I know Max wants me to acknowledge the rich irony here, but I'm too distracted by what Manuel is telling me. Was it Jake that drove Dad so far underground, his mother dying, or something else? I mean, my dad used to have fun, surf, and play professional soccer? It's all pretty hard to get my mind around.

"I think the last time I saw him was '97. Before that, I hadn't seen him in ten years, since he left Ensenada. He came back right after your grandmother moved to the States, to clean out her house. We had a beer and talked about his new baby boy, San Diego, your mom. You were probably only four or five at the time. . . ."

Max and I follow Manuel up the steps of a bungalow

painted a daffodil yellow. There's music coming from an open window and the smells of something cooking. The house sits atop a gently sloping hill, with views of the bay. Before we enter, Manuel stops and points to the rough blue waters in the distance.

"That's Estero Beach over there. Your father and I spent most of our youth on that beach. Swimming, fishing, surfing. It's one of the nicest beaches in Mexico. We call it La Bella Cenicienta del Pacifico."

"Cinderella of the Pacific? That's a weird name for a beach," I say.

"It's often overlooked for the fancier, newer beaches in Cancún or Puerto Vallarta," Manuel adds. "But its charms will suck you in. No matter where I go, I always want to come back to Estero."

I stare out at the jagged blue waves. They do look inviting.

"Ready to go in?" Manuel asks.

"Yep," I say. Ready or not, here I go.

Manuel opens the door and goes inside.

I start to follow after Manuel, but Max pulls me back. "You good?"

"Yeah, I think so. I'm just sorry you got dragged into this whole thing. Yet another crazy situation I've managed to find for us."

"You've got a gift, Flores."

"I'm really, really sorry."

"Don't be. I'm digging this."

"Okay. Thanks. It's just . . . weird that you're here with me."

"I know. But I'm glad I am. Manuel is awesome. And I'm

psyched to hang here for a while. I just . . . want to make sure you're okay. It's a lot." Max puts his hand on my shoulder. "If you want to leave, just say the word, okay?"

"Yeah and . . . thanks again, Max." How weird to be thanking Max Langston twice in the span of thirty seconds.

We step inside, and immediately we are swarmed by people. Young, old, there's even a guy in a wheelchair and a tiny baby in a bassinet. It seems like the whole town is here, cradle to grave.

"Kylie Flores. Javier's daughter. *Dios mío*, you are gorgeous! Like a movie star!" says a tall, slender woman.

I blush sixteen shades of red. Max's eyes must be rolling so far back he can see out the other side of his head. A movie star? She's the one who looks like a movie star, with her thick mane of jet-black superstraight hair that frames her perfectly well-defined features. I would give a kidney for hair like that. Manuel's arm rests protectively around her waist.

"This is Carmela, my wife. She knew Javier as well. We all went to school together," Manuel tells me.

"We miss your dad so much. You must tell him to come visit," Carmela says.

Carmela pulls me into a tight hug. I'm having a little trouble adjusting to all this affection and attention. It's not normally where I reside.

"Il Maestro's daughter. It is an honor," says a man in a blue suit.

"You have your father's eyes," says an older woman with skin like bark. "Let's hope you didn't inherit his mischief-making."

178

"No worries there. Kylie's a good girl," Max offers.

Because I'm the most neurotic person in the world, I will worry about the veiled significance of Max's comments for days to come. Does he mean that in a bad way? A good way?

"And what is your boyfriend's name?" Carmela asks me.

"Oh, no. He's not—"

"I'm Max." Max shakes Carmela's hand. "Thanks for having us over."

I'm glad someone is equipped to deal in this hall of mirrors, because I'm having trouble putting together nouns and verbs. Three adorable children appear at my side, two little boys and a girl. They tug on my sleeve.

"Do you want to play ball?" asks a small boy who looks like a mini Manuel.

"No. She's going to play dolls with me," declares the pre-pubescent girl.

"You are a serious celebrity," Max whispers. His lips graze my ear ever so gently, sending a shiver down my spine. I start to giggle, partly out of nerves, partly out of a sense of the absurd. I've just dragged the hottest boy in school to a BBQ in Ensenada to meet my father's old friends. On the last night of school. It's so not what Max had in mind for tonight.

"What's so funny?" asks the little boy.

"Nothing, I'm just . . . really happy to be here. And a little nervous," I say. "It's nice to meet you all," I announce, because everyone is staring at me, waiting for some kind of response. That's all I've got. This is not my forte, being brilliant on the spur of the moment.

"It's cool. This is going to be fun," Max whispers. "More interesting than a high school house party. C'mon, where would you rather be?"

He's right. This is bound to be interesting. Max manages to put me at ease the way so few people can. It's bizarre. My nerves settle. I smile at everyone.

"We're honored to have you and Max join us today," Carmela says. "Move away, everyone. Give them a little room to breathe. *Ay yi yi.*"

Carmela leads us through the house, which is decorated with wicker furniture and plastered with family photos, and into the backyard. It's lush with flowers, potted plants, and bougainvillea. There's a clear view of the water. Several picnic tables with colorful tablecloths are piled high with plates of food. Paper lanterns are strung from the trees. It's lovely out here. I wouldn't mind settling in for a nice long holiday.

From the table, Manuel grabs a pitcher full of a deep red juice. He fills a number of goblets, and he and Carmela hand them out to everyone. Now that I'm getting a good look at the crowd, I realize it's not quite as overwhelming as I thought. Maybe only about thirty people or so.

"This is wild, huh?" Max asks me. "These people are so psyched to see you. Your dad must have been way cool, back in the day."

"Yeah, maybe back in the day."

We all take glasses and follow Manuel's lead, holding them up in toast.

"To Kylie and Max's visit," Manuel says.

Everyone drinks. I take a huge gulp and my eyes water a

bit. The stuff is strong. It warms my throat as it goes down. It's certainly not juice, whatever it is.

"Carmela makes the best sangria in Baja. But it packs a punch," Manuel says.

I'll say. There must be a bottle of tequila in every glass. My buzz from the bar is almost completely gone. I wouldn't mind getting it back on.

"Yo, slow down, girl. We need to pace ourselves. This could be a long night," Max says. "Speaking of which, we should call Will, let him know where we are."

I borrow Manuel's phone and excuse myself. It would be a nice reality check to talk to him, explain my current surreal state. I give him a call. But, alas, Will's not answering his phone. Maybe he's in a dead zone on the 405. I text him our new details and hurry back outside, worrying that I've left Max to fend for himself. But there's clearly no reason to worry. Max has made himself right at home. He's got a huge wonking plate of fish tacos, and he's listening intently to a story the old man in the wheelchair is telling him. He's also managing to toss a baseball to a little boy, in between bites.

"Hey, Kylie, come here." Max motions me over. "You have to help translate. I think he's saying that he used to be a bull-fighter, for real."

He slaps the old man on the back as if they've known each other forever. Is all of Max's life this effortless? Can he just slip seamlessly into any new situation? This is what it means to be popular. Max has a certain comfort level with himself, with new people, that is deeply ingrained in his DNA, unlike me. He is relaxed, happy, enjoying himself, while I am uncomfortable, awkward, questioning my every move. I'm starting to see the pattern here—Max crumbles in the face of a real threat, but put him in a room full of strangers and he shines. I'm just the opposite, but I'm going to try to be different tonight, because it makes a lot more sense to be like Max. I mean, I spend a lot more time in fairly harmless rooms with strangers than I do in serious peril. My skill set is not so handy in real life. Only in the movies.

I turn to the man and ask him, in Spanish, if it's true, was he a bullfighter?

"*Sí, sí,*" he says. And then he lifts his shirt up and reveals a six-inch scar under his rib cage. Whoa! Serious. Max and I gape at it.

"Holy shit," Max says. "My man, I have never seen anything like that." He whips out his iPhone and snaps a picture of the scar, up close. He shows the photo to the man, who smiles at the image. I didn't know they had bullfighting in Mexico. It turns out there's a lot I don't know.

"This is fantastic, Kylie. I totally dig it here," Max says.

Max refills both our glasses. We toast and knock back the sangria. Max's body is pressed close to mine as we take a seat on the wooden bench. A gentle heat starts in my stomach and slowly spreads out to my extremities, some of it alcohol related, some of it Max related. All of it good.

CHAPTER TWENTY-FOUR

"I know it's difficult for you . . . but please stay here and try not to do anything stupid."
—PIRATES OF THE CARIBBEAN: THE CURSE OF THE BLACK PEARL

will:

"*H*is lips are devil red and his skin's the color mocha. He'll wear you out. Livin' la vida loca.*"

I've got the top down on my Mini, and I'm singing at the top of my lungs as I shoot down the 405, on a bullet to Mexico. I've gone old-school homo with my playlist—Ricky Martin, George Michael, Boy George. I don't normally do music this queer unless I'm alone, in which case, I change the pronouns (because, really, Ricky Martin has no business singing about girls) and blast the suckers. I can make out the border up ahead. In a few minutes I'll be on Mexican soil. *Arriba arriba.* Not even sure what that means, but I like the sound of it. Mexico, get ready, 'cause here I come. . . .

I'm loving the fact that Kylie got herself into this mess. It's unclear to me how exactly this all happened, but who cares? She's trapped in a foreign country, in need of help. So *Bourne Ultimatum.* And so not Kylie, which bodes well for NYU. This is the kind of adventure a boy like me can only dream about—getting caught somewhere exotic-ish (it is Baja, after all, not Bali) with an Adonis like Max Langston. Talk about ending the school year with a bang. And to think, only a few short hours ago, I was so disappointed by the day.

I approach the customs booth and am relieved to see that the cars ahead of me are being waved right through. There's barely a wait. This should be easy. We might even have time for a few drinks, maybe some guacamole and chips seaside before returning stateside.

I slow down as I approach the booth, expecting a simple hand flourish that will mean my entrée into Baja. Instead, the grim little troll in the booth takes one look at me, holds up his hand, and pops out of his cage. I stop the car, and his nasty face is at my window, leering down at me. Calm down, boyfriend, I'm not running drugs or guns. I'm one of the good guys, just your average everyday hero rescuing his damsel-in-distress South of the Border. I deserve praise, not scorn. But that doesn't look like it's happening.

I roll down the window.

"Hi there, big guy," I say, realizing my mistake immediately.

A scowl materializes on his already unhappy face. Oops, my bad. Shouldn't have called the little guy a big guy. He thinks I'm making fun of his size. I'm not. It's just what I say. A peccadillo, if you will. Please don't shoot.

I switch to downright obsequiousness. "How can I help you, sir?"

"I'm going to need to see your passport, license, and registration."

His uniform is too tight and he's sweating profusely in the unforgiving Mexican sun, which can't be helping his mood. He's looking at me like he'd love to make an example of me.

"Nooo problem, officer."

I smile broadly at the hobgoblin. It has no impact on his sour mood. I know enough to check my snarky comments at the door. The border is not the place to try out new comedy material.

I rummage through the glove compartment and gather up all the necessary papers. I'm shockingly well-prepared for just this type of situation. This would not normally be the case, save for the fact that my sisters, my mother, and I drove down through Mexicali last year en route to Rancho La Puerta, the bougie spa in Tecate, where we were cosseted, coddled, and catered to for a solid seventy-two hours. Sheer bliss. We were also frisked and questioned at the border, as our trip coincided with a huge spike in drug activity.

I hand over the documents.

"What is the purpose of your trip?"

"I'm visiting a friend in Ensenada."

I know enough not to say that I'm picking someone up and

bringing them back across the border. That would just throw up a slew of red flags. Weirdly, my innocuous comment seems to have the same effect.

"Please step out of the car."

What? Are you kidding me? Everyone else is literally speeding through the pearly gates, barely slowing down. I want to scream at him, *Who, in their right mind, sneaks into Mexico? Seriously?* But I bite my tongue.

"Excuse me, officer, I'm just curious what exactly I did?"

"Please step out of the vehicle."

Uh-oh. We've gone from "car" to "vehicle."

His rigid body stance seems to be saying, *Go ahead, make my day.* No interest, *amigo.* I'm all about keeping the peace. Confrontation gives me a headache.

I open my door and step out of the "vehicle," which is the first time I realize how inappropriately I am dressed for the occasion. I could be in trouble here. I'm dressed more for a Scottish Highlands party than an altercation with Mexican border patrol. I am wearing a Marc Jacobs kilt (bought in the men's section, but I doubt this will make any kind of impression on my friend here, so I choose not to mention that pertinent fact) paired with black combat boots (my guess is that the subtle juxtaposition of styles is lost on him). I have a jaunty little beret on my head, and a T-shirt emblazoned with a skull and crossbones. I shouldn't be wearing this. For the second time today I am slapped in the face with the realization that my outrageous fashion choices may be coming up against the law of diminishing returns.

Officer Grumpy takes in my ensemble. His eyes sweep

down to my toes and move slowly upward until we are staring at one another. His distaste (and that's putting it mildly) is carved into his face. I smile goofily at him, hoping he'll see that I'm not worth his time.

"Listen . . . William," he says, glancing down at my license. "I need you to open your trunk for me."

An obvious joke comes to mind, but I swallow it.

I pop open the trunk, wondering what the hell he thinks he's going to find in there. Cash? Bombs? A dead body? I mean, really? I'm so much less interesting than I look. I smile to myself as I watch Officer Grumpy take in the mind-numbingly dull contents of the trunk.

There's a beach chair, a few textbooks, and an empty Vitamin Water bottle. Ooooh, so raunchy. I'm such a bad boy. Spank me.

He closes the trunk and turns to face me. "Are you planning on driving to Ensenada?"

"Yes, I am."

"Do you have Mexican auto insurance?"

"Uh, no. But I have American auto insurance."

Mexican auto insurance? Are you kidding me? God, this whole encounter is really dampening my enthusiasm for my Mexican holiday.

"Technically, you don't need Mexican insurance, but if you get into an accident and you don't have it, you'll be taken to jail to determine your guilt or innocence and your ability to pay damages. I would suggest you get it. You should also add legal services to your policy. This way you can have a lawyer represent you, if need be."

Jesus, what the hell?

News flash: *You* are lucky I'm even coming down here with my American dollars. I'm doing *you* a favor, guy.

"Why would I need a lawyer while I'm in Mexico?" I ask, just out of curiosity.

Officer Grumpy doesn't even dignify that question with a response. I guess the answer is just too obvious. My mere presence violates the law. Say no more. I get it. I look like the sort of person who would need a lawyer on a regular basis, particularly in a foreign country.

"You might also want a number for a doctor and a decent towing company. Anything can happen in Mexico."

Dude's in the wrong line of business. He should work for the bureau of tourism. He really knows how to sell it. Jail? Doctors? Lawyers? Mexico is one big party. Fun in the sun.

Officer Grumpy hands me a stack of business cards—no doubt his drinking buddies, from whom he gets a nice kickback when some idiot American, like me, actually decides to buy into his bullshit. This guy has quite the scam going.

"Do yourself a favor. Call these guys. Protect yourself."

"Definitely, Officer. I will do it as soon as I get back on the road," I say, taking the cards, with the intention of tossing them into the trash. Seriously, what's the worst that could happen? A little Montezuma's revenge, maybe. But my car's going to be just fine.

"If you're going to be on your phone while driving, make sure to use your headset."

"Absolutely," I say, pulling my headset from my pocket and dangling it from my fingers to illustrate my point. I am all

188

about bowing down and kissing the ring of the law.

With Officer Grumpy's blessing, I get back in the car.

"Next time, William, consider wearing pants."

I hear you, loud and clear. Leave the cross-dressing at home. That's the one piece of advice I actually intend to heed.

I get back on the road, having spent a good half hour with Officer Grumpy. And now I've got to pee like a bandit. I'm going to have to pull off the road and pray I can slip in and out of one of these roadside dumps without attracting too much attention. Damn, time is a wastin'. So much for the beach party. I'm going to have to pick up Kylie and Max, turn right around, and hightail it back to the border before it gets too late.

I pull over at a gas station/restaurant/bar (one too many slashes for my taste). There is one lonely gasoline pump. Several feet away, a few men sit on stools, drinking beer and eating tacos as the delightful smell of *gasolina* wafts through the air. Lovely.

I take the keys from an old woman at the bar and walk around back to the bathroom. There's a father with a small boy at the sink. As I enter, the man grabs his son and dashes out of the bathroom like he's seen a ghost. Whoa! That was rude. And a big, fat depressing drag. I'm scaring people. That's hardly the goal. I know I should be able to dress however I want, but I don't want to frighten anyone. I don't want to be *that* guy. In trying to thrust my sexual preferences into everyone's face, I've become someone I'm not sure I recognize anymore. And what have I accomplished? Does anyone really accept me? Has anyone else at Freiburg come flying out of the closet? Have

I helped make La Jolla a gay-friendly place to be? Sadly, no, no, and no. Out here in the real world, beyond the gates of Freiburg, I'm even more of a freak show.

I realize that this persona I've created isn't even who I want to be. I vow to find a pair of jeans ASAP, even if I have to dig them out of a Dumpster.

CHAPTER TWENTY-FIVE

"You have no idea what I'm talking about, I'm sure. But don't worry, you will someday."
—AMERICAN BEAUTY

max:

So far today I've eaten tripe tacos, Carmela's legendary *sopa de mariscos*, and a plate of stewed goat meat over rice, all of which was amazing. I'm drinking my third glass of sangria and bonding with my new bud Carlos, an eighty-year-old bull-fighter. I'm out of my element and totally into it.

I want to get home in time for graduation, but I'm not really caring about tonight's Freiburg parties anymore. I'd rather hang here and do something different for a change. My life's become so controlled, so contained, I've forgotten how good it feels to go off the grid. This whole crazy Mexican side trip, which was a freaking nightmare only a few hours ago, has turned out to be the best thing I've done in ages. Another country, a different culture, new people—it's something I've been craving without even knowing it.

I wander into the living room and find Kylie staring at pictures of her father like she's in a trance. This must be majorly wigging her out. I'm not sure I could handle it if all this news and information were coming at me.

"Here's one of your dad in high school. He was team captain and we'd just won the countrywide championship. Javier scored the winning goal," Manuel tells us.

Kylie's seventeen-year-old dad is being carried through the streets of Ensenada on the shoulders of his teammates. He's our age and looks like he owns the world. There are pictures of her dad playing soccer for huge crowds. A picture of him holding up some major trophy. One of him signing a poster with his image on it, for a bunch of schoolkids. How could Kylie not know any of this? Kind of mind-blowing.

Kylie pores over the photos, gently touching them. It makes me want to wrap my arms around her, protect her. But I don't. I keep my arms to myself.

"This is the night Javier won the soccer championship for Colef, College of the Northern Border." Manuel holds up a picture of Javier smiling stupidly as his teammates pour beer on his head. "Javier dropped out of Colef right after that, I think it was sophomore year, to play for Mexico in the World Cup. Recruiters started talking to him right after that game. Real Madrid, Manchester United. He'd hit the big time and would have gone on to play professionally if it hadn't been for the accident," Manuel tells us.

"He got hurt playing?" Kylie asks.

"You don't know about the accident?" Manuel asks.

"No." Kylie stares at Manuel, confused.

"He didn't get hurt playing. But, maybe I've said too much. Your father should probably tell you."

"He never says anything," Kylie says. I can tell she's trying really hard to keep her voice neutral. But her eyes betray her discomfort. "We don't always . . . get each other, if you know what I mean." Kylie shifts around in her chair.

"I know exactly what you mean," Manuel says. "Believe it or not, I was a teenager once."

"Yeah, it's not so much a teen thing with my dad. It's just a . . . thing thing with him. He doesn't talk about his past. And my grandmother died a few years ago, so there's really no one around to tell me anything."

"Believe me, I know how difficult Javier can be. We grew up together. There were days when he'd stop speaking to me for some stupid remark I'd made. He was always a moody bastard, but he's got a good heart. I think Javier is probably trying to protect you."

Manuel is trying to gauge things, figure out exactly what to say. He knows Kylie is freaking. Who wouldn't be? This is all pretty heavy, even for me. And I don't know the guy. I feel like I shouldn't be here, like I'm interrupting a private moment, listening in on Kylie's family secrets. But it also seems rude to just get up and walk away. So I stay where I am.

Kylie is still looking at Manuel, hoping he'll confide in her. Manuel sighs audibly as he gazes at Kylie.

"I don't know," he says. "Maybe your dad should tell you."

"He won't. But maybe if you will, it'll help me understand him better," Kylie replies. And then adds, for good measure, "Please?" Looking up at Manuel with those big, beautiful, golden eyes.

It's going to be hard to say no.

"Okay, I'll tell you, but you've got to go slow when you talk to your dad. . . ."

"I promise."

"He's not good with the surprise attack. He shuts down."

"Yeah, tell me about it."

"Hopefully, it'll be good for both of you. Maybe it'll get you two talking more. If nothing else, I think it'll help you appreciate him in a different way."

Manuel settles himself onto the couch and then launches into it. "Javier was in a horrible accident. It was almost thirty years ago, a few months after the World Cup. Mario, Javier's father, was a truck driver. And sometimes he would bring Javier and his brother with him on long hauls. I remember your father learned to drive a truck when he was fifteen. I hated him for that. I thought he was so cool.

"That night, all three of them were in the truck and they were almost home. They'd been on the road for a couple of days. Your father was driving; he must have been around nineteen. Another car veered into his lane and Javier swerved. The truck flipped over. His father and his brother died. But Javier didn't have a scratch on his body."

Manuel pauses. I can see it's still difficult for him to tell this story, even all these years later. He looks at Kylie to see if she's okay. I'm not sure if she is or not.

"Everyone said it was a miracle that Javier survived. Like he was protected by God. But Javier was ruined by it. He felt like he killed his father and his brother. He felt responsible. And he felt guilty for surviving."

Kylie looks stunned. Manuel puts an arm around her, and the two of them sit there silently. I don't know what to do. Talk about a third wheel. I don't want to make things worse, and I don't know how to make them better, so I just keep quiet, watching and waiting for a sign from Kylie.

I can't really imagine what she's going through. I guess my dad's cancer comes close, but that's been a slow dissolve. This must feel more like being punched in the stomach. Maybe we shouldn't have come.

"Is that when he moved away?" Kylie asks Manuel.

"Yeah. He just couldn't take being surrounded by all the memories. He kept going over and over the accident, blaming himself. I don't think he knew how to go on without his dad and his brother. He stopped playing soccer and worked as a bartender for a while in Rosarito. We kept in touch whenever he returned to Ensenada. Which became less and less often.

"Eventually, Javier started talking about going to America. He seemed better as he made his plans. He came to see me one night. His car was packed and he had made the decision. He was going to San Diego. After finding a job, he'd bring his mother. I promised to look after Lola while he was gone. In many ways, Lola had it worse than Javier. She lost her

195

husband and her son. And now her only other son was moving to America. She just sat around the house knitting. I used to take her out to dinner once a week. That's how I heard about you and your mother and your brother. Javier fell out of touch soon after that. He stopped returning my calls. I assumed that was something he had to do to shed his past. So I stayed away. But I never stopped thinking about him."

Manuel stops talking and looks away for a moment. I think he's worried that what he's told Kylie will upset her even more. But Kylie is poised and calm.

"Thank you, Manuel. I appreciate hearing all of this," she says. Someone would be picking me up off the floor right about now. But Kylie's holding it together amazingly well. I'm officially impressed.

"This is a lot to take in, no?" Manuel asks Kylie.

"Yeah. But I'm so glad you told me. It helps to know. And it explains . . . a lot."

"I'm sure your dad has his reasons," Manuel says.

"Yeah. Maybe."

"You're okay?" Manual asks.

"I am. In some strange way, it's a relief to find this out. At least there's an explanation for his behavior. It gives me hope for him. For us. To be honest, I'd kind of written him off."

"Well, then, I'm glad I told you."

"I think I'm going to take a walk, get some air. I'll be back in, like, fifteen minutes," Kylie says.

"Take as long as you need. We'll be here," Manuel promises. "We can talk more later, if you want."

Kylie gets up. I follow her.

"You mind if I come with?" I ask.

"Nope."

We head out into the bright sunshine.

"You want to talk?"

"Just . . . walk with me. You don't have to pretend to care about my messed-up life," Kylie says.

"I do care."

I mean it, which is weird because I usually don't care all that much. I like to keep my distance, keep it light. Too much baggage messes with my game. But Kylie's story has drawn me in, or maybe it's Kylie. I want to know about her family, about her.

Kylie heads up a hill, past a row of earth-toned bungalows. Everyone seems to be having a backyard party. We walk along in silence for a while. I'm trying to figure out what to say that won't sound completely stupid and insincere. So I say nothing. Brilliant.

I'm pushing to keep up as Kylie goes faster and faster. And then, near the top, Kylie collapses onto the grass. She lies there, motionless. I lie down next to her, careful not to touch her or say anything moronic. I'm never usually this self-conscious, but Kylie has me tied in knots.

"I always thought it was Jake that made him shut down. And then, maybe his mother's death," Kylie says. "But now I get that it was so much more. I can't believe I had to come all the way to Ensenada to learn about my dad. I mean, it would have been nice if he could have told me himself."

"Yeah, my dad's not much for sharing either."

"People say you become your parents," Kylie says. "But I don't want that. I mean, I love my parents, but I don't think they're really happy. I don't want to shut out the world like my dad."

"I think it's already too late for me," I say.

"What do you mean?"

"I don't know. I'm not exactly good at opening up to people. I'm a lot like my dad."

"What are you talking about? I'm the one who's always shutting people out. You're amazing with people. You can talk to anyone."

"Maybe, but it's all kind of an act. I don't like people knowing all my shit. Except Charlie. But that's different; we've known each other since nursery school."

"Well, you're telling me your shit now." Kylie looks at me directly.

She's right. I am.

We both look away. It's too intense. I stare up at the sky. It's a perfect, cloudless blue. I take out my phone and snap a photo of it. Maybe I'll use it as background for something.

"At least I don't think he's a complete dick anymore. I mean, he needs therapy, but I get where he's coming from now. His drinking, how disconnected he always is. It makes sense. I don't know why my mother or my grandmother never told me. Jesus. My family is so messed up."

"Welcome to the club. I'll have to teach you the secret handshake."

Kylie smiles. She's twirling a long curl around her finger. "No wonder I'm such a social retard."

"You're not a social retard." I may have thought that yesterday but not today.

"Do you think, when we have kids, we'll mess things up as bad as our parents?"

"Dunno. Hopefully not."

We just lie here for a while, not saying anything.

"Thanks for not . . . I don't know, laughing at this whole thing," Kylie says.

"I don't think it's funny, and I'm guessing you don't either."

Kylie sits up and looks down at me. She's so raw, exposed, beautiful.

"Max Langston," she says as she continues to stare at me.

I like the way she says my name.

"Max Langston." She says it again. And then she starts to laugh.

"What?"

"Out of all the people to find myself stuck with in Ensenada, learning about my dad's secret past. Max Langston. I can't believe it. I mean, it's crazy, right? We don't even know each other."

"We know each other a lot better now."

"That is indisputable, Max Langston."

"C'mon, let's go back down. Will should be here soon."

"Sounds like a plan."

I jump up, grab Kylie by the hand, and pull her to her feet.

CHAPTER TWENTY-SIX

"I saw that going differently in my mind."
—HITCH

jake:

'm on the 5:25 bus to Buchwald and Center. I know I shouldn't be. But once I had the idea, I couldn't stop myself. I can meet Kylie at school and we'll go home together.

I have two Luke Skywalkers, one Darth Bane, three Yodas, a Poggle the Lesser (which is very rare), and a Darth Vader with me. I forgot my Tavion Axmis. I will not forget Tavion Axmis next time. I should have brought four Luke Skywalkers, because I have lined them all up on the seat next to me and they look uneven. I move the Yodas to the front, but I don't like it. I put one of the Luke Skywalkers in a fighting position.

"Excuse me."

Someone is talking to me, but I'm not going to look up.

"Excuse me, may I sit here?"

I'm not looking up. Sometimes I like company, but not now.

"No," I say. I'm not looking up. Are they gone?

I move one of my Yodas right next to Darth Vader. They are contiguous. I love that word. *Contiguous*. I think they're gone.

We're passing One America Plaza. The top of the building looks like a screwdriver. Every time I see it, I can't believe how cool it is. I could stare at it all day. The tallest building in the world is Burj Khalifa in Dubai. It's one hundred and sixty-three stories. Almost five times as high as One America Plaza. Burj Khalifa is also the tallest structure in the world. Which is different than a building. The KVLY-TV mast in Blanchard, North Dakota, is the second-tallest structure in the world, and the CN Tower in Toronto is the second-tallest freestanding structure.

I stare out the window and count buildings. I know Mom will be angry with me that I just walked out of the house, but I need to see Kylie. I've never done anything like this before. But Kylie's never missed dinner without telling me. And Dad did everything wrong. He'll probably be happy I'm gone.

The bus pulls up to Buchwald and Center. It's 6:17. Exactly fifty-two minutes. Excellent time, especially in rush hour. But the buses have special lanes. I walk the seven blocks to Freiburg. I know exactly how to get there. Mom and I used to take Kylie to school all the time. I count the cracks on the sidewalk as I go. Twenty-five cracks every block. One hundred and seventy-five cracks by the time I get to the main stairs of Freiburg.

The school is so big and bright, it looks like a castle. I walk up the main staircase. There's no one around. I try the door.

It's locked. All the doors are locked, chained shut. I knock on them, hard. Maybe Kylie's locked inside. Will she even hear me?

A man with a mop opens one of the doors.

"Can I help you?"

"I'm looking for my sister. Kylie Flores."

"Everyone's gone home. It's the last day of school."

"She's probably in the library. She likes to read."

"No one's in the library. I just finished cleaning the place."

"She said she was staying late at school, so she must still be inside. Can I come in and see?"

"I'm sorry. School rules. No one's allowed inside. Hope you find your sister." The man with the mop shuts the door.

I'm alone. I'm not sure what to do or where to go.

CHAPTER TWENTY-SEVEN

> "We're all pretty bizarre. Some of us are just better at hiding it, that's all."
> —THE BREAKFAST CLUB

kylie:

"I've seriously never eaten this much before," I tell Max. "I am a beached whale."

"I feel you, sister," Max responds.

"You 'feel me, sister'? Who are you, Snoop Dogg?"

"What? I'm too white to talk like that?"

"Uh, yeah. I'm too white to talk like that and I'm half Latina."

"Kylie, there's something you don't know about me."

"What's that?"

"I'm only white on the outside. Underneath, I've got a

dark, hip, urban rapper center. I'm like a vanilla Tootsie Pop."

"You're more like a Blow Pop. With a bright, chewy bubble gum center."

"Okay, I'm pretty sure that's offensive. I'm not crazy about the image."

"Better than being a dumb jock."

Max raises an eyebrow at me. I know he worries that he is a dumb jock, or that people only see that side of him.

"You're not one, by the way," I say. And I mean it. I feel bad for even introducing the subject. I don't think he's a dumb jock. Maybe a few hours ago, but not now.

Max and I are lying in a neon orange hammock, strung from two palm trees in Manuel's backyard, having just finished what seemed like a fifteen-course meal. If I had to write this scene, I'm not sure I'd be able to do it and make it believable. *The school loner and the school heartthrob are pressed together on a hammock, high above the harbor in Ensenada, swinging to the gentle sounds of salsa and cicadas. His foot rests on hers, her shoulder pushes into his.*

It sounds so cheesy, even *I* don't buy it. And it's currently happening to me.

Somewhere between my second cup of sangria and a long session of singing Beatles songs with Manuel, Max, and a guy named Fresco, Max and I fell onto the hammock. And little by little, our limbs began to intertwine, as if by some will of their own. I'm still thinking about my dad, but less and less. A little girl named Felipa, dressed in a Spider-Man costume, crawled into the hammock with us. She curled up at our feet and fell asleep.

This is probably the closest, physically, I've ever been to a boy other than Jake or Will. So far, it's all pretty innocent, except for a few mildly scandalous thoughts (I'm sure only on my part). Thanks to a nice sangria buzz that I've managed to keep going by pacing myself, I'm not nervous. At all. I am wondering what happens next, though.

"I've eaten Mexican food my whole life and never once had turkey *mole*. Are you sure it's the national dish of Mexico?" Max asks a woman sitting on the grass nearby. They've been having an on-and-off conversation for the past few minutes. I've been listening in.

"I'm sure. I teach history in high school," she tells Max.

"Well, then, I guess you'd know. I always assumed it was tacos or burritos," Max says.

The woman laughs. There's that easy rapport again. Hanging around Max, I think a little has rubbed off on me. I've been chatting it up with everyone here, as if that's what I normally do.

As Max talks to the woman, I study his face, committing every detail to memory. I may not pass this way again. His thick, wavy locks are the color of straw. His eyebrows arch perfectly and then taper down ever so subtly. He has a tiny mole on his left ear, right above his earlobe. And he has lovely long eyelashes that make him look like he's always slightly sleepy.

I hear a click.

"This one's definitely going in," Max says, pointing at his iPhone. He's been taking pictures since we got to Mexico. He's creating an album as a kind of record of the trip. He shows me a photo of a baby gecko clinging to the side of the tree where the

205

hammock is hung. The gecko is looking right into the camera, completely ready for his close-up. It's really a brilliant shot.

"Let me see what you've got so far," I say, taking his phone. He's been clicking away, but I've barely seen anything he's taken.

I scroll through the photos. There are so many of me, it's a little freaky—mostly when I wasn't aware he was taking them. I can't help wondering what Lily will think if she sees them.

There's one of me standing in the bus station, pissed. One of me driving the truck, with my hair whipping in my face, the window down. One of a road sign with an image of a giant rotisserie chicken dripping juice into the mouth of a man. Each picture is artistically angled, deliberate and striking. A perfectly captured moment. Max is way talented. I know it's condescending, but I'm surprised by this revelation.

"That's a keeper too," Max says, peering over my shoulder to look. It's a photo of me wearing my dad's yellow soccer jersey. Number twenty-seven. Manuel gave it to me, and I've been wearing it ever since.

"I don't know. I think I look fat."

"Why do girls always say that? You do not look fat."

"My arm is bulging out there, and I look like I have a double chin or something."

"You look great. Even in a thirty-year-old soccer jersey."

Because of the way he says it, I believe he means it.

I turn the phone around and snap a picture of the two of us. We both stare at the shot. It's just our faces tilted toward each other. Neither of us is smiling, but we look relaxed and comfortable. Good together. It's almost too intimate; something about it makes me feel awkward. I'm about to say something snarky to diffuse the moment, but I change my mind when I turn toward Max. He's staring at me so intensely, I swallow my words.

It hits me hard how attracted I am to him. And not just because he's gorgeous, which is undeniable. I'm liking the whole package, much to my surprise. He's not an asshole. It's funny I couldn't see it. Makes me wonder how often I'm missing stuff. Or maybe it's just that Freiburg brings out the worst in people.

We're friends now, I guess. The way hostages bond during capture, maybe. How long it will last, once we're free, remains to be seen. But right here, right now, this feels right. It's just too trippy to even make sense of. He was always the arrogant, silver-spooned, dim-witted jock that ruled the school as a result of his good looks and good fortune. I don't know how to square that image of him with the Max I'm with now, the smart, funny, kind Max. Was he there all along? Or is it just a temporary deviation from form, a Mexican morphing effect? I think about all the times I watched him strut around campus with his arm draped over Lily's shoulder, looking so entitled and cocky, and my infatuation deflates a little.

"You always seemed like such an arrogant prick. How is it that you're not really like that?" Even I'm surprised that I just said that. Nice work. Really subtle. I'm destined to be single forever.

"I'm sure you mean that in the best possible way." Max laughs. "You always seemed like a psychopathic loner. How is it that you're not like that?"

"Is that really what you thought of me?" That stings. Is that what I'm putting out there?

"Not really. To be honest, I didn't think much about you,

Kylie. I was into my boys, Lily, and squash. I didn't have much interest in anything else. Which I guess makes me kind of an arrogant prick. The moral of the story is, always go with your first impressions."

"You said it."

"That's kinda splitting hairs. You said it ten seconds ago."

"I qualified it."

"Yeah, but you were hedging. You think I hang out with assholes, so I must be an asshole."

"No comment," I say, because, why bother? We'll never find common ground on this issue.

"You act like you hate everyone. Except Will. And these are people you've never spent any time with. So how do you know they're such jerks?"

"Those were your words, not mine. I don't hate everyone. It's just, I don't find your crowd particularly interesting."

"But it's not like you've tried with any of us."

How did I manage to turn what was a perfectly lovely, intimate moment into something closer to an argument? I have a real skill at driving people away. Like father, like daughter.

"It's not like anyone's tried with me, either. I know you say Charlie's a great guy, but I've just never seen it. He practically called me trailer trash on the squash court the other day."

"Yeah. That was way off base, knee-jerk. He was just defending me. He gets pretty territorial about friends. He's like a big bear, loyal to the core. He once beat the shit out of a squash player who called me a guido fag after I beat him eleven–zero in three straight sets."

"You're Italian?"

"That wasn't really the point of the story."

"It's just, you don't look Italian. And Langston doesn't sound Italian."

"My mom's half Italian. Her last name is Gradassi. I guess the guy knew that somehow. Anyway, the thing is, Charlie is a good guy. You would like each other if you actually hung out."

"'Kay. If you say so." I seriously doubt it.

"Look, you're right, plenty of people at Freiburg are dicks. Like Richie Simson and Lacey Garson. Even I don't love hanging with some of them. But you can't just write off most of the class."

I'd like to agree to disagree, but if I don't offer more than that, it ends here. We never go into deeper waters, we never get close to bridging the chasm. We've come this far, might as well travel the rest of the way.

"I don't know, maybe it's easier for me to write people off instead of getting to know them. And then having to deal with them. And their stuff. And my stuff. And all the other stuff that goes along with that." I'm rambling now. I should stop, but I don't. I keep going, much to my chagrin. "With Will, I know what to expect. He doesn't judge me. I don't judge him. And, honestly, I don't really want people judging me, and I feel like Freiburg is a really judgmental place." As soon as I've vomited it all out, I regret it. It sounds incoherent and psychobabbly. I feel pathetic and defenseless.

Max looks at me for a moment, quiet. What's he thinking? That I'm even more of a head case than he thought?

"I don't know what I'm talking about. I've stopped making sense. . . ."

"No. I get it. We all do it," Max says.

"Not all of us. Only the most screwed up of us."

"Everyone's screwed up. Just in different ways."

Maybe I don't have to be afraid of him, now or when we get back. Maybe he is actually a good guy. Maybe I'll see him again after Mexico. Maybe, maybe, maybe . . .

"There's not a lot wrong with you, Kylie, from my perspective," Max says.

"I wish I had your perspective." I pull myself up and out of the hammock.

"Where you going, Flores?"

"I've gotta pee," I say. And I also don't want to talk about this anymore. I no longer have the urge to go the distance. I've already over-shared too many times today.

"Well, have a good one. Come back soon. We'll miss you."

"Who's 'we'?"

"Me and the snoring child at my feet? Me and the gecko? Take your pick, Flores."

"Are you drunk, Max?"

"I'm getting there. And what about you? Why aren't you blasted? You've never even drunk before, and here you are, all composed."

"I'm pacing myself. That, and I'm superhuman."

"Can you grab me another beer? You can carry me home, Catwoman."

"Back to La Jolla, on my shoulders."

Max smiles goofily. I smile back at him. The lightness is back. Max resurrected it from the dead. He's got a gift.

I have a quick pee, grab Max a beer, and find myself wanting to return to him after only a few short minutes apart. I think I'm getting a little too attached. Will is going to be here soon, and this fairy tale will come to an abrupt end. I should gird myself for that reality, but instead, realizing how limited our time is together, I want to ask him a million questions. I want to spend what little time we have left together lying in the hammock. I head back outside, toward Max. I'm going to have to fit a lifetime into the next few minutes. Unfortunately, when I get back to the hammock, Max is passed out. The little girl and the gecko are gone. Max looks too beautiful, sleeping peacefully, slowly swinging back and forth in the breeze, to wake him. I gingerly climb into the hammock, slide in beside him, and stare up at the darkening sky, wishing we had more time, wishing this wasn't the end but the beginning. But what's the point of that?

I must have drifted off, because the next thing I know, I see a man leaning over Max, planting a kiss on his lips.

Before I can react, Max opens his eyes, screams, "What the—?" bolts upright, and knocks us both out of the hammock and onto the ground.

"Hey, guys!"

We look up to see Will standing above us waving and laughing. He's wearing . . . overalls? Striped denim overalls? Come again?

"What the hell was that, man?" Max asks Will.

"Just saying hello. Seemed like the best way to wake you, sleeping beauty."

"Will . . ." I scold.

"Don't worry. What happens in Mexico, stays in Mexico," Will says.

"Shit, that was messed up, dude," Max says.

I stand and give Will a hug. "I'm glad you made it!" I say, wishing he hadn't gotten here yet.

"Barely. Just by the skin of my chinny chin chin. But that's a story for later. Much," Will says.

With the abrupt arrival of Will, whatever spell was beginning to form between Max and me has dissipated, and now I'm back to feeling a little awkward.

"This town seems like party central. We should check it out," Will says.

"Will, it's late. We need to head back." I'm saying what I'm supposed to say even thought my heart isn't entirely in it. Because this is what I do. The responsible thing. This is who I am. Allowing Will to lead us down the garden path couldn't possibly be a good idea. Despite the fact that the garden path is calling my name.

"We should say our good-byes," I say to Max, looking to him for confirmation.

"Yeah, guess so." I'm surprised to hear the hesitation in Max's voice.

Still, it's late. We've got to go.

"Don't I, at least, get a little food and drink? I mean, I know I'm just the driver, but still, the help's gotta eat," Will says.

"Suppose we have time for a taco. Let's get you a plate," I

say, looping my arm through Will's and walking him into the house. Max trails us.

"'We're gonna bring this party up to a nice respectable level. Don't worry, we're not gonna hurt anyone. We're not even gonna touch 'em,'" Will says.

"'We're just gonna make 'em cry a little, just by lookin' at 'em,'" I say, finishing the quote.

"What are you guys talking about?" Max wants to know.

"It's just some lines from *Some Kind of Wonderful*," I offer.

"The old movie?"

"The genius old movie by the brilliant Sir John Hughes."

"Oookay, whatever," Max says.

Will has wedged himself between us. Literally and metaphorically. Our ritualistic behavior must seem strange to Max. I'm hoping Will can keep our little routines to a minimum. It's too much information for Max.

"What are you wearing, Will?" I ask. The overalls might be more shocking than anything else that's happened in the last ten hours.

"Carhartt dungarees. They're all the rage in Milano. I picked up a pair in Tijuana."

"Seriously? What?"

"I needed a change of clothes, and this is all I could find at the border. They could use a major retail infusion here. Someone should get word to H&M."

"What happened? You drove down naked? Your clothes got ruined? I mean, really, you look insane."

"Kylie. Leave it alone," Will warns. I rarely hear that tone in his voice.

"Got it. Let's get you a nice big glass of sangria and introduce you around." I will leave it alone, if that's what he wants. Will is my best friend. He's trekked all the way down to Mexico to rescue me, and if he wants to dress like a gay farmer, so be it.

Will sniffs at me. "I gather from the fact that you smell like a sailor on holiday that you've taken up drinking?"

"Yes. Only in moderation."

"I'm shocked! Shocked!"

"You're always on me for not having fun. I'm having fun now."

"I thought you'd be a bloody wreck. Weren't you kidnapped? This gives a whole new meaning to Stockholm syndrome."

"These aren't the people who kidnapped us. These are my dad's old friends. And we didn't really get kidnapped. More like accidental abduction in a truck of stolen electronics."

"Your dad has friends?"

"That's your takeaway?"

"That was the most shocking part of that sentence."

I laugh because Will knows my dad almost as well as I do.

"Apparently her dad had a lot of them. And fans as well. He was a soccer star in Mexico," Max offers.

Will raises one eyebrow and looks at me.

"I can tell you all about it on the way home," I say.

Will, Max, and I enter the kitchen to find Manuel's nephew Juan making a fresh round of sangria. Juan is the poster boy for tall, dark, and handsome. I can practically feel Will's eyes caressing him, hear Will panting after him. The temperature in the room rises twenty degrees as Will moves in on his target, all focus. Oh God. I brace myself for what is sure to be a debacle.

214

Juan is so not gay. But there's no stopping Will once the wheels are in motion.

"Hey, you," Will says, eyes only for Juan.

"Hi there," Juan says, perfectly innocuous, almost perfunctory, to all three of us. But somehow Will takes it as an open invitation.

"How are you doing tonight, gorgeous?" he asks Juan, sounding like a parody of a gay man on some *Saturday Night Live* skit. Max and I share a look, both wincing at the tacky line.

"I'm, uh, good," Juan says. I can tell he has no idea what to make of the flamboyant Will.

"It's good to be good. I'm good too. Better, now that you're here," Will says, full of innuendo that Juan seems oblivious to.

Oh, dear God. This is embarrassing. Where did Will find these lines? In some dusty old book from 1984?

"Juan, this is my friend Will. He just drove down from San Diego to take us back," I say.

As Juan turns to grab a few glasses, Will leans in and whispers to me, "So gay."

"Don't think so," I whisper. "Your gaydar is off."

"It's never off," Will says.

"Sangria?" Juan offers Will a glass.

"I thought you'd never ask." Will takes the glass from Juan, grazing his hand.

Juan looks awkward and quickly moves his hand away. I shoot Will a look, hoping he'll cease and desist before things get downright mortifying.

"So, are you guys going back to San Diego now?" Juan asks.

"Not quite yet," Will says.

"But pretty soon," I add.

"So, what do you do when you're not making sangria, Juan?" Will asks, polishing off his drink and pouring himself another. Guess we just lost our designated driver. Looks like I'll be needing a Big Gulp of coffee en route.

"I'm at architecture school at UCLA."

"Ooooh, I love architects. They have such *big* buildings."

Oh Lord, let the floor open up and suck me into the ground. Better yet, take Will.

"Uh, not all of them are big. Some are quite small. It all depends on the client," Juan says.

"I'm sure yours are very, very big."

"Yeah, well, I'm still in school, so I'm not really building much other than models at the moment." Poor Juan looks hideously uncomfortable.

"I bet you're really good with your hands, all that drawing and building."

"Yeah, we do take a lot of drawing classes, so, you know . . ."

"No, I don't know. Why don't we go outside and you can tell me all about it."

I can see Max choking back laughter. This is turning into some kind of strange performance piece. I'm pretty sure Juan's not enjoying himself. I know I'm not. Time for a curtain call.

"I think we should really get on the road," I say, taking Will's hand and pulling him out of the kitchen. "So, uh, hope to see you again soon, Juan."

"That was awkward," I say.

"You were freaking that guy out," Max tells Will.

"He's gay. Trust me," Will insists. "He wants me."

216

"You're out of your mind," I tell Will.

Manuel approaches.

"We've got to head back to San Diego," I say. "My friend Will just got here."

Will goes to shake Manuel's hand, but Manuel pulls him into a tight embrace. The guy is a hugger. I can't even imagine how he and my dad were best friends.

"Promise you'll be back soon," Manuel says to me.

"I promise."

"And try to bring your dad next time."

"That I can't promise."

"You have to go so soon?" Juan asks, suddenly appearing at our side. "I could tell you a little about architecture school," Juan offers to Will. "If, you know, you're really interested," Juan asks.

"I'm really, really interested," Will responds.

"So, you can stay for a little bit?" Juan wants to know.

"Not really . . . no . . ." I say.

"Forever, if that works," Will pipes in.

"We need to get going. We've got graduation in the morning," Max says.

"You guys could e-mail," I offer helpfully. As much as I want to stay, I know time is ticking away. We don't want to get to the border too late. Mom is expecting me. If we lose Will it could be days before we get out of here.

"We could take a short walk, talk architecture, and then you can leave with your friends," Juan offers.

Before I know what's happening, Will and Juan are heading out the door.

217

"Nice overalls, by the way," Juan tells Will as they walk away.

"I've got a kilt in the car. I could change," I hear Will say.

"Wait. What just happened?" Max asks me.

"No idea," I say, feeling dazed and confused.

"Is your friend gay, by any chance?" Manuel asks.

"I don't think there's anyone gayer," Max responds.

"You may want to go after them if you plan to get back to San Diego tonight. Juan is, how do you say, on the low down."

"You mean the down low?" Max asks.

"He doesn't think we know he's gay. But we know. We've all known forever. We're just waiting for him to tell us."

After hearing this, Max and I charge outside, but we're too late. Will and Juan are speeding down the street and out of sight in Will's Mini.

CHAPTER TWENTY-EIGHT

"Pain can be controlled. You just disconnect it."
—THE TERMINATOR

jake:

have been sitting on the curb outside the school for a long time now. I'm counting seconds; I'm up to 3,841. I don't know what to do or where to go. My plan was to get Kylie and go home. But now that I can't get Kylie, I don't really have a plan. Kylie might be in the school. But the man won't let me in. Maybe Kylie will come out and see me. Maybe she's not in there. But then, where is she?

I keep counting.

Why didn't Kylie come home today? Why doesn't Dad know where she is? Why did Mom leave me with Dad? I liked yesterday and the day before that and the day before that and every day except today.

I stand up and look out at the street. Cars rush by. Everyone is going somewhere except for me. I'm stuck here. I reach into my backpack and grab the two Luke Skywalkers. I don't want them anymore. I throw one across the street. It doesn't even reach the other side. I throw another one, harder this time. It goes a little farther. I empty my backpack onto the ground and start throwing all the figures into the street. I can hear cars crushing them. They're all broken now, in pieces everywhere. Most of my collection is gone, but I don't care. I don't care about anything.

I start counting again. I decide to start over from one. I get to 467 when a car pulls up to the curb. It's Dad. He sees me standing at the top of the stairs and comes toward me. I don't want to see him. He's going to be angry. I turn and walk away.

"Jake," Dad yells as he starts running. "Stop. Wait."

I run faster, around the school. I've got to get away from him. But Dad is fast, faster than I would have thought. He reaches out and grabs my arm. He's strong. I can't move.

"What the hell were you thinking, Jake?" Dad's yelling now.

I don't know what to say except, "Hi, Dad." I don't like yelling.

Dad throws his arms around me and hugs me for twenty-three seconds without saying anything. He breathes out really hard and then takes in a few deep breaths. He lets go of me, and we stand there staring at each other. I wonder what will happen next.

"Jesus, I had no idea what happened to you. You could have been killed or kidnapped or . . . I don't know what. You can't just run away like that, Jake." He's not yelling, but he's talking really loud. Too loud. I'm standing right next to him.

"Here's the list of stuff I don't like: apples, the fork in my bowl, Honey Nut Cheerios, eggplant parmesan, worms, watching baseball, and Taylor Swift." I'm not looking at Dad anymore. He's not saying anything.

"Okay." Dad is speaking softer now. "I think I've got it."

"There's more. That was just one list."

"How many lists are there?"

"Fifteen."

"I think you're going to have to give me all the lists."

"I can do that."

"Bud, why did you leave the house without telling me? I was so worried about you."

"Kylie's not at school. Mom said she was staying late. But a man told me that she isn't here."

"Maybe she's on her way home. I'm just glad you're okay."

"I threw all my *Star Wars* figures onto the street. They're not okay."

"We'll get you new ones."

"That would be good."

Dad isn't acting like Dad. He's acting nicer.

"Jake, you can't do that, you know? You can't just leave the house by yourself. If you want to go somewhere, you need to tell me."

"I went to find Kylie. If I'd found her I wouldn't have been by myself."

"You could have gotten lost. You could have gotten hurt. I was so scared something happened to you, Jake."

"I know how to take the bus. I know how to walk. I'm not stupid, you know?"

Dad just stares at me for a long time. I hate it when he does that. Usually he leaves the room after that. But where would he go now? Back to the car?

"You know what, buddy? You're right. You did good. But next time, you've got to run it by me, okay? Just so I know where you're going."

Dad is smiling at me. He never smiles. His teeth are nice and white. His lips are very red. He should smile more. I smile back at Dad.

"Don't tell Mom, okay?" I say.

"I already told her. I was worried so I called her. It was her idea to come to school and look for you. Don't worry. She won't be mad, I promise."

"You were worried about me?"

"Of course I was, buddy. I would never have forgiven myself if something had happened. You didn't think I'd be worried about you?"

"No. I didn't think you cared."

Dad looks sad. And surprised. I'm not sure why.

"Really, buddy? You didn't think I cared?"

"No."

"Well, I do. A lot."

"Okay."

"I guess I need to do a better job of showing you."

"Yes. You could do a better job."

222

Dad laughs. And he hugs me again.

"You never leave the house like that, Jake, without telling anyone, okay?"

It's hard to answer with Dad still hugging me. I pull away. It was a twenty-seven second hug. That's really long.

"I never need to. Kylie always comes home."

"I know, buddy. I know. But we're going to have to learn to live without her sometimes."

"I don't want to."

"It's gonna be hard. But you can do it. We can do it."

"I don't want to."

"I know how you feel."

"No. You don't."

"You're right. I don't know exactly how you feel. But I think I can come close. I know what it's like to miss a sibling. My brother died. I miss him a lot."

Dad's brother died? I didn't even know he had a brother.

"When did he die?"

"A long time ago, Jake. A long time ago. But I still miss him. A lot."

I don't know why Dad says it twice, but he looks really sad when he says it. Like he might cry. I don't want Dad to cry. I don't like it when people cry. That's one more thing I don't like. I'll have to put that on the list.

"Can we go get pizza. Extra cheese, olives, pepperoni?" I ask. I know Dad likes pizza. And so do I. Maybe it'll make us both feel better.

"Sure. I know you like Diet Dr Pepper, right? We'll get you a big one of those too."

Dad and I walk around the school and down the stairs.

"You parked on the sidewalk," I tell him.

"Yeah, I know. I guess I was in a rush."

"You're not supposed to do that."

"I know. Don't tell anyone, okay?"

"Okay."

Dad and I get in the car. As we bump off the sidewalk and onto the street, I hear a big crunch. I think that was my Poggle the Lesser. I can see his foot sticking out as we drive away.

CHAPTER TWENTY-NINE

"I like you as much as I can like anyone who thinks I'm an asshole."
—BROADCAST NEWS

max:

"They're not nearly as good as yours," Kylie says, staring at the pictures she's just taken with my phone. "You're talented, Langston, what can I say?"

I'm gathering Kylie thinks that all it takes to capture an image is to point and shoot. That's what everyone thinks. But there's a lot more to it. It's taken me years to frame things correctly. People assume you can't take good pictures on an iPhone, but they're wrong. Some of my best shots are on the phone. They're raw and simple, and most of the time no one knows you're taking a picture. It's much better than the thousand-dollar Nikon my dad got me for Christmas. I don't think I've used it in months.

"It must be shocking to discover I'm good at something."

"It is. And I mean that in the best possible way."

Kylie's been taking pictures of everything as we head back into town. Manuel encouraged us to check out the celebrations for St. John the Baptist. He thought we'd probably find Will and Juan somewhere here.

Kylie hands me the phone. "Here, check it out. Revel in my suckiness."

I scan the pictures. She's not going to win any awards. Lights strung up on palm trees, a little overexposed; two kids running down the street, pretty blurry; the harbor at night, kind of obvious. But she's trying and I dig that.

I was bummed that we were leaving when Will showed up. Kylie and I were really vibing, and Ensenada is way cool. It seemed like a drag to go back to La Jolla. But that was when I knew we had a ride. Now that Will has totally bailed on us, I'm getting kind of worried that we're never going to make it back in time for graduation. It was pretty stupid to depend on Will Bixby.

"I don't understand what you do that's so different from what I'm doing." Kylie is all focus as she stares into the lens. She's so passionate about every little thing. How does she do that? It's both exhausting and impressive. Who cares if she can't take a good picture? But the girl is determined to master it. "I see something cool, I point the camera, click, and then . . . it sucks. You can barely make out the image."

"I like your pictures."

"Don't lie to me. They're awful."

"Why do you care?"

"Because I do. Because I like to be good at things. I want to make movies. I want to be able to see things visually. A story. A moment. A place. It's an important skill and I'm terrible at it."

"And you can't stand my being better than you at something?"

"It's so not a contest. I just want you to teach me what you know. Impart your sage iPhone camera wisdom."

This girl makes me laugh. And think. She's way cool. And nothing like Lily. Lily . . . I haven't thought about Lily in hours.

"You know about story. I know about visuals. It's not the same thing."

"I should know both."

"I don't. I couldn't write a good story with a gun to my head."

"I want to understand how you frame a shot. C'mon, tell me your secret."

"It's hard to explain. It's like, I know it when I see it. It's about learning what works. I didn't know what I was doing at first, but I read about Stieglitz, Ansel Adams, Diane Arbus, Helmut Newton. I saw how they used light, composed their shots."

"And I thought you were just a pretty face."

"Yeah, well, I'm full of surprises too. I also watch a lot of old movies. They're like moving photographs."

"That's how you know about *The French Connection?*"

"I caught that on TV. But more like Fellini, Luchino Visconti, Godard. I see them at the Ken Cinema on Adams. Sometimes I go after squash games to just chill and watch the pictures go by. Pretty amazing stuff."

"Why didn't you tell me you were into movies? You know I'm a movie freak."

"I just met you, Kylie, remember?"

"I guess that's true," Kylie says. She's swinging her arms as she walks down the street, like a little kid. She looks so adorable, I want to take her in my arms, but that would be very weird. We know each other a lot better than we did this morning, but still . . .

"I've never seen anything by Visconti or Fellini. Kind of embarrassing, huh? I'm a connoisseur of the brain-dead action film and anything made after 1985," Kylie adds.

"David Fincher is a master."

"I know. I worship *Fight Club*."

"I've seen it three times."

"Six!" Kylie says proudly.

"'Kay, that's a little weird."

"You ever seen *Pan's Labyrinth*?"

"Guillermo del Toro. Genius."

"I know, right? That's what I keep telling Will. He won't go see it. He says it's responsible for the decline of Western civilization."

"It's pretty cool visually."

"Totally groundbreaking."

"You've got to see *The Leopard*. It'll blow you away. It's three and a half hours, but totally worth it."

"I was kind of waiting for NYU. Figured I'd have to see all those old films in class. You ever seen *Blow-up*?" Kylie asks me.

"Sick. Just totally sick. And loved the sex scenes."

"You would."

228

It's wild to talk old movies with someone. I don't know anyone else who's interested. Definitely not Lily. She had a shit fit and walked out of *The 400 Blows*. She said I was trying way too hard. The thing was, I wasn't trying at all. I just thought she'd like it. That was the last time I ever took Lily to the Ken.

"Maybe we could go see something at the Ken this summer, you know, if we're both around?"

"Yeah, sure, maybe," Kylie says, hesitating. She doesn't sound like she means it at all. I guess she's thinking that after tonight, this is it. I get it, it makes sense. We run in completely different circles, no overlap at all. It kinda bums me out, though.

"Okay, over on the lawn." Kylie points to a beach ball on the grass. "How would you photograph that?"

"For starters. I wouldn't."

"Why?"

"Because it doesn't have any life to it. I don't know. It's dull, meaningless. When I take pictures, I'm looking for something I connect with, a feeling, a mood, a vibe. It's like I'm having a conversation with what I'm photographing, or something like that."

I stop, uncomfortable. Why am I talking like this? I sound like some kind of pompous idiot, going on about photography like I'm Cartier-Bresson or something.

"I'm sure that sounds totally pretentious," I say, wanting to take it all back.

"It doesn't at all. It's very cool to hear you talk about it. How long have you been doing it?"

"I don't know. A while. I got a digital camera for my tenth birthday. And then I started playing around on the Mac, developing pictures with a million different programs. It's really the only thing I do, other than squash."

As we approach the harbor, I can hear music and the sounds of people partying. Lights are strung up everywhere. It looks like Christmas. Man, they know how to live it up in Mexico. I need to come south more often. The streets are covered with ribbons and giant paper banners. Colored lights have been strung up across the storefronts, and confetti floats in the air. A crowd of little girls in hot pink dresses comes toward us. They all have their hair pulled back, and flowers tucked behind their ears.

"Oh my God, look." Kylie points to a tiny Chihuahua wearing a sombrero on his back as he flies past our feet. A few seconds later a donkey carrying a huge wooden cross ambles across the street. People lead the donkey toward the church, but he stops and refuses to budge. A man whacks him on the butt, and he reluctantly moves on.

I'm taking pictures like crazy. This place is bursting with life.

"You should be a photographer, Max. Seriously. You have a real eye. I mean, you know more about film than I do."

"Whatever. Plenty of people can take great photos. It's not that big a deal. . . ."

"Yes, it is. It would be a shame if you didn't pursue it."

"Okay," is all I say. Because I don't want to get into it with her.

"You're really good. You must know that." Kylie looks up at me with her big eyes. She is so damn sincere. And earnest. And open. And beautiful . . .

230

"Yeah, I guess."

"I mean, I can write. I know it, and no one can take that away from me. You can take great photos. Better than most people. You should do something with it. See what happens."

"Look, I don't know. I just . . . I don't have your confidence. . . ."

Kylie looks at me, her head cocked to the left, like a dog that's just heard a grating, high-pitched noise. Like she doesn't understand what I've said.

"My confidence?" Kylie laughs like that's the funniest thing I've ever said.

"What?"

"An hour ago I was saying the same thing to you. You're ninety-five percent confidence. I'm like, twenty-five percent, thirty on a good day. I just know I can write and I know you can take photos. It's not confidence, it's fact."

"I told you, it's complicated."

"Yeah, everything is."

The crowds are getting thicker, the music louder, as we hit the center of things. It feels like New Year's Eve. I wonder how we'll ever find Will and Juan in this scene. Kylie and I slow down and try to stay on the outskirts.

"Look, I tried," I say. It comes out before I can take it back.

"What do you mean, you tried?"

"It's just not going to happen, okay?"

"Tell me." Kylie is not backing down. I've put it out there and she's going after it. I look at Kylie and exhale. Why did I even say anything?

"Really, it's no big deal."

"What do you have to lose by telling me? We'll probably never see each other again after today."

I hope that's not true.

"We'll see each other at graduation," I say. But I'd like to see her after that as well. I'm just not sure I should say it. We both know I've got a girlfriend. Suddenly, Lily is feeling like one more thing I wish I didn't have to deal with.

"Okay," she says, "we'll have an intimate moment with about a hundred and twenty other seniors tomorrow. The point is, we don't really hang out. I'm safe territory. You can tell me. And no one else ever has to know."

"I applied to RISD . . . the Rhode Island School of Design . . . and got in."

"Oh my God. That's amazing."

"Yep."

"But you're not going."

Kylie looks at me like I'm a total idiot. And that is exactly why I didn't want to say anything.

"Nope."

"You're doing prelaw at UCLA instead."

"Yep."

"It's not too late to change your mind. You can always—"

"It's done. I didn't even tell my parents I applied. And when I got in, it was right after my dad got really sick. I ripped up the acceptance letter. My dad wants me to be a lawyer. And he's sick. So I'm gonna be a lawyer. I'd have to be a real jerk not to."

"I think you're a jerk if you become a lawyer to make your dad happy."

"Don't hold back. Tell me what you really think."

232

"I'm sorry, it's just, that is so stupid. It's your life, Max. If you don't want to be a lawyer, how can you resign yourself to doing it for the rest of your life? That is so bleak."

"Everything is not about passion and following your dream. Get real, Kylie. Grow up. People do tons of crap they don't want to do. I mean, does someone wake up one day and say, Man, I want to pick up people's garbage more than anything in the world?"

I'm getting a little too intense. I look away.

"Okay. I get it," Kylie says. "Not everyone gets to do exactly what they want to do. But don't most parents want the best for their kids? Wouldn't your dad want you to pursue your passion?"

"Pretty sure he wants me to be a lawyer. He thinks the arts are, 'No way to make a living.' I'm quoting here. You should talk. Doesn't sound like your parents are so into you studying film. And, no offense, but it's a total long shot. I mean, I hope you have a plan B." That comes out a little harsher than I intended.

"Gee, thanks for your support."

Kylie looks annoyed. I try to pull it back, but I'm feeling under attack. "Look, I'm doing the best I can under the circumstances."

"I get the pressure. It's all going to be hard. I may need a plan B, C, and D. But you know what? I would be so pissed at myself if I didn't give it a shot. And just maybe, when I'm thanking my parents in my Oscar acceptance speech, everyone will regret telling me I couldn't do this. Including you."

"You're kind of a walking contradiction. At Freiburg you're like a scared little mouse. At least that's the impression I get.

You keep your distance because you don't want to risk being rejected, or whatever. But then, when it comes to your future, you have this incredible confidence. You know exactly what you want, and even though it's a crazy dream, you're going to do it. Nothing can stop you."

"Does that make me an idiot?"

"No. It makes you very cool."

We look at each other. It breaks the tension, but in its place is an undeniable attraction. I'm not sure what to do about it. I'm trying to keep in mind that I've got a girlfriend, but it's slipping away.

"You're exactly like me, Langston. Just in reverse."

"How do you figure?"

"You're the most confident guy around when it comes to Freiburg. But then, in real life, you don't believe in yourself enough to follow your dreams."

"That sounds like some kind of cheesy line from a movie."

"Don't knock cheesy lines from movies. They can be totally inspirational. Please pass the cheese."

"Photography is more of a hobby."

"Hobbies are for wimps who don't have the guts to follow their passion."

"See what I mean? Your confidence is so strong it's obnoxious."

"Okay. Have fun sitting in an office for the rest of your life, doing something you don't want to do."

"How am I going to support myself being a photographer? Especially after my family cuts me off?"

People pass us by, on their way to the festivities. We should probably shut up and go look for Will. But we're in it now.

"Oh my God, Max. We aren't supposed to say stuff like that when we're eighteen. If everybody just thought about money, and making the safe choice, there would be no art in this world, no music, nothing interesting. I'd rather starve."

"You're used to not having money."

"That's kind of insensitive."

"I didn't mean it like that. In a way, you're lucky. You know you can live without it and be fine. I don't know if I can do that."

"You'd be fine, Max. Plenty of people are happy doing what they want and never making a gazillion dollars."

"Listen, Kylie, you've given it your best shot. And maybe at a different time or place you could have convinced me, but not now. After my brother disappointed my dad, my telling him I don't want to go to law school would kill him, sooner than already expected."

"Okay, well, maybe after law school, then."

I can see by her body language that Kylie is backing down. The mention of my dad's imminent death is making her uncomfortable.

"Maybe your dad will actually be okay. And then you can do what you want. People defy the odds all the time," Kylie says. I know she's trying to be nice, but I'm so sick of everyone refusing to accept the inevitable. What's the point?

"I know it's weird to say that my dad is going to die, but, you know what? It actually makes me feel better. No one ever says it. My mom certainly doesn't. The doctors don't. They talk about the next step, alternative treatments, attacking it from another angle. He's got inoperable cancer in his brain. It's just a matter of time. I'd like someone to just say it."

I'm suddenly fired up again without realizing how I got here. I'm breathing hard. Kylie takes a step toward me and then, tentatively, puts her arms around me. I relax into her body. It feels so good in her arms, I could stay here for a while. I put my face in her hair. My arms wrap around her body. I pull her close. Breathe her in. My cheek presses against her cheek. Her skin is sticky, warm, sweet. I turn my face, and my lips press lightly against her face . . .

And then, *SPLASH!*

Water rains down on us from out of nowhere.

Kylie and I pull apart and both turn to see Manuel's son, Manu, standing in front of us, laughing. He holds an empty bucket. Manuel comes tearing around the corner, wearing a donkey mask, carrying two liter bottles of water like loaded pistols. He douses Manu and the two double over laughing.

Kylie and I stare at them like they've lost their minds. I mean, what up, people?

Manuel pulls off the donkey mask and throws a wet arm around us.

"Time to get soaking wet. Part of the tradition of St. John the Baptist is to throw water at each other, or dunk people in the sea. You two are not nearly wet enough. Manu . . . get 'em."

Manu pulls out two squirt guns from his pocket and fires away. Manuel hands us each a squirt gun. Kylie turns her firepower on Manu, and I shoot Manuel straight through the heart. I don't think I've used a water gun since I was ten.

The water fight has changed the mood. Kylie takes a giant step away from me. It feels like hours ago that our faces were pressed together. That moment's gone.

"Now it's time to get you two to the party. C'mon," Manuel says, taking us both by the arm and dragging us down the street and into the pack of partyers. "Have fun!" Manuel tells us. It sounds like a command rather than a suggestion. And then he disappears into the crowd.

"What should we do about Will?" I ask Kylie.

"Dunno."

"We need to get back for graduation."

"He'll turn up," Kylie says as she walks toward a group of people dancing the merengue in the middle of the street.

I follow her. Kylie watches them, entranced.

"What happened to little Miss 'We have to do Murphy's assignment, or else'?"

"Oh my God. Murphy's assignment. I completely forgot." Kylie laughs. "If she only knew what that assignment did to us. For the record, I'm totally not doing it."

"And what about your speech? You don't care about that, either?"

"Of course I do. Will is going to turn up, trust me. We'll get back. Let's just enjoy the party for now."

And with that, Kylie jumps in. She's dancing to the music. What she lacks in style, she makes up for in enthusiasm. I watch her from the curb. She looks happy, uninhibited, free. Someone she can't be at Freiburg.

She's right. We'll make it back at some point. I join Kylie, throwing myself into the mix.

CHAPTER THIRTY

"Everything I found out, I wanna forget."
—THE BOURNE IDENTITY

lily:

"Lily, grab my cap, grab my cap," Tessa Overby screams at me. "He's going to throw it in the water and I'll have to wear it to graduation all warped."

I'm standing in Luca Sonneban's kitchen as Luca holds Tessa's graduation cap over his head. Tessa is climbing his back like a monkey on a tree, attempting to pry the cap from his hands. She's clutching at his shirt and laughing hysterically. I might have found this amusing yesterday, but now I just want to smack her.

I wander out back to find Justin Brandt standing on the diving board, holding Ella Bing by her ankles, dangling her over the water. They're both clearly wasted out of their minds. Ella's always a little sloppy, but hanging upside down is really pushing things to a new level. Her shirt drapes around her neck, like a scarf, as her breasts dangle freely for everyone to see. It may be the last day of school, but, Jesus, have a little dignity.

"Should I do it?" Justin slurs.

A loud roar goes up from the crowd standing around the pool.

"Do it. Do it. Do it," everyone chants.

Ella gives one last squeal and then Justin lets go. She drops into the pool with a splash. People cheer and hoot. A few seconds later Ella bursts to the surface, laughing and spitting out water. Justin dives in after her, fully clothed. Fifteen or so people leap in as well, all clothed.

Ella throws off her shirt and is slapping around the water, topless. A bunch of other girls toss off their shirts. Boys throw off their jeans, and soon it's one big skinny-dipping bacchanal. More senior rituals I should be partaking in. I've been looking forward to senior night since freshman year. I'd probably have been the first person in the water. If only.

I've now thoroughly scoped out the party, and Max isn't here, which is just so infuriating. And it begs the question, where the hell is he? And why hasn't he bothered to text me all day?

"Hey, girl, where you been? I've been looking all over for you," Stokely says as she throws an arm around me and kisses my cheek.

"Just got here a little while ago."

"It's awesome, isn't it?"

"Totally," I say, trying to sound enthusiastic.

"So . . . Luca asked me if I was going to Charlie's party with anyone."

"What did you tell him?"

"I said I wasn't going with anyone."

"Oh, Stokes, you shouldn't have said that. You should have let there be a little mystery. Make him want it."

"Shit. Do you think I fucked up?"

"No. I'm sure it'll be fine. He's probably just waiting till the last minute to ask you. All of these guys are so lame."

"Totally. Too bad we're not lesbians. It would be so much easier."

Poor Stokely. She's hopeless at the games. I've tried and tried to coach her, but it's just not sinking in, which is weird because she's a smart girl. Just really stupid with guys. I don't know how she'll ever land a boyfriend. She's had a crush on Luca forever, but she can't seem to play it cool around him. Guys love the chase, but Stokely just wants to fall down at their feet.

"You wanna go swimming?" Stokely asks.

"Maybe in a little while. I'm starving. What's there to eat?"

"Oh my God. You have to check it out. They got the sushi chef from Nawazaka. It's unbelievable. C'mon."

Stokely takes my hand and drags me toward the other end of the pool. Under a large cabana, a whole sushi station has been set up, replete with glass-enclosed cases of raw fish. It's insane. A sushi chef makes sashimi and maki, whipping it out as fast as he can. People are downing toro and yellowtail like it's popcorn. Stokely and I squeeze our way through the crowd and pluck a few rolls.

Susan Miles is standing next to me. She starts to wobble, and then turns and hurls onto the grass. Lovely. Raw fish and excessive vodka don't go particularly well together. Amy Singer, Susan's best friend since fourth grade, rushes to her side and holds her hair back as Susan finishes puking her guts out. Several of the waitstaff appear and clean up the mess, even as it's still happening. Everyone walks around the carnage, not wanting the bloodshed to get in the way of their good time. It's senior night; there will be plenty of roadkill. Susan just has the distinguished job of being first.

As Stokely and I head out into the yard, Sandy Lin calls out to me.

"Lily, did you find out what dorm you're in? I just heard I'm in Adams House."

Sandy Lin got into Stanford early decision, just like me, but the similarities end there.

"Um, the thing is, I'm actually thinking about taking a gap year." As soon as I say it, I realize my mistake. I should have just kept my mouth shut and dealt with it later.

"Really? What are you going to do?" I can tell by the curdled look on her face that Sandy thinks this is the worst idea she's ever heard. And I have to agree with her. Why would anyone put off the holy grail of Stanford? Trust me, Sandy, I'm right there with you.

"I'm thinking about traveling to Europe or Asia."

Stokes is looking at me like I've lost my mind. This is the

first she's heard of any of this. First I've heard of it too. But I feel like I've got to have some kind of story, in light of what happened last night. This isn't my greatest spin job, but it's the best I can do on the fly.

"Okay. Well, that sounds . . . cool," Sandy says. Not.

Stokely steers me away from Sandy.

"What are you talking about, Lil," she says. It's more of a statement than a question. I'm not even sure how I should answer her. I've dug myself into this hole and now I've got to climb out.

"I don't know. I'm just not feeling the whole college thing yet. I think a year off would be good for me. Everyone in Europe does it."

"What are you talking about, Lily?"

"You just said that, Stokes."

"I know. 'Cause I don't know what else to say. I mean, this is crazy talk. It's so not you."

"It's not like I'm not going to college or anything. I just want some more life experience."

"Isn't it a little late in the game to be deciding this?"

"It could be good for me, you know?"

"Not really." Stokes can tell I am not kidding, and she looks completely knocked out by the news. For good reason. I've just done a one-eighty on her. Then again, life did a one-eighty on me.

Stokely was hell-bent on going to Duke, just like I was hell-bent on going to Stanford, and when we both got accepted, by chance on the same day, we burst into tears. Which is not exactly my style, but it was just such a relief, I couldn't hold it in.

"Come on, Stokes, let's go down to the beach." I don't want to talk about it anymore. Soon, everything will be public and everyone will be gossiping about me. At least for tonight I want to enjoy my fake gap year.

I head down the path toward the ocean. Luca's parents have more money than my dad used to have—that thought goes down hard. Their house is one of those huge glass boxes that look like a modern art museum. It sits on the bluff above the beach, and everything in it is white. Or at least it used to be, before tonight. Luca's parents made the mistake of letting him host a graduation party, and now everything is covered in a thin gray film of senior night debauchery. But no worries— they can just throw everything out and redecorate tomorrow.

We walk down the wooden stairs and snake our way to the beach. There's a bunch of people on the sand, sitting in front of a huge bonfire that two guys continue to feed. More staff. Why couldn't I be a Sonneban instead of a Wentworth?

"Yo, yo, Lil and Stokes," Charlie says as he and Ben Goodman approach us. "What's up, ladies?"

Their faces are red from either drinking or standing next to the blazing fire or both. Ben clutches a fifth of Jack Daniel's. He takes a long sip and then passes it to Charlie.

"We just threw Billy Stafford's clothes in the fire," Ben tells us. And then he and Charlie high-five.

"Where is Billy?" I ask, not really interested.

"He's in the ocean," Ben says. "Guess he's going to be there for a while." This cracks Ben and Charlie up.

"Have you heard from Max?" I ask Charlie.

"No. This is messed up. He is seriously missing the dankest party of the year."

I'm enraged. I have never been this mad at Max. I would be worried except that I know Max, and it is just like him to disappear on me in my time of need. Plus, if anything happened to him, we would have heard something. La Jolla is the smallest of small towns. News travels at the speed of sound.

"Let me have some of that," I say to Charlie as I grab the bottle of JD from his hand and take a long pull on it. Fuck it. I'm going to get wasted. The whiskey burns my throat, but I force myself to keep drinking. I've never been much of a drinker. If ever there was a time to start, now is certainly it. I haven't eaten all day and I can feel the alcohol taking hold right away. I feel lighter immediately.

Ben and Stokes have gone down to the water to look for Billy. I see Stokes pull her dress off and step into the water. I take a few more sips from the bottle.

"Hey, Charlie, can you match me?" I take a drink and pass him the bottle.

"Aw, Lil, you're talking to the master here." He takes two and passes it back.

My turn.

"You okay, Lil?" Charlie may be drunk, but he knows me well enough to know that something is wrong. I don't normally act like this, drinking straight out of a bottle, matching Charlie, shot for shot. I'm acting like trash. It's embarrassing. But I guess that's where I live now. Might as well get used to it.

"I'm good," I say. "Just pissed at Max."

"Yeah, he can be an asshole sometimes, you know?"

I've never heard Charlie say anything bad about Max before. He's loyal to a fault. I wonder if that's just the alcohol talking.

"He sure as shit can," I say.

Maybe something happened to him. Maybe I'm so caught up in my own stuff, I can't think straight about Max. Nah, I doubt it. I'm pretty sure he's just bailed on senior night. Lately, he's been sort of cold. I can't help thinking this is about another girl. With Max, everything is usually about sex or squash. Maybe he's fucking someone on the squash court. Probably Marsha Spittman. Or, better yet, Lacey Garson. That little bitch. She's wanted to get into Max's pants for as long as she's known him. And, come to think of it, I haven't seen her here.

"Screw him." And that's when I take Charlie's face and pull him to me. I kiss him hard. He's too drunk to protest. His lips are bitter, like vinegar, and his breath is sour. Charlie's tongue is in my mouth, forceful, poking, like he's doing root canal work. It's not particularly pleasant. Nothing like Max, but I'm here. No way out now.

I take Charlie's hands that are hanging limply at his side, seemingly looking for direction, and I shove them under my shirt. He fumbles around on my breasts like he's never been to this place before, like it's unfamiliar territory. What's up with that? I thought Charlie was quite the swordsman. Maybe he's too wasted to know what he's doing. Or maybe he just can't do this to his best friend, he's too good of a person. Not vengeful, petty, or bitter. Like me.

We make out for a few more minutes, but it's not working.

245

For either of us. I pull away and crumple onto the sand. I don't want to look at Charlie ever again. What was I thinking?

Charlie stares down at me, dumbfounded. "What just happened?"

I can't help myself, I start crying.

Charlie falls to the sand beside me. He gently rubs my back. Now, at least, he seems to know what to do with his hands.

"We made a mistake. We were drunk. It didn't mean anything. Max never has to know about it. Promise."

"That's not what I'm crying about," I cough out, in between tears.

Neither of us says anything as we stare at the fire.

And then Charlie's phone rings. He takes it out of his pocket and answers.

"Max . . . hey."

Charlie looks at me, and I look away. Speak of the devil.

CHAPTER THIRTY-ONE

"I was thinking how nothing lasts and what a shame that is."
—THE CURIOUS CASE OF BENJAMIN BUTTON

kylie:

"*Buenas noches, señorita. ¿Cómo estás?*" a man named Augusto asks me, slurring his words. He's so wasted, he's about five minutes from falling off his stool. We're back at Manuel's bar, hoping he can help us track down Will. He's so busy with the madding crowd that he hasn't had time to talk to us yet, so we're waiting at the bar. I don't think we're going to make it home tonight. It's getting too dark to make the drive now. And the funny thing is, I couldn't care less.

Max is off calling his parents to tell them he'll be later than expected. Much later. I'm drinking a beer and waiting for Max to return, wishing Augusto would disappear.

"*Yo no hablo español,*" I say. I'm not in the mood for a lengthy conversation with Augusto, who may or may not be celebrating his birthday. I glance over at him as he sways precariously. Jesus, I really hope he doesn't fall over on me.

Max saunters back from the phone booth, smiling at me. I wonder what it's like being Lily. Always having Max walking toward you, looking like that. Must be nice. Really nice.

"Everything good at your house?" I ask.

"*No problemos.*"

"Lucky you," I say. I don't think it'll be quite the same at my house.

I stand up as Max takes a seat next to Augusto.

"I'm going to call my mom. I would advise you to move over a few seats. Augusto here is getting ready to take a tumble," I tell Max.

"Don't worry about me. I can handle myself."

And then, as if on cue, Augusto falls over onto Max, and they both go down. Max is laughing.

"Wow. You called it," Max says.

"I'm psychic."

Augusto is snoring. Jesus.

"What are we supposed to do with him?" I ask.

"Let's put him in a chair in the back."

Max and I drag Augusto to a worn leather chair in the corner of the bar.

"He can sleep it off here," Max says. "Go call your mom."

As I head into the phone booth, I can't help thinking that Max is a really decent guy. Possibly even a better person than me. All I wanted to do was run fast and far from Augusto, but

248

Max wanted to make sure he was okay. Do I have everyone else at Freiburg wrong as well? I push that out of my mind as I dial Mom's cell. I can only focus on fixing one problem at a time. Mom is up. Then I can revisit my social miscalculations from the past six years.

I never lie to my mom, but there's a first time for everything, so here goes. I brace myself for the conversation, but she doesn't pick up, which is weird. She always picks up my calls. I am calling from a different number, so maybe that's the reason.

"Uh, hi, Mom. It's me. I just wanted to let you know that the meeting went kind of late and I'm going to spend the night at Will's, okay? I'll call you in the morning." And then I hang up fast. I've just dropped a bomb. She's going to be, among other things, pissed. Really pissed. I've never done anything like this, but maybe it's finally time I did.

"So?" Max asks as I slip onto a stool next to him, having passed Augusto along the way, who is curled up on the chair, fast asleep, covered in a colorful blanket. Did Max find a blanket for him as well? Who is he, Gandhi?

"I left her a message. She didn't pick up. Second time today. She almost always picks up her cell."

"I'm sure everything's fine. She's working, right?"

"Yeah, that's probably it," I say. But in the back of my mind, I can't help worrying that something's gone horribly wrong in my absence, because that's my job. I hold things together for my family. But, you know what? I can't do it forever. They need to learn how to take care of themselves, starting tonight. I'm leaving in less than three months. We've all got to learn how to let go, otherwise I might as well just call the whole thing off and go to UCSD.

I make a decision to put everything out of my head except for the here and now. For one night I want to be totally, unconscionably, downright selfish. Does that make me a bad person? I don't think so. I'll deal with everything else tomorrow. Maybe I'm just buzzed enough to pull it off.

"Manuel says we can crash at his house. On the floor or something. And then we'll head out first thing in the morning."

"Yeah. Definitely," I say. But I can't help wondering what the larger meaning is here. I mean, Max and I are spending the night together, in a manner of speaking.

"Don't worry. We're going to get to graduation on time," Max says.

That's the last thing on my mind at the moment.

"Dos cervezas, por favor," Max says to an old bartender who's helping out Manuel.

I laugh at Max's accent.

"What?" Max asks.

"It's *dos*, not *does*, which are female deer."

"Maybe you can give me Spanish lessons when we get back home."

"Maybe," is all I say. But, of course, my mind races with the implications of that innocuous comment. First he mentioned going to the Ken. Now Spanish lessons. Does he think we'll be seeing each other when we get back home? On a regular basis? I definitely need another beer. It's been a long night and the buzz is ebbing and flowing. I need to get a continuous flow going or I'm going to pick apart everything Max says, looking for the hidden meaning. I'm sure he'll forget about seeing me the minute we're back in La Jolla.

A shouting match breaks out at the bar. A drunk guy with dreads is screaming at the old bartender. The bartender yells back. He's a tough old dude. He looks about ready to leap over the bar and smash the guy's face in. Manuel has one eye trained on the guy, watching. The shouting gets louder, and then the guy with dreads throws a glass at the old dude. The old dude rushes out from the bar, but before he can get to dreadlocked guy, Manuel is there. He's got dreadlocked guy in a headlock. The old dude is yelling in Spanish. His face is turning red with fury. Manuel barks out orders. The old dude retreats. Manuel drags dreadlock guy toward the exit and kicks him out of the bar.

Max and I share a look. I don't think either of us would want to mess with Manuel. He's one tough mother.

Manuel walks over to us.

"Enjoying the show?" he asks.

"Totally," I say.

"That was awesome," Max tells Manuel.

"Just another night in Ensenada." Manuel laughs. "Dealing with people like that is part of doing business. Don't own a bar when you grow up, *mis amigos*. People are *loco*. And when they drink, forget about it. Do something that doesn't involve glass or alcohol."

"Got it," Max says.

"I texted Juan. Didn't hear back from him. Probably doesn't want me to know he's with a guy. I wish he'd just come out already. It would make life a lot easier for all of us. I'm sure if you wander around you'll run into him. Either way, you'll crash at our place. I'll make sure Juan gets Will to the house bright and early, even if I have to go to Juan's apartment myself in the morning and fetch Will. I'm sure Juan will insist they're just friends, even if they're butt naked and in bed together." Manuel laughs at his own joke. "Don't worry, I'll get you guys to the border in plenty of time."

"Thanks, Manuel," I say. "For everything."

"It's nothing. I just hope you'll come back to Ensenada. And bring your dad."

"I'm definitely going to try."

"You guys should get out there and enjoy the party. No need to hang around with a boring old man."

"You're the least boring person I've met in years," Max says.

"I second that," I say.

"Okay, now get out of here and have some fun."

"All right, we'll catch you later," Max says, throwing his arm around my shoulder and leading me out the door and back into the crowd.

We weave up and down the streets, connected. For Max, an arm around a shoulder probably means nothing. To me, it means everything. A whole new world. My whole body is buzzing from the sensation of being bound to Max. Never let me go, I think.

"So did you really hate the quote?" I ask Max.

"What quote? What are you talking about?"

"The Golda Meir quote. From my speech." I've been wanting to ask Max about it, but I didn't really feel comfortable bringing it up until now.

"No. I didn't hate it. I was just surprised by it."

"Surprised. Why?"

"I don't know. I guess the quote felt pretty average. Kind of dull, predictable. I figured you'd have some obscure movie lines or some brilliant insights into our future. You don't think like anyone else I know. So I was expecting something different, I guess. Does that make sense?"

I'm pretty sure he means this in a good way. Still, it doesn't bode particularly well for my speech.

"You have to hear the rest of it. It makes perfect sense in context."

"I'm sure it does. And I know it'll be great. I'm hardly the person to give advice. I'm a terrible writer. You should do the opposite of what I say."

"You think people can't relate to the quote?"

"Look, Kylie, I haven't heard the whole speech, so what do I know? It's just, now that I know you, I bet you could stand up there without any speech and just ad-lib and it would blow everyone away. You're funny and smart and insightful. You don't need to quote anyone but yourself."

"Yeah, well, that's not exactly how I roll. I show up prepared for everything."

"Whatever you say is going to be awesome. Don't overthink it. And don't take my opinion too seriously. I'm almost always wrong about stuff like this."

"Okay," I say. But Max's words ring in my ears. Is it too stiff? Not relatable? I don't ad-lib my life, so no chance that I'll just show up and wing it.

We walk by a cluster of people standing on a street corner

singing Mexican folk songs at the top of their lungs. Like mostly everyone else in town, they're drunk. Oddly, they don't sound half bad. As we pass, a woman pulls us into the circle, throwing one arm around each of us. It's exactly what I need to shift the mood. I don't want to think about my potentially disastrous speech tomorrow.

We all sway together, like trees in a breeze, as everyone continues to sing. Even though I don't know one of these people or the song they're singing, I want to be part of it, which is bizarre since I'm so not a group kind of person. I attempt to sing along, catching words and phrases here and there. They finish singing and the circle splinters.

Max and I wander back into the street. We're no longer touching. I wish we were, but I'm not sure how to initiate it. I spend several endless seconds thinking about how I should do it. Do I just grab his hand? Or would it be more subtle to slip my arm through his and then slowly, gently, wind my hand down his arm until my fingers find his? As I'm strategizing, Max casually throws his arm over my shoulders, and once again we are connected. I am freed from the misery of figuring out how to do it myself. Max probably didn't think about it for a minute.

We turn down a small alleyway lined with open-air stalls. Couples kiss in discreet corners. Stragglers loiter on stairs, sharing cigarettes. It's quieter as the revelry from the main street dies down. A dress in a tiny shop window catches my eye. I stop and stare at it. It's a deep fuchsia, delicately embroidered with yellow flowers, with layers of lace on the front, and tiny cap sleeves. The body of the dress hangs in tiers, almost to the

254

floor. It looks as if it's been fashioned out of paper, like an elaborate valentine cut by hand.

"You like it?" Max asks me.

"Yeah, it's sort of fantastic. Tacky and chic at the same time."

"Let's go in. You can try it on," Max insists.

"First of all, I don't wear dresses, especially not one like that. Second of all, I've got practically no money; and third—"

"Slow down, Flores. You know what, I don't care about number three. Or number one or two, for that matter. You like it. You should try it on."

Max opens the door and pushes me into the store. There are racks of brightly colored flouncy dresses crammed into every pocket of the tiny space. The shop is packed so full of dresses there's barely room to maneuver around the clothes. Purses and hats hang from the low ceilings and line the walls.

"*Hola,*" says a round old woman as she approaches us. She's so short she barely makes it to my shoulders. "Let me help you find something, *señorita.*"

Before I can respond, she ushers me toward a rack of dresses. She plucks a lime green macramé number from the mass and holds it up to me. The skirt is speckled with pink pom-poms. Hideous does not begin to describe this frock.

"You like?" The woman peers up at me, hopeful.

I catch Max's eye and can see he's holding back laughter. I grope for something diplomatic to say, but what comes out is, "Uh, no. Not at all."

Upon hearing my blunt response, Max bursts out laughing.

I switch to Spanish so that Max can't understand me. I

try to tell the woman that I'm not really a frilly dress girl, but she's so delighted that she can speak Spanish with me, she isn't really listening. She's on a mission and there's no stopping her. The little round ball of a woman is a whirling dervish as she bounces through the racks in search of the perfect dress for me.

I feel bad. The woman seems sweet and she clearly wants to make a sale, but she's got the wrong girl. I don't want to try any of these dresses on. I can't even remember the last time I wore a dress. I'm all about jeans and T-shirts. Dressing up for me means buying a new pair of high-tops. What am I doing in here? Oh, right—this was Max's idea.

"C'mon," Max whispers to me. "Just try something on. It'll be fun."

"I don't do dresses," I say.

"Make an exception."

"Only if you will."

"What do you mean?" Max asks.

"You try one on. I'll try one on," I offer.

Max stares at me, trying to determine if I'm serious. I am. His eyes crinkle into a smile. He's up for the challenge. I should have figured; he's the kind of guy who's up for anything.

"'Kay. I'll pick yours. You pick mine."

The old woman is pulling out dress after dress, one more hideous than the other. I shake my head at the choices, saying, "*Lo siento*," after each one. She is surprisingly chipper, undaunted by the fact that I've yet to give her any positive reinforcement.

Max, meanwhile, begins to peruse the racks, checking out dress after dress.

The woman disappears into the back and returns with a

plain white cotton gown. It's lovely in its simplicity. Perfect for Max. *"Sí,"* I say. She smiles, pleased with herself.

"But it's not for me. It's for my friend," I say, this time in English so that Max will understand. I'm worried she's going to freak and kick us out of the store. Instead, she smiles broadly.

"Ah, St. John brings out *la niña* in all of us. I get a bigger one for you," she says to Max, sizing him up. She retreats into the back room again.

"What have you got for me, Langston?"

"I think you'll do the pink one in the window, Flores."

"No. It's too . . . too. For me."

"Sorry. Too late. I've made my decision."

The woman returns and hands Max his dress.

"Can you get the pink one in the window for my friend?" Max asks.

The woman yanks the dress off the hanger and holds it up to my body.

"Yes. She's beautiful, no?" she says to Max.

"Yeah, she is," Max replies. It's hard to tell if Max is just being polite or if he means it. Nonetheless, I turn seven shades of red.

Max and I head to "the dressing room." A generous term. It's more of a broom closet. There's only room for one of us at a time, which is a relief. I couldn't deal with us both changing at the same time, my big butt exposed for Max to see.

I let Max go first. He squeezes himself into the room, and after some grunting and groaning, he returns with the dress on. Max's long, buff limbs look strangled in the form-fitting dress.

The old woman claps at Max. "You look so funny. It makes me smile."

"And by that you mean handsome and debonair," Max says to her.

The old woman just laughs.

"What do you think, Flores? Can I go head-to-head with Will?" He looks absurd. Not like Will, whose lithe frame is made for the delicate lines of women's clothes.

"'Fraid not. Will kind of blows you out of the water on the cross-dressing front. But you rock jeans and a T-shirt much better."

"C'mon, you're bringing me down. I am totally feeling this transvestite thing. I thought it could be my new look for UCLA."

Max sashays in between the racks. His lovely tight ass is obscured by the folds of the fabric. Max's ass was invented for jeans.

"I'm sorry, dude. You can't work it like Will does."

"That's cool. I'm good with guy clothes. It seems really hard to walk in a dress. And if you add heels to this, I'd seriously kill myself. Okay, your turn."

Max retreats to the dressing room, throws on his clothes, and comes back out looking even better than when he went in. How is that possible?

Max hands me the pink dress. I wrinkle my nose and start to protest. I worry it'll look silly on me. Like I'm dressing up in my mother's clothes. Like I'm trying to be something I'm not.

"We had a deal. I showed you mine, now show me yours," Max says.

I can tell he won't back down, so I capitulate and head to

the dressing room. I pull my jeans and T-shirt off and shimmy into the dress. It fits me perfectly. I turn to look at myself in the cloudy mirror. Someone has written *Ensenada rules* across the length of it.

The bodice of the dress is tight. It emphasizes my A-cup breasts, making me almost look like a B. The cap sleeves hang off my shoulders just a little, framing my upper arms and giving the illusion of sculpted muscles. The low scoop of the neckline reveals my cleavage, and my instinct immediately is to cross my arms over my chest. But I don't. I stand there and stare at myself, shocked that I don't look as ridiculous as I thought I would.

I step out of the dressing room to find Max and the old woman staring at me. I feel exposed and excited in equal measure as I stand there awkwardly. Max doesn't say anything for a moment, which adds to my insecurity, tipping the scales toward exposed.

"Yeah, like I said, it's not really me."

"No. It's definitely you," Max says. "You look incredible. Really."

And then Max reaches over and pulls the band from my hair. My curls tumble out of the ponytail and onto my shoulders.

"You look like a rose in bloom, like fireworks in the sky," the old woman says to me. Her eyes fill with tears. "So lovely. *Bella*. I have never seen someone look so good in that dress."

Okay, enough with the bad metaphors and the hard sell. I'm kind of wishing she would just go away at this point. It's getting embarrassing.

"Well . . . I'm going to change now," I say, and turn away.

"No, no." The woman rushes up to me and tugs here and there on the dress to adjust it. "This dress is perfect on her, no?" she asks Max, like he's in charge of me, or something. Got to love the Latino culture.

"I'm buying it for you," Max announces.

"No . . . Max, come on. That's ridiculous. I can't let you do that."

I inch my way toward the dressing room. Max takes my hand to stop me. The old woman makes herself scarce, sensing that her sale relies on Max's power of persuasion.

"Kylie, let me buy it for you. As a graduation gift. You can wear it tonight and then throw it away if you want. You've been wearing those jeans all day. You must be dying to change into something clean."

"So, I'm looking dirty?"

"That's not what I meant. I think you know that."

Max is looking at me with such expectation and excitement in his eyes, I am loath to disappoint him.

"Okay," I say, even though I am not the kind of person who ever wears dresses, especially frilly fuchsia dresses, or lets guys buy things for me. Tonight, I will be that person—for Max. And maybe for me as well. "Thanks, Max."

"You're welcome, Kylie."

Our eyes meet. We're standing close. Close enough so I can feel his breath on my face. I am transfixed by his full lips, his green eyes. His hair hangs over his left eye. I want to push it off to the side, touch my hand to his face. What must it be like to kiss Max Langston? Clearly, I'm not going to find out

260

now, because the old woman suddenly materializes next to us, holding a pair of white cotton shoes—espadrilles with woven soles and strings that tie around the ankle.

"To go with the dress," the woman says. I've got to hand it to her; she's milking this for all it's worth.

I take the shoes and slip them on.

"Perfect," Max says.

Max hands the woman U.S. dollars, which she's happy to take, and we leave the store. If I didn't feel like I was wandering through someone else's life before, now I really do. I'm in costume; I'm just not sure what part I'm playing. The obvious allusion to Cinderella does not escape my attention. I've got the ball gown, someone has slipped a new pair of shoes on my feet, and there's Max, the prince. Two big problems with this picture: Max is someone else's prince, and I'm so not a princess, it's laughable.

As I'm burrowing into these thoughts, Max makes a beeline for a small plaza with a stone fountain in the middle. He takes my hand and drags me with him. A couple of teenagers emerge from the fountain, dripping wet, and wander off, laughing. Otherwise, the plaza is relatively deserted. A few old men stand in a circle smoking cigars. Several couples wander by, hand in hand. A man to the side of the fountain is playing the violin, and a woman next to him plays the cello. This is not mariachi music. It's not even Mexican music, as far as I can tell. It's mournful, sweeping, and romantic.

"Dance with me," Max says. It isn't a question. And it isn't a command. His comment lies somewhere in between. He's serious, not even a little bit joking.

I don't say anything. But my eyes say, *Yes, yes, yes. I'd love to. Right here. Right now. In the middle of this street in Ensenada.* And, like we've known each other for years, like we have some kind of secret way of communicating, Max takes me in his arms without my ever saying anything. Without him ever responding.

My heart is beating so loudly I'm afraid Max can hear it. I put my head on his shoulder. Our bodies are pressed close. Every one of my senses is on high alert as we move to the music, slowly, perfectly in sync. I am completely transported. I can't remember being happier than at this moment. I wish I could stop time just for an hour or two.

The musicians and a few other stragglers watch us. A couple wandering by stops and starts to dance as well. I take my head off Max's shoulder, pull back and look at him. He's staring at me intently.

"What?" I say, suddenly self-conscious.

"You should wear your hair down more often. And you should wear that dress, like, every day."

"That would be kind of weird."

"Yeah, maybe. . . ."

"And it would start to smell."

Max doesn't say anything; he just gazes down at me. I realize that he is going to kiss me. We've been on the verge of this for what seems like weeks. The interruptions have only added to the anticipation. I'm literally shaking from the suspense, the desire. Max leans into me, his lips hover over mine. I can feel the warmth from his breath. I want his lips on mine so badly my whole body feels the craving like a deep ache. My pulse races. I try to slow it down, breathing deep. I'm waiting, eager, and scared to death. I've never done this before.

Max's lips move in, and, at the same time, due to nerves or some kind of sudden onset of Tourette's, I turn the slightest bit to the left and his kiss lands on my cheek. I'm mortified and disappointed. Such an amateur. I completely blew it. I'm a total freak.

Max pulls away, not much, just enough to look at me. Is he mad? Hurt? Confused? It would all make sense. I mean, what am I doing sending mixed signals like this? I don't know what I'm doing, that's the problem.

But he's none of those things. He breaks into a big smile.

"How about we try that again?" he asks.

"Excellent idea."

Max takes my face in his hands, to prevent any sudden moves, I'm guessing, and plants his sweet, soft lips on mine, and then I hear—

"Go for it, Kylie!!" Someone yells from a window above the plaza. Someone who sounds suspiciously like Will.

Max takes his lips off of mine. *No. Wait. Please. Don't go. . . .*

Damn. What the hell? Foiled again.

We both look up and scan the buildings nearby. I can see someone leaning out of a fourth-story window, waving a T-shirt in the air like a war surrender.

"Kylie! Over here."

It's Will. I'm happy to see him but pissed at the terrible timing.

"'Darling, I don't know how to tell you this, but there's a Chinese family in our bathroom,'" he yells from the window.

On the upside, we found Will. On the downside, we lost the moment. Maybe we'll find it again.

"Your movie thing?" Max asks me.

"*(500) Days of Summer.*"

"Get your butts up here. Now," Will insists. "We've got a party going on and we've been waiting forever for you guys to show up."

That makes absolutely no sense, which is perfectly consistent with this whole day.

CHAPTER THIRTY-TWO

"This is an incredibly romantic moment, and you're ruining it for me."
—PRETTY IN PINK

max:

"What took you guys so long?" Will is standing in the doorway of an apartment where a party rages behind him. He's wearing jeans, a button-down shirt, and flip-flops. This is not the Will Bixby that's been flying his gay flag as high as he can for six years.

"We've been looking for you for the past two hours," Kylie says.

"Look no further, darlings, 'cause here I am!" Will exclaims, seemingly oblivious to the fact that he left us stranded.

"Yeah, would have been nice to know where you went," Kylie says.

265

"Shit happened, if you know what I mean."

"Why do you look so . . . straight?" Kylie asks.

"I'm trying something new," Will says. "Just like you." He peers at Kylie with a knowing look, and she turns away.

He obviously saw us dancing, kissing. I feel embarrassed for Kylie and for me. I really don't need Will Bixby making jokes at my expense.

"Dude, you totally disappeared on us," I say. "We can't leave till morning now."

"My bad. Sorry. Guess we'll just have to party our asses off until then."

"Seriously, Will, I'm not missing graduation," Kylie says.

"No worries, Kyles. Your chariot awaits in the morning. I'll get you to that podium in plenty of time. I just think we oughta play while we're in the game. You only live once, baby doll."

Will is acting like we're fashionably late to a party we didn't even know about. Normally I'd be pissed, but I can't exactly be mad at the guy who drove to Mexico on a moment's notice to get us.

"Loving the look," Will says to Kylie, referring to her dress. "It's so not you. And that's a very good thing."

"Max made me get it."

"Max Langston has taste. Who knew? I'm impressed. God knows, I couldn't get Kylie into a dress if my life depended on it," Will tells me.

"She should wear them more often, right?" I'm talking to Will but looking at Kylie.

"Okay, message received. I dress like shit most of the time."

"Not most of the time," I say.

"All the time," Will says.

"That's not what I meant," I say, because it isn't.

"I'm officially insulted," Kylie says.

"I'm officially kidding," Will says. "You look hot in jeans and a T-shirt, but even hotter in a crazy-ass Mexican dress." He polishes off the rest of his beer. "Okay. I need another one," he says. "And so do you guys. You're way too sober."

"Trust me, we're not sober. We've been drinking all night," I say.

"Well, you're more sober than me. You guys need to play catch-up. Especially since no one's driving anywhere tonight. The bar's in the kitchen. Help yourself. I'll be floating around the room on a cloud of romance and inebriation. Come find me."

And with that, Will disappears.

"He is one wack dude," I say, hoping Kylie won't take it the wrong way.

"Yep. No doubt about it. And I love that about him."

I look around the room. Techno music throbs from giant speakers. The smell of smoke mingles with the unmistakable scent of aftershave. The room is crammed full of guys, totally cut, wearing tight T-shirts, grinding into one another on a makeshift dance floor.

Shit. I should have figured. This is the ultimate gay boy house party, Mexican style. Will must be in heaven. As I'm having this epiphany, I can't help but notice Kylie taking in the room at the same time. She bites her lip to stop from giggling. I know what she's thinking. That this is not my scene. At all. She couldn't be more right about that. I'm probably the only

267

straight guy in the room, and Kylie is one of the few girls. I want to get out of here.

Will reappears with three beers. "Since you didn't get to the bar yet, I brought the bar to you. No thanks required. But you're on your own from now on."

As Will hands me a beer, he leans in to me, close. A little too close. He's already kissed me once. I'm not down for another shot. I step away, but Will grabs my hand. Damn, he's stronger than he looks.

"Max, break our Kylie's heart and I will hunt you down like a dog. And tear you apart." I never thought of Will Bixby as anything more than a joke. But he's not. He's fierce in his love and concern for Kylie. And kind of scary as his eyes bore into me.

"I won't. Don't worry," I say. He lets me go.

Juan waves from across the room.

"Okay, kiddies, time for me to fly. Try to mingle. And if you can't mingle, dance. And if you can't dance . . . well, you'll come up with something."

Kylie and I watch as Will rushes up to Juan, tosses an arm around his shoulder, and nuzzles into his neck. And then they're kissing. Full on, frontal. Juan seems way, way out of the closet. Hard to believe he's trying to keep any of this a secret from his family.

Juan slips his hands into Will's jeans pockets and pulls him close. They sway to the music. I've never seen two dudes kiss before. Okay, I saw *Brokeback Mountain*, and I was a little weirded out by it. But somehow, in the flesh, it's different. It's not as strange as I would have thought. Not that much different than a guy and a girl. They actually seem kinda sweet together. Still, I don't need to be here watching it all.

"Wow. The caterpillar has finally turned into a butterfly," Kylie says.

"He was always pretty butterfly-ish, no?"

"Less so than you'd think. He talks a big game, but he's never really been with a guy. Until now, I guess."

"He's catching on fast," I say as Kylie and I watch them suck face on the dance floor.

"Yeah, well, Will's always been a quick study."

"Yo, I'm the only straight dude here," I whisper as two guys in wifebeaters walk by and check me out. "It's kinda freaking me out."

"You're fresh meat," she says. "How does it feel to be objectified?"

"I'm not into it."

"It's hard to be hot."

"Yeah, I never really had a problem with it until now."

"Oh my God, you are homophobic."

"Not at all. I just . . . I'm not gay, and everyone here thinks I am."

"Well, you're with me, and I know you're not gay," Kylie says, flashing a smile at me. She finishes her beer, tosses the bottle into the garbage, and grabs my hand. "Let's dance," she says, pulling me toward the center of the room, near the speakers. My body is rigid with discomfort as we squeeze between several couples. I want to relax and get into it, for Kylie's sake, but it's awkward; it's so not my scene. I don't like this kind of music. Too techno. Too much bass. Too much thumping redundancy.

Kylie begins to dance, but I don't do much at first. I'm not used to dancing like this, packed into a room full of guys. I watch Kylie shake to the beat, throwing her whole body into it. I'm not sure she would have done this twenty-four hours ago; something in her is shifting. She looks so sexy and fierce. She's like a giant pink flower in the middle of the room, her dress swinging back and forth on her hips, her hair flying wild. Something in me releases, and I start to loosen up.

I forget about everything but Kylie and her gorgeous body bumping into mine. We move around and into one another, ours shoulders touching, our hips grazing each other's. Everyone in the room is dancing with abandon. It's screamingly loud, the beat is pulsing, and everyone is singing along. I can feel my discomfort washing away. I put my hands on Kylie's hips and pull her to me. Our bodies grind into one another. She feels so good. I don't want to ever let her go. Kylie and I are grinning at each other, talking without saying anything. I've never felt like this with anyone before.

"'Baby, I was born this way . . .'" Will has found us in the crowd and dances up next to us, belting out Lady Gaga. He's got a glow stick in his hand that he's swinging above his head like a lasso. Juan, behind him, is cracking up. And then Will dances off, Juan in tow.

Before I know what's happening, Kylie has disappeared and I'm dancing with a dude in a black fedora and a red bandana around his neck. Whoa! What up? Where is Kylie? The dude puts his hands on my hips. I'm not down with this. At all. Thankfully, Kylie reappears.

270

"You mind if I dance with your date?" Kylie asks the dude.

"He's all yours," he says, shimmying off to another partner.

"Okay, that was weird," I say.

"Sorry, things got a little chaotic. I ended up with a guy who looked like Justin Bieber."

"Think I'd rather have fedora guy."

"I'd rather have you," Kylie says.

And then she takes my face in her hands, pulls me close, and we're kissing. Finally. Thankfully. Amazingly. It's an aggressive move, and I like it. This time, neither of us holds back. Our tongues explore each other's mouths. My hands plunge into her hair. Her hands roam my back, my stomach, my ass. It doesn't matter that the room is filled to capacity; in my mind we're the only two people on earth. I can feel the warmth of her body radiating up her back. I don't know where her mouth ends and mine begins. I want her with everything I've got.

I don't know if it's been five minutes or five hours, when Kylie suddenly pulls away, so fast I nearly fall into her.

"Whoa . . . what's going on?" I ask.

"I'm sorry, I just . . ." Kylie stands there staring at me, as the music and people swirl around us.

"What happened?"

"I just . . . need to get some air." Kylie turns and walks off the dance floor. I follow her.

"Where are you going?"

"I don't know, I need to walk." Kylie makes her way toward the front door.

"You're leaving?"

"I'll be back. I need a minute . . . to think . . . alone. I just . . . this all caught me by surprise."

"Yeah, me too. . . ."

"But you're used to this. I'm new at it. And I . . . I don't know. I'm okay. Really. I just need some air."

"You shouldn't go by yourself. It's dark. You don't know where you are. I'll just walk with you. I won't say anything—"

"I'll be fine. I'm just going down to the harbor. I'll be back soon." And then, she's gone.

Man, this girl . . .

CHAPTER THIRTY-THREE

"Things are not all they appear to be."
—INSIDE MAN

jake:

'm lying in bed, my head under the covers, reading *The Hobbit* with a flashlight, in case Mom or Dad comes in. They don't like it when I stay up past my bedtime. But I do it all the time. Mom only found me once, and I promised her I wouldn't do it again, but that wasn't true. It's like a secret forest. I love it in here, especially late at night.

It's hard to read with Mom and Dad still talking so loudly.

Mom is mad. I don't think she's mad at Dad even though she's yelling at him. I think she's mad at Kylie even though she's not here. I think Kylie might be in big trouble when she comes home. I've never heard Mom so mad. Even Dad is mad. And Dad usually doesn't care enough to get really mad. Although he told me earlier that he does care. I don't think he was lying. He seemed to mean it and he was a lot nicer than he usually is. He let me tell him all about the Garbage Patch while we had pizza, and then we came home and watched *Star Wars* together and he didn't even fall asleep. So maybe he does care. He just forgot how to show it.

Mom came home while we were watching *Star Wars* and said that Kylie was sleeping over at Will's house, which meant I wouldn't see Kylie until the morning. I really wanted to talk to Kylie, so I called her on her cell. I called seven times, but she never picked up. It went straight to voice mail. I waited and waited for Kylie to call back. We finished *Star Wars*. I brushed my teeth and Kylie still hadn't called back. So I called Will's house. His mother answered. She didn't seem like she wanted to talk to me, which was fine because I didn't want to talk to her. I wanted to talk to Kylie. But she said Kylie wasn't there and neither was Will. When I told Mom, she called Will's mom right back, and when she hung up she told me to go to bed, and then she started yelling at Dad. It's been a half hour and she's still yelling. I hope Kylie's okay. I wonder where she is.

CHAPTER THIRTY-FOUR

> "Sometimes the truth isn't good enough. Sometimes people deserve more. Sometimes people deserve to have their faith rewarded."
> —THE DARK KNIGHT

kylie:

"*¡Felicitaciones!*" an old woman says as I pass her.

Congratulations? For what? For running away from the best thing that's ever happened to me? For not knowing how to be young and impulsive and carefree? For falling for a guy with a serious girlfriend? For being completely, totally, emotionally, socially retarded?

I'm walking to the end of a long pier that extends out over

the water. I lost Max somewhere along the boardwalk. I was ducking and weaving through the crowds and then ended up on the pier. I'm pretty sure Max continued to look for me on the boardwalk, heading in the opposite direction. I know it's ridiculous to hide from him like this, but I need to think, to gather my wits. I don't know what I'm doing here, and some-how, someway, I've got to figure it out.

The pier is wooden and narrow, and as I walk the length of it I have the sensation that I'm walking on water. I can see the bay shimmering on all sides, and beneath me, too, between the slats of wood. There's a full moon shining so bright it lights up the whole sky. I pass by a few couples sitting with their legs dangling over the water. I can't help thinking this would be a lovely spot to hang with Max. Too bad I've just abandoned him.

When I finally reach the end of the pier, I'm alone. I turn around and can see all of Ensenada circling the bay, the hills rising above the water, the lights of the town blinking and glowing. I take a seat on the ground. It feels like I'm sitting at the edge of the world. I stare out at the wide expanse of ocean. I can make out a few boats in the distance. I think I see something jump out of the water. A dolphin? I doubt it.

What am I doing? I practically attacked Max on the dance floor and then went scurrying away like a scared little mouse. I am so not normal. I may even be psychotic. Something took hold of me and I couldn't help myself. I had to touch his skin, feel his lips on mine. It felt so good, so right. But then I couldn't help thinking that he's not really mine. He's Lily's. This isn't right.

But if he really belonged to Lily, would any of this have happened? Would it have felt so right? I remind myself, they aren't married. We're just teenagers. This is hardly adultery. There's obviously something happening between us. Why can't I explore it? See what happens, where it goes. Sure, he could break my heart tomorrow. But isn't it worth taking the chance? Why must I always hold back, ruminating, instead of just jumping in with abandon?

"*¡Felicitaciones!*" a couple calls out as they approach.

What is up with all the congratulations? Are people mistaking me for someone else? Someone lucky in love. Someone who deserves congratulations. That's not me, people. I am a fool. I just ran away from a very hot guy who happened to be totally into me, at least for the moment.

The couple approaches. They stand a few feet away, staring down at me. Am I meant to answer them?

"Uh, *gracias*," I say.

"American?" the girl asks me.

"Yes."

As soon as people discover you're American, they're dying to speak English with you. It's such a funny thing. In the States, we'd never speak anything but English with a foreigner. The world of the superpower. It means never having to say you're sorry in anything but English.

"You came down to Ensenada to get married?" the boy asks.

What are they talking about?

"Married? No," I say.

"But you're wearing the dress," the girl says.

I look down at my dress. "I just bought it here. In Ensenada."

That's when I notice we're both wearing the same dress; hers is yellow. Wait. Did I actually buy a wedding dress? Oh, shit. What a royal, freaking mistake. No wonder everyone is congratulating me. I'm parading through the streets in a wedding dress. What an idiot. And Max bought it for me. I have to laugh at the irony.

"It looks nice on you," she says.

"You too," I say.

They walk away, leaving me in the lonely company of my endless stream of anxieties. The alcohol must be wearing off, because the volume in my head has been turned way up. Can't I just shut down my brain and let my heart lead the way? So he's got a girlfriend. Don't people sometimes meet the love of their life when they're already with someone? What about *The Philadelphia Story*? *Sleepless in Seattle*? But those are movies, and this is real life, my real life, where movie endings NEVER happen.

I can't think about this anymore. I lie down on the wood planks and stare up at the sky. It's filled to capacity with stars. I never see this many stars in San Diego. The city lights are too bright; the sky looks murky and muted. But out here it's clear and pristine. I think I can make out the Little Dipper. I start to count stars. It's a good distraction from the dizziness of going round and round.

"Found you," Max says, looking down at me. "Turns out, I'm not so easy to get rid of."

I'm so happy he's here I feel like crying. And yet I have no idea where to begin, based on where we left off.

"I guess not."

"Gotta hand it to you, though. That was a tricky move back there. Took me a few minutes to figure out that you snuck around the crowd and went the other way. Can I sit down?"

"Free country." That came out a little snarkier than I planned.

"Technically, Mexico is a little less of a democracy than the U.S."

"You can still sit down. You're not breaking any laws."

"Thanks. 'Cause, you know, wouldn't want to do anything illegal."

"I can appreciate that."

Max lies down next to me.

"Kylie, I know this is complicated. . . ."

"Yeah, you have a girlfriend. . . ."

"Maybe. But I've been thinking about kissing you all day."

"Really?"

"Really. Whatever's happening between us has nothing to do with Lily. And everything to do with us. That kiss meant something. The whole day has meant something."

"But what about Lily?" I don't want to keep pushing the issue, but I can't help myself.

"Look, I have no idea what's going to happen between us. But I know I can't have these kinds of feelings for you and stay with Lily. Even if we never see each other again—which would suck, by the way—I can't stay with Lily. Today made me realize that I don't really love her. I don't know if I ever did."

Max and I stare at each other.

"Sorry I bailed on you," I say. "It's just, this is not normally what I do." I'm peeling off my defenses, leaving myself raw, exposed, scared. I'm doing this, but that doesn't mean it's easy.

"Me either."

"What are you talking about? You're like a professional boyfriend."

"Thanks. You make me sound like a gigolo."

"That's not what I mean. It's just, you always have a girl-friend. And, well, I've never had a boyfriend."

"But it's never felt like this with anyone. And it's not just about the kiss. Although it was pretty awesome. It's more than that. I know we don't really know each other, but I feel completely connected to you, Kylie. I can't explain it. I can talk to you. Really talk. Being here in Mexico, it's been such an insane experience, in a good way. And being away from La Jolla, away from Freiburg, it's made me realize how boring things have been. How boring I've gotten. I've built a wall around myself and I don't let much in."

Max stops and breathes in. I don't say a thing.

"I don't want that anymore. I want to explore life, and so do you. I love that about you. When we kissed, it just, I don't know, kind of blew me away. I know it all sounds so corny, but you can't deny it. There's something here. And we'd be idiots to just walk away from it. I don't think this happens all the time, Kylie. I mean, I've had a lot of girlfriends and I've never felt like this."

"Please, do tell me more about the multiple girlfriends. That is so sexy."

"Seriously, Kylie. I want to talk about this. And I never want to talk about anything. I don't know if you're scared or you don't feel the same—"

280

"I feel the same," I blurt. "And I'm scared."

"Me too."

Strange as it sounds, I believe him. The great Max Langston is scared and nervous, just like me. We're not all that different.

We look at each other for a moment. I think we're both trying to make sense of things. It's not entirely clear, but as I look at him, it's coming into sharper focus. I realize I've made my decision. I'm going for it, whatever the consequences, Lily or no Lily, even though it may only last for one night. Whatever this is, I don't want it to end. Hopefully, I'm not being naïve. At the very least, we'll have tonight, which is more than I would have had yesterday.

My hand slides over the wooden planks and I place it on top of his, closing the distance between us. He squeezes my hand tightly.

"I can't make you any promises, Kylie. All I'm saying is, I like you. A lot. I can't talk like this to anyone else. You're funny. And smart. Very smart. And sexy. And weird. And a little bit of a head case."

"I'm a total head case."

"Maybe, but it's sexy. Really sexy."

Max flashes me a huge grin. God, he's gorgeous.

"So can we just be with each other and see what happens?"

"Yes. We can. We totally can," I say.

And then, without thinking too much about it, I climb on top of Max and slowly, very slowly, lean down until our faces are nearly touching. I float over him for a moment, studying his face, his features, and then I kiss him. And he kisses me. And our mouths open and the world disappears, and it's just

281

me and Max alone in the universe. Nothing matters except for tonight. And if that's all we end up with after everything is said and done, it's enough. Because right here, right now, is all that matters. I don't want to be anyone but Kylie Flores kissing Max Langston in Ensenada.

CHAPTER THIRTY-FIVE

"... but by God, there'll be dancing."
—MY BEST FRIEND'S WEDDING

will:

"**Y**ou having fun?" Juan whispers in my ear as we bump and grind with a bunch of boys.

"Yes," I say, trying to sound cool, calm, and collected. But what I really want to do is shout it to the world. "Yes! Yes! Yes!" I've been waiting for this moment to arrive forever, and now that it's finally here, it's even better than I could have imagined.

I've got my hands in the air, I'm dancing up a storm, sweating like a pig. Some of my moves feel a little rusty, but, frankly my dear, I don't give a damn. I'm enjoying myself far too much to care. This is the best night of my life. If only it didn't have to end in the morning.

I saw Kylie and Max making out on the dance floor (which was almost as shocking as the fact that I've been making out on the dance floor), but the next thing I knew, they were flying out the door, like fighter jets off to war. Normally, I'd be worried and chasing Kylie down the street, making sure she's okay. But I haven't got time for the pain. I've got one night only. One night to make Juan mine. And if I do, who knows what can happen next? A whole world of wonderful. At least that's what I'm gunning for.

Hopefully, girlfriend can take care of herself while I'm taking care of myself. Or, rather, Juan is taking care of me. How awesome would that be if Kylie and I both lost our virginity on the very last night of school? Talk about bringing back a rocking souvenir from Mexico. Fingers crossed.

"Can I have this dance, gorgeous?" Juan's high school friend Antonio asks me.

I turn to Juan to make sure it's okay. "You cool with that?" I ask him.

"By all means. Everyone wants a piece of the beautiful new boy in town," Juan says.

Beautiful new boy? Who? Me? I look around to make sure Juan isn't talking about someone behind me, in front of me, to the left or the right of me. He's not. He's looking straight at me with his baby blues. Hot much? Be still, my heart.

Antonio, meanwhile, is quite the specimen. They know how to grow these boys in Mexico. And he wants to dance with me. Me! That is the freaking craziest thing I've ever heard. It's like an alternate universe here in Ensenada, where the duckling

284

is a swan. I'm handsome, suave, and popular. I could get used to this.

As Antonio and I shake our booties to the Scissor Sisters, I'm beginning to question my decision to return to La Jolla in the morning. I promised Kylie a ride back, but if tonight goes well, why bother trucking over the border when I've found paradise right here in Ensenada? Does it get any better than this? I highly doubt it.

Juan is staying in Ensenada for the summer. Maybe I should stand by my man. Though Kylie has to be at graduation, there is no pressing need for me to be there. Or anywhere but here, for that matter. The only sticking point is that Juan isn't exactly out to his family. The macho Latino culture is a bitch. But I can help with that. Coming out is my forte.

Sure, Mom and Dad will be bummed that I've missed graduation, but I'll make it up to them by losing the women's clothes and dressing like a guy, for the first time in years. Dad will be so happy he'll probably start handing out cigars. I just hope Kylie will understand when I hand her the passports and put her and Max on the first bus back to San Diego.

CHAPTER THIRTY-SIX

"Yeah,
I can fly!"
—IRON MAN

kylie:

have no idea how long we've been making out on the pier. As far as I'm concerned, the world could end here and now. Because everything I never knew I wanted, I just received. Thank you, more please, Max Langston.

We're sitting up now, having gotten a few splinters from rolling around on the wood. I'm on Max's lap and his arms are wrapped around my waist as his lips work their way toward my ear. His tongue plays with the fleshy part of the lobe and it's so pleasurable I'm not sure I can bear it. Who knew my earlobes were so sensitive? How can someone be this good at kissing? His lips, his tongue, his teeth, they all work as a team, constantly doing new things, reinventing themselves. Just when I

286

think he's exhausted his repertoire, he'll gently bite my lip and then his tongue will work magic somewhere new in my mouth, or on my neck, finding sweet spots I never knew existed.

"Look." Max points out toward the horizon. His face pulls away from mine, and I feel like someone has cut off my oxygen.

And then I see it. A pod of dolphins has swum into the harbor and is leaping out of the water, spinning in the air and splashing back down. Max and I watch, mesmerized by their show. A few fireworks pop in the sky. Ensenada is going all out tonight. I guess it *was* a dolphin I saw earlier. My luck appears to be turning around, at least for today. I'm seeing stars, dolphins, and fireworks. And liking it. I've suddenly gone all soft, which is fine by me.

I jump up and look down at Max. "I'm going swimming, Langston. You coming?"

I don't even care if Max sees my big old butt. Maybe he'll like it. Maybe he won't. I just want to splash around in the ocean, under the stars, while a full moon lights up the night sky. This is one moment that's not going to pass me by.

"Hell, yeah!" Max says. "But what about the eels?"

"I had forgotten about them, but thanks for reminding me."

"Sorry, my bad. Still going in?"

"I'm going to take on the eels. You with me?"

"All the way," Max says, standing up and pulling off his shirt. His chest is so exquisite, so perfectly sculpted, my heart skips a beat. Is this really happening?

I pull my dress off, standing in front of Max in my bra and underwear. If he's going to think I'm fat, might as well let him have at it.

Max's eyes graze my body. I can feel them moving from my neck down over my breasts and resting on my stomach. He reaches out and touches me softly with his fingers. His hands wander over my body. I want to kiss him again, but he's keeping me at a distance, just touching me. It feels so nice. His hands wind their way along my sides until both palms rest on either side of my butt.

Why isn't he saying anything? Does he think I'm fat? I'm certainly plumper than bony Lily Wentworth. I mean, baby got back. I'm Latino. And Jewish. I like to eat. What can I say? I'm not a stick and I never will be. Say something, Max.

"You have the most beautiful body, Kylie. I can't believe you hide it away in those baggy jeans."

What? "Shut up," is all that comes to mind. Brilliant.

"I'm serious, Kylie. I love your ass. All the girls at Freiburg are so skinny. You've got a perfect ass."

"No way." Another genius retort. It's official, I'm a blathering idiot.

And then, because I can't really discuss my ass any longer, I rush toward the edge of the pier, soar off the edge and into the water. It's warm, silky, and bubbly. It feels like swimming in champagne. Max throws off his jeans and dives in after me. He swims up to me, takes hold of my hands, and we float together as the gentle waves toss us about. The dolphins play a few hundred yards away. The fireworks have finished—the literal ones, that is. Metaphorical ones are going off at an ever increasing speed.

"If you put your head underwater, you'll be able to hear the dolphins speaking to each other," Max says.

"Really?"

"Yeah. I used to do it as a kid. It kind of sounds like little clicking noises. Wait, I'll try."

Max plunges under the water, stays down for a few seconds, then pops back up.

"You can totally hear them. Go see."

I take a deep breath and submerge myself. After a second or two I hear it, little clicks and screeches. It's unmistakable. It sounds like they're chattering away in a foreign language. I come back up to the surface.

"Very cool!"

"I know. It's hard to hear them in San Diego. Too many people. They don't come this close to shore."

"What do you think they're saying?"

"Probably talking about corruption in Mexico. I don't think they're fans of Felipe Calderón."

"Listen to you, talking Mexican geopolitics."

"Just trying to impress you. How am I doing?"

"You've impressed me, Langston. Enough already. I'm starting to feel like an underachiever here."

Max leans in and kisses me. We bob up and down and side to side as we attempt to kiss, breathe, and somehow stay afloat.

Max points to the pier. "Check it out. Total crowd scene happening out there."

I look to the pier and notice that people have gathered on the dock, men in suits, woman in dresses like mine.

"You think they're watching us?" I ask.

"Definitely. They heard about the Americans swimming in their underwear in the harbor and they've come down to check it out."

"Oh my God."

"Kylie, no one cares about us."

"I've never gone swimming in the ocean at night before. Ever."

"Seriously? Night swimming is the best."

"This is amazing. If I lived here I would do this every night," I tell Max.

"If I lived here I would have a little boat, and I'd take us out on the water at night, maybe a little sangria, some of those tripe tacos. We'd lay back and look at the stars as we tool around the harbor. It'd be sweet."

"You are sweet, Max Langston."

"You are amazing, Kylie Flores."

I can't help myself, I'm giddy and grinning from ear to ear. I'm barely recognizable even to myself, and I'm liking that a lot.

"What are you smiling at?" Max asks me.

"I'm having a great night."

"Me too."

I lie on my back in the water, moving my hands just enough to keep me afloat. The stars are blazing above me. I feel like the luckiest girl in the world. Even though I know there might be an expiration date on this kind of thing.

CHAPTER THIRTY-SEVEN

"Shit happens when you party naked."
—BAD SANTA

max:

"*Felicidades!*" someone yells out for the fifth time in ten minutes, and we all drink. Again. A guy appears and refills our plastic cups. Where did he come from? And how much tequila do they have? An endless supply? We've been knocking back shots with the crowd on the pier since we got out of the water, about a half hour ago. People have gathered here for some kind of massive wedding.

We hopped out of the water, practically naked and smack into the ceremony. We tried to bail, but no one was having it. So we got dressed and joined the party, as we've joined every party that would have us since arriving in Ensenada. Man, these people know how to live it up.

Kylie holds her glass up to mine. "To Saint John the Baptist. I think he seems like a very cool dude. And he throws a kick-ass party."

Kylie clinks glasses with me and downs what must be her fourth shot. I've had three and am really starting to feel it, so she's got to be pretty blasted at this point.

"Maxie, wassup? You're not drinking?" Kylie asks me.

Maxie? Definitely way wasted.

"I'm taking a break. You might want to do that as well."

"Don't think so. I'm feeling gooood. Wanna feel even better."

"You don't want to get sick."

Suddenly I'm the responsible dude. This is not my thing, but I'm worried about Kylie, and I never really worry about anyone. Usually I let people take care of themselves, but there's something about Kylie that's vulnerable and fragile. I want to protect her. Giving her valedictorian speech with a nasty headache is going to be brutal. She has no idea.

"Oh my God, look at you. You're such a little worrywart," Kylie says, slurring her words. She's got it bad. She's going to have one wicked hangover in the morning, but, man, she is hot as hell right now, with her eyes at half-mast and that one dimple on her left cheek.

Kylie goes to grab my arm, misses, and nearly falls over. I catch her. She collapses into me. I don't mind. I love the feel of her body next to mine. It just . . . fits. She smells like an ocean-and-tequila cocktail. It's a potent mix. I want to lie down right here on the pier with her. Unfortunately, we're in the middle of a massive group wedding. My timing is a little off. Maybe later.

A priest is in the process of marrying couple after couple. It's a tradition, at midnight, on St. John the Baptist. After each mini-wedding, everyone drinks, and Kylie has thrown herself into things with abandon. So far, ten new marriages. Five more to go. Most of the brides wear dresses just like Kylie's. And the grooms wear tuxedos. I can't tell if this is serious or not. Are these people married now? Is this just some elaborate party ritual? Because the tequila is a big part of it, that's for sure. I think the priest might even be taking a shot every now and then.

The crowd yells out, "*¡Felicidades!*" again.

"*¡Felicidades!*" Kylie screams, practically in my ear.

Everyone lifts their glass. Another one bites the dust. The couple kisses and then swerves off down the pier.

"That priest is churning 'em out," Kylie says. "You think he gets some kind of kickback for each wedding? Maybe he works on commission?"

I laugh. She's still damn funny, even toasted.

A man approaches us with a fresh bottle of tequila. We've moved on from Patrón to the off-label stuff, maybe brewed at home. Things are deteriorating rapidly. Kylie shoves her glass out for the man to fill. I put my hand over it.

"I'm cutting you off," I say.

Kylie frowns. She looks so freaking cute, I move in to kiss her, but she pulls away.

"I want to get my drink on," Kylie says.

"I'm saving you from yourself. How are you going to speak tomorrow?"

"I'll worry about that tomorrow."

"Okay," I say. "Fill us up."

He does and we both drink. The liquor burns my throat, but the warmth that flows afterward feels good. I'm really buzzed. Things are getting a little fuzzy around the edges.

"Are you two next?" I turn around to see the priest standing behind us.

"Yes! Totally!" Kylie says.

I turn to Kylie. "What are you doing?"

"We're getting married, Maxie," Kylie says, pulling me into a hug. "I want to do this." She stares at me. Her big golden eyes couldn't be more serious. Is this the alcohol or Kylie talking? Or a combination? She wants to get married? Seriously?

As I stare into Kylie's face, I realize I've never wanted to do anything more. Kylie looks so fucking beautiful. This is the most romantic, exciting, awesome night of my life. I think I've fallen for Kylie Flores. Hard.

"I dare you to marry me, Langston," Kylie says.

"You're on," I say. "Let's do this."

Kylie and I come crashing together in our drunkenness and euphoria. We kiss wet and sloppy. I get down on one knee.

"Marry me, Flores," I say.

"I thought you'd never ask, Langston."

"Do you have the rings?" the priest asks.

"We forgot our rings. Do you have any extra?" Kylie asks.

"I always bring extra. People forget the most important thing," the priest says, handing Kylie two gold rings that probably came out of an old-fashioned gum ball machine. Kylie holds on to one and hands me the other.

"One for me. One for Maxie," she says.

I look at Kylie wearing that rocking dress, backlit by the moon, and I can't help but wonder how I didn't notice this girl years ago.

The priest says something to us in Spanish. He waves his hand above our heads and touches his chest with his fingers. We exchange rings, fumbling to get them on each other.

"I now pronounce you husband and wife," the priest tells us. "You may kiss the bride." And that's exactly what I do.

Everyone shouts out, *"¡Felicidades!"* as Kylie and I kiss and kiss and kiss and kiss. An older woman comes up and hugs us both. Several others join in, and soon we're in the center of a group hug. I'm still holding on to Kylie, but she's sliding out of my arms and down onto the ground. I hold her tighter, trying to keep her upright.

"Kylie, you okay?"

"Hey, you," she says. She's half asleep. She can't fight the alcohol anymore. And then she completely passes out. Her head falls to the side. I grab her under the arms so she doesn't hit the ground. I've got to get her into bed. So much for the wedding night.

GRADUATION DAY:
FRIDAY, JUNE 25

CHAPTER THIRTY-EIGHT

"*I have had people walk out on me before, but not . . . when I was being so charming.*"
—*BLADE RUNNER*

lily:

"**L**il, what are you doing here?" Charlie asks, when he sees me sitting on the hood of his Jeep.

It's a valid question at five thirty in the morning.

"I'm coming with you," I say, trying to sound all chipper, like I'm going to make the best damn driving buddy a guy could want. As if.

"We talked about this. You agreed."

Technically, he's right. I tacitly agreed by not arguing, as I normally would have. I didn't have the energy. I wasn't exactly on my game last night. I was already losing my shit over Dad's

299

news, and then Max's bizarro phone call to Charlie telling him he was in Mexico, with no further explanation and absolutely no interest in talking to me, only added insult to injury. So I didn't force the issue because I hadn't fully realized just how enraged I was at Max. Blowing me off on the last day of school to go hang in Baja, probably to surf and get drunk all day.

"A girl can change her mind," I say.

"I don't think it's a good idea. . . ."

"You shouldn't drive alone. It's not safe. Besides, it'll be fun. A little end-of-the-year road trip. And"—I hold out a shopping bag filled with junk food—"I brought snacks. Your favorite. Oreos and Yoo-hoo. You can't kick a girl out with Yoo-hoo."

I'm thinking the best sell is positive spin and lots of ammunition. I came locked and loaded. I figured I was going to need it. And I was right. Charlie is such a stupid slave to Max. Blindly following his every request like it's the frigging word of God. He may be a nice guy, but nice guys finish last, my friend.

I still can't believe Max didn't even bother to text or call me. All day. So rude. And hurtful. Especially in light of what I'm going through (not that he knows, but still, Max needs to start putting my feelings first a little more often). Petty as it is, I kind of feel like I need my pound of flesh. And I'm going to Mexico to extract it.

"Look, I don't know what's going on with him, but Max really wanted me to come alone. I feel like I should respect that," says Charlie.

"I know. You made it abundantly clear. Which is insulting, but I'm choosing to rise above and accompany you anyway.

300

With Yoo-hoo and Oreos. That's just the kind of loyal friend I am. You're welcome, by the way."

Charlie isn't making this easy, and I don't have the patience to play nice much longer. Here's the deal. I'm going. My boyfriend blew me off the entire last day of school. He has inexplicably and suspiciously found himself stranded in Mexico. I am not going to sit in La Jolla and wait for him to come find me. Given that the rest of my life has gone to shit, I'm not going to let Max slip away without a fight. I am hightailing it south, and then, on the off chance that Max hasn't done anything too offensive, I will be there for him in his time of need. In the event that Max has been a total selfish asshole (far more probable), I will be there, front and center, to ream him out and then graciously consider forgiving him, which should earn me a few Brownie points.

"He really wants me to come alone."

"Yeah, you just said that. Several times. And I'm not so interested in what Max wants."

Okay. That was quick. I've already gone dark. I polish off the last of my venti capp (thank God the new Starbucks at the mall opens at five a.m. or things would be really gruesome right now), slide off the hood of the Jeep, and jump into shotgun before Charlie has a chance to say anything more.

Charlie climbs in, closes the door, but doesn't start up the engine. Oh, no—here it comes. Charlie is a talker. Which is pretty ironic considering he's Max's best friend. I can only imagine the one-sided conversations that take place in the locker room. Probably pretty similar to Max's and mine. Normally I'm happy to chew the fat with Charlie—he's been almost like a girlfriend, listening to my shit when Max won't—but I'm not in the mood this morning.

"Maybe Max wanted some time off, you know, to think about . . . stuff."

"Stuff? What kind of stuff?"

"College. Squash tryouts. His dad?"

"His dad? What about his dad?" I ask. "I thought he was getting better."

Charlie just stares at me.

"What?" I ask.

"You should probably ask Max. It's not my business."

Yet another thing Max and I haven't properly discussed. I could fill a room with the things we can't talk about.

"This whole thing is probably no big deal," Charlie continues. "Maybe he just wanted to catch some good breaks. There's great surfing in Baja. The thing is, I don't think he wants any drama right now. It's not anything he said, so don't ask me what I know. It's just a vibe I'm getting. The two of us showing up is gonna be drama."

"Absolutely no drama. I'm on board with that."

"C'mon, Lil. You know that's not true. If you come, there is going to be drama. There always is. Just wait here. I promise I'll bring him back quickly, and then you can go at him all you want."

"I'm coming, Charlie. . . ."

"And it's graduation. What if we're late? You don't want to be late. Seriously, Lil, this is not a good idea."

"I'm coming, Charlie." I pull a Yoo-hoo out of the bag and

offer it to Charlie. I throw my feet onto the dashboard and sink into my seat. Let's go, bro.

Charlie takes the Yoo-hoo, opens it, and gulps it down. He's still not starting the car. I'm tempted to grab the keys and fire up the ignition myself. Charlie is really beginning to get on my nerves.

"I feel like you're ready for a fight before you've even heard Max's side of things," Charlie says.

Oh my God, more talking. Please, stop.

"Max's side of things is always up for grabs. I want to see for myself what's going on."

I am working myself up into a total lather. This was not the plan, but Charlie is not starting the car, and I am not getting out until I'm in Mexico.

Charlie sighs. Debate is not his strong suit. He's always a little too concerned about everyone's feelings.

"Start the car, Charlie. You know you can't win this one. I will wear you down."

"I just want to go on record as saying this is a really bad idea."

"Noted."

Charlie starts the car and takes, like, five years to back out of his driveway. He turns on to the street and we're crawling toward the intersection. Oh. My. God. At this rate, we'll be in Mexico early next week.

"Are we going to drive twenty the whole way?" I ask.

"It's not even six in the morning. I don't want to wake the neighbors. I know everyone on the street."

I roll my eyes because that is just so Charlie. Always concerned about someone or something. Jesus, dude, you're eighteen. Who fucking cares what the neighbors think? The world is not your problem.

There's silence for a whole minute, and then Charlie turns to me.

"Are we okay?"

"What do you mean?"

"You know, after last night."

Last night? Shit. I had forgotten about that whole disaster. Do we really need to dredge that up again?

"Oh, yeah. Totally," I reassure him.

"'Cause I still feel kind of weird about everything."

"You so shouldn't give it another thought. It just happened. We were both drunk. It was . . . whatever. Don't worry about it. We're fine. No one needs to know."

"I know, but . . . maybe we should tell Max? I don't want it to get back to him from someone else. I feel bad—"

"Nothing happened, Charlie. What is there to tell? Besides, who knows what he did in Mexico. He probably has a lot more to unload than I do."

Charlie keeps looking over at me. I can tell he still wants to talk about things. *Please, Charlie, I'm begging you, can we just drop it?*

"You seemed really pissed at me last night when, you know, I couldn't . . . do anything. And I just, um, wanted to say that—"

"Charlie, it's so not a big deal. Put it out of your mind. I seemed pissed because I was pissed. At Max. Not at you. We messed up. It happens. There is no larger meaning here. Don't look for it."

"I guess you're right," Charlie says.

"I know I'm right. We're seniors. This is the kind of thing people do senior year. So they have something to tell their grandkids."

"Okay, I just, well, I thought I should explain why I couldn't—"

"The less said, the better."

"Maybe you're right."

"We all have our junk."

What is this, Oprah? Enough with the over-sharing. Now I get why Max finds my need to constantly communicate my feelings annoying.

"Before you go all postal on Max, you should probably listen to what he's got to say."

"Sure." As if.

CHAPTER THIRTY-NINE

"Happy endings are just stories that haven't finished yet."
—MR. & MRS. SMITH

kylie:

am jolted awake by sunlight flooding the room.

What time is it? Where am I?

Disoriented, I attempt to open my eyes. The light is stabbing. My head is throbbing, my throat is raw, and my stomach is roiling. Is this what a hangover feels like?

I wouldn't know. I've never had one. Until now.

I close my eyes, take a few deep breaths, and lie still, trying to get my bearings. Last night was one of the greatest nights of my life. I think. But then again, it could have turned into one of the worst. I don't remember much past a certain point.

I give it another go. I glance around, taking in my

surroundings. A partial view of an unfamiliar bedroom comes into focus. There's a dresser in the corner where a mess of snow globes, stuffed animals, and Barbie dolls fight for space. A poster of a fuzzy white kitten with a huge purple bow around its neck is taped to the wall, between two windows. One window has a shade pulled halfway down, the other has no shade at all. Light pours in, mercilessly. Is it always this sunny in the morning?

I turn my head to avert my eyes, and that's when I see him. Asleep. Oh. My. God. Max. I am now wide awake and it's all coming back to me.

I try to sit up, but the effort makes me woozy, and I lie back down. Why on earth would anyone drink if this is what it feels like the morning after? Maybe because the night before felt pretty damn great. That much I remember.

CHAPTER FORTY

"Dreams feel real while we're in them. It's only when we wake up that we realize something was actually strange."
—INCEPTION

max:

feel the hangover immediately. But it's not nearly as brutal as I thought it would be, considering the amount of tequila we downed.

I can tell it's going to be another gorgeous day in Ensenada from the way the sunlight hits the wall. Surf is probably up. I bet the breaks are sweet. Wouldn't mind picking up a board and going out. I'm sure Kylie's never surfed. I could teach her. How fun would that be?

I look down and catch a glimpse of my watch. Shit. It's six thirty. I wish we had more time, but we don't; we have to motivate. Graduation is in less than six hours.

Suddenly it doesn't seem so important. I briefly think about missing it entirely, staying in Ensenada with Kylie. But that's a no go. Kylie needs to be there. Reality rules, which is a bummer. I'm afraid of what happens when we get back to real life and Lily is waiting there for me. I shove that thought to the back of my mind. I'll deal with it later. I've got six more hours with Kylie. I don't want to think about Lily until I absolutely have to.

I turn over to see Kylie gazing at me through those impossibly long lashes. The sun bathes her brown skin in a golden glow. Damn, that's a nice sight to wake up to.

I curl into Kylie, wrapping my arms her. I can feel the curves of her body as they melt into mine. She's perfectly rounded. All positive space. The soft arcs of Kylie's flesh feel so much more like home than Lily's hard edges. Man, I've fallen hard. It's only been twenty-four hours, but it feels like a lifetime.

CHAPTER FORTY-ONE

"Am I missing a tooth?"
—THE HANGOVER

kylie:

"**H**ey, you," Max says, smiling lazily. "We got pretty messed up last night."

"Yeah," I say, hoping he'll offer more, giving me a better picture of what exactly happened toward the end of the evening, when my disc got erased.

"I hope we didn't do anything stupid," I say, fishing for information.

"Yeah, pretty sure we did." Max laughs softly and his eyes close again.

That's all I get?

Max takes my hand in his, which is when I see them— two identical gold bands. One on his hand. One on mine.

The rings catch the sun; light shoots off the gold and bounces around the room.

What exactly happened last night? I am ablaze with an unsettling mix of passion and panic. I'm sweating now, which can't possibly be appealing. What have I done? I've got high school graduation, a summer internship at the San Diego Arts Council, New York University in the fall, and parents who are going to freak. I've been MIA for the past twenty-four hours. I'm in Mexico with Max. And we're wearing rings that look suspiciously like wedding bands. This is bad. Very, very bad.

I've never even been on a date.

Or had sex.

Or have I?

I sit up, intent on hatching a plan, and that's when I see Lily Wentworth standing in the doorway, staring at me.

CHAPTER FORTY-TWO

> "If you wake up at a different time in a different place, could you wake up as a different person?"
> —FIGHT CLUB

max:

"What. The. Fuck. Max?"

I hear her before I see her: the unmistakably piercing sound of Lily.

I am going to kill Charlie. What part of "come alone" wasn't clear?

It's a rude awakening to what is bound to become a bear of a day.

I lift my head to see Lily standing in the doorway. If this

were a cartoon, smoke would be rising from her head. Her body would be engulfed in flames.

I am in some serious shit.

I look over at Kylie looking at Lily, and sure enough, she is flipping out. Her eyes are as big as saucers. If *she* were a cartoon, her eyeballs would be popping out of her head and rolling onto the floor. Unfortunately, none of us are cartoons. This is not a comic book. It's real life. And what was once a romance is now a horror show.

I have no idea what to do. I am not the guy who smoothes out these kinds of situations. I'm not a peacekeeper, like Charlie. I'm the guy who looks for the exit at times like this.

I can see Charlie standing awkwardly next to Lily.

"Dude?" I say to him.

"Sorry, man."

Damn. I am so pissed at Charlie.

CHAPTER FORTY-THREE

> "Do excuse me
> while I kill the man
> who ruined my life."
> —PIRATES OF
> THE CARIBBEAN:
> DEAD MAN'S CHEST

lily:

This cannot be happening. It's like some cruel joke. Or a bad dream. Or a mirage. On the off chance that my brain has scrambled the image, I close my eyes. When I reopen them, the same gruesome tableau is still there, the bodies splayed out before me like the goddamn Alamo.

Max and Kylie. Kylie and Max. In bed together. In bed together.

I'm trying to process it, but I can't make sense of it. It's too bizarre. Too infuriating. Too everything.

Maybe there's some kind of logical explanation for why they're in bed together, other than the fact that they've just had sex. Yeah, as if.

This is where Max has been on the last day of school? While I've been living in my own private hell, suffering my dad's indignities all alone, he's been hanging out in Ensenada? Screwing Kylie Flores, of all people?

I am so livid I can't think straight. I want to pull my hair out. I want to pull Max's hair out.

I mean, seriously. What. The. Fuck?

Max is such an asshole.

"Let's give him a minute," Charlie says. I forgot he was even here.

"Let's not!" I insist. I mean, Max has had twenty-four freaking hours. What does he need with another minute?

CHAPTER FORTY-FOUR

"I got a baaaad feeling on this one there, Fats."
—TROPIC THUNDER

will:

I see Lily Wentworth and Charlie Peters standing in the hallway as soon as Juan and I enter Manuel's house. What are they doing here?

Lily's skinny arms are folded across her chest in a power pose, outside an open bedroom. I have to assume Kylie and Max are in there, post-whatever.

Be afraid. Be very afraid.

There will be blood.

Instinctively, I know I must get to Kylie, to help, protect, and serve. An invisible tether pulls me toward her. I rush past Juan, completely forgetting our discussion. Clearly, he has not.

316

He grabs my hand to stop me. Juan has been gearing up for his big moment with Manuel for the past hour. He wants to proclaim his homosexuality, and he's asked me to stand by his side for moral support, which I promised to do; but now my allegiance has shifted. Potential boyfriend or not, I have to get to my girl.

"I thought you were going to help me tell Manuel," Juan says.

"Tell Manuel what?" Manuel asks, sidling up next to us.

"Juan is gay," I blurt out. I feel bad letting the cat out of the bag like that, but I've got a sneaking suspicion this will not come as a surprise.

"Oh, I knew that," Manuel says. "I think everyone knows. I'm glad you're finally ready to tell us."

"You don't have a problem with it?" Juan asks, shocked.

"Of course not," Manuel says.

"Problem solved," I say, extricating myself from Juan's grasp and hurrying down the hall, Manuel and Juan on my heels.

"What's *she* doing here?" I hear Kylie say. I can't see her, but I can feel her. And she's mad as hell.

"The girl says she's here to pick up Max. I didn't know what to do. She insisted on coming in," Manuel says.

"I'm sure it'll be okay," I say, pretty sure that won't be the case.

If only I'd gotten here a half hour earlier, when Manuel first called, I could have put Max and Kylie on a bus, and we would have avoided this little reunion. But Juan wanted to rehearse his whole coming-out speech. A lot of good that did us.

"What's going on?" Juan asks.

"Sadly, I think this is going to mean a little change of plans, darling," I tell him. "I'm going to have to drive Kylie back to La Jolla."

My holiday in Ensenada has come to an abrupt end. I won't be dropping Kylie and Max at the bus station and kicking back in Mexico for an extended vacation. I'll be escorting Kylie to graduation because, first off, she's going to need her best friend by her side, and second, there ain't no way I'll let her travel back with Lily and Max. There's either going to be a homicide or a suicide in that car, and I don't want Kylie involved.

"No problem," says my perfect man. "I can come with. I love a good graduation."

Did I actually get this lucky, or is Juan a serial killer?

CHAPTER FORTY-FIVE

"I can take life as quickly as I can give it."
—FIRED UP!

kylie:

already had a litany of things to worry about, like the fact that my graduation speech may totally blow despite months of work, or that my brother Jake may be lying in a ditch somewhere due to my negligence, or that I may or may not have married Max Langston last night, along with losing my virginity. I didn't need to add a psychotic girlfriend to the mix.

"What am *I* doing here?" Lily barks at me. "What are *you* doing here?"

Max jumps out of bed so fast, he blurs by me. He's at Lily's side, trying to calm her down. Old habits die hard, I guess.

"Oh. My. God. Can you please put on some pants? It's only making it worse," Lily insists.

As Max throws on his jeans, he turns to Lily, all apologetic, seemingly oblivious to the fact that he's just left me in bed.

"I'm really sorry, Lil. It's kind of a long, crazy story. I can tell you all about it on the way back." Max speaks softly, calmly. Like he cares. Like last night, with me, was just a bunch of bullshit.

"Yeah, I guess now's not a good time, because you're a little too busy cheating on me with Kylie Flores! I suppose that's why you told Charlie to come alone."

Lily is gesticulating wildy, fuming, spitting at the mouth. Max puts his arm around her, in an effort to calm her down, I assume. Still, it feels like a dagger straight to my heart.

"It's not like that at all," Max says. "I was going to explain everything when I saw you."

Max shoots Charlie a look. Charlie looks sheepish. "Sorry, dude. I told her not to come. She wouldn't get out of the car," he says. "You know what? Think I'll go wait in the car." Charlie slinks out.

"Good idea," Max says. "Listen, Lil, I called Charlie because I didn't want you to flip out. It's all a huge misunderstanding. Not a big deal, honestly. . . ."

Wait. Hold on. Rewind. There are so many things wrong with that sentence, I don't know where to begin. Max called Charlie? When? And it's not a big deal? Wow. What a difference a day makes. I'd love to ask Max about this little news bulletin, but the volleys are flying so fast, I can't get a word in.

"It sure seems like a pretty big deal, Max," Lily says.

"Just let me grab my stuff and Kylie can get dressed, and then we'll head out and I'll tell you what happened—"

320

"Kylie can get dressed? Get dressed?! Why are you doing this to me?" Lily's voice morphs into a semi-hysterical scream.

"I'm really sorry, Lily. I didn't mean to hurt you—"

"Rise and shine, everyone!" It's Will, popping his head into the room.

"What the hell are you doing here, Will?" Lily yells, turning her wrath on him.

"I'm sorry, Lily, but I don't recall sending you an invitation to our little soiree in Ensenada," Will responds.

"Bite me," Lily spits.

"Lovely to see you too."

"You called Charlie?" I finally eke out. I glare at Max. The anger is building inside me, especially as I notice he still hasn't removed his arm from Lily's waist. The arm that was around my body just five minutes ago. I want to lop off that arm with a machete.

"When did you manage to call Charlie?"

"When I told you I was calling my mom," Max says.

Nice. Lying jerk. Can I trust anything he said last night? "Did you even call your mom?" I ask.

"No. I was afraid Will would flake on us," Max says. "He hasn't exactly been reliable."

"Standing right here," Will adds.

"I'm sorry. I guess I should have told you. I was just trying to make sure we got back for graduation."

He guesses he should have told me? What a dick. I've lost all interest in talking to Max. I just want out of here. Away from Max. I can feel myself shutting down, reaching for the armor for protection. I never should have opened up in the first place.

"I'm really sorry, I had no idea Charlie would bring Lily, I swear," Max says looking at me.

"Yeah. Right," I say, because, really? Really? He had no idea? He called Charlie and didn't think Lily would come. They're the Three Musketeers. Of course Lily would come. And where was that supposed to leave me? I'm sure my feelings never figured into it. I was afraid I'd get hurt. I had no idea how fast it would happen. I'm an idiot for thinking this would end any other way.

"Yo, I'm your girlfriend, in case you forgot. If anyone should be here, it should be me, not *her*," Lily screeches, pointing at me with her forefinger. "And, for Christ's sake, can you please stop apologizing to *her* like *she's* your girlfriend or something. Or, I don't know. Maybe she is. Is she, Max? Is she?" Lily taunts. "Is she your girlfriend now? Is that what's going on here?"

"No," Max says quickly. A little too quickly.

"Yeah," I snap. "We're nothing to each other, Lily."

"Well, then, stay away from him from now on. Don't go poaching other girls' boyfriends just 'cause you can't find one of your own."

"I wouldn't want him if he was the last guy on earth."

"Kylie . . ." Max says, as if there's anything he can say to make this better.

"What?" I ask.

"I don't know. Nothing. . . ."

Lily and I stare daggers at each other, both breathing hard. I hate her with every morsel of my being. Max just stands there, looking back and forth from me to Lily with a stupid, sad look

322

on his face, like a little kid who's lost his mother at the mall. What a loser. What did I even see in him? Talk about not rising to the occasion. Just like in the truck—when the shit really hits the fan, Max folds. It's not an attractive quality.

"Let's all take a few deep breaths and see if we can't figure this thing out calmly and—"

"Fuck you, Will," Lily snaps.

"You know what? I was trying to be civil. But forget it, you little wench. In case you haven't gotten the picture yet, let me paint it for you. Your presence isn't wanted here. Why don't you run back to La Jolla, girlie?"

And that's when Lily rushes not at Will but at me. She gets in one good smack at my face before Max and Will drag her off me. For a fancy princess, she's pretty trashy. She could give the girls in the 'hood a run for their money.

"Mess with her, and I will mess you up, bitch," Will says.

"Leave her out of this, Lily," Max says in a measured voice. "You want to hit someone, hit me."

"Shut. Up. All of you," I yell. I am standing on the bed. "Max was right. This was all a big fucking misunderstanding. A big mistake. And I don't want to be part of your stupid, petty games, so, if you'll excuse me, I'll be leaving now. I have a speech to give."

I jump off the bed and head for the door.

"Wait. Kylie . . ." Max comes toward me.

I turn around and look at him.

"What now, Max?"

"I just, I don't know. Drive back with us."

Us? Are you kidding me? Us is not an appealing prospect, dude. Us was you and me last night. And now it's you, Lily, and Charlie. Count me out.

"I don't think so," I say.

Will reaches into his pocket and pulls out a passport, which he hurls toward Max.

"Here you go. See you on the other side," he says.

As I stare at Max for probably the last time, last night descends on me—swimming in the ocean, kissing on the pier, thinking I had fallen in love. Instead of feeling good about it, I feel like shit. This is not the same boy I was with yesterday, the boy who convinced me that everything was possible. It's morning. I'm not the princess. And he's no prince. He's just the same old Max Langston I've known for years. Selfish prick. God, what an idiot I am.

I still can't remember how we got back to Manuel's or what happened when we did. Hopefully, nothing much. But if I did actually lose my virginity, I'm just going to have to chalk it up to drunken stupidity. And if I got married, well, I'll get it annulled, move on with my life, and never, ever think about it again. Luckily, I don't ever have to see Max after graduation. New York City will erase the shame of this whole affair. I'd rather walk back to La Jolla than get in a car with Max, Charlie, and Lily.

I grab my backpack and head for the door, but Will takes my arm, stopping me. "Sweetie, you might want to throw on some clothes before we head back to Cali. Trust me, the border police are a pretty conservative bunch."

I look down and realize I'm only wearing my bra and panties.

I search the floor and see the Mexican dress from last night. It's the last thing I want to put on, but I have no idea where my other clothes are. I snatch it off the floor, and I'm about to throw it on when I'm hit with a wave of nausea that nearly knocks me over.

I run to the bathroom, lean over the toilet, and puke my guts out.

A lovely image, I'm sure. I'm practically naked, vomiting, possibly married, potentially a huge slut, and most likely late for graduation. Ending the year with a bang.

"I've got it," I hear Will say.

Someone takes my hair and pulls it away from my face. I look up to see Will standing above me. Disappointment blasts through my body. I thought it might be Max. What kind of fool allows herself to be deceived over and over and over again?

"You okay?" Max asks. Like he gives a shit. He's standing in the doorway, keeping his distance, I'm sure.

"Yeah, great, peachy," I say.

"MAX!" Lily yells from the bedroom. "We've got to get out of here. We're going to be late."

"Be right back," Max says to me. And like some kind of automaton, he races out to her.

"Don't bother," I say.

I can hear Lily berating Max. I'm not really listening to the words; they all run together in a high-pitched, earsplitting blur. But I do hear two words from Max that make my blood curdle and my heart collapse—"temporary insanity." It's pride-swallowing, soul-crushing to hear him characterize our night that way.

Fuck him. Fuck him. Fuck him.

And I thought it was love. Boy, was I way off.

I lean over the toilet and throw up again.

CHAPTER FORTY-SIX

"The rumors of my promiscuity have been greatly exaggerated."
—EASY A

max:

"Hey, man, everything okay?" Manuel says, as Lily and I pass him on our way out the door.

"Uh, yeah. Sorry about all the noise. Big misunderstanding."

"No worries." Manuel looks at me for a beat. He knows what went down, but he's too cool to say anything.

"Thanks for everything, Manuel."

"No problem, *amigo*. Hope I see you again soon."

"You will, man. You will."

"You want some coffee or some food for the road?" Manuel asks. He's such a good guy, I actually get a lump in my throat. I don't deserve his kindness.

"No, no. We're good. We'll probably just stop in town."

Manuel disappears down the hall, probably to talk to Kylie. I feel bad that Manuel's generosity has been met by drama and tears. He doesn't need this shit in his house. No one does.

"Who's he?" Lily wants to know.

"Manuel. It's his house. We met him yesterday. He's a friend of Kylie's dad. Awesome guy."

"I'm so sure," Lily says, no interest in concealing her disdain for anyone having anything to do with Kylie.

"You're an idiot, Max," she says as we exit Manuel's house. She's referring to the fact that I've just told her what happened, in the most abridged version possible.

"It was stupid. I know," I admit.

I can see Charlie sitting in the car, waiting for us. Lily is walking slowly, shaking her head, like she still thinks I'm lying to her. She's in no rush to get to the car. She's not done carving out her pound of flesh.

I'm sure a huge fire is raging through her body right now. Luckily, she's keeping things in check, so I'm just getting residual smoke. We're speaking—it's not pleasant, but it's a huge improvement over fifteen minutes ago when I was pretty sure she was going to strangle me with her bare hands. Seriously, all one hundred pounds of her could have taken me. Lily is a force to be reckoned with, which is exactly why I told Charlie to come alone. Man, what part of that didn't he understand?

"It all sounds like complete bullshit," Lily says again.

"I know. Even to me. It was just, one thing led to another and then we were stranded in Mexico. No passports. No way home."

328

I'm just being contrite. Not saying much. Lily needs a punching bag. Anything I say can, and will, be used against me. I've just got to take my medicine and then, hopefully, get the hell back to La Jolla. At least I caught sight of the wedding ring in time and slipped it off my finger and into my pocket. A ring on my finger in the middle of this argument would not have helped things. At all.

"That is the stupidest thing you've ever done. I mean, what were you thinking?"

"I guess I wasn't. I just kind of followed Kylie. I thought she was gonna get herself killed, and so—"

"And so you went after her like Superman or something? All that for some weirdo you barely know. What is wrong with you?"

Lily's description of Kylie hits me hard. I want to defend her. But I don't. I know that's not going to help things at the moment. It's only going to make it worse.

"Look, I don't know. Temporary insanity, like I said." I don't have the will to fight Lily, to bother telling her the truth. What would it matter anyway? Kylie wants nothing to do with me, so what is there left to fight for?

The one thing I don't say is that I wish it had never happened. Because that's not true. If I hadn't jumped into the truck, I never would have spent the day and night with Kylie. It may have only been one day, but it was the best date of my life.

"Maybe you were thinking with your dick."

"I told you, I just felt bad for Kylie. We didn't have sex."

"Since when did you give a shit about crazy Kylie Flores?"

"Since I got to know her. She's not the weirdo we thought.

She's actually pretty cool." I can't help myself. I won't let Lily keep bashing Kylie.

"Spare me. I don't want to hear about how you guys are suddenly besties."

"Look, Lil, it was messed up but it wasn't intentional. I wanted to be there with you for the last day of school. I'm really sorry."

"Yeah, you didn't seem super sorry. Especially when you were curled up in bed with Kylie."

I'm not sure how to respond to that. I'm sorry I almost got myself killed. I'm sorry I hurt Lily. I'm not sorry about Kylie. How exactly do I say that? I don't.

"Like I told you, we had a lot to drink and then we just fell asleep. I feel bad you had to walk in on that."

"Yeah, me too. The image will forever be etched into my brain. Were you trying to hurt me?"

"Of course not." I sigh deeply because this is such a typical Lily conversation. "Everything is not about you, Lily."

"I wish people would stop telling me that."

"Sometimes shit happens. For no reason at all. This is one of those times."

I look over at Lily and see the tears pooling in her eyes. She looks like broken glass. I don't want to hurt her any more than I already have. She doesn't deserve it. I don't need to shove whatever this thing is with Kylie down her throat.

"Honestly, Lil, nothing happened. That's why I told Charlie to come alone. I wanted to explain everything when I saw you. It looks worse than it is."

330

Lily doesn't say anything. My head is pounding like crazy. It feels like we've been talking for three years now. I don't know how many more rounds of this I can take. I can't help wondering what Kylie is thinking right now. Is she thinking about me? About last night? Regretting everything? Will she ever want to see me again?

I wanted to stay with Kylie, make sure she was all right, but Will practically shoved us out the door.

I get it. My girlfriend walking in on us wasn't exactly the best scenario for the morning after. I fucked up. I've disappointed everyone, including myself.

Lily's delicate shoulders start to shake with sobs as she cries quietly, her thin arms wrapped tightly around her stomach to calm herself. I have to push out thoughts of Kylie right now. What's the point? I've got to man up, take care of Lily.

"Lil, I'm not going to lie to you, stuff happened between me and Kylie, but it wasn't about sex. It was more like talking."

"Talking? You never want to talk," Lily says accusingly, like I've just pulled a gun on her.

"I like to talk. Just not all the time." This is a lie. But I don't have a good defense.

"Are you breaking up with me, Max? Because, if you are, I don't think I can handle it right now. Please don't. I'm begging you. I've got a lot going on and . . ." Lily's voice drifts off, and she starts sobbing again.

My heart breaks for her. Lily may not be my soul mate, in the way I thought Kylie was last night, but she's been my girlfriend for almost a year. I can't do this to her. It's not fair.

"I'm not breaking up with you, Lil. Yesterday was a . . . mistake." Right now, I just want to make Lily feel better. And get in the car and head back to Freiburg. I'll worry about the rest later.

"Okay. Good." Lily collapses into me. I pull her close. She smells like lemon and ginger, the shampoo she always uses. This is such a familiar place, it's hard not to just relax and fall into the same old patterns.

"It's okay, Lil," I say as I stroke her hair.

"Is it, Max?"

Lily looks up at me, beaten, broken. Last night, with Kylie, I would have said without a moment's hesitation that things between Lily and me were done. But now, in the harsh light of day, with Kylie hating me and Lily in pieces, the night has given way to the realities of the morning.

Lily leans in and kisses me on the lips. It doesn't feel the least bit sexual. More like a kiss from a friend. But maybe I'm just feeling numb from everything.

"Don't break up with me," Lily pleads.

"Okay," I say.

"You're my soul mate. If we're going to make it, we'll have much more than this to weather."

Maybe last night was just a blip on the radar. A crazy Mexican dream.

"You know what, Max? We don't have to tell each other all our dirty little secrets. It's cool. If you say nothing happened, then nothing happened."

"Nothing happened," I say again. Less and less convinced that it's true. Everything happened.

"I just want to know we're okay."

"We're okay," I say.

"'Kay, let's head back to La Jolla," Lily says.

And just like that, Lily has rallied. I shouldn't be surprised. It's so Lily—a whirlwind of ever-changing moods. It's better than her staying pissed. Only problem is, are we really okay? I don't know. I look at her—her gorgeous body showing through her thin T-shirt and shorts, her long blond hair pulled into a messy ponytail, revealing her flawless face. She's beautiful, like a *Sports Illustrated* swimsuit model, like a Barbie doll. Are we okay? Maybe. I know all her junk, and, in a way, that's a relief to not have to learn someone else's stuff from the beginning. But is that enough? Maybe not. Shit. I am out of my league here. I thought I could handle these types of situations, but I'm crumbling.

"I love you so much, Max. I don't want to ever lose you. I'll do whatever it takes to make this work."

"Yeah, me too," I say. As soon as it's out of my mouth, I know I don't mean it. Maybe I did at one time. But not anymore. The problem is, I don't know what else I can say. I'm losing my grip on things. It's harder and harder for me to see what's real. Maybe when the hangover lets up. Maybe when I've had some time to think and put it all in perspective. Or maybe it is what it is—one awesome night in Mexico with a girl I barely know. Maybe life is full of moments like this—fleeting, genius moments that don't bleed into real life. And don't mean much when they're over.

CHAPTER FORTY-SEVEN

"This is me leaving. This is me leaving."
—OLD SCHOOL

kylie:

"I can't believe they didn't take any of my music. That's just insulting." Will and Juan and I are standing in front of Will's Mini Cooper, staring at the driver's-side window, which has been smashed to smithereens.

"That's what you're worried about?" Usually Will's humor is charming, but right now I want to rip his scalp off. Not only have the windows of his car been decimated by thieves, but all four tires are gone. Gone. His car looks like a toy that's been mangled by a toddler. We're not going anywhere.

"You have to admit, it's offensive. How could they not have wanted any of my CDs? I have great taste in music." Will looks at me, dead serious.

334

I want to throttle him. I am so not in the mood.

"Who gives a shit about your music, Will? We have such bigger issues. How the hell are we going to get to graduation now?" I'm going to lose it on Will. He's hardly earned it, but he's the only likely candidate for my rage.

Juan has the good sense not to get involved. He looks out at the ocean, waiting, I assume, for us to resolve this nightmare somehow or seek his counsel.

"Kylie, this is not my fault, darling. How could I have known my car would get vandalized? Damn. The border cop actually told me to get insurance, and I thought he was just trying to scam me. Who knew? I should have listened to him. My dad is going to kill me. He just bought the Mini a few months ago."

I can feel myself losing it. "Listen, Will, I feel bad about the car, but you can deal with it later. I'm sure your dad can figure this out. Right now, we've got to focus on finding a way back to school. Shit. Shit. Shit. What are we going to do? This is so typical. You know what, Will? You attract trouble."

I know it's not Will's fault, but somehow, somehow . . . I feel like it is.

"What? Let me remind you that *you're* the one who got kidnapped and taken to Mexico, not me. *I'm* the one who hauled ass and came down here to rescue you. So I think you better just lose the 'tude."

Will's righteous anger tugs me back to reality. Why am I treating my best friend like shit? Because I let some guy treat me like shit, that's why. It's not fair. I'm better than this. Will deserves better than this.

"I'm sorry, you're right. I just don't know what to do."

"It's all right, *chica*, I know you're stressing. We're going to get back; we'll figure this out." Will puts his arm around my shoulder. "'Make anyone cry today?'"

"'Sadly, no. But it's only four thirty,'" I say. *10 Things I Hate About You* always brings a smile to my face. I love that movie. And Heath Ledger in it. And Will for bringing it up.

I have to stop acting like such a tool. And feeling sorry for myself. Yes I got my heart broken, but at least I put it out there. Maybe next time I'll pick a better contender, like Will did. Right now, I've got to throw everything I've got into Plan B.

I turn to Juan. "I don't suppose you have a car, Juan?"

Juan smiles weakly. "No. I've got a bike."

I'm sure Max, Lily, and Charlie have already hightailed it out of town. Max seemed eager to be far, far away from me.

"We've got to see when the next bus leaves. It's our best option," I say. "Let's go back to Manuel's. He can help us figure out the schedule."

We turn and trudge back toward Manuel's. It's hard to buck up. The self-pity is creeping back in like roaches at a seedy motel.

At this point, I know it doesn't even matter, but I must look like such a train wreck. My hair is frizzing out and the ends are coated with dried vomit. I'm still wearing this goddamn wedding dress, but the lace hangs off the hem, shredded. My white espadrilles are gray at this point, and my skin has a greenish hue. It's certainly an original look for the Freiburg valedictorian.

I dig into my backpack, pull out a tube of lip balm, and swipe it across my lips. I may look like hell, but at least my lips will be moist. It's not much, but it's something. As I'm putting the lip balm back, I catch sight of my key chain from Jake, attached to the zipper. It's a plastic palm tree with the words SAN DIEGO written up the trunk. I have no idea why he thought I'd like it so much, but I do. I treasure it. The thought of Jake pulls at my stomach. I've been so busy making a mess of my life, I haven't thought about him in a while. I wonder how he's doing without me. What did Mom tell him? Jesus. I can't go there, not now.

I feel the ring on my hand and glance down at it briefly. I'm not even sure what it means. I search the recesses of my brain and find, deeply hidden, a vague recollection from the pier last night. There was a priest, couples, a wedding ceremony. Is it even possible? We couldn't have gotten married. Could we? And even if we did something that stupid and reckless, doesn't it take a lot more than some priest on a pier for an American to get legally married in Mexico? It was probably just a joke. An idiotic, foolhardy, drunken joke. Whatever it was, I'm sure it's fixable. The rest of the mess is less easily mended.

I stare down at the ring. I should hurl it across the street. It's a potent symbol of my folly. And yet I don't want to take it off. Stupid, stupid girl. Are you waiting on a miracle? Get over him. It's not happening.

I head back into Manuel's house, Will and Juan right behind me. They're holding hands like they've been together for years, an old married couple. It's surreal.

"What time is it, Will?" I ask, dreading the answer.

"Uh . . . seven thirty-five."

A little more than four hours to get to graduation. Our chances are shrinking by the minute.

"Hello?" I walk through the front door of the house to find Manuel and Manu watching TV on the couch.

"You're back?"

The sight of Manuel with his arm around his son, somehow pierces at my heart, and I erupt in tears. Oh my God. I'm turning into a character from a Mexican *telenovela*. I cannot stop crying. What is wrong with me? I've probably cried at least six times in the past twenty-four hours. I do not understand it, but Manuel has struck a chord in me, maybe because of my dad, maybe because he was such a huge part of such a huge night in my life, maybe because I am flat-out exhausted. In any case, I run up to him and throw my arms around him.

"Whoa there, *mamacita*, what's wrong?"

"I'm sorry. I'll be fine. Just tired. I feel like I didn't properly apologize for the craziness this morning, Manuel. I'm so sorry."

"Is that why you came back, to apologize. Again? Because you already did. Several times." Manuel is chuckling. He must think I am a complete lunatic. Which I am. "You really don't have time to waste. The border could be crowded. You need to get going."

"Will's car was vandalized. We need to get a bus."

"I bet you can catch your . . . friends. Can I call them that?"

"Not really," I say.

"Well, whatever they are, I bet they're still in town. They went to buy food. Max told me on his way out."

"No way. That's great. Thanks. Thanks again and again, Manuel. For everything."

"You'll come back with Javier. This summer. Before you go off to New York City."

338

"I promise I'll be back. I can't speak for my dad. You know what he's like."

I'm running for the door when Manuel calls to me.

"Kylie, that girl doesn't hold a candle to you."

I smile at Manuel. If I stayed any longer I'd start crying again.

I fly out the door. Will and Juan are waiting outside.

"C'mon. Manuel thinks Max, Lily, and Charlie went to get food in town. We've got to find them." As sickening as it will be to drive all the way back to school with them, it's the best idea we've got.

"We're all going to drive home together?" Will asks, equally horrified at the prospect.

"Yes. Unless you have a better idea."

"I've got nothing."

I tear off down the hill. I can see town up ahead. I run past the houses and the kids playing in the street and the ticky-tacky souvenir shops. Back into this town that I've come to love. And there it is, Charlie's Jeep sitting on the main street, across from the harbor, idling.

I'm still a few blocks away as I watch Max and Lily climb inside and shut the doors. And then the Jeep pulls away from the curb.

I charge after it, yelling and waving my arms furiously.

"Wait! Stop! Max!"

The Jeep picks up speed.

Will and Juan run after me, but they're too slow. Our great hope to make it to graduation, pulling down the street . . .

Shit. Shit. Shit. What are we going to do? I feel my anxiety rising to dangerous levels. My breath quickens. I'm gulping air. I see an old guy on a Vespa heading into the plaza, and decide in a crazy last-ditch effort to flag him down.

He stops.

"Por favor, ¿me prestas tu Vespa?" I say to him.

He stares at me, not sure how to answer. I want to borrow his Vespa. Naturally, he doesn't look pleased by the idea. Damn, I don't have time to debate this.

"Por un momento, lo prometo," I say, hoping that will make a bit of a difference. I look at him beseechingly and, miraculously, the guy climbs off.

I have a real skill in vehicle jacking. There's my Plan B if the screenwriting thing doesn't work out. The poor guy just stares after me, bewildered. He'll get it back momentarily; he just doesn't know that yet.

Having never ridden a Vespa before, I'm a bit wobbly, but my determination wins out over my lack of skills, and quickly I'm on the road, right behind the Jeep. The thought occurs to me that, once again, I've found myself in yet another cliché-ridden movie scene. Although, if this were a movie instead of my pathetic life, things would probably end differently. I would be chasing my love, racing against time to tell him that I was wrong, that I do love him and can't live without him. He would jump out of the car and proclaim his undying love for me as well. Everyone would applaud and we would live happily ever after. But that is so not happening here.

I pull alongside the Jeep.

"Max! Max!" I yell. "Stop!"

Max, sitting in the passenger seat, turns to see me.

"Kylie, what are you doing?" he yells through the open window.

"Just stop the car."

Charlie pulls the Jeep to the side of the road, and I jump off the Vespa. Max looks at me. Our eyes meet, and for an instant it's yesterday again. It's just him and me and I'm happy and in love. But then my eyes shift ever so slightly to the left, and I see Lily sitting in the back, her pinched little face pushing into the front seat, and I'm thrown back to reality.

All three of them jump out. Great. The Three Musketeers. The thought of riding home with them makes my stomach turn.

"Hey, Kylie, nice Vespa," Charlie says. Is he being nice? Or just attempting to make a horribly awkward situation incrementally less awkward? Who knows? I've never gotten Charlie.

"Uh, listen, we need a ride back to school. Will's car got vandalized."

"What do you mean?" Max asks.

"She means Will's car no longer has tires. Or windows," Will says as he and Juan run up, panting. "But they left all my CDs. That's just weird, isn't it?"

"That guy really wants his Vespa back," Juan says to me. "He's pretty pissed."

"I told him I'd bring it back," I say.

"Yeah, well, shockingly, he didn't believe it," Will says.

"You stole a Vespa?" Max asks.

"I borrowed it."

"Cool," Charlie says. Man, he is such an idiot. Why is Max friends with him? Then again, maybe I'm giving Max too much credit.

The Vespa owner marches up and snatches his scooter from me, whispering under his breath, *"Loca!"*

I don't think he means that in a good way.

"Gracias," I say, trying to make amends. *"Muchas gracias."*

He gives me the finger, jumps on his bike, and speeds off.

"'Kay, so can we come with you guys?" I ask again since no one has actually answered me. Are they really going to make me beg?

"Sure," Max says. Charlie and Lily don't say anything.

One yes is better than none.

Lily scowls at me. She looks miserable. And, believe me, I get it. It would be so easy to hate her at this very moment, but I can't. We've both just had our hearts broken by the same boy, and now we are bonded together, like it or not.

"I don't think there's room. I mean, there are three of them," Lily says.

"Oh come on, Lily. We'll make room. It's graduation." It's Charlie, coming to our rescue. Who'd have thought?

"Max, there is no way I am getting into that car with her." Lily has suddenly shifted from downtrodden to crazy pissed. The hate is on again. And I'm feeling it too.

"Well, then I guess you're staying in Ensenada." Will cocks his head at Lily and smiles.

"Oh shut up, Will," Lily snaps.

Oh. My. God. I do not want this to devolve into another shouting match. Charlie glances over at Max like it's Max's decision to make. I look at Max, daring him to say no, while Lily stares him down, daring him to say yes. It's a Mexican standoff, literally.

342

"Of course there's room," Max says, steadfastly refusing to look at either me or Lily. Still, if we're playing, and everything is a game after all, I'd say one point for me.

"Someone will have to sit in the rear seat, in the way back," Charlie says.

"Not me," Lily insists.

"Of course not. We wouldn't dream of asking you, princess," Will says.

"I'll do it," Juan says. "I don't mind."

The decision is made. All of us will cram into the goddamn car and travel to graduation together. What a frigging nightmare. Shoot me now.

Max is opening the back door for Juan when a look of fear flashes across his face. I know that look. What's going on?

He leans in to me. "Kylie, look. Over there. Across the street."

I follow his gaze. And there they are, the two dudes from yesterday, standing on the other side of the street, next to their U-Haul. There's no mistaking them. Bald, muscled, and inked up. Practically twins, except the tall one is twice the size of the little one.

You have got to be kidding me. What are the chances?

I suddenly realize this is exactly where we left the U-Haul. I cannot believe our terrible luck. Still, how did they find it? And how did we end up right back where we started? It's like *Groundhog Day*. We're just going to keep running into these guys every single day for the rest of our lives. They'll appear in La Jolla, San Diego, New York City, tracking us down for our one transgression. Okay, there's no way that's going to happen.

343

I'm totally being melodramatic. Still, our bad luck is pretty epic.

"Get in the car, get in the car," Max says, literally herding everyone into the Jeep.

"How did they find the truck?" I ask Max.

"I don't know. They must have a tracking device in there or something. Shit."

"I am not sitting next to her," Lily says, pointing at me.

"Lily, just get in the car," Max says.

No one has any idea what is going on, and there's really no time to catch them up on the situation. I would bet that if Lily knew the extent of things, she'd still complain about having to sit next to me. I have a sneaking suspicion she's petty to the core, even in the face of grave danger.

I've turned away from the two guys and am climbing into the Jeep. I'm banking on the crazy idea that if I don't look at them, they can't see me. But when I glance over, they're studying Max closely, trying to remember how they know him. And then there's a moment of recognition on both their faces as they realize who he is.

CHAPTER FORTY-EIGHT

"This is either a really smart move or by far the stupidest thing we have ever tried."
—HAROLD AND KUMAR GO TO WHITE CASTLE

max:

"Charlie, give me the keys. I'm driving." Kylie says evenly.

I look at Kylie and I can see her snap into the same fear-fueled state of focus she experienced in the U-Haul yesterday. I know she's completely freaked out, but instead of being paralyzed, she's somehow calm and decisive. I will myself to be stronger this time around.

I snatch the keys from Charlie and toss them to Kylie. She

hustles into the driver's seat. I shove Charlie into the back, slam the door, and get in shotgun.

"What the fuck, dude?" Charlie says.

Kylie tears off down the street. Maybe they won't follow us. They've got their stuff, they've got their truck. What would they want from us anyway? Revenge?

"The guys who stole the stuff, that was them across the street," I tell Charlie.

He hears the urgency in my voice. The mood shifts.

"Shit, man," Charlie says.

"I know. What are the chances?" I say.

"Improbably low," Kylie says.

"Why does Kylie get to drive?" Lily asks.

"Because she drives better than any of us, that's why. And she knows the town!" Man, that is so Lily to be sweating the small stuff when it's the big stuff that's gonna get us any minute.

Kylie turns right onto a small side street and winds her way into the heart of the town. I check the rearview mirror and I don't see the U-Haul. I'm beginning to think we're in the clear.

"I cannot believe you guys got us into this. How are we going to make it to graduation?" Lily says to no one in particular.

"Lily, if you'd like to get out, be my guest." Kylie is still calm and focused, but in no mood for Lily's shit.

"'I've got a trig midterm tomorrow, and I'm being chased by Guido the killer pimp,'" Will says. "I love it."

"What the hell's he talking about?" Charlie says.

"It's a line from *Risky Business*," Kylie says.

346

Will is one bizarro dude. He seems totally amused by the situation. I don't think he grasps that it's not fun or funny at all. It's scary and hugely stressful.

"Oh shit," I yell. "Kylie, over there."

The U-Haul is coming straight at us from another side street. Kylie swerves left and barrels down a narrow street, and then turns right again, back onto the main road. There's an enormous truck in front of us, and I watch as Kylie makes the split decision to pass it, hoping to lose the U-Haul. She successfully makes her way around the truck, but the U-Haul is directly behind us.

Kylie drives fast down the street, but there's not much she can do to lose the truck.

Juan is yelling something from the back.

"What?" I can't hear him well, he's too far back.

Juan climbs over the seat and squishes himself in between Lily and Will.

"Oh my God. What do you think you're doing?" Lily squawks at him.

"I'm talking to myself back there. No one can hear me. I know the police chief. I can help you out of this. I just called the cops. Kylie, you need to stay on this road until it intersects with the toll road to Tijuana. The police will meet us there."

Juan has suddenly become the hero. I had forgotten he was in the car. Earlier, I was wondering why the hell he even had to come. But now I'm just thankful he's here.

"Are you sure?" Kylie yells out.

"Yes. I'm on the phone with them now. My dad and the police chief are best friends."

Juan speaks into his phone in clipped Spanish, telling someone, presumably the police, what is going on.

The U-Haul speeds up and is driving alongside us, despite the fact that there are cars racing toward it from the opposite lane. Vehicles are honking and swerving to the left and right to get out of the way. It's complete chaos. I don't want to look at the guys, so I turn the other way. I'm trying to control my shit, but I scream when I see how close cars are coming to us. For now, Kylie is maneuvering with agility. She has the look of contained fear on her face that she had in the U-Haul. But this scene is beyond her. It's out of control, and even perfect driving can't save us. There are way too many variables.

Lily has her head buried in her hands, Charlie is staring straight ahead, his face drained of color, and Will isn't enjoying himself anymore; he's just sitting stone still, his hands clenched into fists. Other than Kylie, Juan is the only person in the car who's helpful, as he continues talking into his phone. Sadly, I'm as useless as everyone else. For the second time in two days, I am engaged in a high-speed car chase, now fleeing from bad guys. And I am not doing a damn thing to help the situation. Although, to be fair, I don't think there's much I can do.

The U-Haul rams into us from the side, and we all slam into one another from the force of the impact. Kylie accelerates and punches ahead. The U-Haul is forced to pull away to avoid being hit by another car, and for a moment we're ahead of them and we have the advantage. Kylie must have watched so many action scenes in her life that they are hardwired into her brain, because she is outperforming herself here. It's mind-blowing.

"You are a total overachiever," I say to her. If I can't be

helpful, the least I can do is be supportive.

Kylie doesn't take her eyes off the road, but I see the sides of her lips lift into a smile. Man, I am totally into this chick. She is way cool. Whatever happened this morning between us hasn't diminished anything for me. I've never felt this way about anyone. She may want nothing to do with me, but my feelings are undeniable.

"Kylie, stay to the right, the toll road is up ahead. When you get there, just stop," Juan says.

"Just stop? Really?" Kylie asks.

The disbelief spreads through the car, and we all look at Juan with doubt. Just stop? Does this guy know what he's doing? Can we stake our life on it?

"I don't know, man," Charlie says. "I think we should keep going."

"I'm telling you, we need to stop. The police are right behind us; they're going to take care of it. Trust me," Juan says.

It sure doesn't sound like a great idea. But it's the only one we've got.

As we come upon the intersection, Juan yells, "PULL OVER!"

"Now?" Kylie says.

"Now!" Juan insists.

Kylie pulls to the curb. Seconds later, the U-Haul speeds up from behind and screeches next to us. We all panic and scream, as if on cue. The two guys fling their doors open and are on us like a shot. Kylie is about to pull away again when we hear the high pitch of a siren approaching. I look in the rearview mirror, and just like in the movies, I see a police car speed into view. The cavalry. The two dudes hear the siren as well and immediately retreat. They're climbing back into the U-Haul when the police car skids up to us and two police officers jump out.

One of the officers approaches Kylie's window and says, "Go, go. We'll take it from here. You don't want to miss your graduation."

Kylie doesn't hesitate. She pulls out and makes a beeline for the toll road. Within seconds, we're on the road and cruising toward the border. For a few seconds, no one says a word. We've just traveled through a tunnel of doom and come out the other side.

"Oh my God. Oh my God. Oh my God," Will chants.

I'm not sure how long Will has been chanting this under his breath, but now he's upping the volume a little.

"You okay, Will?" Kylie turns around to look at him.

"I'm fine. Now."

"Juan! That was awesome. Man, how did you do that?" I, for one, am overjoyed.

"Because he's a rock star!!" Will says. "He's *my* rock star!" Will smothers Juan's face in kisses. Juan is giggling. Lily recoils.

"You grow up in a small town in Mexico, it has its advantages," Juan says.

"What did you tell the police?" Kylie asks.

"I told them there were two criminals chasing us, with a shitload of stolen stuff in their truck. Like I said, the police chief is my dad's best friend. He's like my uncle. He didn't really question it. He knows I would never do that unless it was for real."

350

"You're my own personal Chow Yun Fat," Will says to Juan.

"Who?" Charlie asks.

"Chinese action star," Kylie and I say at the same time.

Kylie and I share a look. I try to convey a million little things, but I don't think I'm particularly successful. Kylie looks away, either not feeling it or not wanting to acknowledge it.

CHAPTER FORTY-NINE

"You think because you don't yell, you're not mean. This is mean."
—KNOCKED UP

lily:

know I should probably be relieved or grateful or something that we got out of that situation, but all I can think about is the look I saw Max give Kylie. A fairly significant look, I think. Max may think I missed it because I'm sitting in the back and they're in the front together. Maybe I'm being paranoid; God knows it's in my nature. And Max did seem really sorry when we were talking earlier. Still, I've got to change the dynamic here. I can feel things slipping away.

"That was awesome," Charlie tells Kylie.

"All I did was drive," Kylie says, trying to seem humble. Who is she kidding?

"You rock, girlie. But then again, I already knew that," Will says.

"Man, I totally thought we were toast," Charlie says. "But you drove like a pro." *Yeah, we get it, Charlie. Enough already.*

Max insisted Kylie drive, and now everyone is propping her up. As if it wasn't bad enough seeing her wake up with Max, I'm meant to suffer a hundred indignities as we all congratulate Kylie to within an inch of her life. This is too much.

"I think we have the cops to thank for saving us," I say. Everyone goes silent. At least I've changed the tenor. "And Juan."

"Yeah, thanks, dude," Charlie says to Juan. "We owe you one."

"It's no problem. You don't owe me anything," Juan says.

Thank God, the conversation has turned. I have no clue who this Juan guy is, but I'd rather he be the focus of attention than Kylie.

I'm trying to keep my composure, but I can feel it weakening with every second. I'm, like, thirty seconds away from total hysteria. It's been a long day and it's not even nine a.m.

"Maybe Charlie should drive now," I say. "I mean, it's his car and we are in Mexico. Don't want to take any chances. The police can be sticklers down here." I don't need the two of them sitting in the front seat together.

"I'm happy to get in the way back," Juan says. "It's getting a little crowded in here."

"Fine with me. I need to look over my speech anyway," Kylie says.

Kylie pulls over at a turnoff and Charlie jumps into the

driver's seat. Max stays in the passenger seat. I'm sure the plan is for Kylie to just pop in back with me. But that's a no go, I'm afraid.

"Maxie, could you sit next to me? I'm not feeling so great," I say.

"Uh, sure," Max says. I don't know if he really wants it. But I figure two hours of me and Max sitting next to one another will help bridge whatever gap may still remain between us.

"It's cool. I can sit in front," Kylie says, like she's the most agreeable girl in the world.

Please. Honey, you don't fool me, I saw you on that squash court. I know what a raving lunatic you are. And you know what a bitch I can be. So let the games begin.

Kylie gets in front, Juan gets in back, and Max climbs in next to me. We've still got Will in the row with us, unfortunately, but there's no other place for him, except in the trunk, which would be fine with me. I'm guessing it's not going to fly with everyone else, though. I'll just have to pretend Will isn't here. Easier said than done.

"You seem tense, sweetie," I say to Max. "You want a neck massage?"

"I'm okay," Max says. He seems almost uncomfortable around me. This is so not good.

"C'mon, I insist. It's been a rough ride. It'll make you feel better."

Max hesitates a second before answering. "Uh . . . okay." He doesn't want to say no. But he doesn't want to say yes.

I massage his neck, working my hands over his shoulders. "Feel nice?"

354

"Yeah, thanks, Lil," he says. And then, literally thirty seconds later: "I think I'm good now."

What a joke. No way I'm stopping. I need to make this work for me. Show who's the alpha dog here. My hands move around his shoulder and down his arms, over his torso, toward his legs. Will is watching us with obvious disdain.

Kylie takes a quick look over her shoulder.

Max moves his leg away. I ease off, but I've accomplished something. Things may not be entirely good between Max and me, but, at the very least, I've staked my claim. Kylie saw my hands all over him. Hopefully, she got the message.

CHAPTER FIFTY

> "Lies, deceit, mixed messages . . . This is turning into a real marriage."
> —FACE/OFF

kylie:

I am sitting in the front seat, hunched over my laptop, eating stale potato chips—which are somehow all the food we've got in the car—and staring at the screen. I'm trying to focus on my speech, but it's hard with Max and Lily directly behind me practically having sex. Talk about inappropriate. They could at least wait until we're all out of the car. I can't stop asking myself how I could have been so wrong about him.

I will my eyes to concentrate on the words in front of me, tuning out everything else, and I begin to read:

Golda Meir once said, "Create the kind of self that you will be happy to live with all your life. Make the most of yourself by fanning the tiny, inner sparks of possibility into flames of achievement." Today is the day we create ourselves. The decisions we make from now on will impact the rest of our lives. Every generation is handed the torch. It's our turn now to take it and run with it, to show the world what we've got.

I'm having serious second thoughts. What I imagined was brilliant and heartfelt yesterday sounds clichéd and pretentious this morning.

I glance at the speech again.

We don't have one second to waste. We can't afford to make mistakes. Think carefully, choose wisely, set a tone. And get busy, class of 2012!

Maybe Max was right and the quote is off. I'm not sure anyone will relate to it. I'm not sure I do.

We can't afford to make mistakes. Do I really feel that way? It sounds so severe. I mean, the last twenty-four hours were a huge mistake, but do I regret it? I don't think I do. My answer surprises me a bit. But the truth is, despite the fact that it's morning and things haven't exactly gone in my favor, I learned I can survive outside of my tiny little world. I learned that even if it hurts sometimes, I'd rather be out there in the big, wide world than hidden safely inside my own cage. My heart may be broken, my clothes may be lost, my speech may no longer be relevant, but I'm stronger for it. Still, it's not very helpful at the moment. I mean, what am I going to do about the damn speech? I don't have time to rewrite the whole thing. And I'm certainly not going to just ad-lib a new one from the podium. I have no real choice. I'm going to have to go with it. It's one speech, for a school I hated. I'll say the words, get off the stage, and move on with my life. It won't go down in the annals of Freiburg history as the world's best valedictorian speech, but I'll live.

We've now been driving for a while; we're nearly in Tijuana. We're making good time. If all goes well, we should be back by ten thirty, eleven. Maybe I'll even have time to change. I realize I'm going to have to call my mom and come up with some kind of explanation for why I'm still not home, where I've been, and why I'm wearing a bright pink dress that looks distinctly South of the Border.

"You working on your speech, Kylie?" Max leans over from the back. His head is nearly flush with mine; his hair grazes mine. I feel a shiver shoot up my spine. I wish he didn't do that to me. It would be much easier to pretend I don't give a shit if my body would just play along.

I glance at him and can't help catching an eyeful of Lily as well. She looks as sour as ever. Max is suddenly pretending to care. Please. Fool me once. Not twice. When Lily arrived he fell right back into old patterns. Last night was just a temporary deviation from form, or as he told Lily, "temporary insanity." Once an asshole, always an asshole.

I'm not interested in conversation. That ship has sailed. We are no longer whatever we were last night. We're not even friends. I may not regret the experience, but that doesn't mean I want his pity.

"Uh, yeah," I say.

"Want to read it to us? Try it out?"

"No. I don't." I turn around and give my computer my

full attention, hoping something brilliant will come to mind. Maybe I can add a line here or there, incrementally improve things.

"The whole valedictorian thing is so stupid and overrated," Lily says to no one in particular.

"I doubt you'd think it was overrated if you were the one chosen, like me," I say. I'm in no mood for her attitude, and I'm in no mood to let her get away with it, either.

"Whatever. I so don't care."

"Lily, you care more than anyone," Charlie adds. "You just weren't first. Like Kylie."

Charlie hasn't said much this whole car ride, but what he has said hasn't been anything like what I assumed he'd say. It's a shock to my system. He's not such an awful guy. I'm actually starting to like him. Guess I shouldn't have kicked him in the shin.

"I wanted to come in first, but I never wanted the responsibility of the speech. It's too much pressure. You spend all this time working on it, and then no one really listens, and the few people who do rip it to shreds. You just can't win," Lily says. "I feel bad for you, Kylie. I really do. I know how much work you've probably put into it. And I know how hard it's going to be to pull it off."

Lily isn't fooling me. She's trying to psych me out. Not going to work.

"Kylie's speech is going to blow people away. I've heard it and it rocks. So shut your piehole, Lily," Will snaps.

"I heard some of it too, and I'm sure Kylie's going to be great," Max says.

What a lie. He hated what he heard. Don't bother defending me. I can fight my own battles, dude.

"You know what, Lily, I don't really care what you or anyone else thinks. It's one speech. One day. It's like a sneeze in our lives." I refuse to let Lily think she's won. Sure, she's gotten to Max. But she hasn't gotten to me.

"It can be pretty embarrassing if it doesn't go well. Three years ago, Janelle Davis gave such a bad speech, I heard that she's still too embarrassed to come visit."

"Lily!" Max scolds.

"What? I'm just saying . . ."

"Kylie, I meant to ask you guys earlier, but then it completely slipped my mind, with Guido the killer pimp after us. Why are you and Max wearing wedding rings? Must have gotten pretty serious last night," Will says.

Oh, no. I know what Will's doing. Trying to bitch slap Lily. But this isn't the way.

"What?" Lily says, turning to Max. "You have a wedding ring?"

"Uh, not exactly," Max says, sheepish.

I can't help myself: I turn around and look at Max's hand and discover he isn't wearing his anymore. I slip mine off and put it in my pocket.

"Pretty sure I saw one on each of you this morning," Will says. "Wait, wasn't there a massive group wedding on the pier last night? You guys didn't actually tie the knot in a crazy fit of spontaneity, did you? Because, I mean, you were both pretty wasted."

I get a sick feeling in my stomach. I don't want to do this.

Not here. Not now. The space is too claustrophobic. I turn around and shoot Will a look, but he ignores me.

"I mean, it wouldn't surprise me. You looked pretty in love—"

"No! Nothing like that happened," I say, cutting Will off, even though I'm not sure what exactly happened. My recollection is a little vague. I want to ask Max in privacy and then deal with the consequences later. Not in the car, with everyone listening.

"Actually, we did. We got married. On the pier. With about thirty other couples," Max says. Jesus, what is he doing?

"What?!" Lily and I say it at the exact same time.

"Jinx," Will says.

"Are you kidding me?" Lily spews her venom on Max. "You said nothing happened. It was all a mistake, temporary insanity. This is not nothing."

"Which is a double negative, meaning something happened," Will adds.

I need to stop this.

"Trust me, it was nothing," I say. "We're not really married. It was like a game on the pier. We both know it wasn't real, right, Max?"

"I guess so," Max says, without conviction. *C'mon, help me out here.*

"It was nothing," I say again, wanting to emphasize my point.

"From what I saw last night, it sure didn't look like nothing," Will adds, not helping the situation at all.

"Well, it was," I tell Will, shooting him yet another look,

hoping he'll actually get the point this time and shut the hell up.

"You can't just get married without a license or anything," I say. "Right?" I'm actually asking because I'm not quite sure, and I could use a bit of reassurance.

"Right," Max says. "You need a license."

"I cannot believe this. Just when I think it can't get any worse. What the fuck were you thinking?" Lily comes at him like a bull out of a pen.

"Lily, calm down," I say. "You heard Max. We're not really married. You need a license. It was a goof. No big deal. A joke." I don't know why I'm trying to appease her. I guess because I don't want this thing blowing up any more than it already has. What good can it do? I want to get to school without further damage.

"Max, why are you doing this to me?" Lily's voice has risen ten octaves. It's hurting my ears.

"Lily, we talked about this. Nothing happened. Chill."

"Don't tell me to chill," Lily spits out. "I think I deserve some details about last night." Her anger is in full bloom.

I know I've been pushing Max away, not interested in ever speaking to him again, but something about the way he says "nothing" infuriates me. And the truth is, I still don't know what happened last night, after we got back to Manuel's. I've been giving him the benefit of the doubt, hoping he was a gentleman. But now I want details too. I spin around in my seat and look at Max.

"You know what, Max," I say. "I would actually like to know what happened, too. What does that mean, 'nothing'?"

362

I should not be going down this road, but I'm exhausted, hurt, hungry, and angry. Not a great combination. So much for minimal damage.

"Let's get it all out in the open," I say.

"I'm all for that," Lily chimes in.

Max looks panicked, furious. He's being pressed on all sides.

"Maybe you guys should talk about this later? When we're all not around and things have calmed down," Charlie says.

"You know what? Charlie makes a good point," Juan says. *Too late, Juan. We're in it. Bummer you had to be here.*

"Fine." Max looks from me to Lily. "Kylie, you want to know what happened last night? Lily, you want to know?"

"Yes," we both say in unison.

"Nothing." Max spits this out. "Okay? Nothing. What that means is that Kylie and I did not have sex. We slept together. As in fell asleep. That's all. We were too drunk to do anything else." As he says this particular piece, he looks me directly in the eye. "And we got married, but as Kylie pointed out, it doesn't mean a thing. It wasn't real. Nothing about the night was real. It was a stupid, drunken game. We barely know each other."

Max's voice has an edge to it, like he's angry at me. Which is absurd. If anyone should be angry, it should be me.

"Excellent," I say. "Thanks for clarifying that." I turn around and stare at the road.

"You know what I don't get?" Lily is not giving up the fight. "If you're gonna sleep around behind my back, why would you do it with Kylie Flores? She's not even hot. She's just weird. And skanky."

Before I have a chance to bite back, Will goes ballistic.

"Listen, you vile little rodent. Kylie has more intelligence, class, and God-given beauty in her pinkie finger than you'll ever dream of having."

"As if I care what you think," Lily tells Will.

"Don't go after Kylie, Lily. This is not about her," Max threatens.

"What's it about, then?" Lily demands.

"Us. You. Me."

"I don't get it." Lily has now started crying. "Why are you defending her? If nothing happened, then why aren't you taking my side?"

"There are no sides in this, Lily. Stop turning it into a war." Max is talking to Lily but looking at me now.

I can't stay silent any longer. "Lily, you have nothing to worry about. Okay? Max is all yours. News flash: I don't want him."

CHAPTER FIFTY-ONE

"You're not an asshole, Mark. You're just trying so hard to be."
—THE SOCIAL NETWORK

max:

can't stand Kylie.

That's not true. But I wish it were. It would make things a shitload easier.

How could I have thought she was anything other than completely psycho? How can she just stare at me like nothing at all happened last night? Sure, Lily's arrival has thrown a wrench into things, but Kylie doesn't even seem to understand what a tough spot I'm in.

Whatever we had is done. Finished. It obviously didn't mean a thing to her.

Lily is crying harder now. I feel bad she had to walk into the middle of my nightmare. If only she'd stayed back in La Jolla like I wanted her to. Charlie and I could have gotten through this by ourselves. But with Lily and Will along, things are spiraling out of control. I'm not sure how to make things better, but I know I need to try. It's the best course of action at this point.

I put an arm around Lily. "C'mon, Lil, it's not that bad. It's one sucky car ride, but there's graduation, parties, and the whole summer to get psyched about."

This seems to make Lily cry even harder.

Funny how Will and Kylie aren't saying anything now. Like they're waiting for me to take care of this. If only I'd never agreed to do Murphy's stupid assignment, none of us would be here.

"Lil, I'm sorry about all this. Try to calm down. It's seriously going to be okay," I say, knowing it's pretty pathetic comfort at the moment. I wish I could go back to loving Lily and barely knowing Kylie existed. But it's too late for that.

"No. It's not going to be okay! Nothing is going to be okay ever again," Lily shouts. "My life is over. Completely fucked!"

Whoa! This seems like an overreaction even for Lily. What's going on? She looks so desperate, like something inside her has broken. That can't be all about me, can it?

"This is going to be something we all laugh about in a few weeks," I say, not entirely convinced that's true. "You're just being melodramatic—"

"I am not being melodramatic. I am being honest. For once. Things are bad. Worse even than they seem right now. My entire life is shit."

"Lily, what are you talking about? Everything's going to be fine. You'll see, after graduation—"

"My dad is going to jail." Lily says this between sobs.

"Your dad's going to jail?" I say.

"Jail?" Kylie says.

"Seriously?" Will asks.

I pray Will doesn't say anything else. I swear I will beat the shit out of him if he makes this worse.

"What do you mean? Why is he going to jail?" I put my arm around Lily. I need to get her to calm down, to talk to me. She's really freaking me out.

"I just found out. Two days ago. But since you weren't around all day yesterday, I haven't been able to tell you. He's been arrested for fraud, or money laundering, or, I don't even know what." Lily is sobbing. Hard. "I didn't want anyone to know, but what does it matter? Everyone's going to find out when he goes to trial."

"Jesus Christ." This is from Juan, in the way back. I'm sure he wished he never got on this crazy train to begin with.

"Lily, I'm so sorry I haven't been there for you. . . ." I say, at a loss for more words. There's no way to make this right. It's all so wrong. "How did you find out?"

"Mom unloaded everything last night. But things have been weird for a while. You never want to talk, so I didn't say anything. Maybe that's why you haven't told me how sick your dad is. In fact, if I remember correctly, you said he was going to be fine. I guess that's your fallback response. Everything's going to be fine. Don't worry. Be happy." Lily is now half crying, half yelling at me. This has become a very private fight in the middle of a very public car full of people.

"I'm really sorry, Lily. I should have told you," I say.

This is all coming at me too fast. I have no idea how to react.

CHAPTER FIFTY-TWO

"I'm sorry I farted into your purse."
—BABY MAMA

will:

What have I wrought? I was just trying to teach Lily a lesson, but now the shit has really hit the fan, and Kylie seems royally pissed at me. Max just seems depressed, and Lily, as always, seems like a nasty piece of work, but at least she's got some real live problems to moan about. Even I'm feeling sorry for her now. And what must Juan be thinking? He probably wants to get away from us, from me, as fast as he can. He's ruing his decision to ever get in the car. Ruing the day he met me. Me and my big mouth.

"Jesus, Max, if you and I could talk, really talk, maybe we wouldn't be in this stupid, fucking situation in the first place," Lily says, still crying, snot running down her tearstained face.

She's unraveling. I think I prefer her as a psycho killer rather than a pitiable, crying mess.

"Maybe not," Max says. He looks beaten down to a bloody pulp. Poor guy.

I need to introduce a cocktail of levity and a plate of titillating niblets into the mix. I created this mess. Now I've got to clean it up. Or at least brush it under the rug.

"I lost my virginity last night. To Juan," I blurt out.

"No one cares," Lily snaps.

"Will . . ." Kylie shoots me a warning look.

"What?" I say to her. "I was attempting to change the subject. Jesus, no medals for trying."

No one says anything. I thought the least they could do was offer up a little congratulations. Lily is such a bitch. I take back my pity.

"You're so selfish," Lily says, obviously intent on blasting Max until he's dust.

"Look, I'm really sorry about your dad. Really sorry about last night. Really sorry about everything. I don't what know more I can say. . . ." Max offers.

"Lily, lay off Max. At least for right now. You guys need to talk about this, but alone," Charlie cuts in.

"That's right, Charlie. Defend your buddy. That's pretty ironic, isn't it?" Lily turns to Charlie.

"Okay, Lily, enough," Charlie warns.

"Don't you think it's already gone too far, Charlie?" Lily is holding a box of matches and seems determined to torch the whole ship.

Charlie doesn't say anything. Neither does Max, who appears to have shut down operations.

"You want more secrets?" Lily ramps it up.

Oh God, I'm not sure we can handle it.

"I don't think we do, Lily," Kylie says.

"Too damn bad," Lily says. "Charlie and I hooked up yesterday, at Luca's party."

Yikes. Lily has lit the first match, it lays on the deck, waiting to catch fire.

"What?" Max says, visibly shaken.

I turn to Juan, who's staring wide-eyed at the proceedings, and say, "I'm sorry. I'm really, really sorry." This is even too much theatrics for me.

Juan puts his finger to his mouth and says simply, "Shh!" I guess he's enjoying the show. Why not? They're all just actors to him.

"Dude," Charlie says. "It's not what you think."

"So, you did hook up?" Max says.

"No. I mean, we were drunk. Lily was upset about you. She didn't know where you were. We kissed. That's it."

"What the fuck?" Max is pissed. The irony here cannot be ignored. Unfortunately, Max doesn't seem as keenly aware of it as I am.

"Max, it didn't mean anything." Charlie says this more emphatically, but Max is still staring at him in disbelief.

Charlie is throwing Max's own words back in his face. Am I the only one who sees what a sham these people are? What hypocrites? All of them messing around on each other, none of it meant to be taken seriously. I wish Kylie hadn't gotten involved.

"Dude, you're my best friend," Max says.

"Max. It. Didn't. Mean. Anything. It was, like, one kiss."

Max sits silently. We all do. Lily just watches. I can't tell if she's enjoying the havoc she's wreaked or if she's so far gone she's inured to it all.

"It was like kissing a friend," Charlie says.

"Your best friend's girlfriend. Which is really fucked up. I mean, where does that leave us?" Max demands.

"You're like my brother. Max, I was wasted. I'm sorry." Charlie seems on the verge of tears.

"You macked on my girlfriend. That is unbelievable. You're my best friend. My best friend." Max is talking more to himself than to Charlie.

"And you spent the night with another girl. So why do you get to judge me?"

Uh-oh. Here we go. . . . Buckle up, it's going to get bumpy.

"Wow . . . okay. Is that how we're going to do this?" Max asks Charlie.

There's a long, awkward moment where it feels like we're all holding our breath, and then Charlie lets out an audible sigh.

"No. It's not. Look, I don't want to go there, dude. Bottom line, it shouldn't have happened. But it did and I'm really sorry." Charlie says this in a very measured tone. "I swear to you, it didn't mean anything because I'm . . . gay. I'm gay."

He says it twice. As if we didn't hear it the first time. Trust me, it made a *huge* impression on the first go-round.

Even Lily looks stunned by this doozy.

372

Gay? Charlie? I'd like to say "I told you so," but this doesn't exactly seem like the right moment.

"You're what?" Max asks Charlie.

I guess Max does need to hear it a few times before it sinks in. Straight guys can be so dense.

"I'm gay. Okay? I'm gay."

I hear you, my friend. No need to hit *me* over the head.

CHAPTER FIFTY-THREE

"Is life always this hard, or is it just when you're a kid?"
—THE PROFESSIONAL

max:

"**W**ell, that explains a lot," Lily says.

"I think it's awesome news," Will says.

"Yeah, I bet," Charlie replies.

Will throws his fist into the air. "Score one for our team!"

My silence is certainly not helping matters. It's just, I'm not sure what to say. Or how to say it. *Way to go? Good job? I'm happy for you?* Of course, one of the first things that comes to mind is, is he crushing on me? What about all those times in the locker room? I know it's a horrible straight-boy cliché. I wish my mind were a slightly more evolved place, but I guess it's not. I'm having some trouble getting my head around the situation. My best friend is gay. Charlie is gay. I say it in my head a few times, hoping it will register. It doesn't. I still can't believe it. It's not that I'm homophobic, because I'm not. It's just that you think you know someone so well, and then it turns out you don't know them at all.

I'm not sure where we are, but we must be closing in on the border, because I see signs everywhere. I have to fight the urge to just jump out of this car and make a run for it. I'd be happy to wander around in Mexico for the afternoon and try to make sense of everything that's happened. Although, I think it would take a lot more than an afternoon. It might take a lifetime.

I can't help thinking that maybe I wouldn't be in this freaking mess if I weren't so tuned out. How could Lily and I not have talked about her dad? Or my dad? How could I not know that my best friend is gay? It turns out I don't know shit about anything, myself included.

Everyone is silent. They're waiting for me to say something.

"Dude, why didn't you tell me? We spend, like, twenty hours a day together." It's not the best I could have come up with, but it's what comes out, unfiltered.

"I sort of didn't believe it myself for a while. I'm still trying to figure it out. It's not the easiest thing to talk about—"

"And Max is not the easiest guy to talk to, as I think we've established," Lily says.

I so don't need her commentary here. I would love to put off this conversation for a few hours, until Charlie and I can grab some time alone.

"Lily, you're not helping things," Charlie says.

"Yeah. I know." Typical Lily.

"At first I thought I could will myself straight—"

"Been there," Juan shouts out from the back.

"Not me," Will says.

"But it is what it is. It's who I am. I've been wanting to talk about it all year. There's never really a right time, though. And I didn't want everyone to start freaking out, seeing me as some guy they couldn't hang with, someone they couldn't be in the locker room with, someone who was going to start crushing on them."

Fuck. Guilty. I suck.

"You have no idea how many gay jokes I've heard over the years, from everyone, including you. It's not the most tolerant environment, Freiburg."

"Tell me about it," Will adds.

I feel awful. I am sure I've made a million inappropriate remarks. My first instinct is to say as little as possible and then shut down and hide behind that, but I don't want to be a wimp anymore. Charlie's just done something braver than I'll probably ever do. He deserves better than that from me.

"I'm here for you, man," I say, lame as it is. This is me, trying. I want to mean it. I've never had this conversation before; I'm not sure how it goes. But I still don't entirely get it.

"What about Janice Smart? And Tracy Lestahl?" I ask. Was Charlie faking it? He seemed so straight for so long.

"It's been a long process, okay?"

"'Kay, I get it," I say. I don't really. But I'm gonna try, for Charlie's sake.

No one's talking. They're just letting us have this awkward conversation all alone, in a car filled with people.

"So, whatever you need. Just say the word. Nothing changes between us, seriously," I say.

"Thanks, bro. That means a lot."

Everybody's watching, waiting. Suddenly, I start laughing. I don't know if it's from the awkwardness of the situation or the absurdity. Or both.

"What?" Charlie asks.

"It's just, I can't believe you picked now to tell me. I mean, I'm glad you said something. It's just, funny. Here in the car. With everyone."

"I know. It's crazy." Charlie laughs along with me. It feels good to laugh. Maybe everything will be okay.

"It kinda gives new meaning to the expression, 'It's me, not you,'" Lily says. Her lips curl up into a smile and she chuckles to herself. The heaviness lifts, if only a little.

"This has to go down as the most wacked road trip in history," Kylie says, the edge softening in her voice. Maybe we all will make it out alive.

"Have you told your parents?" Will asks.

"No. Not yet."

"I have so much to teach you," Will says.

"Charlie may be gay, Will, but that doesn't mean you're suddenly besties or anything. He still finds *you* totally annoying," Lily says.

"And I still find you totally annoying, you odious harridan," Will tells Lily.

"What's a harridan? Sounds like a religious freak," Charlie says.

"A fancy word for hag," Will says.

"I love it. I'm totally going to use it," Lily tells Will.

"Don't. I'll sue," Will promises.

"Yeah, good luck with that. We're bankrupt." And then Lily actually laughs, long and hard. "Totally, fucking bankrupt. Bankrupt. Bankrupt. Bankrupt. It feels kind of good to just come out and say it."

Will laughs as well. "The Wentworths have gone bust. I never would have imagined it." He actually sounds sympathetic. "I think I first tasted caviar at your house."

"Oh, God, I remember that. In kindergarten. Mom had it flown in from Petrossian. It was so gross. She gave it to us for a snack with juice," Lily recounts.

"I was hoping for Oreos. I got caviar. It was so disappointing, I don't think I've touched it since that day," Will says. "Kids don't generally like fish eggs."

"Tell me about it. The one upside here is no more caviar." Lily and Will both giggle at this. Which comes pretty close to one of the trippiest things I've seen in a while.

I'm relieved. I couldn't take the stress much longer. I relax my shoulders and inhale a few times. It feels good to get air in my lungs. I think I may have stopped breathing.

"Oh, shit," Kylie says, pointing out at the road.

What now?

I lean forward, look out the front window, and see immediately what Kylie sees—a huge, snaking line of traffic. The border is at least half a mile up ahead. I check the clock. We have a little over an hour to get to graduation. And we've come to a complete standstill.

378

CHAPTER FIFTY-FOUR

"You know, I have one simple request. And that is to have sharks with frickin' laser beams attached to their heads."
—AUSTIN POWERS: INTERNATIONAL MAN OF MYSTERY

kylie:

check my watch. Eleven fifteen. Graduation begins in forty-five minutes. We've been sitting here, clawing our way forward, for the past twenty-five minutes. I take in the reality with a sharp breath.

"We're not going to make it," I say, to no one in particular.

"Sure we are. We're five cars away from the booth," Max tells

379

me. It's the first time he's spoken to me in a while. Not that I care.

"And then we're going to go ninety-five all the way to school," Will says. "Right, Charlie?"

"Let's say ninety," Charlie replies.

No one else seems willing to face the cold hard facts. Lily's been pretty quiet, keeping to herself. Her anger has subsided, and in its place a sort of glumness has settled in. I actually feel sorry for her. Finding out your dad is a small-time Bernie Madoff has to be pretty hard.

Today has been at the top of my agenda for months. I have been preparing for it forever, and yet I've managed to screw it up so royally it almost seems intentional. Was this really so difficult? Couldn't things have gone as planned? We should have been able to get in a car and get back to school in time for graduation. I should have been able to read my brilliant speech that I've worked on since the dawn of time, and received a standing ovation. Instead, we're going to miss graduation entirely. I should have never insisted on doing Murphy's assignment. I risked everything and didn't even get it done. I suck.

If nothing else, the past twenty-four hours have made me realize that all work and no play isn't such a good idea after all. It's better to mix it up a little more. Before today, I spent all my time thinking about the future and none of my time living in the present. As of now, I'm not going to do that anymore. Maybe NYU really will be different.

I look at my watch again. Three minutes have passed. The numbers are against us. We've got thirty-seven minutes. We're still four cars from the border; it's taking each car three minutes to get through, so at this rate we won't get through until eleven thirty, and then it's a forty-minute ride to school. With absolutely no traffic we'd be ten minutes late. And that's the best-case scenario. We're screwed. In light of my looming speech disaster, that should be good news. But it's not.

One more car creeps over the border. We're now three cars from the booth. We're so not going to make it. As much as I keep telling myself it doesn't really matter, I can feel my heart breaking for the second or third time today. I might hate Freiburg, but that doesn't mean I don't want to celebrate all that I've achieved there. I've been looking forward to this day for four years. It was supposed to make all my hard work worthwhile and all my social shortcomings seem irrelevant.

For the past several minutes no one has said a word. The tension is building. I think everyone is starting to realize that I may be right. I wish I weren't. It's not particularly fun to be right all the time. I'd like to be wrong for a while. I start to chew on my cuticles—a bad habit I rid myself of a few months ago, but it's back with a vengeance.

"Will, can I use your cell phone?" I say. "Mine is dead. I need to call my mom and tell her we're not going to make it."

"We're going to make it; don't be silly," Will says, sounding entirely unconvinced.

"We're not going to make it. I need to tell my family."

I turn around to take Will's phone, but he isn't handing it over. Max is staring at me like he wants to say something. I quickly turn away. What's the point?

"It doesn't matter," Lily says. "It's just a ceremony. We still graduate." Lily has had her eyes closed for a while now, and they're still closed, lizardlike.

381

"It matters to me," Charlie says. "I don't want to miss graduation. Shit." And he pounds the wheel with his hand, something he's now done a few times. It doesn't move us along any faster, but I guess it makes him feel better.

"I need to be there," Max says. "For my dad's sake."

"I hate to break it to you, but there's no way." This comes out meaner than I intended. Max doesn't respond. "Will, please, give me your phone." I hold my hand out in front of him.

"No. I'm not giving it to you. We're going to make it."

"Oh my God, Will. Just give me the phone."

"No."

"Here, Kylie, you can use mine." Lily holds out her phone. I'm almost afraid to touch it. Like it'll blow up in my hand or something.

An olive branch? From Lily? So strange.

I stare at the phone for a minute, realizing I don't have the strength to talk to my mom. So I text.

HI MOM, IT'S ME. I'M W WILL. WE'RE RUNNING LATE N WILL MEET U AT GRADUATION.

As I wait for Mom's response, we pull up to the booth. Oh. My. God. We're here. One minute ahead of schedule. If Border Patrol just lets us through, if they don't stop us and search our car, if Charlie floors it, we may actually get to school, late, but we could still make it.

"Good morning to all of you. Passports please, people," says an annoyingly chipper woman.

We all hand our passports to Charlie, who hands them to the woman at the window. I hold my breath and cross my fingers. I'm not going to breathe until I know we are good to go.

The woman flips through our passports for what seems like an interminable period of time. Is she going to ask us to get out of the car? Does she sense we came here illegally? Why is she taking so damn long?

"Did you all have a nice time in Mexico?" she asks.

"We sure did," Charlie says.

Oh. My. God. Are we really going to have to make small talk?

"Where did you all go?"

"We were in Ensenada," Charlie answers evenly. He doesn't even sound stressed. Thank God for Charlie because I'm not sure the rest of us could have pulled it off. I'm tempted to lunge out the window, place my hands around the woman's neck, and scream, *Let. Us. Go.*

"Love Ensenada. I go there every chance I get," the woman says. "Did you make it to the beach?"

Are. You. Kidding. Me?

"Sure did. It was lovely," Charlie replies, meeting her chipper and raising her one.

"Be sure to come back and visit."

"We sure will," Charlie says.

"Okay, folks, you're free to go." Finally, she ushers us through.

I gulp air. I feel light-headed from holding my breath.

We pass through the extensive border area, and then we're in California, heading onto the 405 Freeway. The long slog is over, and we instantly speed up as if shot out of a cannon. We all let out a huge sigh of relief. Will and Lily high-five, which ranks fairly close to the top of all the strange things that have happened today.

"You just might make it," Juan shouts from the back. Juan? I forgot about him.

And all of a sudden the dark cloud that had settled over the car lifts. Lily has opened her eyes and come out of hibernation. Will is perched forward like an alert puppy.

Lily's phone, still clutched in my hand, buzzes with an incoming text from Mom.

WHERE ARE YOU? I KNOW YOU'RE NOT WITH WILL. I TALKED TO HIS MOM LAST NIGHT. I CALLED THE POLICE AND PUT OUT A MISSING PERSON'S REPORT. WHY HAVEN'T YOU TEXTED UNTIL NOW?

Uh-oh! I'm in trouble six ways to Sunday.

"My mom knows I didn't spend the night at your house," I say to Will. "She talked to your mom."

"Shit!"

"Tell me about it." Jesus. A missing person's report?

KYLIE: IT'S A LONG STORY. I'M FINE. ON MY WAY BACK FROM ENSENADA.

MOM: ENSENADA?! MEXICO? HOW COULD YOU JEOPARDIZE GRADUATION?

KYLIE: I DIDN'T DO IT ON PURPOSE. UR GOING TO HAV TO TRUST ME ON THIS. I MADE A MISTAKE. BUT I'M FINE AND I'LL MEET U AT GRADUATION.

MOM: YOU'VE GOT A LOT OF EXPLAINING TO DO. AND YOU'RE GROUNDED.

I can't believe Mom and I are having this discussion right now, via text message. But for once, I don't feel like backing down. I always back down with Mom.

KYLIE: I KNOW. BUT U HAV TO BELIEVE I KNOW WHAT I'M DOING. OTHERWISE, HOW CAN U TRUST ME TO GO ALL THE WAY ACROSS THE COUNTRY IN 2 MONTHS?

384

MOM: I THOUGHT YOU KNEW WHAT YOU WERE DOING BUT NOW I'M NOT SO SURE. YOU RAN OFF TO MEXICO.

KYLIE: THINGS R GOING TO HAPPEN N I'M GOING TO DEAL W THEM THE BEST I CAN. U CAN'T GROUND ME IN NYC.

MOM: WE'LL TALK ABOUT THIS AFTER GRADUATION.

KYLIE: I LOVE U. TELL JAKE I'M ALMOST THERE.

MOM: I LOVE YOU TOO. GOOD LUCK.

Now wasn't the time to tell my mom that I may not make graduation. She was already pissed enough. Charlie has been going ninety, as promised, for the past several minutes. He's looking nervous and his hands have a death grip on the wheel. I kind of wish I were driving. I'm definitely better at it. But this is hardly the time to switch drivers.

Everyone is calling and texting their parents to let them know they'll meet them at school. It's still kind of unlikely we'll make it anytime soon. But at least we'll make it. And then I hear a loud, wailing police siren fast approaching. I look out my window and see a police car directly behind us.

"Shit, we're getting pulled over for speeding," Charlie says.

Naturally, my good luck has run out. It lasted for a whole five minutes.

CHAPTER FIFTY-FIVE

"Take a deep breath. You only got one shot. Make it count."

—QUANTUM OF SOLACE

max:

Charlie pulls over to the side, and the police car pulls up behind us. The cop gets out of his car and takes what feels like ten years to get to us. I can feel the car empty out of air as we all suck in a deep breath, waiting.

As the cop approaches, Charlie feels around in the glove compartment for everything he knows he will need. Charlie and I have been here before—last year, to be exact. Charlie got a speeding ticket. We must have been going eighty-five in a forty mph zone. His dad had it expunged from his record, but he was beyond pissed and threatened to take Charlie's car away if he got another one. Looks like that's about to happen.

"Goddamnit," Charlie says, loud enough for us all to hear. He's freaking, thinking this could mean no more car. I feel for him. Everyone else is freaking, thinking this means no graduation as the minutes tick away. I can see Kylie in the front seat, chewing on her thumb, staring blankly at her closed computer. This is her big day and it's all gone horribly wrong. I feel for her. Lily's big blue eyes fill with tears as she looks out the window and into the nothingness of the San Diego landscape. I feel for her too. Man, I'm feeling a little too much. I liked it better when I was shutting out the world.

"What are we going to do?" Will asks.

"Dunno; what we can do?" Kylie says.

"We're sort of screwed," Lily says. "It's eleven forty-five. There's no way we're getting to graduation at this point."

"Are you aware you were going eighty-seven?" the cop asks Charlie.

"Uh, I'm not aware of the exact speed, but I know it was pretty fast," Charlie offers.

"Can I see your license and registration?" Before he's even done asking for it, Charlie hands the papers to him through the window.

The silence in the car is oppressive. Even Will doesn't have a snarky comment. I look around and realize that everyone has given up. So this is the way we spend graduation? Waiting for a cop to write out a speeding ticket? This blows. I can't let it happen. I suddenly feel responsible, like I've got to do something. I don't really have a solid plan when I open the door and jump out of the car.

"Excuse me, sir," I say to the cop. I'm winging it here.

Which is probably a terrible idea when you're trying to sweet-talk a police officer.

"Please remain in the vehicle," the cop tells me. I know the drill. I should just get back in the "vehicle." But I don't.

"Can I just have one minute of your time to explain, sir?" I am determined, in a way I rarely am, to make one last attempt to get us to graduation. Not even really for me, because I've lost all interest. But I know Kylie hasn't. And Lily hasn't. And my dad hasn't.

"Let me see your license," the cop says to me. "If you don't get back in the car, I could take you in for obstruction."

Shit. I'm in over my head here.

"Dude, what are you doing? Get back in the car," Charlie pleads.

I hand over my license. I should just calmly climb back into the Jeep. But a force beyond my control is pushing me forward. Yeah, it was definitely better when I didn't give a shit.

The cop looks to be in his forties or fifties. I see a wedding ring on his finger.

"Do you have kids, sir?" I ask the cop.

"Excuse me?"

"It's just, if you have kids, then you know how important high school graduation is. To them and to you."

"Yeah, I've got three kids." That's all he says.

"Today's our graduation. Right now, in fact. And we're late. We went to Mexico last night and now we're on our way back to school, but we got stuck at the border. Our parents are waiting there for us. Our relatives. Our whole class. See that girl in the front seat?" I point to Kylie. I'm whipping through sentences, keeping my fingers crossed. I have no idea what I'm doing. "She's the valedictorian. She's supposed to be speaking right now. That's why we were speeding—"

"That doesn't mean you can break the law," he says.

"I know, sir."

"Everyone always has a good excuse for speeding. But there's an enforced speed limit for a reason. You weren't driving at a safe speed. It's not safe for you or other people on the road. Graduation or no graduation, I can't let you get away with it."

"I know," I say. At this point, I'm giving up. I'm not getting the sense I'm making any progress with this guy. He's had a million people try to talk their way out of a speeding ticket. Why did I think this was going to work? I'm not even doing a good job.

The cop stares me down, "Can you get back in the car, son?"

"Yes, sir," I say. I climb back into the Jeep. I shouldn't have gotten out in the first place.

The cop begins to write up our ticket, which is when Lily pops open the door and jumps out. Oh, no. Bad idea.

"We're late because we were doing our civic duty," Lily announces to the cop.

"Get back in the vehicle, miss," the cop says.

Lily doesn't move. "We helped catch some thieves in Ensenada."

"Sure you did. Could you get back in the vehicle?" The officer rolls his eyes; he's heard it all before.

"Seriously. We helped the police arrest two dangerous criminals. Juan, could you get out here?" Lily demands.

389

"As I've already explained to your friend, I can't make any exceptions here."

Juan scrambles out of the rear seat, dives over the middle row, and clambers out of the car, like he's at Lily's service or something. She has that effect on people.

"Can you get your friend, the police chief of Ensenada on the phone?" Lily asks Juan. "And could you have him tell"— Lily leans in and reads the officer's name tag. The officer scowls at her, not pleased with whatever her game is—"Officer Kwan, here, how we helped catch the criminals, the ones who stole thousands of dollars of merchandise from your jurisdiction, actually, from the San Diego area." Lily looks at Officer Kwan with a knowing nod, like she's happy to be so informative.

"I'm going to ask you one last time to get back in the vehicle. Or I'm going to have to take you all in to the station."

Lily crosses her arms and stands her ground. Shit. We're all going to end up in jail. Juan takes out his phone and dials. He says a few words in Spanish and then hands the phone over to Officer Kwan.

Officer Kwan looks at the phone like he's being handed a dead pigeon. He doesn't dare take it.

"Please, sir. It's the police chief from Ensenada. Will you just talk to him for a minute?" Juan pleads, pushing the phone on him. "He'll explain everything."

Officer Kwan stares down at Juan. There's a long beat where we all wait anxiously to see what Officer Kwan will do. Slowly, reluctantly, he takes the phone and dubiously puts it to his ear. He turns away from us, walks a few feet down the road, and listens for what seems like hours. Time moves in slow motion as we all keep our eyes on the officer, wondering what happens next. Finally, Officer Kwan heads back our way, talking on his radio.

"I need a Suburban. Now. Any in the area?" Officer Kwan says. "Okay, send it."

He walks back over, hands the phone to Juan, and approaches Charlie, who's still sitting in the driver's seat.

"So what time is graduation?" he asks Charlie.

"It's at noon, sir," Charlie says. I don't think I've ever heard Charlie use the word "sir."

"Where is it?"

"Freiburg Academy. La Jolla," Lily answers.

"You kids are in a real pickle, huh?"

"Yes, sir," Charlie responds.

"Okay, it's gonna be tight, but we'll see what we can do."

And just at that moment, a huge black-and-white police van screeches to the curb right behind us, and stops. With caged windows and massive bolt locks on the back doors, it's like an armored vehicle. Scratch that—it *is* an armored vehicle. It's the kind of van police use to transport large numbers of prisoners to jail. I remember Mr. Dewhurst calling it a paddy wagon in history class. Shit. Is this the way we're going to arrive at graduation?

"Get in the vehicle, kids," Officer Kwan instructs us. "It's the only one big enough that's available right now. Officer Spittani is going to drive you back to school. If you have a shot in hell of getting to graduation at all, you're going to have to leave the driving up to us. I'll have someone bring your car around later."

391

Without saying much of anything, probably because we're too much in shock, we all file into the van. There are rusted benches on either side, and as Officer Kwan shuts the heavy metal doors at the back, Charlie, Lily, and I settle onto one bench while Kylie, Will, and Juan sit on the other, across from us. All we're missing are the handcuffs.

A police officer sits in the driver's seat. This is obviously Officer Spittani. He turns and talks to us through the wire cage that separates the front from the cargo area.

"You kids ready to rock and roll? Seat belts on, we're gonna go pretty fast."

Officer Kwan waves as we peel out and back onto the highway, sirens blaring.

Despite the minor detail that we will be arriving at school looking a lot like common criminals, I am psyched. Because we actually might make it in time for graduation. The mood starts to shift.

"I don't believe it," Charlie says. "Juan, you the man."

"I try," Juan offers, smiling.

Will reaches over and squeezes Lily's shoulder, "You rock, Lily Wentworth. Even though you can be a huge beyatch, I feel like kissing you."

"Yeah, don't push it, Bixby," Lily says.

Kylie looks at me and smiles for the first time since Manuel's house. "Thanks," she says.

"I didn't do anything," I say. "It was all Lily and Juan."

"You tried. Thanks for that. And thanks, Lily," Kylie says. She and Lily lock eyes for a minute. I'm sure a million thoughts are exchanged between them in those six seconds. Things I'll never understand.

"You're welcome. Now, do your part and rock out that speech. Make us pay attention," Lily says.

"'Kay," is all Kylie offers.

We all sit back, glued to our seats by the sheer force of velocity. The siren blasts. Red-and-white beams flash and whirl from the top of the van as we speed through San Diego at light speed.

CHAPTER FIFTY-SIX

"Sand is overrated.
It's just tiny little rocks."
—ETERNAL SUNSHINE OF
THE SPOTLESS MIND

jake:

"**C**heck it out, buddy," Dad says, pointing to Kylie's name in the program. I already saw it. She's the thirty-fifth name on the list. I looked for it as soon as we got the programs. Her name is also listed on the front, as valedictorian. And on page six, under *Honors*.

According to the program, Kylie gives her speech and then the headmaster and then the commencement speaker, who is some guy named John Block. Then, I think, they name all the seniors, and people come up and get their diplomas.

Last night, I decided I wasn't coming to graduation. I didn't care about seeing Kylie. I stopped wanting to see her at

9:15 p.m. when I found out she lied to us. She's never done that before. Mom said she must have a really good reason. Mom told me that if I didn't come, Kylie would be disappointed. I didn't care. But then I woke up this morning and I wanted to see her again. She still wasn't home so I decided to come to graduation.

Mom made me put on my khaki pants and my blue blazer and a tie. My neck feels really big in this tie. I want to take it off and throw it in the bushes. But Mom would be mad. It's my only tie. My sunglasses keep slipping down my nose.

When we got here Kylie wasn't here. We've been waiting twenty-eight minutes and she still isn't here. Mom says she's on her way. We're sitting on foldout chairs on the big lawn near the library. All the graduating seniors are sitting in foldout chairs across the lawn. Almost all the chairs have filled up, but there are still five empty chairs. One of them must be Kylie's.

"Do you think Kylie's coming?" I ask Mom.

"Of course she is," Mom says. Mom and Dad keep looking at each other. They're worried about Kylie. They're wondering why she's not here. Just like me.

If I were graduating from high school I would be the very first one in my chair.

Why is she taking so long? She's never away from home. And now it feels like she's never home. I guess this is what it's going to feel like when she goes away to college. I don't like it. I'm going to miss her. A whole lot.

There's a guy on the stage who keeps tapping the microphone. This horrible screeching sound is coming out of it that makes me want to put my fingers in my ears, but I know Mom doesn't like when I do that. She says it's disrespectful. I hope he fixes it.

Dad made us stop on the way here to buy some flowers for Kylie. I got to choose them. I picked out yellow roses with these tiny white flowers mixed in. I've been holding them for forty-six minutes. They're starting to wilt because it's really hot. They probably should be in water. I'm afraid they're going to die. I keep spitting on them to keep them wet, but I don't think it's working.

I am wearing two watches—one digital on my left arm and one analog on my right arm—and they both say the same time, 12:16. Where is Kylie? The headmaster takes the stage. People applaud. I don't. I can't. I'm still holding the flowers.

"Welcome, everyone," the headmaster says. "Sorry to get started a little late; we were just giving our graduation speaker some extra time. We're not quite sure where she is."

He's talking about Kylie. He's wondering about her, too, just like me and Mom and Dad. I look for Will. I don't see him, either. They must be together. I don't know anyone else to look for. What if Kylie never comes? What if they call her to give her speech and she's still not here? I wonder what will happen.

I hear a police siren. It's loud and getting louder, coming closer and closer. I stand up and look out at the street. A police van stops in front of the school. Everyone is turning around in their seats and staring at it. It's practically on the lawn. A police officer climbs out of the front seat and goes around to the back to open the doors. That's when Kylie gets out.

CHAPTER FIFTY-SEVEN

"The number one fear of people isn't dying; it's public speaking."
—AMERICAN GANGSTER

kylie:

The van screeches to a stop outside of Freiburg, careering over the sidewalk and onto the lawn. Officer Spittani gets out and unlocks the door for us. I'm about to jump out when Lily grabs my hand, stopping me.

"What?" I ask her.

"Just wait a minute." Lily pulls a tube of lipstick out of her bag. Expertly, she dots my cheeks and lips, rubbing in the color with the focus of a makeup artist. She runs her hands through my hair, fluffing my curls. And then she takes out hand lotion, using it to smooth away flyaways.

"Okay. Go," Lily instructs. "Do this thing."

"'Kay, thanks . . ." I say, too thrown to say much else.

I scramble out of the police van and burst onto the lawn to find my entire graduating class, their friends and family, staring at me. Shit. What an entrance. Not exactly what I was going for. I was kind of hoping to just walk up to the podium quietly, no spotlight, and plow through my mediocre speech as quickly as possible. But that's all gone to hell.

Max, Charlie, Lily, Will, and Juan stumble out after me. We all stand motionless for a moment. Shock and awe is probably the best way to describe our communal reaction. We stare out at the audience. They stare back at us. I try to spot Jake, Mom, and Dad in the crowd, but can't find them.

I can only imagine what everyone is thinking. I'm wearing the bright fuchsia Mexican wedding dress. Will has his Carhartt overalls on, and Max, Lily, and Charlie give new meaning to graduation casual in their shorts, jeans, and T-shirts. Lily has got to be bummed she didn't have time to change. She's always got the perfect outfit for every social occasion. This is nowhere near graduation chic. And, of course, we've all just climbed out of a police van most often used to transport prisoners, not graduating seniors.

Headmaster Alvarez marches toward us, and to say he doesn't look happy would be understating it by a mile.

"What is going on here, Officer? Is there a problem?" Alvarez asks Officer Spittani, who, as it turns out, is a man of very few words. He didn't say a thing the entire way to school, but he did haul ass, getting us here in record time. He's clearly a man of action.

"No problem at all. The kids just needed a little help getting to graduation on time," Officer Spittani replies. He turns to us. "Good luck, guys. And congratulations."

We all offer up an earnest round of thanks. Officer Spittani hops back into the van and drives off, leaving us with Alvarez.

"Anyone care to explain?" Alvarez asks.

I'm groping for something helpful to say, because that's what I do; I'm the good girl who plays by the rules, the teacher's pet. I'm about to apologize and prostrate myself in front of Alvarez and my whole class in the vain hope that it will somehow wipe away the stink of the current situation, when I hear my name being called.

I turn and see Jake, his head above the sea of faces. He's climbed up on his chair and is waving both his arms in the air, yelling out my name. Just seeing his face and hearing his voice gives me an incredible rush of happiness. Mom and Dad stand up, flanking him. They wave to me. They may be pissed, but they're keeping it under the hood, and I'm grateful. I decide to forget about Alvarez. Screw it. I'm tired of being the good girl. I rush toward Jake.

Before I can get to him, he leaps off his chair and runs toward me at full speed. He comes at me so fast, I go down, with him landing on top of me.

"Kylie, you made it," Jake says.

"Of course I made it, Jakie. You didn't think I'd miss my own graduation?"

"You're sixteen minutes late."

"I know. I wish I'd gotten here on time."

"I missed you, Kylie."

"I missed you too, Jakie. Were you okay last night?"

"Yeah. Dad and I went for pizza."

"Dad?" I say, though I'm less surprised than I would have been two days ago. I know there's more to Dad than meets the eye.

Headmaster Alvarez approaches. "Kylie, you might have this little family reunion some other time. We've got five hundred people waiting."

"Right," I say.

He hands me a cap and robe. "You're going to need this."

"Thanks." I throw it all on, take my computer out of my backpack, hand the backpack to Jake, and make my way to the stage with Alvarez.

This is it. My speech. The biggest moment of my life. Shit.

I'm just going to read it as fast as I can and then get off the stage. One speech, one day, who cares? One speech, one day, who cares? That's my mantra and I'm sticking with it, in an attempt to push out all the bad juju that's forming.

Will rushes up to me and falls in step beside me.

"How we doin'?" Will asks.

"No comment."

"Shut up. You're going to blow everyone away."

"No comment," I say again, because I seriously don't even know what to tell Will. I love him for trying to boost me up when I need it most, but I don't want to tell him how hopeless the whole endeavor is.

Alvarez, Will, and I stop at the stage. Will takes both my hands in his.

"'I don't wanna kill anybody. But if I gotta get out that door, and you're standing in my way, one way or the other—'"

400

"'—you're gettin' outta my way,'" I say, finishing the line from *Reservoir Dogs*.

"Get up there and kill it," Will says, hugging me. "You look smokin'. And you just spent the night with Max Langston. Own it."

"'Kay, I'll try," I say, wishing I had Will's attitude instead of my own wilting faith in things.

As Alvarez and I head toward the stage, Lily and Charlie, robes and caps on, rush by en route to their seats. Max is behind them. He pauses. Our eyes meet. And in one look, in that single moment, I realize that last night meant something to him. What, I'm not exactly sure, and I don't have time to contemplate it as Alvarez guides me to the lectern.

And then, here I am. On the stage. All alone. Hundreds of people look up at me, waiting. Here goes nothing. . . .

I place my computer on the lectern and look down at the speech. I take a deep breath, tuck my curls behind my ears, lick my lips, open and shut my eyes once, twice. I'm buying time, but it's not cheap. I'm paying a stiff price.

I hear the crowd shifting in their seats. I'm already losing them. I will myself to jump in. Say it. Read what I've written. No one cares. It's one day, one speech. It doesn't matter. I look up and out at the crowd. I see Lacey Garson lean over and whisper something to Sonia Smithson. Sonia rolls her eyes and laughs. Okay, I cannot just stand here any longer. I have to do something.

"Golda Meir once said, 'Create the kind of self that you will be happy to live with all your life. Make the most of yourself by fanning the tiny, inner sparks of possibility into flames of

401

achievement.' Today is the day we create ourselves. The decisions we make from now on will impact the rest of our lives, other people's lives, the world. Every generation is handed the torch . . ."

My voice fades. I'm not feeling this at all. It's not what I want to say. It may only be one day and it may not matter to anyone else, but I've got to say something meaningful to me, or die trying. Otherwise, what's the point?

I glance up from the computer screen and, somehow, miraculously, in the crowd, my eyes find Max. He's looking right at me, which I suppose is to be expected. Everyone is looking at me. I'm the valedictorian speaker and I've stopped speaking. It's not normal. But then again, people expect that from me. Crazy Kylie, living up to my reputation. Maybe that's all I'll ever be to them, but I want to be more, if not for them, then for me, Jake, Mom, and Dad. I want to prove that what I'm made of is more interesting than crazy and brainy.

Max's focus hasn't swayed from the stage. As everyone around him starts whispering among themselves, wondering what the hell I'm doing, his eyes remain on me. His chin lifts ever so slightly, willing me to go on. He mouths, "You can do it." And while he may be five hundred feet away, I feel him like he's standing next to me. My face flushes. A shudder pulses through me. I want to be in his arms. I love him. I hate him. He's a prince. An asshole. My soul mate. The bane of my existence. Shit. This is no time to try to work through this.

I look at Max. He's right. I *can* do this, provided I haven't lost the crowd at this point. I have plenty to say even though none of it is in my carefully crafted speech. The murmur from the crowd builds to a low roar. I can see Alvarez getting up

402

from his seat and walking toward me. He's ready to shut me down. No need, dude, I'm on it.

I clear my throat into the microphone. The noise dies down. Okay, let's do this.

"That was the beginning of the speech I had prepared for today. I spent the past three months writing it. You might have really liked it. The problem is, I didn't. It was full of pithy quotes from brilliant people and sage advice I'd gleaned from books, but it didn't feel very authentic. It's stuff I'm supposed to say, not stuff I want to say. The truth is, I don't have any answers for you today. All I have are questions because, like you, I don't have a clue what's ahead for us. I could tell you that the best is yet to come; time and tide wait for no one; you'll accomplish great things; life is what you make it; we have the power to change the world; do what you love, the rest will follow; individuality is the key to success, blah, blah, blah. But you've heard it all before, and if you haven't, it'll probably roll right over you. Because, really, what does any of that mean to a high school senior? All you want to do is get out of here and start partying. Am I right?"

A loud roar goes up from the seniors. Headmaster Alvarez has sat down, but he's perched on the edge of his chair, wavering, wondering if he should get back up and give me the hook.

CHAPTER FIFTY-EIGHT

"You are hanging on by a very thin thread, and I dig that about you."
—JERRY MAGUIRE

max:

Kylie pauses as people yell out their approval. They weren't expecting it, but they liked that last line. She looks surprised by the reaction. It's funny, she's spent six years hiding away from everyone, and now she's putting it all out there at the very last possible moment. People think they know her, but they're about to discover, like me, that they don't know her at all.

"Whoa, girl is losing it," Carl Krauss says, who's sitting to my left. "Get ready to watch self-destruction begin. Should be fun." What an asshole. Jessica Littleton, who's on my right, laughs at Carl, a little too loud and a little too long. I know she's just trying to get my attention, but it's annoying. She's been trying to get my attention for twelve years.

Whenever we're alphabetically ordered, it's Carl, me, and Jessica. This is the last time we'll be together. Despite the fact that I'm not into either of them, I find myself missing them. Or the idea of them. I mean, it's all over now, and it suddenly seems really sad. Maybe we'll all sit together at our twenty-fifth reunion, for old time's sake. We'll bring our spouses and kids, we'll fly in from wherever, pass around our business cards, show photos of the vacation home, the boat. Shit. Will that be me? Is that what I want? I look into the future and I don't like the scene that's set there. Kylie's right: hobbies are for wimps. I don't want to be the guy who plays golf on the weekends, works my ass off all day in a job I'm not digging, and has to have two martinis every night to dull the pain.

The noise dies down; people are ready for more, but Kylie just stares out at us, quiet. She seems frozen. I hope she's got a second act. It may have been a good start, but she can't just leave it there. A few seconds pass, Kylie's still not revving it up. Damn, what's happening? Is she backing down? I have to stop myself from rushing the stage and walking her out of here. It's the wrong plan—she wouldn't want it and it wouldn't do any good. I just have to hope she can pull it together and continue. I'm breathing hard, like I'm right up there on the stage with her. I know Kylie can do this. *Think, think,* I try to convey to her even though she's not looking my way. *You know what you want to say, Kylie. Don't give up.*

People are getting impatient. Someone throws a paper airplane, made from a program, at Kylie. It lands at her feet.

"Why'd she stop talking?" Carl asks.

"Maybe she remembered what a loser she is and that no one cares what she has to say," Jessica says.

Carl and Jessica bump fists. I feel my face getting hot.

"Shut up," I say. "She's not a loser. She's way cool. So don't talk shit about her."

Jessica and Carl look at me like I've sprouted horns. And maybe I have. I don't know why I care so freaking much about this girl. It certainly doesn't seem like she feels the same way about me.

"What's it matter to you what we say about Crazy Kylie?" Carl asks.

"It just does, dude. So don't say it. And she's not crazy."

"'Kay," Carl says. He shuts up and turns away.

He may have gotten a soccer scholarship to UCSB, but he's still a douche bag, and he doesn't want to get on my bad side before Charlie's party tonight.

Alvarez is freaking out. He must be wondering how this could be happening to him. Kylie Flores seemed like the surest thing ever as valedictorian. Who would think she'd go off the rails now? Alvarez stands and approaches Kylie. Is he going to walk her off the stage? But just as he gets to her, Kylie leans in to the microphone.

"I've spent the past six years at Freiburg working incredibly hard. And I did well. Super well in school. Better than all of you. I mean, I'm standing here, and you're not, so I must have done something right. I certainly did everything I was supposed to do. And more. I never got a B, I aced my SATs, and got a full ride to a top college, but I spent all of my time at Freiburg in the library, not talking to anyone. I'm not sure that was

406

the best way to go. When you over-prepare and micromanage everything, there's no time for spontaneity. No time for life to play out. Life is something we have to experience, really feel, not just study for with books in a library. Learning is about so much more than school. If we're too busy studying, we miss out on the experience. What I've only just realized is that I've been missing out. And I don't want to do that anymore!"

Kylie is rallying. I feel a huge sense of relief. Maybe she's going to pull this one out of the hat. Just in case she doesn't, Alvarez stands nervously by her side. He's not taking any more chances.

"In the past twenty-four hours, I've learned more about myself and my potential than I learned in all my years at Freiburg. With my apologies to Headmaster Alvarez."

Kylie glances at the headmaster, who looks like his head is about ready to explode. This is not the kind of speech a headmaster hopes for. This is the kind of speech they fire head-masters for.

"As I said, I don't have a lot of advice. But I do have a few suggestions. Sometimes having no script, having no idea what is going to happen next, having no map, might be the way to go. Because life just happens, and when it does, how you handle it will teach you more about who you are than any class or test ever can. The best preparation for the rest of your life is, maybe, no preparation at all. Dive right in. Make mistakes. Break a few rules. Wing it.

"Figuring out what you want comes from failing, and then trying again. It comes from questioning everything, falling in love, fighting the power, living without limits. It doesn't come from getting straight A's, playing by the rules, and listening obediently."

Kylie glances over at Headmaster Alvarez. He looks ready to kill her. "I'm sure Headmaster Alvarez isn't exactly pleased with everything I'm saying. It's not what he expected. It's not what I intended. But let me just add, I'm not saying don't plan for your future and don't work hard. I'm just saying, don't let that be all you do. Because that's not enough. Trust me, I've been there. And I have no plans to go back. Things are happening right now, right here, and if you're not in the mix, you're missing out. Who's with me?"

"I am," people call out, one after the other. Kylie's got the crowd in a way I never would have imagined. In a way she never did during school. I see her lips curl into a grin. She's into it, living her moment. She takes the microphone out of the stand. She looks comfortable on the stage, relaxed. Alvarez, not so much. I don't think he likes the freewheeling microphone thing. He looks like he wants to snatch it from her clutches, but she takes a few steps away from him.

"So, kiss the girl. Buy the dress. Take a vacation. Join the circus. Order the fried frog legs. Try out for the play. Learn to snowboard. Do something that scares the shit out of you. Or something that makes you happy. Or something that makes you cry. Whatever it is, do something that makes you feel something. Because feeling nothing is no way to go through life."

I'm watching Kylie, I'm listening, and all of a sudden, I don't want to disappoint her. I don't want to disappoint myself. I am overwhelmed by a love for this girl I barely know. I wish she felt the same.

408

CHAPTER FIFTY-NINE

"Maybe I come on too strong, but . . . I don't know who else to be. I just have to put my whole heart into things."
—JOHN TUCKER MUST DIE

will:

I can't believe Kylie is still talking. And talking. Off the cuff, saying what she feels, no filter. No editing. It's so not her. And I'm eating it up. Every last word. There's so much take-away I don't have enough doggy bags for it all.

"I've spent a lot of time watching movies. Maybe too much time. I've convinced myself I'm going to be a screenwriter, and while it's more likely that I'll end up selling popcorn at the Regal Cinema on Osprey, I don't care. I'm going for it. Against all odds. Despite what anyone says. I plan to write myself a

409

rocking lead role in life. Chances are, the movie of my life won't get made. But I don't want to think about that now. My recommendation is that you don't either. Write yourself a kick-ass movie to star in, and don't listen to what anyone says. At least not right now. Now is the time to try. It might feel like we have forever. But the sad truth is, we don't. And we won't always feel this optimistic about the future. So, go for it. Before there's too much standing in your way."

"Sing it, sister," I shout out. "That's my girl up there!" I tell everyone sitting within twenty feet.

"Jesus, Bixby, you just screamed in my ear! Can you shut up, please," Patrick Bains says to me.

"Stuff it, Bains," I say. I've sat next to Patrick Bains in every single assembly since first grade and I am so sick of him I could puke. He's been president of the student council three years running, and so full of himself it's criminal for a guy with an inexcusable lack of fashion savvy and a pretty serious case of halitosis. I can't wait to never see his mug again.

"What is your problem?" Patrick asks me.

"You are my problem," I say, and then I turn back to Kylie and yell: "I. LOVE. YOU. KYLIE!"

" 'I didn't invent the rainy day, man. I just own the best umbrella,' " Kylie says. "That's one of my favorite lines of all time. It's from a movie called *Almost Famous*. I think what it means is that life is going to throw all kinds of stuff at you, good and bad. But all you can do is get out there and try to stay dry."

I give a big whoop for *Almost Famous* because it's a genius line to quote in a graduation speech. And no one but Kylie would think to use it.

410

Bains glares at me. Dude, you might want to talk to a digestive specialist about that breath problem. It's not going to help you any at college.

"So get a good umbrella, class of 2012! You're going to need it! And congratulations!" With that, Kylie leaves the stage and goes to her seat.

For a second, no one does a thing. There's silence. And then the place erupts in applause. Loud and hard and long. A bunch of people jump to their feet, others follow suit. It's a standing O. Holy. Shit! My girl got herself a standing O! I am so proud of her, my eyes well up and a lump forms in my throat.

Kylie outdid herself. I am whistling and cheering. I can see Max a few rows away, hands in the air, clapping furiously. Juan, who has been sitting near the stage the entire time, is on his feet, fists pumping. My eyes are trained on Kylie as she takes her seat. Her face explodes into a giant grin. Girlfriend knows she nailed it. We all know she nailed it. Take that, Freiburg. Put it in your pipe and smoke it. No more Kylie Flores to kick around.

CHAPTER SIXTY

"Seems like you had a better time in Morocco than you let on."
—WHAT A GIRL WANTS

lily:

I've been watching Max watch Kylie, and I feel like I'm going to throw up. He's way into her, so far down the road there's no turning back. Clearly, something happened in Mexico. Something that changed absolutely everything. Whatever it was, it wasn't just a fling. Max couldn't take his eyes off Kylie in the car, and then during her speech, and even now as she's sitting two rows in front of him. I thought we still had a chance, but I realize now that he's gone, baby, gone. And there's not a thing I can do.

Max keeps glancing over at Kylie as Alvarez speaks. It certainly didn't help things that Kylie managed to miraculously come up with a great valedictorian speech. I mean, it wasn't hard to do; there's not exactly stiff competition. Last year's speaker, Benjy Samuels, fainted halfway through his speech. And the year before that, Emma Ralston showed up wasted. Most of the other speakers in recent history have been so deadly dull, no one remembers what they said. I'm sure we'll barely remember Kylie's tomorrow morning. Still, the standing O was beyond irritating. I am so screwed. Kylie has managed to pull herself out of the abyss of social obscurity just in time for me to fall in.

I notice Luca Sonneban staring at me. He's sitting at the beginning of my row. Can he tell something is going on with Max and Kylie? Is he gauging my reaction to this whole public disaster? Or is he checking me out, as usual? I smile and wave, and he blushes a deep scarlet. It looks good with his perennially tanned skin. He's hot. Funny, I never really noticed. Well, I'm noticing now.

Luca has been crushing on me since ninth grade. He's asked me out at least half a dozen times. I've always said no. He's just not my type—a little too surfer dude, with the long stringy blond hair and the constant board shorts. Enough already. We get it. You surf.

We kissed once at a party in tenth grade. There was waaaay too much tongue. It was slobbery, like making out with my Labradoodle. But he could be trained. And he's got plenty of money. So there's that. The problem is, Stokely has the hots for him, which is unfortunate. Normally I'd steer clear—sisterhood and all that. But things have reached critical mass, and as much as I don't want to hurt Stokely, I need to put myself first.

413

"Congratulations, class of 2012!" Alvarez yells out.

A loud roar goes up from the senior class, and we all jump out of our seats and toss our caps in the air. Big whoop!

I'm so outta here. I stand and make a beeline for Max. We've got business to take care of. I've got to save face, if nothing else. As usual he's surrounded by his loyal posse. It's hard to squeeze my way in, but I do, and the sea parts. Max looks down at me, nervous. He's not even remotely happy to see me. The reality smacks me in the face. This is so not where I live.

"Lil . . . hey," he says. He's palpably uncomfortable.

I'm going to make this so easy for him. He doesn't need to be sweating it.

My eyes scan his face. God, he's gorgeous. I really love him—truly and intensely—in a way I've never loved anyone or anything. Sure, there have been ulterior motives circling around, but my love for him is as pure as it gets with me. I suddenly feel like crying. I don't want to say good-bye, but there's really no choice.

I lean in to Max. I feel his body go rigid. How is it possible things have changed so much in such a short span of time?

"Listen, Lil, we need to talk. How about we go out for lunch—"

"Save it, Max," I say. "We don't need to talk about anything. It's over. I can't forgive you for yesterday. We're done. There's nothing more to say."

Max looks at me like I've just pulled the Astroturf out from under him. *Sorry, Max, I got there first. You can't fire me, I quit.*

"We should talk, Lily. We can't just end things like this."

414

"You should have thought of that last night," I say, my voice starting to quiver.

I will not let him see me cry. I will not give him the satisfaction. I lean in and kiss him on the cheek.

"I'm sorry, Lil. Really sorry . . ." Max says as I turn away swallowing the bitter aftertaste of rejection. I make a beeline for Luca, who's standing nearby, talking to Sam Butterworth.

"Hey, Sonneban," I say, pulling him into a hug. "Congratulations, dude."

"You too, Lil," Luca says, holding me tight, tighter than he probably should, considering, for all he knows, I'm still one of his best friend's girlfriends. This is going to be easy. Like taking candy from a baby.

Stokes walks up as Luca and I are hugging. She stares, waiting for us to release each other. We do, but not before I give him a little peck on the cheek for good measure, sealing the deal.

"You going to Charlie's with anyone tonight?" I ask Luca.

"Uh, not really," Luca says.

"Then how about you pick me up at seven?" I say.

"You're not going with Max?" Luca asks.

"Nope. I'm going with you, if you'll have me."

"Totally," Luca says. He can barely contain his excitement. His smile spreads from ear to ear, like a goofy stuffed animal. I miss Max already.

Stokes pastes on a smile, but I can see the hurt and confusion in her eyes. Why aren't I going to the party with Max? And what am I doing with Luca? I feel bad, but what can I do? Life sucks. I know it only too well.

CHAPTER SIXTY-ONE

"If you're going to let one stupid prick ruin your life . . . you're not the girl I thought you were."
—LEGALLY BLONDE

kylie:

As soon as the ceremony is over, I make my way down the row and look for Max, hoping we can talk before I have to go. He was the first person I wanted to see after finishing my speech. The only person I thought would understand what a feat it was, flying through the air without a net. My hesitations about Max have been washed away by the euphoria of gradua-tion. I want to hug him, congratulate him, hear his voice, feel his touch. I'm craving his company, more than Will or Jake or my parents.

But I'm too late. I can already see the force field building around him. It's a hero's welcome as everyone descends on him. I stand on the periphery and look for a way in. He's surrounded. I can't even make a dent. I catch a glimpse of him and wave. He either doesn't see me or ignores me. What am I doing? Standing here like a fool, begging for affection?

I thought I'd misjudged things this morning, acted too rashly. I was willing to give him a second chance, try again. I thought we were connecting during my speech. I could feel him urging me on, encouraging me. But it was obviously all in my head. He's not looking for me. He's not even thinking about me. He's with Lily and his friends, and I'm just some distant memory. I'm such an idiot. How many times can I fall for the same guy?

I turn and make my way toward the family section when a body slams into me. I almost fall to the ground.

"I love you, man," Will says to me, kissing both my cheeks, repeatedly.

"'I love you too, bud,'" I say.

"'I love you, Bro Montana.'"

"'I love you, homes.'"

"'I love you, Broseph Goebbels.'"

"'I love you, *muchacha*.'"

"'I love you, Tycho Brohe.'"

We both fall back laughing. Juan looks down at us, thoroughly confused. I'm guessing he's not intimately familiar with the dialogue from *I Love You, Man*. Sadly, we are. We've got to get out more. I silently make a vow to do that this summer. Will and I are going to get the hell off the couch and spend some serious time trying to have a social life, as gruesome as that may be. I can't stay inside and watch movies for the rest of my life. I kind of like kissing a little too much to do that. There are plenty of boys in La Jolla; I'm sure I can find someone to practice with before I'm off to NYC.

"You were un-frickin-believable up there, Kyles! I don't know what you had actually written, but it couldn't have been any better than what you said," Will says. "It was seriously mind-blowing. Did you plan any of it?"

"No. I was just kind of rambling off the top of my head."

"You're a superhero. I'm in awe of your powers."

"It didn't sound rambling at all," Juan says. "Best valedictorian speech I've ever heard."

"Wow. Thanks, Juan," I say.

"Truly genius, girlfriend. You're my role model. Always were. Always will be."

"Thanks, Will." I'm getting teary. It's been a day. I am going to miss Will Bixby so much.

"Okay, enough with the sentimental journey. We need a little hair of the dog." I know he's trying to lighten the moment. Will isn't one for waterworks.

"Shut up," I laugh, shoving him.

"Did you talk to Max yet? He's right over there."

"No. And I'm not going to."

"You can't leave things hanging. You two make sense together, regardless of Lily Wentworth's meager existence. If you're not going to do anything, then I am," Will says, obviously eager to stir whatever pot he can get his hands on.

"Will . . . no. Don't do anything. Max and I are—we're nothing. And I don't want you getting involved, do you understand?"

418

"But I know how to fix these things."

"Nothing needs fixing. Stay out of it, Will. Promise me."

"Okay. You have my word."

"Seriously, I don't want to see him again. I just want to move on."

"I get it. We'll find you a better man this summer. Max Langston is in our rearview mirror."

"Kylie, Kylie, Kylie, Kylie." Jake is chanting my name as he rushes toward us.

I open my arms and he runs into my embrace. "Jakie, Jakie, Jakie."

We hold on to each other for a few seconds. With Will standing nearby, it suddenly feels really good to be back on familiar territory, with the people I love. I can live without Max Langston. I can totally live without Max Langston. I've got all I need.

"Aren't you going to say hello to Uncle Will?" Will asks Jake.

Jake disentangles himself from me and looks at Will. "You're not my uncle."

"I know," Will says, pulling Jake into a bear hug. "I'm your stepbrother."

"No. You're not," Jake responds, in all seriousness.

"Right again, Jakie. I'm just boring old Will, Kylie's friend."

Mom and Dad approach.

"Congratulations, sweetie," Mom says. "We're so proud of you."

The two of them encircle me. Their hands are on me, smoothing my hair, touching my face, rubbing my back, petting my shoulders, as though I've been off at war. They finally release me, and I know the questions will start soon. Where have I been? Why am I wearing this crazy dress? I decide to take the lead.

"Mom, Dad, I know I messed up. I'm sorry if you were worried. It was completely unintentional. . . ."

Mom looks at me like she's trying to muster some anger, but she's so busy feeling proud of me that she can't.

"Kylie, we were really scared," Dad says.

Dad, scared? Really?

"When Will's mom said you weren't sleeping over . . . that was not good." Mom looks away like she's going to cry. I feel awful.

"It's all my fault," Will says.

"And how's that, Will?" Mom says. "Care to explain?"

I can practically hear the gears grinding in Will's brain as he tries to come up with some kind of wacky spin that will deftly get me out of my jam. But I don't want him to do that. It's not necessary. I can get myself out of my own mess.

"That's a lie. It's not Will's fault at all. He actually came to my rescue."

"Okay," Mom says, not knowing what to make of all this.

"I'm so sorry. I didn't mean to freak you guys out. It was an accident. A kind of crazy accident that spun wildly out of control."

"You've got quite a bit of explaining to do," Mom says.

"I know," I say. "Can we wait till we get home? And then, I promise, I'll tell you everything."

"I loved the speech, Kyles," Dad says.

"You did? Really?" I ask, because it seems strange coming from him.

"It was from the heart. And beautifully written, as always. Just like everything you've ever written," Dad says.

That last comment really takes me by surprise. I didn't realize Dad had read any of my writing. Man, he can keep some major secrets.

"It was beautiful, sweetie. A little salty at times for my taste, with some of the foul language, but otherwise perfect, really. But that isn't what you've been working on all these months, is it?" Mom asks.

"No. I just kind of winged it. Like I said, the speech I'd been writing didn't really work anymore. All part of the long story."

Headmaster Alvarez waves and saunters over. Is he going to chastise me for my speech? For telling everyone to forget school and live life? I'm sure I must be the biggest disappointment ever.

"Congratulations," he says to my parents, shaking both their hands.

Alvarez turns to me. He puts his hands on my shoulders and looks at me. I cringe inside as I wait for it.

"Great job, Kylie," he says. "I couldn't have said it any better myself. Though I might have put a bit more emphasis on the school part."

"You're not angry?"

"I was a little surprised at first. But it was refreshing to see a different side of you emerge. Maybe someday you'll make it back here and give the commencement speech. I have a feeling you're going to be very famous one day. Just don't forget about us, okay?"

"Never," I say.

And then Alvarez turns to Will. "I like the overalls, Bixby. It's a nice change of pace."

CHAPTER SIXTY-TWO

"Feeling screwed up at a screwed-up time in a screwed-up place does not necessarily make you screwed up."
—PUMP UP THE VOLUME

max:

"Yo, Langs, where you going, G?" Jesse Stern asks me as I brush past him and Charlie.

"Looking for someone," I say.

Charlie doesn't say anything. He knows what I'm doing, who I'm looking for. Thankfully, he doesn't offer his opinion. It took me a while to untangle myself from the crowd, and I'm still reeling from my conversation with Lily, but I have to catch Kylie before she leaves.

"You coming to the beach with us, homes?" Jesse asks. "Gonna catch some breaks."

Jesse Stern, nice Jewish boy from La Jolla who thinks he's a gangster. Wonder if he'll keep up the game at Amherst.

"I'll meet you there. Wanna hang with my dad for a while this afternoon."

"'Kay. Peace out," Jesse says.

I head toward the parking lot. Charlie jogs to catch up with me.

"You think this is a good idea, dude?" he asks. Guess I'm going to hear his opinion, like it or not.

"Honestly, I dunno."

"I can't believe I'm saying this. . . . She's a great girl. But serious. Major serious. The girl is going to want you to commit. You really want to do that this summer?"

"Yeah, I know. It's a lot."

"Maybe let it ride for a while."

"I know that's what I should do. But I don't want to." And then I head for the parking lot, leaving Charlie standing on the lawn.

He's right. I should let it go. I'm moving on from Lily. I haven't been single in almost a year. I should mess around. And I've got a ton of shit to figure out this summer. The last thing I need is to throw myself into a relationship. What am I doing? I stop for a minute and just stare out at the parking lot. Is this a mistake?

I don't think so. I can't get this girl out of my head.

As I step into the parking lot, I see Kylie getting into an old Honda Civic.

"Kylie!" I call out.

She doesn't seem to hear me as she climbs into the car and closes the door. The car pulls out, and I charge after it like a lunatic.

"KYLIE, WAIT . . ." People standing nearby look at me like I've lost my mind. But I don't care.

The car makes a left onto Prospect and picks up speed.

"KYLIE . . . KYLIE . . ." She never turns around. The car disappears around the corner. It's a losing battle. I stop and walk back to the parking lot.

Did she hear me as I was running after her, screaming at the top of my lungs like some pathetic dude from one of those lame chick flicks? I think so. But what can I do about it? Not much. I fucked up this morning.

I wander back through the parking lot. People look at me out of the corner of their eyes, wondering what's up. What's up is I've fallen for a girl who just majorly blew me off. That was humiliating, everyone. I get it, trust me. I've crossed over into this other world where I'm doing things I never would have done in the world I come from.

I'm making my way back to campus when Luca Sonneban approaches me.

"Hey, Max. How's it going?"

I like Luca; he's been a buddy for years, but I'm not really in the mood to shoot the shit right now.

"Pretty good."

Luca looks down at his feet and thrusts his hands into his pockets.

"I was just making sure you're cool, you know, with me and Lily."

What? I have no idea what he's talking about.

"You and Lily?"

"Uh, yeah. We're gonna go to Charlie's party tonight. I thought, I don't know, I thought you knew. You guys broke up, right?"

How is it possible that in the span of twenty minutes Lily and I broke up, the news traveled around the world, and she and Luca are now together? Whatever. The truth is I don't care. At least I know she'll be okay tonight. I don't have to worry about her.

"Yeah, we broke up. She's all yours, man."

"Okay, cool, 'cause I wouldn't want to—"

"We're cool, Luca, don't worry." I just want him to go away.

"All right, I'll catch you later." Luca shuffles off, relieved, I'm sure.

I pull out my phone to text Kylie. One last play. And then I remember her phone's dead. Damn. Why must this be so hard? Maybe it's not meant to be. What happens in Mexico stays in Mexico.

I see Will, Juan, two younger girls who must be Will's sisters, and their parents getting into a massive Range Rover. That is some serious gas the Bixbys are guzzling.

"Hey, Will," I say. "Did I ever thank you for coming to Mexico?"

"Not that I can recall," Will says.

"Thanks, man. Appreciate it."

"Well, it didn't do much good since I couldn't actually give you a ride home."

"Doesn't matter. It was cool of you to come."

"I did it for Kylie."

"I know."

"You know, Max, I saw your photographs. . . ."

"Where?"

"In your room. When I was getting your passport. You're good. Annoyingly good."

"Dude, you snooped through my room?"

"Yeah, sorry."

"Will . . ." Juan chastises.

"I know. I shouldn't have. And I'm sorry about the mirror."

"What mirror?"

"You'll see it when you get home," Will promises.

Great. Can't wait. Man, Will Bixby is a freak.

"I like her, Will," I blurt out. Because, really, why else would I be standing here talking to him? It's not like we bonded in Mexico. I need help and he's the guy. Plain and simple.

"I know," he says. And that's it.

I wait for a minute, but he doesn't say anything else. Damn, I am really having to work for it here. This is not my thing. So not my thing.

"What should I do, man? I don't know what to do. Tell me what to do. . . ." I'm getting a little desperate. I know he can hear it in my voice. I need to pull it back. Get my shit together. This girl is running me through the ringer. I'm starting to think I don't need this. Or her. Or her crazy friend.

Suddenly Will lets out a long beeping sound. What the hell?

"'At the beep, please leave your name, number, and a brief justification for the ontological necessity of modern man's

427

existential dilemma, and we'll get back to you,'" Will says.

"I'm sorry, but what are you talking about?" I ask. Dude is completely mental.

"It's a line from *Reality Bites*," Will says.

"Uh . . . okay."

"The thing is, Max, I can't say anything. I promised her I'd stay out of it. I swore to it, and my allegiance is to her. Not to you."

"Stay out of what?"

"Anything having to do with the two of you. She says she wants to move on."

"Do you think she means it?"

"My lips are sealed."

"Will, are you ready to go? We're late for lunch," Will's mom says, leaning her head out of the car.

"Yeah. Ready," Will says. "Look, Max, I'm sorry. Truly. I would love nothing more than to get involved, but I can't break my promise." And with that, Will climbs into the car.

"A pleasure meeting you," Juan says, and then jumps into the Range Rover after Will.

I'm at the end of the line here. I don't know what more I can do except go home and see my dad.

CHAPTER SIXTY-THREE

"I never realize how much I like being home unless I've been somewhere really different for a while."
—JUNO

kylie:

"**G**ot it," I say as I kick the ball toward the makeshift goal.

Dad expertly blocks my shot and sends the ball sailing back to Jake. We're actually playing soccer together. It's pretty mind-bendingly weird. Granted, it was my idea and I practically had to drag Dad into the backyard to get him to do it, but once we were here, he was into it. Maybe that's what I should have been doing all along, forcing Dad, kicking and screaming, to pay attention

429

to us. I've been letting him set the pace all these years when what he really needed was for someone else to shove him out of his own way. It's hard to ignore the similarities between us.

Dad's wearing the yellow soccer jersey from Manuel. He stared at it for about ten minutes when I first pulled it out of my backpack, and then he disappeared into the bathroom for a while. When he came back out, he was wearing the jersey.

I told Dad and Mom all about the stolen computer, Ensenada, and Manuel. I left out some of the grittier details, but I did mention Max here and there. I played it down because I don't need the third degree. Dad didn't want to talk much about the accident. So I let it rest. For now.

The mere fact that he and Jake made it through a long evening together (okay, Jake did run away, but at least Dad found him), in which they went out to dinner, without Mom, is a huge relief. Dad probably isn't ever going to be this warm and fuzzy guy, but today is already better than yesterday, and maybe tomorrow will be better than today. At least I know why Dad is damaged, and I don't feel the same antipathy toward him.

Jake stops the ball with his foot, picks it up, and throws it to Dad.

"You can't touch the ball with your hands," Dad says. "Only your feet touch the ball in soccer." I can hear the annoyance creeping into his voice. Maybe this wasn't such a good idea.

"I know that. I play soccer in school," Jake says. "I just like catch better. I'm tired of playing soccer."

"Okay," Dad says. "Then let's play catch."

"Catch is a game for two people," Jake says.

"Three can play catch," Dad insists. I'm not sure he'll ever

430

come to terms with the particulars that make Jake Jake. Catch will never be a three-person game to Jake. His rules are hard and fast. He's grown a lot in the last few years, but Asperger's has its limits. And Dad has his limits. Hopefully, in the Venn diagram of their lives, they can find a little more overlap.

"It's okay. I'm going inside to get dressed. You two play catch," I say.

I head into my room to change. Will and Juan are coming over for our John Woo movie marathon. For once, we're going to hang at my house instead of Cloudbank, Will's McMansion of ridiculous proportions, and I'm psyched about it. It's nice to be back home.

The Mexican wedding dress is lying in a heap at the foot of my bed. I pick it up and finger the frayed hem, smooth out the wrinkles. It's a lovely dress. I was going to toss it in the trash because I didn't want any reminders of my night with Max. But now, looking at it—the delicate embroidery, the hand-dyed color, the beautiful cut—I want to keep it. Or maybe I'll have it chopped into a mini and wear it with platform sandals in New York City.

I throw on my familiar uniform of jeans and a T-shirt and check myself in the mirror. My hair is back in a tight ponytail. My face is scrubbed clean of Lily's makeup. It's all so familiar. This is the reflection that has stared back at me for as long as I can remember. But is this the me I want to show the world? I can do better. What's the harm in putting a little effort into it? Tonight may only be Will and Juan, but, hell, I just graduated high school, rocked out my valedictorian speech, and I'm off to New York City in two months. Life is just getting started, and

I'm dressing like I'm retired. I pull my hair out of the ponytail and muss it up. I grab a stretchy black minidress off a hanger, one of the many gifts from Will that have been going to waste in my closet. I throw off the jeans and T-shirt, and shimmy into the dress. It's formfitting in all the right places. I probably should have listened to Will a long time ago. I add a belt, flip-flops, and a little gloss. Better. Much better. I spin around in front of the mirror. I can look hot if I try. Why have I been trying so hard not to?

My phone buzzes with an incoming text. It's Charlie inviting me to his party. I don't bother to respond. I can't imagine feeling very welcome there with everyone toasting Max and Lily, the prince and princess of the ball. Thanks, but no thanks.

No texts from Max. But what did I expect? A note proclaiming his undying love? He and Lily are most likely having sex right now.

There's a knock on my door and Mom pokes her head in.

"Can I come in?" she asks.

"Sure."

Mom takes in my outfit. "You look so pretty. You should go to a party. You don't need to hang out here tonight."

"I thought I was grounded."

"Yeah, I don't think that's really necessary anymore."

She sits down on the bed and puts her hands on my cheeks, like she used to do when I was little. "Kylie, I'm sorry I've put so much pressure on you." She's gearing up for a big talk, the kind of talk we never have. Normally, I'd love it, but I'm kind of talked out today. I just want to kick back and turn off. "It wasn't fair to rely on you to take care of your brother every day. I should have figured something out so you had more freedom." She's determined to have the talk.

"Don't beat yourself up, Mom. Seriously. I like hanging out with Jake."

"I feel like you should have been hanging out with friends more, and I didn't make that enough of a priority."

"Maybe that's my fault as much as yours. I kind of used all the stuff I had to do at home as an excuse to hide away. I mean, I probably should have pushed back a little, right? Maybe said no every now and then, like a normal teenager. But I didn't. Because it was safer to be here than dealing with everyone at school."

"I hope you won't do that at NYU."

"I hope so too."

Mom smiles. "You can be just like your dad sometimes."

"I know." I say this like I'm not thrilled with the similarities, and Mom picks right up on that.

"That's not such a bad thing, you know. He loves you and your brother very much. He's just been hurt by life and he's still picking up the pieces. But he'll get there. And, you know, we're going to be okay next year. I don't want you worrying about us. We're going to miss you a whole lot, but you just need to focus on making the most of NYU and New York City." Mom puts her arms around me and pulls me close. "You make us so proud, Kyles. You always have. And I know you always will."

Tears pool in my eyes. I wrap my arms around Mom and squeeze her tightly. I can't remember the last time we held each other like this. It's nice to be with her when she's not distracted or in a rush or worrying about Jake. Those moments have been few and far between over the years.

The doorbell rings, and thank God for that, because another second here with Mom and I would have turned into a blubbering idiot.

"I'll get it," I say, releasing Mom. "It's Will." I rush out of the room, wiping away the tears with the back of my hand.

I fling open the door to find Max standing there. Oh my God. My heart flips around in my chest like a fish out of water. I struggle to breathe.

Max smiles, his cheeks dimple, and I fall in love all over again. Man, what is wrong with me? I'm such a sucker. How will I ever make it in the big city?

"What are you doing here?"

"We need to talk."

"Let's go outside," I say.

I step outside and close the door so we are alone.

Max doesn't say anything for a few moments. He's nervous and fidgety as his hands try to find a place to rest comfortably. They finally slip inside his front pockets. It's jarring to see Max like this.

"You look . . . really nice," he finally says.

"Thanks."

"Listen, Kylie, if you don't want me here, I get it, I just . . ."

"Who says I don't want you here?"

Max takes a deep breath; I can see him steeling himself.

"I can't stop thinking about you. I know you might not feel the same way. But I had to tell you that. I wanted to say something after the ceremony. I looked for you—"

"You did?"

"Yeah. Did you look for me?"

I can see the fear in Max's eyes, and it surprises me. The fact that I have this power, any power, really, over Max is shocking. "I went to find you as soon as it was over, but you were with Lily and everyone. I couldn't even penetrate the circle."

"Lily and I were breaking up. Actually, she broke up with me. She kind of got there first. I think she knew, after seeing us together, that it was over."

This jolts me. Maybe I read everything wrong. "You were going to break up with her?"

"I told you last night. There was no way I could stay with her after being with you. It didn't feel right anymore."

"Yeah, but this morning you seemed—"

"This morning I was half out of my mind. I was just doing damage control. I thought Lily would go berserk, so I tried to appease her. I screwed up."

I had convinced myself that I didn't care about Max, but as soon as I hear that he and Lily are really over, the walls come tumbling down. Maybe next time I shouldn't build those walls so quickly.

"In the parking lot, I ran after your car like a maniac."

"You did?"

"You didn't hear me?"

"No." I'm not sure what to say. It feels like this isn't really happening. Girls like me don't get the guy.

"Will told me to leave you alone," Max says. "Said you were pretty adamant."

"Well, that's true. Then again, I'm adamant about everything."

"Yeah, so I've gathered."

"Honestly, I didn't think you cared," I say. "Or I had convinced myself that you didn't."

"I care. A lot. I kind of thought you didn't."

We both smile at the classic misunderstanding. It's all so cliché-ridden, it's embarrassing. I wish our story could have some more original twists and turns. Maybe one of us will turn into a vampire or something.

"We were both wrong," Max says. He lets out a deep breath, and his body seems to relax from the strain. He looks more like the cool, confident Max I'm used to.

"So, where does that leave us?" I ask. I'm not trying to be dense. I really don't know what to do. I'm scared to take the next step. Max is going to have to lead.

"I want to be with you, Kylie. I've been trying to say that for a while now, but you kept shutting me down." He takes my hand in his and pulls me to him. A swell of heat rises in me. I feel like I could burst into flames at any minute.

"But I've got an internship this summer," I say. "And you're supposed to be in Europe and then I'm off to New York and you're at UCLA—"

"And the world could blow up. Or I could get hit by lightning. A lot of shit could happen, Kylie. Don't spin things out and start making problems before we have to. I'm not going to Europe. I'm hanging here. So let's just start by, I don't know, going out for dinner? A movie? Figure the rest out later. I mean, we're already married. We should at least go on a date." Max smiles with his whole face.

I laugh nervously. "Wait, we aren't really married, are we?"

"No. Not really. It wasn't legal. I asked my dad."

"I didn't think so." Still, I breathe a small sigh of relief.

"But I've still got my ring," Max says, pulling the cheap piece of gold out of his pocket and slipping it onto his finger.

"Me too. As a souvenir, you know? I forgot to pick up a snow globe."

"So, what do you think about dinner? A movie?"

Max is right. I'm jumping way too far ahead, as usual, finding things to worry about when there aren't any. I throw my arms around him and pull him as close to me as I can.

Max kisses me.

Yes. Yes. Yes, I want to shout. *Of course we can go on a date. And another. And another. And another. As long as you promise to kiss me like this every time.*

I hear the door open. It's Mom and Dad. I quickly disentangle myself from Max and take a giant step away. Awkward.

Mom's never seen me with a boy. *I've* never seen me with a boy, so I can only imagine how she feels.

"Do you want to invite your friend inside?" she asks.

"Hi, Mr. and Mrs. Flores. I'm Max. A friend of Kylie's from school." Max extends his hand and shakes both Mom and Dad's hand. "A pleasure to meet you."

The boy has manners. Nice.

My parents, slightly in awe of the beautiful boy on our front porch, stare at him like he's Prince Harry.

"Do you want to come in, Max?" Mom asks again.

"Sure, thank you." Max begins to step inside, but I pull him back by the arm.

"Actually . . . I think Max and I are going to go out to a party, if that's okay."

Both Mom and Max look equally surprised by my announcement.

"Really?" Max says.

"You're missing the biggest party of the year, and so am I."

"You hate parties," Max says.

"Yeah, I'm thinking of changing my position on that."

"Don't do it for me. I can live without it."

"I'm not just doing it for you."

"You sure?"

"Yeah."

Max turns to my parents. "Would you mind if I took Kylie to the party?"

"It's fine by us," Mom says. "It's really up to Kylie."

"I just need to do one thing before we go, okay?" I head back into the house and find Jake in front of the TV watching *Star Wars*.

"Jakie, I want to go out to a party tonight. I know I said I'd stay here with you. But we could hang out all day tomorrow instead. What do you think?"

"You can go, Kylie. Just come back."

"I will. Promise."

I give my parents a peck on the cheek and head out of the house with Max before I can change my mind.

CHAPTER SIXTY-FOUR

"Just follow your heart. That's what I do."
—NAPOLEON DYNAMITE

will:

*T*ouch me. I'm going to scream if you don't . . .

The lyrics to the My Morning Jacket song keep going around and around in my head as Juan and I sit in the car, driving to Kylie's. It's been an hour since we kissed in my bedroom, and I'm literally going insane. Juan is my drug and I need a fix.

My phone buzzes with an incoming text. Despite the fact that I'm on the 405, I take the phone out of my pocket, but Juan snatches it out of my hand before I can read it.

"Kylie says she and Max are going to Charlie's party and she wants us to come," Juan says.

"Girlfriend, say what? That is insane!"

"Why?"

"For starters, we don't do Freiburg parties. I hate to break this to you, but I wasn't exactly the prom king. And secondly, we just bought a boatload of In-N-Out burgers for the John Woo film festival. What are we supposed to do with them?"

"We'll throw them out and probably live ten years longer," Juan says.

Throw out In-N-Out burgers? I'm horrified by Juan's suggestion. Nobody's perfect, I suppose.

"Tell her we'll be there. With bells on," I say.

"Bells?" Juan asks.

"Kidding."

"I never know with you."

"No bells. Promise," I say. "But you're sure you're good with going to a high school party? Isn't it all a little juvenile?"

"If it is, we'll make our own party."

I take it back—my man is flawless. In fact, everything's been kind of peachy since I met Juan. To be honest, it's kind of freaking me out. I'm not used to life going so swimmingly. I'm kind of waiting for the other high heel to drop.

At lunch with my parents today, I almost had a heart attack as I watched my dad yakkity-yak architecture with Juan. I know my parents were thrilled to see me in pants, but that doesn't really account for the way my dad just sat there chatting it up with my new boyfriend as if he'd known him for years. I think at one point he even invited him to play golf at the club. And now I'm off to *the* graduation party of the year

440

with my boyfriend, and Kylie is going with Max. It's opposite world. At least for the moment, I'm not the huge, wonking loser I've played my whole life. I'm a leading man. Hopefully, it all won't end tragically. Like maybe with some kind of shoot-out at Charlie's.

CHAPTER SIXTY-FIVE

> "I can only show
> you the door. You're the one
> who has to walk through it."
> —THE MATRIX

Kylie:

When Max and I pull up to Charlie's house, which is a monumentally large Spanish-style villa, I feel my body stiffen with tension. Anxiety floods my system. This is the sort of place I avoid, the kind of situation that makes me want to crawl right back into my corner and scowl at everyone. There are cars everywhere—on the street, in the vast driveway (that looks more like a helicopter landing pad), and on the lawn—Range Rovers, BMWs, and Audi sports cars. I'm in a foreign land without a guidebook, despite the fact that I'm with Max. This is his country. I wish Will was here, waiting to greet me as I step out of the car, but he's not. And who knows when and if he and Juan will get here.

I briefly consider asking Max to turn around and take me home, but something in me shuts that idea down. If not now, when? I survived Mexico, I survived my speech, I can survive this.

Charlie comes out of the house to greet us, but before he can say anything, Jason Simon rides up on a beach bike and nearly runs Charlie down. "Duuude! We need more salsa and chips at the beach!"

He's drunk, wearing a wet pair of surfer shorts, and his eyes are rheumy. I don't really know Jason, but I assume he's surprised to see me here. I gird myself for a rude comment.

But all he says is: "Hey, Kylie. Rockin' speech."

"Thanks," I say.

"I'll let someone know," Charlie tells Jason, and then he turns to us as Jason zooms out of sight.

"Hey, hey, hey." He and Max bump shoulders. "Glad you guys are here."

"Thanks for, uh, having me," I say. Jesus, I've got to stop thanking people.

"Um . . . about what I said in the car . . . I don't really want to get into it tonight," Charlie says to me, after throwing Max a significant look. I gather he and Max have already discussed this.

"I would never say anything," I promise.

"I just need to do this in my own way, in my own time," he says.

"I get it. Totally," I say. And I do. I respect Charlie enormously for what he's done, but I'm aware that it's a long road and he's only at the beginning of it.

Charlie leads us through a lush courtyard and into the house.

"I need a beer," Max says.

"Outside by the pool, bro. But it's a friggin' packed house, so it could take a while. I'll catch you guys later."

Charlie disappears into the crowd. Max takes my arm and leads me through a sumptuous hallway and into a living room the size of my whole house. There are people everywhere, hanging out on huge leather couches, their feet splayed across heavy wooden coffee tables. The room bleeds into a high-tech open kitchen and dining room, with a table that must seat twenty. This place could seriously give Cloudbank a run for its money.

I feel like I'm getting the stink eye from people as Max and I make our way through the living room. Maybe I'm imagining it. People are going out of their way to say hi to Max, but no one really acknowledges me. Sonia Smithson rushes over and hugs Max. She pulls back and stares at me.

"What are you doing here, Kylie?" she asks. I guess I'm not imagining it. What did I expect? I hate her.

"I'm a part of the catering staff—you know, summer job," I say.

"That's awkward," Sonia states, without any sense of irony.

Max laughs. "She's here with me, Sonia." He throws a proprietary arm around me.

Sonia's eyes go wide, like she's seen a ghost. And then she sort of backs away.

"Ignore her, she's an idiot," Max tells me.

He ushers me out to the back patio, which has an unimpeded view of the ocean that momentarily takes my breath

444

away. Wow. I can't even fathom waking up to this view every day. There's a pool on the expansive lawn, and a guy wearing a chef's hat is barbecuing at a huge outdoor grill, flipping burgers and shrimp kebabs.

"Pretty awesome, huh?" Max asks as he sees me taking in the scenery.

"Yeah. Totally."

Max and I take a seat on a lawn chair, looking out at the pool. Lacey Garson and Richie Simson play tongue hockey on chairs across from us. Other couples lie on the lawn, drinking and making out. A few guys toss around a football out by the cabana. A small crowd of people are dancing on the far side of the lawn, where a DJ is set up. It's my first high school party. Possibly my last. Maybe this wasn't such a great idea.

"You okay?" Max asks.

"I'm fine."

"Really?"

"I am. I just, I don't know. I guess I need to get used to . . . everything. Being here. Us. Them. You know, it's all new to me." I smile at Max to reassure him. I know I'm giving him a false sense of security. But what else can I do? I'm trying.

Max pulls me close, holding me tight. I see Lacey gawking at us. She leans in to Richie and whispers. He turns to stare at us as well. Here we go.

"Lacey and Richie are looking at us like we've just robbed a bank," I say. Max doesn't even bother to look at them.

"Who cares?" he says, and then he leans in and kisses me for the whole world to see. At that moment I understand with total clarity that he believes in me, in us, and it gives me a

445

shot of confidence. He's right; who cares?

"I'm sorry about Lily," I say. "Is she okay? Is she here?"

"You didn't see her when we came in, sitting on Luca Sonneban's lap?" Max laughs. He doesn't seem bothered at all by the turn of events.

"I missed that. Probably the stage fright. I think I was focused on the floor."

"Yeah, you were pretty freaked out. It was cute."

"I'm glad I amuse you, Langston."

"What can I say, Flores? You're a quirky chick. And I dig that about you."

I laugh, because it's true and it's probably not going to change anytime soon. Good thing Max likes it.

"That was fast, Lily hooking Luca," I say.

"Not for Lily. She's kind of a record holder in that category."

"Isn't that awkward? I mean, you and Luca are friends."

"Not for me. Luca's really into her and has been for years, and I'm really into you, so it's all good."

"I'm really into you too," I say.

"Well, isn't that special. . . ."

Max and I look up to see Will looming above us.

"You two lovebirds are a sight to behold," he says. Next to him stands Juan. They're both wearing well-tailored suits. Will's is a dark gray with pinstripes, Juan's is navy blue.

"You're wearing a suit!" I say.

"You know how I love Tom Ford's work," Will says.

"Your idea?" I ask Juan.

"All Will. He insisted on buying us matching suits. I didn't really have much to wear, but I would have settled for clean shorts and a T-shirt," Juan says. "I think we're ridiculously overdressed."

"We come bearing In-N-Out burgers," Will says, holding up a large bag.

"Excellent," Max says.

Will reaches into the bag and plucks out a burger. He hands one to Max and then passes out burgers to me and Juan.

"No way I'm eating one of those. Have you seen the spread here?" Juan says.

"You have no idea what you're missing," Max says.

"He's from Mexico. Forgive him," Will says.

"Those burgers will kill you," Juan says.

"Maybe, but they're worth it," Max says, polishing off the burger. "Loved the mirror. Impressive work," Max tells Will.

"I thought you'd appreciate it," Will says.

"I'm keeping it as is," Max says. "For posterity."

Will laughs. I have no idea what they're talking about.

From across the lawn I see Jemma Pembolt, one of Lily's faithful lieutenants, striding toward us. She looks determined and pissed. Shit. She comes right up to Max.

"You are such an asshole, Max. I can't believe you brought Kylie to the party. I mean, the body's still warm."

"Lily's here with Luca. I think she's okay with it," Max says.

"You're such a self-centered prick. Of course she's not 'okay' with it. She's just letting Luca lick her wounds," Jemma says, her well-toned arms folded across her chest like some kind of South American despot.

"Jemma, chill." It's Lily who has suddenly materialized, with Luca at her side. While he stands dutifully next to her,

Luca looks like he'd rather be anywhere but here.

Lily gives me a level gaze. It's not hateful, but there's no warmth to it either. I get it. She's doing the best she can to preserve her dignity, and I'm certainly not going to make it any harder on her.

"Jemma's just being protective. But I can take care of myself," Lily says. "C'mon, J, let's get you a drink."

"Whatever. He's still an asshole," Jemma says, giving Max one last icy look, and then the three of them walk away.

I feel bad for Lily. This is her turf, and my being here with Max can't be easy for her.

"Do you think we should leave?" I ask Max.

"No. She's fine. She's happy to parade Luca around with her. And Charlie's my best friend; I have a right to be here. And we've got a whole lot of summer parties ahead of us. Might as well get used to running into each other."

"We're going to feed Juan some real food," Will tells me. "We'll be back." He and Juan wander off.

"How about I get us some beer?" Max asks.

"I think I need to detox tonight." I also want to see if we can have fun without the alcohol.

"Told you tequila can give you a nasty hangover. Maybe you'll listen to me next time."

"I doubt it. I'm stubborn like that," I say. "I'll just have some water."

What I don't say is, "Don't leave," even though that's what I'm feeling when Max gets up and heads over to the bar. With Max as my life raft, I can float. Without him, I feel a little like I'm drowning. The encounters with Sonia and Jemma have

448

diminished whatever confidence was building.

I spot Sharon Lee approaching, and I vow to say something as soon as she's close enough. It's like my own personal test. Can I do this? If not, I should seriously forget ever leaving the house again. Sharon's always been super popular, but I don't think she's evil. How hard can this be?

"Hey, Sharon," I say.

"Hey, Kylie. What's up?"

"Not much." I rack my brain for something else to add to that. Jeez, I am hopeless at the art of conversation today.

"You're going to NYU, right?" Sharon asks after a pause.

"Yeah."

"I'm going to Barnard. We should totally get together in New York."

"Uh, yeah. Sure," I say, trying to hide the surprise in my voice.

"I'm so psyched to get out of La Jolla and be in a big city, you know? This can be such a small town sometimes."

"I know exactly what you mean." And I say that from the bottom of my heart. "I loved New York when I visited last summer. It had such an amazing energy. I've never seen anything like it. I felt like I was buzzing with ideas after spending the day walking around in the city. I usually feel the opposite after being in San Diego for a while."

Sharon laughs. "I know, right?"

Claudia Kleemon and her boyfriend, Harry Thomas, walk by.

"Hey, Sharon. Hey, Kylie," Claudia says.

We both say hi.

I can do this. I can converse with the human race and not have it be an embarrassment of idiocy and awkwardness.

"E-mail me. 'Kay?" Sharon says.

"I will," I promise.

And then she walks away. That was not bad at all. In fact, I would have to say that was a stunning success, considering how badly things started out.

"You okay? Still breathing?" Max asks as he takes a seat, beer in hand.

"I'm fine. Much better than when you left, actually."

"So was it me?"

"No. It just takes me a little longer than normal people."

Will and Juan are back. Juan is holding a shrimp kebab in one hand and corn on the cob in the other.

"We cannot stand idly by," Will says. "Our feet have been called to action."

"You two go," I say.

"Oh, no. You're not getting out of this, missy. We've got to lose our minds on the dance floor in order to make graduation official," Will says.

"I don't think so. . . ." I try to protest, but it's no use. Will pulls me, and Juan grabs Max's arm, and together they escort us to the far corner of the lawn.

"There will be dancing," Will says.

There are only about fifteen people dancing. I'm loath to put myself out there for all to see. But I really don't have a choice as Will and Juan pull all of us toward the DJ. Some Eminem/Rihanna/Prince mash-up is playing. Will and Juan sandwich Max and me in the middle, so there's no way out.

Will and Juan exaggerate their moves, throwing their hands in the air, grinding their hips into ours, singing loudly along with the lyrics. It's embarrassing and ridiculous, but pretty hilarious, like a bad YouTube video. Max and I look at each other and crack up. Max takes my hand and pulls me away as Will and Juan, eyes focused on each other, dance to their own private party.

"How we doing?" Max asks as we walk over toward the pool, both giving up on dancing.

"I'm glad I came," I say.

"Me too."

Max puts his fingers under my chin and tilts my head toward him. I look into his face and I am overwhelmed by a rush of emotion. I may love this boy. Or maybe it's just infatuation. Whatever it is, it's powerful and highly addictive. I could get used to having him around.

There's a rebel yell, and suddenly Charlie cannonballs into the pool. A huge cheer goes up, and then, one after another, people jump in after him. Most of them are in their clothes, but a few have stripped down to their underwear. The DJ turns up the music, and now there are more people in the pool than on the dance floor. The sun is setting, about to dip below the horizon, and the lights in the pool illuminate the water so that it shimmers a deep blue.

Max and I walk to the water's edge.

"Want to go in? No eels. I promise."

"Okay," I say. "Let's do it."

I grab Max's hand, and together we take a flying leap into the pool.

SIX MONTHS LATER

CHAPTER SIXTY-SIX

"Adventure is out there."
—UP

jake:

said I'd be okay when Kylie left, and I am, but it took a while. For the first twenty-three days, I sat on my bed after school and bounced a Nerf ball off the ceiling until dinner was ready. Mom got mad at me, a lot. And I got mad back. Some days a woman named Gloria babysat me. I like Gloria, mainly because she brings me Airheads.

Then we figured out that I could Skype with Kylie, and now we do that almost every day at 3:00, which is 6:00 on the East Coast, where she lives now. Sometimes she's eating dinner when we're talking. She eats a lot of chicken ramen. And apples. She showed me her dorm room, and I met her roommate.

Once Kylie stuck her computer out the window so I could see what she sees. Lots and lots of buildings. A long street with stores and cars and buses everywhere. I saw a CVS sign and a McDonald's sign.

Dad is still gone a lot, working, but he learned to put the fork in the right place, and my milk, and he taught me so many soccer tricks, I think I might play in the World Cup someday. I'm really, really good. I even started playing on a team every Saturday morning. Three times now Max has come over and played soccer with us, like he did all summer. I'm better than he is.

Today is Thanksgiving and Dad told me he would let me carve the turkey with him using the electric carving knife that Mom got him. It's kind of like a chain saw for meat. Too bad Kylie's not here. She loves stuffing and cranberry sauce almost as much as I love Airheads.

I can't wait to see her at Christmas.

CHAPTER SIXTY-SEVEN

"There are millions of people in this world, but in the end it all comes down to one."
—CRAZY/BEAUTIFUL

kylie:

"**W**alter, you can't smuggle food into a café and just sit here and eat it," Gabrielle says.

"They're just lucky I'm not homeless and reeking of urine. This is New York. Far worse things than this occur," Walter insists.

"It's just weird. Buy a sandwich. Or a muffin. I don't get why you have to bring in food from the dorm," Gabrielle says.

"Why pay when we get all the food we can eat for free? Besides, I'm not doing anything clandestine." Walter holds up a sandwich, purloined from the dorm, for the world to see.

"Peanut butter sandwich, people, right here. If they have a problem, they can come talk to me. Or handcuff me. Whatever they see fit. I'll take my punishment like a man. Until then, let me eat my peanut butter in peace."

"Give me half." Gabrielle holds her hand out.

"You harass me and then you want my food. I'm afraid it doesn't work that way."

We're sitting at Café Drip, in the East Village, a bit removed from the crush of NYU coffee drinkers, and we like it like that. We're here every Monday and Wednesday to study Western Civ. The only class we all have together. It's the Wednesday before Thanksgiving, so we're actually done with school and not studying today. We're just hanging until Gabrielle and Walter have to go to the airport to catch their flights home. Walter's from D.C. His dad is some bigwig at the State Department. Gabrielle is from Chicago. Unlike me, they're both flying home for the holiday. I'm staying here, with a little takeout turkey in my dorm room. Mom and Dad could only afford the flight at Christmas. Cue the sounds of a violin playing in the background to accompany my self-pity. This is going to be one sucky Thanksgiving. I console myself with the fact that it's only four days.

When I first walked into my dorm room and discovered Gabrielle was my roommate, I was horrified. Gabrielle is scary beautiful with flawless chocolate skin and a five-foot-nine-inch body. I figured she'd either be a vapid girly-girl or a pretentious snob. But she's neither. She's wry and sharp and curious about everything.

Walter is a lot like Will, in that he's gay, he's brilliant, and he's my friend, but in other ways he's nothing like Will. He's the most serious, intense, motivated person I've ever met. His daily movie viewings, on top of all our homework, make me feel like a sloth. And don't get me wrong, I'm busting my butt here; I just don't have it in me to keep going and going and going the way Walter does. I can't imagine life without Gabrielle and Walter, and yet a mere three and a half months ago we didn't even know one another.

I still miss Will and Max ferociously. I thought it would abate as the months passed, but it's as painful as the day I left. It helps that Will texts me throughout the day, offering up a running commentary on life at Berkeley.

Remarkably, against all odds, he and Juan are still together. "Deeply in love. Inextricably attached," Will says. They see each other twice a month, which is a lot more than I've seen Max, who I haven't laid eyes on since the day I left for New York (unless you count Skype, which I don't), almost four months ago. We text, we talk, we Skype every day, sometimes twice a day when we can manage it with the time difference, but it's just not the same as being there. But what can we do? It is what it is. If we can survive this, we can survive anything.

Walter looks at his watch. "We should go, Gabs."

"You gonna be okay? All by your lonesome?" Gabrielle asks me.

"I'm gonna be fine. I'm going to study for Carter's exam, see a bunch of movies. It'll be nice to have a mellow weekend." I'm not looking forward to it at all, but I'd never admit it.

We all walk outside onto Avenue A, where Walter hails a cab. We hug and then they climb into the cab. I feel like crying as I watch the car disappear into the traffic. Mostly, New York feels like home in a way San Diego never did, but on rare occasions, when I miss Max or Jake or my parents, and the city seems full of other people laughing, walking arm in arm, full of purpose, it can feel like the loneliest place in the world.

I decide to walk the eight or so blocks back to my dorm. I love the street life in the East Village. Men in dapper suits and old-school punkers with multiple piercings fight for space on these blocks. As I take in the smells of roasting peanuts and the sounds of ambulances and cars honking, I remind myself how lucky I am. I'm in New York City. So I don't have plans for Thanksgiving. If that's the worst fate to befall me, I'm doing pretty well this year.

My conviction doesn't quite dull the pain in the way I'd hoped.

I buy a slice, a few garlic rolls, and a Diet Coke for my dinner. I can't help but wonder what Max is doing now. Playing squash? Classes? A tiny part of me always worries that some beautiful, sun-kissed Southern Cal girl will sweep him off his feet one of these days, but I can't dwell on that.

I reach the big blocky building I now call home, and take the elevator up to the sixth floor. The halls are empty, and my footsteps echo as I clomp toward my room in my Doc Martens, the de rigueur NYU shoe. I don't think I've ever seen the place this desolate. As I reach my door, I notice a piece of paper tacked to it.

I step closer and pluck it off. It's a letter addressed to Max. What?

I start to read, and realize it's an acceptance letter from the

Pratt Institute in Brooklyn, for January. . . . I'm thoroughly confused.

I open my door to find . . . Max sitting on my bed, waiting for me.

"Oh. My. God. What are you doing here?" I say.

"Happy to see me?"

"Thrilled out of my brain . . . but how . . . what—"

"Gabrielle gave me her key. I forgot how articulate you are when you're thrown off guard."

Is it possible he looks even better than when I left? I'm pretty sure I don't. I've definitely gained the freshman five. Too many cereal choices at breakfast.

"I didn't have plans for Thanksgiving, and rumor has it, neither do you." Max holds up a can of cranberry sauce. "You like cranberry sauce? 'Cause at the moment, that's kind of all we've got."

I hold up the letter and wave it at Max. "What's this?"

"I'm transferring to Pratt."

"Here. In New York?"

"No, I've decided on the campus in Dubai. Better weather. Good squash team."

"Shut up."

"Turns out, I hate prelaw. Someone I know warned me that might happen. Gonna try my hand at photography. See what happens. You know what they say: hobbies are for wimps." Max smiles, his cheeks dimpling, his eyes twinkling.

How is it this beautiful boy likes me? Has flown across the country to spend Thanksgiving with me? Is transferring schools to be in New York City? I am the luckiest girl in the

461

world. Maybe there's no expiration date on my good fortune. Maybe this is my life from now on.

"What about your dad?"

Since the summer, Max's dad has only gotten sicker. He's been in and out of the hospital the past two months.

"I bit the bullet and talked about it with him. He wants me to be happy."

"Oh my God. Why didn't you tell me any of this?"

"I didn't want to say anything until I got in. And then I wanted to tell you in person."

I can't believe we're still at opposite ends of the room. I quickly close the distance between us by taking a flying leap into his arms. Max catches me, laughing. I wrap my legs around him and hang on to him with everything I've got. He staggers back but then regains his balance. My head nestles into his neck and I breathe him in. He smells like toothpaste and airplane food. God, I've missed him.

And then Max's lips are on mine, soft and sweet and tasting like latte. I open my mouth and our tongues find each other. There's no more me. Just us. And there's no place I'd rather be than right here, right now. In a dorm room in New York City. With Max. This is the best Thanksgiving ever. Thank you very much. More, please.

ACKNOWLEDGMENTS

"We are the people who make sure things happen according to plan."
—THE ADJUSTMENT BUREAU

Nothing would have gone according to plan for us without our agent, Erin Malone, whose astute advice and unwavering support have kept us going through it all; our brilliant editor, Emily Meehan, whose smart and savvy notes made the book better at every turn; our families, whose unflagging enthusiasm and love encouraged us to write in the first place; and our children, whose drunken Mexican adventures inspired this story (kidding—they're all under the age of thirteen).

From graduation day
to prom night . . . Keep reading
for a sneak peek at

DiTCHED

Finally, a Snickers

I SUPPOSE IF I have to get ditched somewhere, I'm glad it's at *this* 7-Eleven, not the sucky 7-Eleven near downtown. This is the awesome one—the one on 4th and Hill with the nacho cheese bar and the endless row of magazines. Ian and I would stop by here on Fridays to celebrate. "No homework. No track practice. Time for jalapeño nachos!" he would always say. And I'd say, "Just a Snickers."

It's not that I don't love nachos . . . what's not to love? But I never got them on our Friday 7-Eleven stops because that was the day my weekly thimble-sized allowance was hovering in the cents column, and a candy bar was all I could afford. Ian would've bought nachos for me—he's a carefree buyer with an unlimited allowance, along with most of the student body at Huntington High School, but I didn't want him to worry that it symbolized more. The last thing I wanted was to weird out our friendship because of a plate of convenience-store nachos.

As I cross through the familiar gas station parking lot, my chest discovers gravity, and my organs and bones weigh me down with sadness, my feet barely moving forward.

Of all the 7-Elevens, *this* one.

Where are you, Ian Clark?

Then music. It's blaring through outdoor speakers, which seems odd this early in the morning. There's no one to listen to it because there are no customers. Except for me.

The bell rings as the sliding glass door opens and a gush of stale air-conditioned air rushes over me. Country music blasts through the indoor speakers, too.

"Need something?"

The cashier stares at my shoes. My two-and-three-quarter-inch heels are covered in dirt and mud—the same ones I had proudly dyed iridescent royal blue just two days ago. But that was before I found out *nobody* dyes their shoes to match their dress anymore. And before I realized listening to the advice of a relative—not my best friend and not an enlightened editor of a prom magazine—was an unwise idea.

Thank you, Mom.

It makes sense that the cashier would stare. I'm guessing not too many girls waltz into the 7-Eleven at 6:15 on a Sunday morning wearing heels that match their shimmering iridescent blue dress, looking like they'd just lost a match with a vindictive sewer rat.

"Got any Snickers?" My voice is weak.

Her eyes drift up to mine. She softens. She must notice my extreme lack of lip gloss. "You hungry?" She looks over my shoulder, probably to see if I am alone.

"Very."

She is wearing high-waisted jeans (*very* high-waisted), a belt with a large silver buckle, and a long-sleeve white shirt tucked tightly into her jeans. Her ultra-long hair is pulled back in a perfect French braid—totally symmetrical—with hints of gray peeking through. She looks like she belongs in a music video for the country song playing over the speakers. Like she'd play the part of the consoling wise aunt who doles out good obvious advice: *Stop drinkin' and smokin' and gettin' so many abortions, honey!*

I can already tell I like her.

She reaches into a box in front of the counter and lays a jumbo-size Snickers on the counter. I was right—there really is kindness in the world. I glance at her name tag. "Thanks, Gilda."

I give her a big smile and reach for the candy bar.

"That's $1.09," she says.

"I . . . I . . ." I can't believe Gilda isn't going to take some pity on me and give me the damn candy bar! Do I look like a monster? She's the one with pants pulled up to her boobs! She'd never be cast in a music video. Actors are *nice*. Which clearly, she is *not*.

I keep my mouth shut about her ill-fitting clothes and lack of human decency, and pat my dress down as if my purse will suddenly appear. But it's gone and I have no idea where I left it. Of course all my money is in there. And my lip gloss. And those directions to Lurch's party. The one Ian and I were supposed to go to the next night. He said he wanted us to go do something fun, just to make sure there wasn't any weirdness after the prom. He even said *weirdness* with air quotes, like I didn't know what it meant. I had hoped "weirdness" referred to all the making out we were going to do—so I guess I didn't know what it meant.

I had no idea "weirdness" to him meant actual weirdness. Dang it.

But in thinking over what happened last night, I have to say, "weirdness" was an understatement of epic proportions. Unreasonably huge . . . an understatement that is Hummer huge. Because Lurch's party—and especially the excessive making-out part—is *never* going to happen.

Which is a pity. Lurch always has the best parties.

"I don't have any money." My voice cracks. It sounds pitiful. Like someone you might even want to take mercy on. But it doesn't sway Gilda.

Gilda places the Snickers back in its box. Then she looks me up and down and tilts her head. "You need a phone or something?"

"Yes! Where?" I feel like a Jack Russell terrier—yippy, anxious.

"Out back. By the hoses. Fifty cents a call."

I'm not exactly sure why she thinks I can suddenly come

up with fifty cents if I couldn't afford the Snickers. "Thanks." I wince at her and secretly think about spraying her down with one of those hoses and wiping that unsupportive smirk right off her face. But all I really want is to get home, so I retreat and hobble back through the sliding glass doors, across the parking lot.

The pay phone is *right* next to the hoses, just like Mean-Ass Gilda said, and I have to hike up my disgusting dress to get around them. I'm not sure why I care about saving my dress from any further grossness. This is absurd.

As I step up to the phone, I hear a car—the rattling, knocking sound of a diesel engine. I whip around, hoping it's Ian, but deep down knowing that he's never coming to get me. A man pulls up in a Mercedes to pump gas. His car is old, just like Ian's, but it's a coupe, not a sedan. He doesn't even notice me. Good.

I start to read the directions on the pay phone, but the words turn blurry. I can feel the tears gaining momentum—I press my temples with my palms, trying my best to contain them.

Get it together. You've gotten this far without falling apart.

My pep talk starts to work—the tears dry up and I glance back at the building to see Gilda planted at the window, glaring at me with her arms folded, standing firm like a redwood tree. She must think I'm going to steal these hoses. Gilda might be the type who takes her job too seriously.

I quickly turn back and finish reading the directions on how to make a collect call. I've never made one and it looks complicated.

I dial wrong three times, but then finally push all the right buttons in the right order and the phone rings.

Come on, Mom. Pick up.

"You've reached the Griffith residence. Please leave a message. . . ."

I can't believe this. She's still asleep. Doesn't she know I'm not there? No, this can't be right. Maybe she's out on a hunt with the police. They're probably using drug-sniffing dogs and everything. Given the people I've been hanging out with the past few hours, those drug dogs will sniff me out in two shakes of a spleef. Should be rescued any moment now. . . .

But I try the collect call one more time. "You've reached the Griffith residence . . ."

Crap! This can't be happening. She's asleep. She doesn't even know Ian just ruined my life. I never wanted to go to this stupid prom at that stupid hotel. I told him that: I like running, not dancing. I like veggie burritos, not rubbery hotel chicken. And definitely not rubbery hotel salad. But he convinced me that prom would be different. It would be a night I would never forget, and he promised I'd love the food. Well, he was sure as hell right about one thing: I will *never* forget this. But the food? I'm freaking starving.

All of a sudden, I can't hold the tears back anymore, my eyes feeling like the Colorado River after a spring melt—the flow just keeps coming. No pep talk can fix this. I fall to the ground, sobbing. *Why me, Ian? Why couldn't you have—*

"Eat this."

There's a tap on my shoulder. Gilda drops a Snickers on my lap.

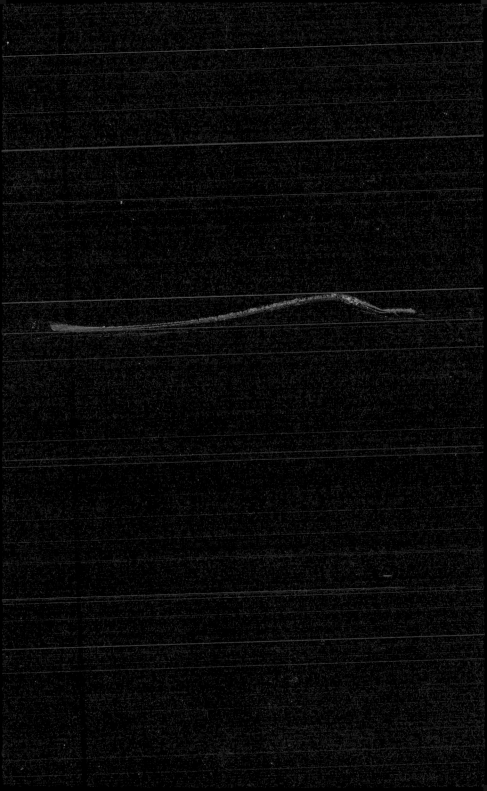